MEMORIES OF TWILIGHT

RYAN D GEBHART

Other Books by

Ryan D Gebhart

The Jewel of Life

Splendor of Dawn

Hidden Within

Fading Lights

Burning Desire

Spires of Arenthyl

Shadow of the Lost:
A Novel in the Jewel of Life Series

MEMORIES OF TWILIGHT

PART SIX

OF

THE JEWEL OF LIFE

RYAN D GEBHART

Hardcover ISBN 979-8-9853738-3-7

Paperback ISBN 979-8-9853738-4-4

Distributed by Ingram Publisher Services

Printed in the United States of America

Cover design by Fiona Jayde Media

For my aunts, all of them,
for your unfailing strength and encouragement

TABLE OF CONTENTS

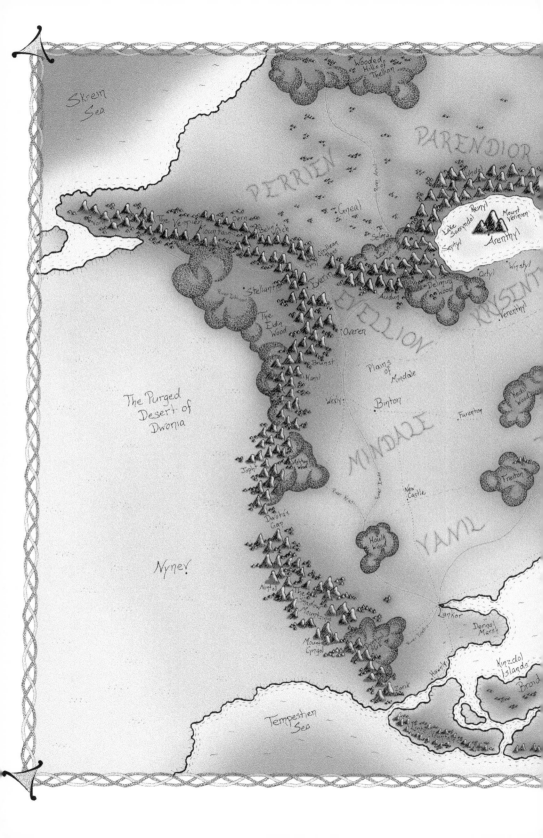

ALDINARE

Thaerwn knelt before the mosaic depicting her goddess, Lerathel. The mosaic was so detailed that Thaerwn could see the beautiful woman's—no, not a woman, a goddess—pearly skin shining like starlight and violet hair falling in luxurious loops all over her head. Thaerwn patted her own bald scalp. What would it be like to push her hands through thick hair of her own?

Caught by the shrine's beauty and the colored tiles depicting her goddess, Thaerwn wondered if, as her priests claimed, Lerathel had designed the shrine. Had she really left her sanctum and placed every tile here? Thaerwn doubted it. Her goddess had more important matters than laying mosaics. Lerathel might have designed it, but she also had thousands of priests to carry out her will.

The shrine was the only thing in Zarathyl the Darkness hadn't corrupted. Nothing was as it once had been; buildings had corroded, trees and flowers had wilted, and the elves had become the aelith. She knew of her people's glorious past only because of the shrine's mosaics. She didn't understand how the shrine was protected; the gods, most likely. But why had their gods saved their shrine and not the rest of the city?

The Aryl of Zarathyl claimed that every disconnected Aldinari city had a shrine. She didn't think any could rival this one. Even without the sun, the mosaics depicting Aldinare's eight gods sparkled.

Like the shrine, the city had once been grand and impressive. The bones were still there and at one point, its domes had glimmered in the setting sun. Perhaps they still would if the sun could touch Aldinare once more. Much like the pearly skin her people once had, nothing glittered on Aldinare now. The Darkness had corrupted everything; like everyone on Aldinare, her skin was a deep purple with blue markings veining across. The markings were not her actual veins; she had no idea how blood pumped through her body.

The followers of Aldarch Nialth, goddess of philosophy, endlessly debated the veracity of current beliefs. How could they think the aelith hadn't once been elves? Who else would have lived on Aldinare if not for their ancestors?

Thaerwn knew what her people had once been, and no priest of Nialth could tell her otherwise. As a follower of Aldarch Lerathel, goddess of art, she knew her predecessors would never have falsely depicted her people in the sacred mosaics. They showed the ancient Aldinari as pearly skinned sons and daughters of the gods, with silver hair spun from starlight.

Much had been lost since the Darkness had fallen over Aldinare. Lerathel's priests still created wondrous works of art, none rivaling what had been created when the sun still touched Aldinare, as though their creative link to Lerathel had dimmed and their goddess had turned away.

Thaerwn refused to accept that.

The gods would never abandon the aelith. Thaerwn knew the Darkness had changed her people, that they were no longer what they once had been. They might still live on Aldinare, but no one claimed to be an elf any longer—they were aelith now.

Thaerwn bent to kiss the stone at her goddess' feet. She cared little for the other gods. Each was important and had their place, even the dead god, Aldarch Theseryn, whose priests still filled the cities and slept in the shrines. One of them now nodded approvingly as she bowed to Lerathel.

The dead god's priests oversaw the aelith's worship to their gods and orchestrated sacrifices. That was too bloody for Thaerwn. She was happy someone had volunteered to officiate the sacrifices. Someone had to do it; the alternative frightened her. What would happen if they turned their backs on the gods as so many aelith believed the gods had done to them? Only their gods' intervention stopped the Darkness from breaching Zarathyl. Would the gods withdraw their blessing from Zarathyl if the aelith stopped worshipping them?

"Lerathel values your devotion," the dead god's priest intoned. "Listen for her words."

Grimacing at the priest's sanctimonious utterings, Thaerwn stood to leave the shrine without responding. She had stayed long enough. The shrine had no doors; instead, open portals stood between each of the eight alcoves. As was proper, she walked out Lerathel's portal, and smiled at her goddess' priests as she left. They worshipped Lerathel and the other gods by creating art. She preferred them over the dead god's priests any day.

Thaerwn had long considered joining them. Devoting her life more fully to Lerathel felt right. She'd been a follower for centuries, having vowed her life to Aldarch Lerathel when she came of age, just as all aelith dedicated themselves to one or another of the gods. But becoming a priest was much different than simply being a follower and Thaerwn hadn't shown any signs of Lerathel's magic. Choosing to become a priest to serve a god meant abandoning your family and answering only to the will of the god.

Outside the shrine, beggars huddled, their minds long ago withered to nothing. If the stories were true, they had been alive when the Darkness fell on Aldinare. Most aelith pitied them but Thaerwn hated them. They had been born as Aldinari elves; they knew what it was to be an elf of the greatest Skyland. She wasn't simply jealous of what they once had, she hated them for it. They had had everything and had lost it.

After the Darkness had fallen, the gods had blessed the cities with magic to push the Darkness back. But that was after the elves had been corrupted, after they lost their hair and their skin had turned purple and blue. These beggars had once been elves but now looked like every other aelith, only much older, and with their minds deteriorated. If Thaerwn left Zarathyl's protection, the same would happen to her. The Darkness would creep into and destroy her mind, just as it had done to these beggars. How long before their bodies were also corrupted?

Ignoring the beggars as best she could, she brushed past a dirty old man. It had been a long time since he'd bathed, and he clearly had no family to do it for him. The beggars had also lost the ability to speak. They could only grunt, frustrated about forgetting their language. But something was different about this old man. He seemed desperate and terrified as he reached out. She was quicker though and swung her skirt away before the old man could soil it.

She wondered why the aryl tolerated these mindless beggars who couldn't even remember which god they followed! They should cast them out of Zarathyl to join the maddened neridu tribes outside the city's wards, where they would surely be killed. The neridu thrived in the Darkness, violent barbarians who killed their elderly, believing it better to die than go mad and linger for eternity.

While the aelith were protected from the Darkness in their cities, the neridu had no such protection and they had been changed by the Darkness in ways that the aelith had not. Their minds could only withstand the Darkness for so long before rotting away.

The neridu somehow knew that the gods protected the cities and they constantly attacked to claim one for themselves. Thaerwn had no idea whether other cities were attacked as often as her own, but the assaults on Zarathyl were constant. The aelith only left their city's protection to repel the neridu. Thaerwn hoped she would never be conscripted to join Zarathyl's defenses. She hated fighting and preferred to create art. Let the followers of Orien and Aeryth and Irithel fight off the neridu. They enjoyed fighting. No one would ask the dead god's followers to fight, so why ask her goddess' followers to fight? They were artists, not soldiers.

Once away from the shrine and its beggars, she slowed her pace. The beggars never drifted far from the shrine and certainly never walked along the canals. They likely wouldn't be able to find their way back. Preferring to walk along one of the canals, Thaerwn watched the gondolas pass, young lovers embracing in the comfort of the cushions as the slow current pulled them along.

Aside from the mosaics at the shrine, the canals were Thaerwn's favorite part of Zarathyl. To her, the canal water felt sacred, one of the few natural things that the Darkness hadn't corrupted. The currents were manufactured; they had to circulate within Zarathyl's wards to remain clean. Any water from outside was as good as drinking poison. She lingered, the canal's gentle current reminding her of glass. Smooth ripples broke the surface as the gondolas passed.

Enticed, Thaerwn removed her sandals and sat on the edge to dip one foot into the water. The water rippled as she twirled her toes, but the ripples didn't stop where her foot had broken the surface. The entire canal vibrated, and the ripples grew larger, turning into waves splashing against the sides. Something was wrong. She breathed in deeply, feeling something awaken in her, as though she could feel the water inside her. It had to be Lerathel's magic—was she being called to become a priest? Is this how it felt? Was it the same for everyone?

Panicked, she stood and backed away from the canal until her back was against a building. Wind howled around her—around everything. Something terrible was happening. She felt as though she was falling, but the ground did not disappear from under her.

All around, people were screaming. Whatever was happening, it wasn't just to her. Grasping at the crevices in the wall to steady herself, Thaerwn looked up to see the Darkness above twirling, spinning like a cyclone, greedily trying to claw past the gods' barrier around the city. And then in a single breath, it was gone. The ever-present dark and stormy clouds surrounding the city had become a distant cluster of smoke rising higher and higher into the sky.

The sky brightened to cerulean and for the first time in Thaerwn's life, she saw the sun. Her heart froze in her chest and her blood chilled in her veins as she looked at the most wondrous bright orb she had ever seen. Even as she squinted at the brightness and her eyes burned, she couldn't look away. It hung in the sky, but it seemed that she and Aldinare were no longer doing so.

Aldinare was a Skyland; it floated in the clouds. As the Darkness and the sun seemed to get higher and further away, Thaerwn was sure that Aldinare was falling. Was that even possible?

The screaming continued. Was she screaming too? Nausea set in, and her stomach heaved. She soon felt a force pulling in the opposite direction; Aldinare was indeed falling and whatever had brought it out of the sky was now trying to slow it down.

BOOM.

The ground shook violently with the impact and threw Thaerwn off her feet. Dust rose all around her and hung in the air. She was dizzy and had difficulty seeing straight. Her head pounded. Reaching up, she touched her scalp and felt a warm liquid. Pulling her fingers away, she saw a sticky blue fluid. She couldn't recall the last time she had bled due to an injury. It had been many years since she had scraped her knees as a child.

Coming back to herself, Thaerwn looked to the sky and once again saw the sun. It was beautiful but its brightness stung her eyes.

Do not gaze into it, my child.

The voice was not her own, but it did come from inside her mind. Thaerwn looked around. There were few people on the street along the canal as most stayed on the thoroughfares where the shops and markets were. The canals were for lovers and thieves, those hoping to avoid the attention of other aelith. Despite her apprehension, the voice sounded trustworthy.

Come to me, my devoted child.

Was it her goddess? Did she speak directly to her followers?

"Where are you?"

You know where to find me; it's where I've always been. The Darkness can no longer harm you.

Lerathel's sanctum, Val'quin, was rumored to be in the west, but Thaerwn had no idea where in the west. The old maps couldn't help; whatever roads Aldinare once had were long gone. Surely the neridu wouldn't have maintained the roads. Their bloodlust only sought destruction.

"How will I find you? I don't know the way."

I will show you the way. Now come to me, for time is short.

PROMISES

Mountain air laced with an icy mist rushed past Devlyn's face, too cold to be mistaken for the summer breeze it should be. The sun still hadn't risen, and Devlyn hoped it wouldn't until Reinyl was secured and in the possession of its aryl. The aryls of every Krysenthien city had sent messages informing Devlyn and Ellendren that their cities were now secured, increasing Therrin and Zara's impatience to reclaim their own city. The Luminari elves had coordinated with the dwarves, and together they had strategized on how best to retake the city.

The Shroud was gone and Krysenthiel belonged once more to the Luminari, but shadow elves and Deurghol still flew their dragons over Lake Saeryndol. Devlyn had recovered from fighting a Deurghol when reclaiming Arenthyl, but he was in no state to repeat that battle. He wanted to draw as little attention as possible to their presence while they crossed the frozen lake.

The ice slowed their pace. Devlyn tried not to concern himself over it, but the longer they remained out in the open, the more he worried. The thought of a Deurghol appearing in the night sky sent shivers up and down his spine. This caravan might be smaller and easier to protect than when the entirety of the Luminari elves had travelled to Krysenthiel, but they were still vulnerable. A dragon could easily swoop down and wreak havoc.

Stop worrying. I can feel your anxiety from up here. We've planned on several contingencies and we're nearly there. Besides, we haven't seen any signs of dragons, Ellendren shared from the front of the caravan. They weren't alone in protecting it. A score of Guardian knights and Eldinari star wardens on griffins, including Viren and Wyn, accompanied them. Aren had come along as well, although few people were comfortable around the Dark Phaedryn. It was hard to forget that not so long ago, he'd been intent on ending Devlyn's life.

I'll feel better once everyone is behind the city walls.

The dwarves will expect Therrin and Zara to throw a feast, you know.

With what provisions? Devlyn asked.

I've already seen to it. Those wagons are to be deserted if we run into trouble. Don't tell the dwarves that.

I don't think we'll have to. Look.

Reinyl's lumaryl walls and spires glowed through the mist rising off the frozen lake. The fog dampened the impression, but the city remained resplendent. While only a fraction of Arenthyl's size, Reinyl possessed the whimsical nature Devlyn had come to expect from elven architecture. As much as he wanted to fly ahead and explore the city, he had to reach out to the dwarves first. It had taken considerable negotiating before the Schtamite had agreed to assist Everin, but Undol Schtam was eager to see Reinyl restored to the Luminari and kept out of Erynor's clutches. They missed the privilege they had once enjoyed when their tunnels had provided safe passage through the mountains, connecting Perrien and Parendior to Krysenthiel. That route would only be more valuable now.

The dwarves formed a perimeter around the elves as they reached the shore, ready for battle in their plated armor and polished axes. Devlyn stayed at the rear of the column, scanning every direction, waiting for something to go wrong. The Reyndien aryl, also anticipating trouble, wasted little time on ceremony and quickly lifted the seal on the city. The caravan moved slowly through the city gates to safety, dragging the wagons and possessions with them.

Not seeing any trouble on the horizon as the last of the elves reached safety, Devlyn flew down to the dwarves. Gauging by the amount of gold and jewels adorning the dwarf in command, he had to be Matriarch Muriel's son. Several names flashed through Devlyn's head as he tried to remember his name. The Matriarch of Undol Schtam only had the one son.

Furyk, Ellendren shared.

Thank you, Devlyn sent back, wishing he had paid better attention to her tutoring on the various peoples of note across the continent.

"It appears Undol Schtam scared off the Erynien Empire," Devlyn said in greeting, clasping Furyk's hand. Dwarves cared little for subtle elven gestures.

"Ha! That or the shadow elves don't want to meet your Guardians in battle again so soon, especially with Shroudsbane in their company," Furyk bellowed in reply.

"Toryn will be delighted to hear that word of her sword's legacy is spreading across Eklean like wildfire."

"I'll want to get a good look at it before we return to Undol Schtam. I won't be the only dwarf who'll want to see the mighty weapon that destroyed the blasted Shroud darkening our southern slopes for so long. Which reminds me, my mother sends her regards. We nearly had to restrain her from donning her armor. She might be willing to make the ultimate sacrifice and return to the stone, but I'm not ready to take her place if needed. She was ready to swing her axe at me and remove my head clean from my neck. If I'd stayed any longer, she just might have!"

Devlyn blanched at the dwarf, many years his senior, declaring that he was not ready to lead his Schtam. While Devlyn and Ellendren had accepted the mantle of leadership thrust upon them, neither of them should have been asked to lead for many years to come. What would it have been like to spend the latter half of his teenage years without knowing he was a Lorenthien? He let the thoughts slip away; he couldn't afford them.

"Matriarch Muriel is very kind to have wanted to be here with us.

Seeing as we have extra time, I'm sure Toryn will be happy to indulge you," Devlyn said, wondering if she would be.

"Aye. Mother would've been furious if she had come expecting a battle and the enemy never showed. I can't wait to tell her it would've been a waste of her time. Our armor is more cumbersome to squeeze into than what you elves favor. She would've grumbled for a month if she had spent all that time getting ready for battle only for the enemy not to show. None of us here are overly happy about it either. At least we don't have to return any of our own to the stone today," Furyk said, shaking his head. "Strange that we didn't meet any resistance though."

"Think it means anything?" Devlyn asked.

"I'm more concerned with where Erynor has sent his legions. We've had reports of Dwonian deserters taking Binton."

"We've heard the same," Devlyn admitted, worried about what Mindale's future held. The kingdom had long supported Erynor but had yet to engage in any of the empire's battles. Had they done something to anger their emperor or did the Dwonian deserters act on their own?

"And here we thought they were on the same side," Furyk said.

"Do you think the Dwonian deserters act with Erynor's blessing?"

"Hard to say. All we can know for certain is that there haven't been any sightings of any Erynien legions in Mindale. Erynor's never been known to let his lackeys lick their wounds and recover. Mark my words, we haven't seen the last of them," Furyk said.

"I suppose we wouldn't be in this situation if he was a benevolent emperor."

"Ha!" Furyk smacked Devlyn hard on the back. "Well, let's get the rest of us into that golden city and see what you elves call a feast!" Furyk called out in his own tongue and his regiment snapped into action.

Seeing all the dwarves, Devlyn fretted. Did they have enough provisions to sate their appetites and expectations?

After the feast, Devlyn, Ellendren, and the others who had safeguarded the caravan to Reinyl returned to Arenthyl through the seguian portal. Travel between the cities would be significantly easier now that it was open. They passed through the lumaryl seguian arch and walked out onto Arenthyl's lowest tier which featured three crescent docks.

Arenthyl rose before them, shining like a beacon. The aryl's palace, Aerodhal, was at the highest point. Everything in Arenthyl had a name; every tier, every building, every street, even the different parts of buildings had their own names if they were large enough. Devlyn was still learning the various names for spaces in Aerodhal, all of them in High Aelish.

He wanted to shift up to Aerodhal, skipping the long trek up the seven tiers. But Ellendren mentally reminded him that they had just returned from reclaiming another city, and as the future Exalted Aryl of Krysenthiel, they were expected to parade up through the city. Anticipating their return, elves already lined the streets to wave at the carriage taking Devlyn and Ellendren up the many zig-zagging ramps of the tiers. Viren, Wyn, Guardian knights, and star wardens walked behind the carriage. Their impractical carriage only had a bench for two people.

"Remind me why we have to take the ramps? They're the slowest and least direct route to Aerodhal." Devlyn forced a weary smile as he waved.

"The stairs that cut through the ramps and streets are hardly appropriate as a parade route," Ellendren replied. She didn't show any level of exhaustion, despite Devlyn knowing that she was. They were all exhausted. They had left Arenthyl for Reinyl late the previous night and had reached the city only an hour before dawn. Their entire entourage wanted nothing more than to sleep; even the elves who still had their Life Immortal longed to close their eyes.

"What's expected of us when we reach the palace?" Devlyn stifled another yawn.

"I'm sure some of the minor aryls will be buzzing about the palace, already preparing their grievances for how their residences aren't befitting their elevated stations. They have their eyes set on the vacant palaces on the sixth tier," Ellendren said.

"Why not grant them? Aren't they empty?" Devlyn asked. He didn't see any value in allowing them to just gather dust.

"They belong to Guardian senators. Every civilization has their own palace. We can't hope to reestablish the Guardian Senate by divvying their palaces and giving them to the highest bidder."

They at last reached the seventh and highest tier and passed through an open gate to the aryl's palace and gardens. Spires rose from the palace's foundations and glassy domes allowed sunlight to pour in from above. The palace and the city around it were wrought entirely of lumaryl, and they glowed in the sunlight, like a beacon at the base of Mount Verinien. If Devlyn had seen Aerodhal before he had left Cor'lera, he would have assumed it was the entirety of Arenthyl, and nothing could have outshone it. Arenthyl was so much more than a palace complex though, and it was like a crown set atop the city.

Devlyn and Ellendren went into the palace together, Viren and Wyn trailing behind. As Ellendren had said, Arenthyl's minor aryls waited in the grand entry. It too had a name, one that Devlyn had yet to learn. The long and wide hall offered easy access to the palace's most public spaces, the throne room, various ballrooms, the library, and other grand state rooms. However, it did not lead to the aryls' meeting chambers further inside.

While that space required as much ceremony and pomp as the throne room, it was also a place of bureaucracy, supported by hundreds of clerks who had once worked for the Luminari aryls to ensure Krysenthiel was governed smoothly. Truly, Aerodhal was only as big as it was because of the many elves who had once been employed there. The clerks had even maintained their own archives and had a full division of staff to administer to them. Devlyn wondered how long it would take for Arenthyl to return to its former capacity.

Trying not to think of his ancestors' bureaucracy, Devlyn smiled and greeted the minor aryls. Petitions came from every side and Devlyn longed for the privacy of the aryl's residence. He and Ellendren had quickly implemented a policy that banned any official business from their residence.

Politely asking the elves to submit official requests through the proper channels, the four of them soon reached an inner garden. Devlyn sighed, thinking the garden empty.

"Exhausting day?" Silvia inquired, startling him. She sat beside a fountain with Kaela and her son, Trethien.

"Ei'terel," Devlyn placed one hand on his chest in respect and bowed, the others following suit. Even Wyn bowed respectfully despite Trethien's arm around Kaela in a show of affection for Silvia Narielle, a show meant to gain her support in recognizing Kaela and her house as stewards in the Lorenthien's absence. "Fortunately, we met no resistance from the Erynien Empire."

"Admitting such might inspire others into thinking that you still have the energy for a chamber meeting." Silvia offered a sympathetic smile and must have seen the flash of worry cross Devlyn's features. "Not to worry, we can keep it our little secret."

"What brings you to Arenthyl, Ei'terel, and away from Winstyl? We don't have any scheduled meetings, do we?" Ellendren made the face that meant she scanned her memories for something she might have forgotten. She showed a hint of embarrassment as she furrowed her brow since Ellendren rarely forgot anything, especially an engagement with the aryls.

"Trethien insisted on a visit, since he hadn't come to Arenthyl yet. He could have told me he was more interested in seeing Kaela than the city, though," Sylvia said, her tone impossible to interpret. Devlyn couldn't tell whether she was proud that her son was courting the former Roendryn princess or annoyed since Kaela no longer held an official title.

Trethien offered his most bashful smile to his mother, an expression Devlyn had never seen on his former schoolmate. The faked expression would surely give them away. But Silvia's smile warmed to something—almost motherly.

"You are too kind to have come all this way with Trethien," Kaela said.

"I've already told you, it's no trouble at all. Do know, you'll be expected to come to Winstyl if you and Trethien continue this courtship," Silvia said.

"That would be lovely. I'm sure the city is spectacular, and even more so with your return," Kaela said, taking a slice of the fruit on the table.

She's going to give herself away, Ellendren shared with Devlyn.

I think Silvia is believing it. I had no idea flattery was the key to Silvia's favor.

Flattery and well-matched spouses for her children, Ellendren shared.

"My time away from Arenthyl will have to be limited though. Surely, you're familiar with my petition, with House Roendryn's petition," Kaela said.

"The motion has been brought before us. I still don't see the need for a steward though, unless Devlyn and Ellendren intend to run off somewhere." Silvia shot her words at Devlyn, who until reclaiming Krysenthiel, had often been away from the Luminari elves.

"I believe it to be a motion of symbolism for the house I was born in," Ellendren said, thoughtfully. "House Roendryn served our people in the Lorenthien's stead, never dreaming of them surviving Erynor's last reign. By acknowledging House Roendryn as a house of stewards, we honor my family's legacy for their service to the Luminari elves."

"No one will forget what House Roendryn did for our people. Perhaps a statue should be commissioned of Lucillia and her twin sons." Silvia glanced at her son, pausing to consider his future. Ellendren and Kaela knew that Silvia would never agree to their proposal on its merits alone. No, Silvia had to get something out of it. And nothing was more valuable to Silvia Narielle than her children's standing through marriage. "I will consider it. But do know, the decision does not belong to me alone. Toral must also agree."

Devlyn wondered whether Silvia was referring to Kaela becoming a minor aryl and their steward, or to Trethien courting another Roend-ryn. "If you'll excuse us, we're going to retire for the night." Devlyn bowed to Kaela, Silvia, and Trethien, and the rest joined him in crossing the garden. It wasn't the most direct route to their residence, but it typically had the fewest petitioners. If Devlyn had known who was in the garden, he would have suffered the petitioners for Wyn's sake. It couldn't be easy seeing the elf you loved fake a courtship for political gain.

When they reached the privacy of their residence and the doors to the public realm of the palace were closed behind them, Devlyn turned to Wyn. "How are you handling it?"

"I can't say I've been in more awkward situations," Wyn admitted.

"Oh, Wyn, that must have been so difficult. Hopefully they won't have to keep up the charade for much longer. Unfortunately, unless something forces a vote sooner rather than later, they're bound to sit on it." Ellendren rubbed Wyn's arm for comfort.

"Thank you, both of you. I'll be fine; besides, Silvia isn't always here." Wyn smirked.

"Is that wise?" Ellendren asked. "You deserve to be happy and not have to suffer at Kaela's expense, but surely you know Sylvia will have her informants watching my sister."

"I'm tutoring her in tapping her inner senses," Wyn said.

"There's a reason elders typically instruct in the inner sense," Viren said. While Wyn might have seen two hundred winters, he was still a teenager in Viren's eyes.

"We're being careful, and our sessions are in public settings, lest we stir scandal in Aerodhal's lumaryl court."

ROOTS

Devlyn and Ellendren sat with their legs crossed on the cool grass in the cathedral gardens among a mix of elves being led through a meditation by Etrien. With them were Arlyn, Viren, Wyn, and some ei'ceuril, all attuning themselves to Verakryl, the Tree of Life. The cathedral and its gardens were on Arenthyl's fourth tier where the ei'ceuril complex filled the entire space between the fourth and fifth tiers' wall. The grounds were filled with auxiliary buildings and cloisters for the ei'ceuril, all brilliant and beautiful, but bowing to the cathedral.

The cathedral itself was built partly along the fourth tier's terracing, giving the impression of a much taller structure. Its foundations spilled over the fourth tier's terracing into the third tier below. Ramps and stairs wove up the terraced wall, providing access to the cathedral from three separate tiers. Columned spires and sculptural buttresses interrupted the fluid tier below the cathedral, a trait common throughout the city. Where the Temple of Ceur in Ceurenyl was identifiably Aldinari, Arenthyl's cathedral was unmistakably Luminari, and contributed to the many lumaryl spires that formed Arenthyl.

The cathedral's location provided a whimsical, unsymmetrical balance to the city, although its location had not been chosen for the sake of urban planning, but for the large, exposed root in the cathedral gardens. Unlike the roots of other trees, this root looked as though it was carved from crystal, and if not for its impressive girth, would've been transparent.

Verakryl's roots were only visible on Mount Verinien. Gardens and parks were set wherever the crystalline roots appeared in Arenthyl, the one in the cathedral gardens being the largest. The rest of the garden's flora bowed to Verakryl's presence; kryseniels blanketed the ground in florid displays, all poised toward the root. Kirenae trees bloomed in a ring around it, offering colorful arrays. The trees provided smaller spaces in the larger garden, segmenting areas for private contemplation or discussion.

Eyes closed, Devlyn tried to narrow his concentration on the Tree of Life but blocking out the surrounding cathedral grounds and elves proved difficult. Stray thoughts from curious elves reached him, all wondering why the Lorenthien aryl were visiting the cathedral gardens. Verakryl's exposed roots were no secret to the Luminari, but the Tree of Life and its exposed roots had faded to myth and legend before the elves had returned to Arenthyl. And even though they could now see and touch its roots, doubt persisted.

Any elf could repeat the story found in the Theseryn. The holy tome held that all life on Teraeniel flowed from the tree, and that the tree was the original center of the Lost Valley where the Children first woke. However, only the Aldinari trapped in Arenthyl had communed directly with the Tree of Life while Erynel's Shroud had claimed Krysenthiel. Maintaining that intimate connection with Verakryl had sustained the Aldinari elves' hope over the past fourteen hundred years while they were severed from the rest of the world.

Devlyn risked a peek at Ellendren. Her eyes were closed and her chest rose and fell in a slow, steady rhythm. *She's much better at this than I am*, he conveyed to Aliel.

Perhaps it's because she practices more, Aliel returned, a glint of amusement in their unique form of communication.

Everything Aliel shared flowed as a single thought. No words passed between the bonded phoenix and elf that made a Phaedryn, nor were images or ideas present. Within the quiet of his heart, Devlyn knew what Aliel conveyed, and it wasn't simple phrases. Their communication was profound and rich, rising from the deepest part of one's self that stirred inspiration.

Devlyn closed his eyes, returning his vision to the hidden reality. Even with his heightened vision, he thought his eyes prevented him from seeing more fully. A hidden light blossomed whenever he opened himself to the world with his eyes closed, similar to when he fully bonded with Aliel. The two experiences weren't the same, but near enough to know they were linked.

Verakryl's root blossomed in his mind, a brilliant light dwarfing the many lights surrounding the elves. The various lights representing elven spirits were no different from this larger light, for the tree was the source of their own inner lights. Verakryl's light felt warm, reminding him of the Chamber of Light in the Temple of Ceur, but this crystalline root was solid. Devlyn could physically touch it and feel the warmth emitting from it.

Quieting his mind, he opened his awareness to the root. Alethea's lessons came to mind as he tried to walk the steps she had so often led him through. An incredible vibrancy of life pulsed from the root as his spirit mingled with Verakryl, as though it was the most alive thing he had ever interacted with. His own vitality felt dormant when beside this eternal font. He soon lost himself in contemplation, no longer aware of even his practiced breathing.

Something changed abruptly. The tree's inner fire vanished, and his fingers turned cold. He shivered, teeth clattering. The breeze stilled and the summer sun that had warmed him a moment before chilled to ice, suddenly feeling as though a fire could never be relit. Devlyn opened his eyes; no one else seemed to be bothered and only he shivered. Rubbing his hands together for warmth, his concentration shattered, he stood to warm himself through movement.

"Is everything all right?" Ellendren asked, her eyes still closed.

"You don't feel the chill?" he asked, expecting to see his breath.

"How are you cold? Sure, there's an icy wind from the frozen lake, but that's not stopping the sun from reaching us," she said, concerned. "It's the middle of Reventh."

Devlyn left the grove dedicated to the crystalline root. The Aldinari elves began to stir from their own meditation and Etrien followed him. Devlyn's gaze followed the cathedral's intricate vertical lines woven from lumaryl and threading upward in braided designs. Buttresses, reliefs, and statues lined the cathedral's walls, all reaching for the heavens. He wanted to distract himself with the cathedral's symbolism and architecture, to find meaning in it, rather than dwell on what he had just experienced.

"The cold that you felt, it's from the lake. Verakryl's roots are encased in that ice, just as frozen as the water. Hopefully the sun will start to thaw those roots, for they are not meant to remain still and solid," Etrien said.

"How long do you imagine it will take for the entire lake to melt?" Devlyn asked.

"I couldn't begin to assume. Lake Saeryndol is large and deep," Etrien replied.

"Can we quicken the process?"

"I've learned in my time with your ancestors to never doubt a Lorenthien," Etrien said, his tone almost grandfatherly. "I doubt you'll want to waste any resources on something that will occur naturally on its own."

"Why do I feel an urgency then? It feels like a warning."

"I cannot say. Verakryl has not revealed any such alarm to me. I would not ignore the feeling though. It amazes me how little formal training you've received yet you are capable of what required us centuries to learn."

"How do you mean?"

"Communing with Verakryl is not something just anyone can do. The Aldinari here are capable of it, but only because we had nothing to do for fourteen centuries. Even the youngest among our members are just learning the intricacies. Perhaps it's connected to your bloodline, for not even Ellendren communes so naturally with the Tree of Life, and forgive my saying so, Ei'denai, her mind and heart are much more prone to sitting with the tree in silence."

"Do you think it has anything to do with me calling forth a sprout in the Illumined Wood? Perhaps the Tree likes me already," Devlyn offered.

"You called forth a verathel?" Etrien stared blankly at Devlyn, shocked.

"Well, the whole forest helped me, but that was a few years ago now."

"Curious indeed. Whether it's your connection with the phoenix or your ancestry, you clearly have Anaweh's favor," Etrien said. "There is another matter I wish to speak to you and Ellendren about, on behalf of the Aldinari here."

Devlyn turned and saw Ellendren still sitting on the ground near the root, her legs crossed and her face a mirror of serenity incarnate. *Elle?*

Her face twitched, her concentration broken. *I believe I know what Etrien wishes to speak to us about.* She joined them, raising her palm to her heart and bowing slightly to Etrien. "Thank you for your guidance, Ei'denai Etrien; with every contemplation under your direction, I grow closer and more in tune with the Tree of Life, and the mysteries it contains."

"Your words are too kind and do little to consider your own gifts." Etrien smiled warmly. "When the Shroud was lifted, the Aldinari elves here felt something. Only some of us are old enough to have lived on Aldinare, but we have never forgotten its touch. We feel it again, as though it has been freed from the Darkness that encased it."

Devlyn's eyes flashed, darting between Ellendren and Etrien.

"I felt something too, deep in my heart, familiar but distant and unrecognizable," Ellendren said.

"Yes, you are of Luminare and Aldinare, it's possible for you to have felt it." Etrien paused as he turned, instinctually knowing where Aldinare was located. "The western call has strengthened since you've returned. The Shroud's destruction could be the reason. I cannot say, but I believe we must heed that call. To ignore it would be a mistake."

"Arenthyl will ever be home to the Aldinari and our resources are yours. We will help you follow this call, but we might have to wait," Ellendren said, catching sight of Aren stepping into the cathedral gardens.

"Thank you, Ei'terel. I would not suggest investigating until we are prepared and can spare the resources," Etrien bowed his head, noting Aren's arrival. Devlyn and Ellendren were training with him. Learning from a Phaedryn and past aryl who had lived on Luminare seemed the best way to prepare for the Erynien Empire's next attack. After the Luminari had reclaimed Krysenthiel and the Deurghol had been killed, the Erynien legions had simply abandoned the battlefield. Given the chaos at the time as they reclaimed their cities, no one had seen where the enemy had fled. For all Devlyn knew, they could have gone back to the Sorenth ruins hidden in an illusioned forest.

He'd expected an attack when they had reclaimed Reinyl. But there had been no conflict and they could've crossed the frozen lake weaponless. Why had the Erynien legions disengaged from the battle and allowed the Luminari elves to reclaim the entirety of Krysenthiel after they reached Arenthyl? Was Erynor rebuilding his army and gathering his allies for a larger assault?

Devlyn worried Erynor was scheming something more nefarious. Could he bring back the Shroud? Etrien had said the Shroud had only come about due to Ceurendol's corruption—Devlyn shuddered at the reminder. How could the Jewel of Life be corrupted? What did it mean for the Luminari and all those who dreamt of Life Immortal? Could the corruption be removed?

"Are you ready?" Aren asked, snapping Devlyn out of his thoughts.

Devlyn and Ellendren both nodded and thanked Etrien for his time.

Aren flung himself into the sky before Devlyn or Ellendren could ask where the Dark Phaedryn intended to train them today. They quickly bonded with their phoenix and followed him. They had yet to explore the entire city, and Aren notably had not taken up residence in Aerodhal. Before Devlyn could ask where he was staying, they flew into a courtyard on the eastern side of the sixth tier. A lumaryl spire rose from the terraced wall, looking east.

Several building masses formed the palatial complex. As they flew around the complex, Devlyn was hard pressed to see any entrance to the spire, except for the elliptical courtyard at the base. Aren dove and landed in the courtyard. Whimsical arcades surrounded it on every side. Aren was followed by Ellendren, but Devlyn dawdled, unwilling to abandon his flight just yet. With a final swoop, he alit gracefully, feet silently touching the ground.

"Welcome to Parenhal. The Phaedryn once called it their home. As I'm sure you've already noticed, the only entrance is through the ellipse. These halls were only ever meant for Phaedryn, and a traditional street entrance was never something they required or desired."

"This place is wonderful," Ellendren said, taking in the sculpted phoenix motifs intwined in the architectural elements.

Aren steadied himself. "You can appreciate the architecture at a later time." He didn't offer them a chance to rest before pressing into the erendinth.

Devlyn forced himself to focus on the wield Aren had started and opened himself more fully to the erendinth. He felt a swirling about him, but it was not the wind he sensed; it was aerys, mixed with aquaeys. Devlyn sensed Aren use ignys to drain both erendinth of any warmth and the humidity in the air condensed and turned to ice.

Frozen pellets flew at Devlyn.

He considered several different wields to counter the attack. Overpowering Aren's wield with ignys and melting the ice seemed the obvious reaction, yet overwhelming Aren's grasp over ignys would require an immense amount of power. Aren was not only a skilled wielder, but a Phaedryn, with thousands of springs behind him. His corrupted nature due to the Void only added to his prowess, making him capable of abilities forbidden among the Luminari elves. Devlyn had yet to see Aren wield tenebrys since his memories had returned and he'd broken free of his interior prison, but that didn't mean he'd forgotten how.

Overpowering Aren wasn't viable. Devlyn would have to do something simpler. He couldn't overexert himself with every wield. One of the most important lessons Alethea had taught him was that there were two ways of doing everything: the hard way or the right way.

Devlyn pressed into the elemental erendinth and felt his surroundings more intimately. The air caressed his body and his senses heightened as he breathed in and out. He could sense new blades of grass struggling to poke through the thawing ground, reaching for the sunlight. Pressing into the currents created by Aren's wield, Devlyn channeled the air around himself, encircling his body before redirecting it and launching it back at Aren. As the icy pellets neared Aren, Devlyn pulled the pellets together with aquaeys, increasing their length, transforming them into long pointed icicles.

The wield required little strength, but a great amount of control. Hoping to receive a small amount of recognition, he looked to see Aren's reaction, but the Dark Phaedryn's expression remained passive. Aren never smiled; the closest thing resembling an emotion that Devlyn had seen was whenever Aren looked east; a sense of longing lay deep in his eyes.

Black wings swirled about Aren, and the icicles transformed, their sleek spear-like appearance shifting. Devlyn felt Aren wield terys and umbrys, encasing the icicles and redirecting them at Ellendren. Their movement grew erratic, and Devlyn felt his heart thrum in his chest as he watched her prepare her own wield.

Ellendren was an incredible wielder, and possessed a level of control that Devlyn envied, but Aren had little interest in testing her control. He sensed Ellendren embrace the erendinth within herself, felt the elemental erendinth fill her being. Unleashing a wave of ignys, Ellendren instantly pressed into animys, and swarmed Aren's wield.

Animys filled Devlyn's vision, the transcendental erendinth crackling between the two elves. He felt both wields, each wielder pushing more force behind their own. Through his connection with Ellendren, he sensed her delve deep within her heart, that hidden intimate place filled with a song belonging to another realm.

Knowing precisely what she intended, Devlyn watched expectantly as a burst of light washed across the clearing. Fully bonded with Tariel, Ellendren's form was already illumined. Her golden hair flew back, and her lucent skin filled Devlyn's eyes.

Both wields vanished; lumenys faded from Ellendren's control.

Aren seemed pleased with this start, and their session continued. When their practice finally came to an end, Aren led them in new jienzu forms. Each form touched a muscle that Devlyn had never known existed.

"Why don't we practice jienzu first?" Devlyn asked. Jienzu centered him in ways that meditating in a garden never could. Despite being exhausted after completing a jienzu form, he felt he could do anything. "Our sessions might go smoother if we reversed the order."

"Would you ask a Deurghol to give you enough time to center yourself with a jienzu form before being attacked?" Aren asked in response.

"It sure wouldn't hurt," Devlyn said, trying to hide his embarrassment.

RUINED ESTATE

Jaerol chanced a look through the knot hole in his uncle's mostly vacant home. The current state of Teran's estate was in stark contrast to Jaerol's early memories. Visitors had once constantly flowed in and out of Teran's home, for both pleasure and business, to say nothing of the many who'd attended his uncle's famous fetes.

Teran's lifestyle had crumbled when the Cyndinari had learned of Jaerol's betrayal. His staff had abandoned him, leaving him to care for his sizable estate alone. Teran's only fault was being related to Jaerol. No one in Cynethol wanted to be associated with a sympathizer to enemies of the Erynien Empire, not in the heart of the empire.

When Jaerol, Liam, and Rusyl had arrived with Evellyn, Teran had eagerly welcomed them. Jaerol worried about the risk his uncle was taking, but they didn't have anywhere else to go. They had planned to fly across the Erynien Bay and into Yanil the same night they had rescued Evellyn from the imperial palace, but the many dragons already in the sky had kept them firmly on the ground. Despite being a day's ride from Broid, they hadn't had a good opportunity to flee the island and every day that passed seemed to make their chances of fleeing Cynethol all the slimmer.

Dragons constantly soared overhead, forcing them to hide from their predators' view. The dragons had largely remained in the sky and left the estate alone. That had all changed today when Teran had hurried the fugitives behind a bookcase in the library and into a hidden room.

Jaerol waited anxiously as his uncle provided the shadow elf with a tour. The dragon roared outside, making Jaerol flinch. Rusyl ground his teeth and muttered, "Abomination."

"Quiet," Jaerol whispered.

"That dragon has betrayed their flight for the Dark Flight," Rusyl growled.

"We won't survive to do anything about it if that shadow elf hears us. We're still in enemy territory," Jaerol whispered sharply.

"They're coming," Evellyn said just before Jaerol heard footsteps. He sucked in his breath as the shadow elf entered the library without Teran.

"Where are you, Jaerol?" He recognized her voice immediately. Olivia crossed the library, her feet padding on the wood floor. "Do you remember me, Jaerol? You've gotten quite the reputation since you left the Imperium and betrayed us. Is it true that you killed Razcul?"

Olivia's voice drew closer and Jaerol stepped away from the knot hole. He thought about wielding to make himself and the others invisible but didn't think that was necessary yet. Hiding wasn't their only option and Jaerol did consider the alternative. Attacking Olivia, even though they outnumbered her, would prove disastrous for Teran. The dragon would burn the estate to a pile of ash if they harmed her, and if, for some unfathomable reason, the dragon didn't, other shadow elves would come to seek revenge on the elf who harbored a traitor and enemies to the Erynien Empire. Teran couldn't stay here if the local authorities discovered the fugitives.

"What was it like killing another classmate? Did you take his soul and accept the strength that is rightfully ours? Razcul had collected more souls than any of our classmates. Did you claim them all?" Olivia paced around the library. "Just imagine how much more powerful you would have been if you had taken Kiron's soul all those years ago at the Grand Tourney. You could have avoided this messy business with the Luminari elves if you had only followed through and been the elf you were born to be."

Fists clenched, Jaerol felt his body go rigid. He would never forgive himself for killing Kiron, but he had come to acknowledge the gift that Kiron had given him. It didn't make living with the burden any easier, but neither did allowing Kiron's soul to pass to Lumaeniel make him weak. If anything, it had made him stronger. Jaerol had always known how wrong the shadow elves were in that regard. Even their own bodies knew they were abominations as they corroded. Their bodies were only held together by the stolen souls trapped inside their frames.

Jaerol had liked Olivia when they had been classmates, but as a shadow elf for well over a decade, she was no different from the others. She only knew hatred and cruelty and the hunger of every shadow elf, devouring others to live longer. Her body hadn't deteriorated to the same degree as Razcul's, but Jaerol could hear from the mocking tone of her voice that she was just as cruel.

"If you refuse to do your part for the empire—for your people— then at least have the dignity to submit and allow someone stronger to benefit from your soul and bring glory to the Erynien Empire."

Jaerol wanted to argue with her, wanted to point out the flaws in her logic. She had once been an intelligent and capable student. Her mind was too gone for any sort of discourse now. Nothing Jaerol said would convince her that the Erynien Empire was at fault. None of the evils committed by Erynor and his shadow elves would register with her. All that mattered was power and that lust had blinded the Cyndinari to who they once were—of who they could be again. Would the Cyndinari who had lived before the Sha'ghol even recognize their descendants?

Olivia's footsteps moved away toward the door. She hadn't found them. Jaerol felt his shoulders slacken in relief. He hadn't realized how tense he had been.

"If you are here, Jaerol," Olivia said, making him look through the knot hole again. It was safe now; she was far enough away from the hidden room and the operable shelf. "Your uncle's soul had more strength than I had anticipated from an old, weak, and disgraced elf."

Whatever had held him back snapped. He pressed fully into ignys and embraced umbrys, pushed his way out of the hidden room and launched shadowy bolts of fire at Olivia. Liam screamed, too slow to react to Jaerol's unexpected attack. They had promised to stay hidden and attack only as a last resort. But that was before Olivia admitted to stealing his uncle's soul, a soul now enslaved to this shadow elf, trapped until she was killed. Jaerol refused to allow that and launched more wields at Olivia, who cackled in delight as she wielded tenebrys.

"There you are!" she squealed. "And there's that Luminari wench that Erynor is so desperate to have back. I'll be rewarded for killing you and bringing her back."

"You forget you're outnumbered," Liam said as he too started to fight off the shadow elf.

"And you forget, disgusting lethien, that I have a dragon," she screamed. A crash rattled the house. The dark dragon was ripping at the roof, his claws tearing away anything between him and his meal. Jaerol could feel Rusyl seething in anticipation, more than ready to reveal himself.

As the roof gave way and the dark dragon's angry maw was finally visible, Rusyl transformed and shot out of the hole and into the other dragon above. The dark dragon was surprised for only a moment before the two collided, biting and clawing, their maws filled with fire as they disappeared behind part of the house that still stood.

"You are full of surprises." Olivia sounded as though a madness had taken over her. Jaerol wondered if the corruption that came from stealing another's soul to elongate a shadow elf's life deteriorated not just their physical bodies but also their minds. Was Olivia still the same elf he had attended the Imperium with? She could very well be gone mentally, never to return or be healed from what she had willingly done.

Eyes on Liam, she asked, "Is this your new Kiron? You replaced a pure Cyndinari with a lethien—a half elf?" With a flick of her wrist, she sent a bolt of tenebrys at Liam. Jaerol was already engaged and Liam couldn't wield a defense quickly enough as he was lending his strength to Jaerol. Everything happened so fast but before Jaerol could throw himself between Olivia's wield and Liam, the room was filled by brilliant light. Evellyn's arms wove as she wielded lumenys, negating Olivia's wield and shooting that same wield toward the shadow elf.

Olivia screamed and shielded her eyes, unable to defend herself as lumenys tore through her corrupted body. The spirits trapped inside flung themselves at the thinning barrier of their prison. A flash of light followed Olivia's last scream and the trapped souls rushed away. Jaerol hoped the way was still open to Lumaeniel, that these souls would not have to wander lost as the Evil One gained more control.

The dragons roaring and screeching outside brought him back to the present. He hurried to the hole in the roof and saw the two dragons flash by as they fought in the sky. Both Rusyl and the dark dragon clawed and bit, flipping and tumbling through the air as they each tried to gain dominance. In the brief glimpses of the fight, Jaerol saw them snap at each other's wings.

"How can we help?" Liam asked, having grown just as close to Rusyl as Jaerol had.

"They're moving too quickly. Anything we wield could just as easily strike Rusyl."

"What about a net?" Evellyn suggested.

"How would we cast it only over the dark dragon?" Liam asked.

"We wouldn't. But it's the safest way to bring the other down without harming Rusyl," Evellyn said, focused on the two dragons as they zoomed past the opening again.

"I'm not sure if I'm strong enough to snare two dragons on my own." Jaerol didn't see any other option for helping Rusyl.

"We'll join our strength to yours. At least the shadow elf can't sever our trap," Evellyn said.

"Right." Jaerol immediately felt Liam and Evellyn's strength pouring into him. His eyes popped open at Evellyn's power. If he hadn't taken the lead, she could have easily brought both dragons down on her own. Before he could ponder how someone who had no formal training in the erendinth had become so strong, he pressed into aerys and embraced animys, wielding tiny threads of the erendinth together before it took on the larger shape of a net.

As he flung his snare over the two dragons, they both fought against it. Even with the added strength from Liam and Evellyn, this was proving to be an impossible feat. Jaerol strained as he wielded more strength into his net.

Reaching out to Rusyl, he sent images of where the wielded net was coming from. Images of fury came back, but Rusyl's resistance faded and Jaerol had a better hold over the net and was able to tug the two dragons down. Their wings snapped against their bodies, and they thudded to the ground like two large boulders.

Jaerol, Liam, and Evellyn hurried out of the ruined library and through the house. A startled Teran appeared in the corridor leading to outside, and Jaerol forgot about the dragons.

"I thought the plan was to hide and wait for our guest to leave," Teran said.

"I thought you were dead—she said she killed you and stole your soul," Jaerol choked, overcome by emotion. Relief flooded through him.

"Shadow elves are known to lie, but they are more known to kill. Honestly, I expected her to do just that when I let her in the house," Teran said.

Irritated images filled Jaerol's mind. Rusyl was not enjoying captivity, especially by a trusted friend. The dark dragon continued to fight the wielded net and Jaerol had to concentrate to hold it in place. He gave Teran an apologetic look then ran out toward the two hulking masses, one blue and one dark. The dark dragon thrashed against his bonds but couldn't break free.

Jaerol focused his energy on the other dragon as he carefully removed the net from Rusyl. Before Jaerol could think of what they were going to do with a dragon of the Dark Flight, Rusyl pounced and clamped his jaw around the beast's neck. The confined dragon's thrashing stilled as its life spilled out. Rusyl only released his hold when he was positive the dark dragon was dead. Blood dripped from Rusyl's maw and he stepped away to transform into his smaller form.

"The next time you want to pull a stunt like that, tell me first. That dragon could have crushed my neck or broken one of my wings," Rusyl roared. Jaerol had never seen Rusyl angry before and realized that making a dragon furious at you was most unadvisable.

"I'm sorry, Rusyl. We didn't know any other way to help," Jaerol said.

"It's best that you did it. I couldn't hold out much longer. But I thought the wield was coming from the shadow elf." Rusyl's sweaty chest heaved with exhaustion and anger.

"She's gone," Evellyn said. "And the souls she had stolen are now free."

"Judging by the state of this place, we had better put as much distance between us and here as possible," Rusyl said.

"Should we wait for nightfall?" Liam asked.

"It won't make a difference with the Dark Flight here. If they're looking for us, which they are, they'll just as easily spot us at night as during the day," Rusyl said.

"Will you come with us, Teran? You cannot stay here," Evellyn said.

"I suppose it is time for me to leave. I will miss my estate dearly; not that I've been able to make a good vintage since the empire shunned me."

"Hopefully, it will only be for a short while," Evellyn said.

"Will you be able to carry the four of us across the bay?" Jaerol asked Rusyl.

"I would prefer to carry two at a time and return for the other two, but that option isn't open to us. Anyone left here will be taken and likely killed."

"I should stay then; I'll run for the hills and seek out my old contacts in the Goblin Guild. They might offer shelter," Teran said.

"I said prefer. I might be a young dragon and have more growing to do, but I'll manage. You'd be found before you could cross the sound. We'll take the shorter flight to Jadien and then to Sudern and travel on foot up Dagger's Point continuing north until we reach Krysenthiel," Rusyl said.

"Do we know where Jadien's loyalties lie?" Liam asked.

"Seeing as it's our only option, we're going to find out." Rusyl returned to his larger form, his blue scales shimmering in the bright Cynethol sunlight. He bent his front legs and invited the others to climb onto his back.

Once they were situated, Rusyl pushed off the ground with a grunt. He sagged for a moment, having difficulty gaining momentum under the added weight. Despite that, he climbed higher into the sky.

Concerned about being seen, Jaerol wielded aquaeys and aerys to form clouds around them. If anyone knew to look, they would easily see through the wielded clouds, but it was better than nothing. The Dark Flight wouldn't hesitate to bring down a blue dragon.

CHILD AND TREE

Devlyn stood between Ellendren and Aren on the highest balcony of Aerodhal. Viren hung back, unsuccessfully containing his irritation since the Phaedryn intended to fly beyond his protection.

The entirety of Arenthyl fanned out below and the lumaryl buildings glimmered in the morning light. Spires and domes and wondrous citadels rose from each of the seven tiers. The city built entirely of lumaryl had a vitality that thrummed, as though the golden glowing stone could move. Even though the tiers appeared to be based on occupation, with traders and craftspeople occupying the lowest tiers, closest to the water and docks for easy trade, each tier was resplendent, forming a beautiful and whimsical whole. Every level appeared just as richly adorned as the seventh and highest tier where the palace of Aerodhal sat. The only difference was that the palace took up the entire tier, its scale larger than any other structure in the city.

The seven-tiered city spilled down from Aerodhal, each level with its own terraces that mimicked defensive walls, set with watchtowers and spires piercing the sky. The peninsula jutting out from Mount Verinien that Arenthyl had been built on defined the tiered city's extents. The defensive wall at the lowest tier rose from the rocky crags of the peninsula that breached Lake Saeryndol's frozen surface.

Devlyn turned back to Viren. The Guardian knight scowled and his crossed arms couldn't be any tighter. "Don't die," Viren said, acknowledging Devlyn's semi-apologetic expression.

Tapping the interior place within his heart, that secret and intimate seat of his spirit, Devlyn and Aliel bonded, flooding the already luminous balcony with more golden light. Ellendren and Tariel quickly followed, but Aren was always bonded with his phoenix. The Dark Phaedryn never spoke of why he never parted from his phoenix, Tyiel, but his black wings were ever present. Shadow no longer oozed off him, but Devlyn assumed that Aren could resume the effect if desired. It's not like he had forgotten how to wield tenebrys, rather that he chose not to.

Bending his knees, Devlyn jumped up before diving off the balcony, his golden wings folded against his back as he plummeted down the sheer vertical wall of the spire. He waited until the spire melded with another portion of the palace before unfurling his wings to lift him up and over the roof. He knew Viren was looking over the balustrade, silently cursing Devlyn as he came too close to a fatal fall but the thrill had him grinning from ear to ear.

Flying was exhilarating, especially over the city that had for so long been swallowed by the Shroud. He and Ellendren were the Aryl of Arenthyl—this was their city. It was the crystal heartbeat of Krysenthiel, humming with life once more after the Luminari had successfully defeated Erynel and destroyed the Shroud. The credit didn't belong only to him, Ellendren, and Arlyn, for the entire Luminari population had joined in spirit to destroy the Shroud. And Toryn was the brave soul who had sharpened her own spirit to plunge her sword into the Shroud.

Rushing over and across the city, Devlyn flew low, enjoying the sites beneath. An ill-intended archer could easily be in range. Devlyn heard Viren's caution in the back of his mind. He flew past the many gardens and the cathedral on the fourth tier where his uncle, Arlyn, was busy restoring its rituals after Ceurtriarch Aaron Roendryn had named him archsteward of Arenthyl. The vacant Guardian Senate chambers rose from the sixth tier, near Aerodhal. While the palace was devoted to governing Krysenthiel and much of its vast halls were filled with attendants to do so, the Guardian Senate had its own palatial complex entirely dedicated to the wellbeing of Teraeniel.

Ellendren and Aren followed Devlyn through the city. *We don't have time for this*, Aren chastised, and he was right. Etrien had told them how to reach Verakryl, the Tree of Life and that was the only reason Viren had entertained their aerial trip without him. With a final look at the city, Devlyn flung himself upward. Wind rushed past his face, past his pointed ears, and pulled his hair back as he flew toward the mountain.

The air thinned and chilled the higher he flew and frigid air poured into his lungs with an exhilarating force. Vegetation was slowly returning to the mountain's slopes; hesitant blades of grass poked through the rocky terrain on the lower reaches that had been barren and frozen for fourteen hundred years. Life returning to Mount Verinien sparked a flame of hope in Devlyn. If Krysenthiel could return to how it once was, surely Eklean could as well. The various warring kingdoms could strike treaties and work together for the betterment of Teraeniel.

The air grew colder the higher they flew and soon, thick sheets of snow and ice blanketed the upper third of Mount Verinien. On the lower portions, the ice melt trickled to form streams and waterfalls to the lake. It wouldn't be long before the rivers flowed from the lake again, further connecting Krysenthiel to the rest of the continent. Though those resurrected rivers would prove little use if Lake Saeryndol didn't also melt.

Peering at the mountainside, he looked for the inconspicuous cavern opening. Etrien had shared the exact location, and Devlyn wondered if he'd sense it before spotting it. He was relieved they didn't have to fly to the top of the mountain, its highest reaches poking into far distant clouds.

There, Ellendren shared, bringing Devlyn's attention to an unadorned, shadowed outcropping. Aren and Ellendren landed, but Devlyn hovered momentarily. With a final swoop, he alit gracefully, his feet soundlessly touching the ground. The three Phaedryn stepped into the cavern, Devlyn and Ellendren immediately brightening its interior.

They glanced around, and Devlyn noted the cavern didn't appear to be special in any way. Could this really be the entrance to the home of the Tree of Life?

"Are we sure this is the right spot?" he asked, too aware of the darkened interior.

"Mount Verinien is massive and Verakryl grows at its heart. We won't see its effects for some time," Aren said, looking forward.

The cavern was too low and narrow for them to fly, so they walked. As a precaution, Devlyn and Ellendren remained bonded with Aliel and Tariel. Even as his body illumined the cavernous tunnel and his sight filled with golden light, Devlyn couldn't help but feel darkness weighing him down. It reminded him of both the Temple of Ceur's darkened entry hall and the Empyrean Sphere when the seraph had had his wings wrapped about Ellendren and himself, blocking out the light of Lumaeniel. Just so, this claustrophobic darkness pressed against them.

There wasn't anything sinister about this darkness but disrupting the dark quiet to speak idly felt wrong here. They walked for what felt like hours, not breaking the silence in the imposing space. Then the lighting started to change, subtly pushing the heavy shadows away.

With light trickling into the tunnel, they saw a boy ahead, blocking their path. He wore a simple tunic that stopped just above his ankles. The boy didn't smile, his face emotionless as he looked at the newcomers. "Leaves wither and the long night threatens life as the Lorenthien aryl, past and present, forsaken and renewed, return to these hallowed halls."

Devlyn thought there was something familiar about the Child, something he'd seen before. But that girl's temperament was wholly different than this boy's. Saecrien wasn't giddy or gleeful, but she carried a lightheartedness that the boy lacked, and perhaps had never known.

"Erynel raged against the Tree's protections. For fourteen hundred years, she lashed against the barriers she could not understand. Death is not welcome inside the mountain; only Life and Creation have a place here." The boy remained planted where he stood, his voice chilly.

"Are you one of the Children—Saecrien's brother?" Devlyn asked.

"We awoke here in the Valley of Saeryndol, given life from the Tree. We were some of the first creatures to grow from the Tree. The dragons came before us, and the anadel before them, active agents in shaping the world to be habitable. The dragons had thought the world would be theirs, and some still think it is. Ramiel had once only wanted dominion over that which he helped create. Like the Dark Flight, he believed the world belonged to him since he was the first to come into the Void. His desires have twisted since then and he actively seeks ways to end creation, to break the cycle of life and death. Somnaeniel all but belongs to him now. Before long, if not already, those who wish to transition to the World-Beyond will be unable to do so—the way will be blocked and Ramiel will be lord of the living and the dead."

The air went out of Devlyn's lungs and he struggled to breathe. His focus on the Child paused at the name. Speaking Ramiel's name brought his and his servants' attention toward the fool brazen enough to speak it. "Is it safe to say the name aloud here?" he asked.

"There isn't a servant of Shadow that doesn't know you've reclaimed Krysenthiel. Your location is not a secret. Saying Ramiel's name will not bring you any harm," Aren said.

Relieved, Devlyn asked, "What can be done about Ramiel?"

"Done?" The boy cocked his head. "Life will end. You are not equipped to stop it nor overcome the consequences."

Devlyn looked at Ellendren. Her expression reflected the terror he felt.

"Come, Verakryl awaits." The boy turned, leading them on through the tunnel.

Nothing Etrien or anyone else had told Devlyn about the Tree of Life could have prepared him for stepping out of the confining tunnel and into the voluminous cavern beyond. Color and wondrous lights filled the spaces. The cavern stretched higher than any citadel or castle he'd ever seen and was perhaps larger than most mountains.

The crystalline tree emitted brilliant lights, casting colors of every shade and hue on the glassy walls. Verakryl looked more like a jewel—a diamond either cut from a single monstrous gem the size of a small mountain, or a combination of thousands of diamonds set together. But the Tree of Life wasn't carved from anything, it simply was. No one had formed it. Not even the anadel who had a hand in creating Teraeniel had been involved with its coming about; rather it was the source of all creation and life in Teraeniel.

Devlyn stepped forward, hesitantly walking beneath the bejeweled leafy canopy. A flower fell from the Tree, wafting down as though it weighed no more than a normal flower, and not one that seemed to be formed of dozens of diamonds. But it glided down, its petals shifting in the tree's light. Devlyn extended his hand to catch the flower.

As it landed in his palm, images of fire without light filled his mind and the world darkened. He screamed at the images of destruction and chaos and the dead walking the land of the living. The flower fell from his hands, its jeweled petals wilting once it touched the ground.

"What does it mean?" Devlyn gasped, his voice strained.

"I've already told you," the boy replied.

"Is there time for them to be formally trained?" Aren asked, oddly calm in the situation.

"Time? I was not among the masses of Children who asked Anaweh for time—pleaded for it. The elder ones so desperately wanted to grow and to change. They received what they wanted, and they all perished as a result, and not all transitioned to Lumaeniel. The Void is fraught with those who have lost their way. Tell me, Aren Lorenthien, do you have the time to find those lost to the Void? What of those you know and once loved?"

Aren, the elf of legend and the namesake for the very city that became the capital of the Luminari elves when they had come to Eklean, remained silent, pensive, sadness falling across his face. Aren was the last aryl, with his wife, Jaequlyn, to serve as the Exalted Aryl of Mar'anathyl, before the elves had been forced to abandon their Skylands due to the encroaching Darkness. None of the old stories mentioned Aren's reign in Mar'anathyl; they only touched on his involvement in shepherding the elves to their new home on the land below. The historians must have had plenty to pen on their scrolls at that time if they never included what Aren had been like as a ruler.

"What sort of training?" he asked, having never heard Aren mention additional training beyond what he was already teaching them.

"Training that you cannot receive in Krysenthiel," the boy said.

"What training, and where?" Ellendren asked firmly. "We must be ready for what is coming."

"Training that has been delayed too long," Aren said.

Devlyn shared another worried look with Ellendren. They had only just retaken Krysenthiel, and now Aren wanted them to leave for training.

"What have we been doing this entire time? Sure, Devlyn has a few years on me, but I believe our training has been rather comprehensive and can continue to be so," Ellendren said.

"If I could properly train you, there would be no need to leave, but it is beyond my talent. We'll have to leave; you must learn as all Phaedryn learn."

"We can't simply leave Arenthyl," Devlyn said, indignant. The aryls had made it clear they would not tolerate Devlyn abandoning them again. "We've only just reclaimed Krysenthiel. If we leave now, how long before a Deurghol shows up at the city gates? Shadow elves will flock here if they learn of our absence."

"Fully trained Phaedryn who had seen thousands of springs fell to Erynor and his dragon. All had completed their training, had learned and embraced everything passed on to them, and they still failed—the elf killed and the phoenix trapped in Ythinor's belly. Do you think you'll be able succeed without proper training in defeating Erynor where they failed despite it?" Aren asked.

Chilled by Aren's words, Devlyn's gaze fell.

"I understand the need for training; I spent years at Gwilnor, and still, I feel inadequate," Ellendren said, calm, collected, and rational. "However, we cannot abandon Krysenthiel. Our people need us—the Guardian Senate needs us."

"The Guardian Senate will fall into ruin and Krysenthiel will be lost with every people bound in chains and Darkness if you do not receive proper training. You cannot know what the enemy is capable of," Aren said.

"Erynor is but a pawn in this war," interrupted the boy, his expression hard. Devlyn knew they were up against more than just Erynor. He knew that the Erynien Emperor was but a single figure in Ramiel's schemes to expand the Void and swallow Teraeniel.

"Erynor was never my master." A silent wind passed by, eerie and otherworldly.

"Aren is right to be afraid," Auriel said, appearing from nowhere. He walked past Devlyn and the boy to stand between Aren and Ellendren. Auriel paused to incline his head at the Tree, then at the boy. "Verinien, your vigilance honors Anaweh beyond compare."

"May the Creating Light protect us from what is to come," the child, Verinien, said.

"Uriel was trapped in the waters for fourteen centuries—that should not have been possible. This war is much bigger than Erynor; Ceurendol is only a symbol of this war," Auriel said.

"Is another kingdom involved? Something with the dwarves in the Shadow Mountains?" asked Ellendren, focusing on the geopolitical ramifications.

"What do you know of the Great Blessing?" Auriel asked.

"Are you referring to the creation of the different races?" she asked.

"That was one result, but not the cause."

"The account in the Theseryn captures the events as best as any could," Aren said.

"Aldarch Theseryn?" Devlyn had learned that Theseryn was one of the draelyn children of the Gold House in the original city of Tenethyl who had been saved from its destruction when Ramiel had brought his monsters to kill and destroy everything and everyone in the city. Theseryn had been Thien and Vivien's brother. Thien had gone to Luminare, Vivien had helped build a new Tenethyl, and Theseryn had gone to Aldinare and become an aldarch.

"He is our distant relative and the first Ceurtriarch," Aren said.

"We'll reread his account when we return to Arenthyl; I'm sure I have a copy in my study." Ellendren's expression was blank, a look Devlyn knew well. She was picturing her study, recalling every detail and seeking the location of the holy tome.

"Still," Devlyn said, thinking back on Arenthyl. "We can't abandon Krysenthiel."

"If you wish to overcome the storm, you must. Ramiel has only grown stronger and more twisted in the Void, as have the Deurghol and beasts he's corrupted," Auriel said.

"What if the Erynien Empire attacks again? We can't simply abandon our people, hoping Erynor will leave Krysenthiel alone," Devlyn said.

"He'll certainly attack, both Arenthyl and every other Luminari city," Auriel said.

"And you still expect us to leave? Knowing full well that he'll target Krysenthiel?"

"You must. Or all will be lost." Auriel vanished, fading into the light. An afterimage lingered, the enthiel's appearance in elven form seared into Devlyn's eyes.

"How long will we have to be away?" Ellendren asked.

"I cannot speak of the formation, nor even where it is located. No one will be able to reach you while you are gone," Aren said.

"So, we're to just leave Arenthyl, tell everybody we'll return at some point without giving them any indication of how long we'll be gone?" Devlyn heard the heat in his voice, and doubtless Aren saw the fire in his eyes. Oddly, that was the first time he saw the slightest twitch of a smile from his distant ancestor.

"If there was another solution, I would have it otherwise. I'm sorry; it's the only way."

TROUBLE WITH TOMES

Running his hand along the lumaryl walls, Devlyn walked along another gently curved corridor. Every wall in the palace had a slight curvature, only noticeable when looking down a long corridor and realizing you couldn't see the end. He wondered if anyone still alive knew the reason for the odd construction.

Despite his limited education in elven architecture, Ellendren had told him that the ancient Luminari had done everything with meaning; even their buildings were imbued with philosophy and some hidden significance.

"Ei'denai," Jeanne Darkel, First of the Guardians, called, "Ellendren asked me to find you."

"Is everything all right?"

"Nothing to concern yourself about. She asked me to find you before the eighth bell today, assuming she would have finished reading the Theseryn by then."

"Is she still in her study?" Ellendren had locked herself away, allowing entrance only to her attendants.

"Yes; I'll take you there," Jeanne bowed.

"You really don't have to; I'm sure you have other priorities to see to."

With a pointed glare, Jeanne turned and waited for Devlyn to start moving. *Should've known better*, he thought. Unlike the palace's corridors,

Jeanne was unbending.

Dozens of palace guards and attendants bowed as Devlyn walked past. Still uncomfortable with the formality, he responded as Ellendren had encouraged and simply went on with his head held high. It had been easier to ignore the formality when they had lived in the camps. The wilderness and messiness there hadn't lent itself to pomp and pageantry. That was not the case in Aerodhal though. Devlyn wouldn't call the palace stuffy; nothing about Arenthyl was stuffy, but the nobles and workers always buzzing about the palace were exhausting.

They passed through the throne room, its expansive high dome springing upward in a shimmering display above the circular space; balconies dotted the walls. The Crystal Throne—two seats, separate but one—stood at the center of the space, demanding attention and recognition. The Aryl of Arenthyl—the Exalted Aryl of Krysenthiel might be composed of two elves, but the aryl was a single entity and their throne served as a constant reminder. Devlyn didn't think the space would ever stop captivating him.

The guards at the entry to the aryl's residence bowed as they opened the double doors. Devlyn had no idea how they did both at once. Devlyn and Jeanne went through two more corridors and up several flights of stairs, before Jeanne finally rapped on the door to Ellendren's study. The door remained shut, but Devlyn thought he heard movement behind it. That wasn't possible though, as sound couldn't pass through any of the kirenae wood doors of the palace. *Come in.* Ellendren's thoughts carried from the room beyond.

Pushing the door open, Devlyn entered to find scrolls and books littered across every surface. "I thought you only had to read the one book." He looked around the disorderly study. Kevn quickly came to mind, reminding him of the mountainous piles of parchment and books strewn about his friend's room when they had briefly lived together.

"That's precisely who I need, since every copy here is written in the original High Aelish, and in a dialect I'm not familiar with." Ellendren lifted one of the books to cross reference it with another. "Do you think he made it to Septyl? We still haven't received any news from the Seven Chairs; we should send someone to investigate. I wonder if Prya and Liara could make the trip."

"I was thinking the same." Devlyn took another cautious glance about the room before timidly asking, "Were you able to learn anything?"

"I know enough Aelish to get by. It's not a perfect translation, but listen to this, 'Clouds had darkened much of the land, blocking out the sun and the stars, permitting Ramiel's corrupted cordel to freely roam the surface.'"

Ellendren flipped several pages. "'None knew of the cordel corrupted beneath Teraeniel's crust and what Ramiel had done to them until they had returned to the surface in great numbers. Unable to interfere with anything physical, the anadel watched in horror as the beasts tore the land asunder, killing cordel and anacordel alike.'" Turning more pages, "'Learning of the return of night to the Valley, Ramiel incited violence in the hearts of those beyond the Valley, knowing he could not reach those within, even with the night returned. Those within the Valley were too close to Uriel. Battle came to the edge of the Valley, and those anadel aligned with Ramiel walked among his corrupted cordel and the anacordel whose hearts were consumed by hate and vengeance.'

"'When the first drop of death's blood fell on the Sacred Valley, a great beam of light exploded across Teraeniel, delving into the deepest crevices of every anacordel's heart. A ring of silent death entrapped the Valley, the aftermath of anacordel killing anacordel. Shame filled the anacordel as Anaweh's silent presence was made known to all creation. The Creating Light sprung with force in every heart, making all creation tremble with fear. They knew within their hearts that they had sinned against their brethren and feared Anaweh's retribution.'

"'Unable to bear Anaweh's presence, Ramiel and those anadel and cordel aligned with him fled from the surface's blinding light, searing them all the way to the deepest depths of Teraeniel. None of the ana-cordel deceived by Ramiel followed below but remained in shame on the surface. With Anaweh's illumined presence, Uriel beseeched Theniel, Sariel, and Kariel to lock Ramiel and his kin below the surface. At every portal, a great mountain spewing fire came to be, preventing any below from passing above, and any above from delving below.'

"'In the Valley, the ground around the Tree of Life rose to a great height, higher than any other, and in the newly formed mountain stood the tree, protected from any who might cause it harm. The tree's roots covered Ramiel's first and greatest portal into the depths beneath the surface.' The Great Blessing follows, and the creation of the different races," Ellendren added, no longer quoting from the Theseryn, but her eyes still darting across the pages.

Devlyn walked from Ellendren's desk to a window where he could look toward the massive mountain. Its rigid slopes were dotted with veg-etation. "Isn't the Tree of Life sealing Ramiel away?" Devlyn asked, his gaze fixed on Mount Verinien and the Tree concealed within.

"What was that?" Ellendren was still buried in the holy tome. Dev-lyn repeated himself, unconcerned by her divided attention. "We've been warned that it's possible for him to escape. There are other accounts of those ancient days, when those corrupted cordel roamed Teraeniel, some doing the bidding of anacordel, others the bidding of the Evil One alone."

"I've seen them, or rather, a memory of them."

"During your trials at Tenethyl? Are they worse than shadow elves and Deurghol?"

"Much worse. Elle, those beasts are terrifying. Some of them are larger than dragons."

Ellendren leaned forward and pinched the bridge of her nose. "I don't think we can refuse Aren. We can't afford not to have every ad-vantage provided. If Ramiel escapes the Void, what hope will we have if we're not fully trained?"

Devlyn agreed. Auriel appearing to them and urging them to leave Krysenthiel for training had to be unprecedented. The enthiel only revealed themselves when it was of the utmost importance. "Is it decided then?" Devlyn asked.

"I believe so." Ellendren looked at him. "Aren will take us to who knows where and we'll have to leave our people. My parents never left Lucillia for longer than a month during their reign. Those trips were diplomatic missions, intent on avoiding the wars to come—the war we live in. What if we went at alternating times? That way we wouldn't both abandon Krysenthiel."

"I think it's important that this is done together, Elle. I don't know why it's important, but it feels like something we should do together." Devlyn squeezed her hand. "Nor do I think we have the luxury of doubling the time one of the us is away from Krysenthiel."

"What if Erynor learns of our absence and assaults Krysenthiel? We have a responsibility to our allies as well. If we want the Guardian Senate to have any chance of success, we can't abandon our allies in need. Erynor will take advantage of our absence."

"The Guardian knights' numbers are increasing. The former Lucillian military is training with them and will serve beside them either as Guardian knights or part of the city guard."

"There's too much to do before we leave." Ellendren sighed. "We haven't even started to prepare for our coronation. We'll have to appoint someone to oversee that while we're gone."

"Do you think the aryls will try to delay our coronation? They've been more tolerable with their cities returned but imagine what sort of harm they'll be capable of with us gone."

"Kaela will ensure that doesn't happen."

"Alex will never forgive us if we miss his wedding," said Devlyn.

"We cannot miss that wedding. Hopefully Elothkar's reconstruction won't conclude until after we return. Alex and Diana's wedding all but solidifies Alex's claim to the Thellish throne. Although Alex is a descendant of Dennion, Evellion's younger brother, it's hardly the strongest claim to the Thellish throne. But Diana is a direct descendant of Evellion, the last King of Thellion, so their children and heirs will be uncontested." Ellendren grabbed another book from her pile. "Not attending is not an option. A renewed Thellion will ripple across Teraeniel. Not to mention the impact it will have on the Guardian Senate."

Devlyn turned away from the window, his expression questioning. But Ellendren somehow always knew when she had lost him. He had expected their bond would have clarified everything, but having her thoughts revealed to him only made her more confusing.

"As a kingdom comprised of three separate kingdoms, Thellion will have a greater influence on the Senate than Yanil as a single kingdom ever will. Yanil will have to garner more support from other senators to prevent Thellion from getting their way, and that's to say nothing of the elven voices on the council."

Devlyn's expression remained quizzical.

"Each of our aryls holds the weight of a minor kingdom. The Luminari have seven, the Eldinari have four, and I think the Aldinari also have four, despite their diminished, but recovering numbers. We'll have to decide what to do about the Cyndinari; perhaps we can elevate an aryldom from those that were loyal to Lucillia. Perhaps Velaria's family will be a decent candidate."

"Can we do that?" Devlyn asked.

"We cannot, but they can."

"I've never heard Velaria mention her family before; have you?"

Ellendren shook her head. "Jaerol is another candidate, of course. Granted, I doubt the Cyndinari would recognize him any time soon. Even the Cyndinari loyal to us won't trust him yet since he was born in Broid."

"He also intends to join the Azurelles." Devlyn thought of the impossible mission he had set for Jaerol, Liam, and Rusyl. He had yet to hear from them and it had been months since he had left them on

Cynethol, the island home of the Cyndinari elves and heart of the Erynien Empire.

Knowing where his thoughts had gone, Ellendren touched his arm. "They'll be fine. There's no one more suited to rescue your mother than those three."

Devlyn forced a smile, suppressing his fears of not only his mother being Erynor's captive and slave, but Jaerol, Liam, and Rusyl also joining that fate.

Pevrel, Ellendren's attendant, stepped in. "Ei'terel, Kaela and Trethien are waiting for you in the salon."

"Of course; thank you, Pevrel. Were they seen together?"

"Multiple times."

"Poor Wyn," Devlyn said.

"He and Kaela will survive this, despite how convincing she and Trethien are. They only need to hold the charade until Kaela officially becomes an aryl and our steward, which has become a more pressing issue if we're to leave. Now, shall we greet our guests?" Ellendren flashed a smile as she moved away and Devlyn hurried to follow her.

Unlike the trek he'd taken up and through the palace, their private salon was only a floor below. Kaela and Trethien chatted amicably there.

"Hello there, sister." Kaela stood and embraced Ellendren and Devlyn in turn.

"Ei'denai, Ei'terel," Trethien said.

"Please, no titles; especially when there aren't any scrutinizing eyes present. We've known each other too long," Ellendren said.

"As you wish." Trethien nodded.

"Has there been any progress with your mother? She seemed quite taken with Kaela in the palace gardens the other day," Ellendren said.

"A rare public show of affection. She's otherwise been cold and aloof as always. But she has insisted Kaela visit Winstyl. My father has shared some choice words with me privately, ensuring I don't break another betrothal. It's impossible to tell from my mother, but my sisters adore Kaela. They'll never forgive me once they learn it was all a farce."

"Wonderful. I believe we have the required support for Kaela to become steward, and it's all but guaranteed if House Narielle also supports the proposal that House Roendryn becomes a house of stewards. As you well know, we're running out of time. The aryls are to meet in chamber to vote on the matter tomorrow," Ellendren said.

"House Lucillia," Kaela said, garnering a prolonged hush from the others in the room. "Roendryn's line ensured our people's security, but if there is to be a new aryldom, it should honor Lucillia over one of her son's."

"You're sure about this?" Ellendren asked; the choice belonged entirely to her sister.

"I don't discredit what Roendryn had done for his people, but I never understood why we took the son's name and not the mother's."

"It might also help your cause in showing that you have no interest in becoming a monarch." Ellendren tapped her cheek with a finger as she held her face in thought.

"How will Silvia respond after learning this was all politics?" Devlyn asked, worried about the repercussions. Silvia and her husband had always been one of their loudest rivals in chamber.

"Silvia would recognize it as a political stunt if I pushed Trethien away and that would end poorly for us all. She'd be impossible to work with in the future. So, Trethien has agreed it would be best for him to end the arrangement," Kaela said.

"And once that's seen to, I'll return to Gwilnor, assuming Danielle has returned there to complete her studies. My parents will be impossible to be around after that," Trethien said.

"I've already spoken with her and she's aware of everything. She won't hold this against you and is quite eager to see you again," Ellendren said.

"Thank you. Still, I don't envy your position on the council once my mother realizes the proposal was a farce," Trethien said.

"Because she was always a delight when sitting in chamber before," Devlyn said, hoping not to offend Trethien.

"My father would say the same." Trethien laughed after a pause that felt too long.

Empty Halls

Velaria Treyven, Chair of Azurelle, looked on in awe as the brilliant palace-city of Septyl rose before her. She felt like a story-book hero as she approached the long-abandoned home of the ei'ana. Like all elven children, she had heard tales describing the Luminari cities built solely from lumaryl, and had seen countless artistic depictions of Septyl, but never in her most wondrous dreams had she been prepared to see the reality.

Slender spires and domes rose from the city's foundations, an unseen pattern mandating their placement as lumaryl structures formed the palace-city. Behind Velaria, a parade of Azurelle ei'ana accompanied by Septyl knights eagerly sought to reclaim their rightful home by virtue of their Counsels.

Every young girl who entered Gwilnor Academy to study to become an ei'ana had fantasized of returning to Septyl. For fifteen hundred years, thousands of women grew old and died, never seeing that dream realized. Velaria had counted herself among them when she had first begun her studies at the age of ten. Now, the noble gates of Cyrelle Azurelle rose before his namesake ei'ana, while the other Schools sought entrance through their own gates.

Before leaving Ceurenyl and beginning the march to Septyl, the Albiens had uncovered every tome and scroll referencing the palace-city. Among the various accounts, more recent editions contained many conflicting interpretations, particularly regarding the pattern woven into Septyl's construction. The records confirmed that Septyl had seven districts; each School had its own district and gate into the city. Among the theories revolving around Septyl, the Albiens had posited that the Seven Chairs would have to lift the seal over their respective city gates.

During their march, Velaria had worried about how they would determine which entrances belonged to which Schools. Gwilnor's halls were lined with tapestries and paintings of Septyl. While gold lumaryl dominated the artwork, each division of the palace-city had a different hue. She had assumed that the varying colors were part of the artistic expression, denoting the seven Schools. She never imagined the colors were reflected in the city itself. But the closer Velaria drew to Septyl, the more she noticed the different hues in the lumaryl road.

The road had divided when Septyl had risen before them, leading to the different gates. The road didn't divide into seven paths all at once; some routes had multiple colors threaded into the stonework, promising a later division.

A crescent-shaped structure enveloped the gate of Cyrelle Azurelle, forming an elliptical plaza soon filled with Azurelles. A central alcove was carved from the center of the grand gate, sheltering those wishing entrance. Velaria recognized the pointed arched gate; Gwilnor favored a similar architecture, as did Lucillia, Eandyl, and the Luminari cities the ei'ana had briefly visited on the journey here. Her mind strayed to the legendary Erendinth Architects that spanned every School, wondering if the lost talent would resurface. Perhaps the fabled library here would shed some light on them.

Two Septyl knights walked beside Velaria, their burnished metal shining in the sun and their blue tunics billowing in the wind. "Mother Velaria, would you like us to investigate the gate first? To ensure your safety?"

"Thank you for your concern, Darnl, but I don't think it necessary." Velaria turned to look at the mass of Azurelle ei'ana and knights behind her; a sea of people wearing blue clothing that denoted their School. These were the men and women who had remained at Gwilnor when the Tenebrae began taking control. Many had fled the school and city when Chancellor Oranna had been murdered. Velaria didn't blame them. Later, she had wanted as many to flee the castle as possible. Still, she had no idea who she could trust anymore. Any one of the ei'ana here or abroad could have deceived her and the other Chairs.

Velaria looked up to see Yelaris soaring above; the blue dragon was just as excited. She eagerly dove toward the gate, which was large enough for her to pass through easily, even if she grew four times larger. Like Rusyl, Yelaris was still considered young and would continue to grow with every passing summer. She landed a short distance in front of Velaria, next to the gate.

Expansive lumaryl doors rose before them, intricate sculpted vines and flowers leaping from the surface in a whimsical dance frozen in time. Sculpted persons appeared ready to walk out from the doors' surface. Velaria had never seen sculptures so lifelike. Only the statue of Lucillia at the place of her sacrifice rivaled these, and that statue had been sung from the forest by tree spirits and other anadel.

Velaria approached the gate and touched the lumaryl surface, finding it surprisingly warm, as though alive. Withdrawing her hand, she examined the gate again. It had been sheltered by the alcove, but the entire city had been encased in the Shroud. Despite the weeks it had taken to reach the city after the Shroud's destruction, Velaria was startled by the gate's temperature.

How can it be warm? she thought. Yelaris sent images to Velaria, showing a fire in her stomach that, as long she lived, would never go cold.

Pressing both hands on either door of the gate, Velaria impressed her authority into the contact. Her very being revealed her identity as the Chair of Azurelle. Both doors warmed more at her touch. She felt something within them—something intelligent. The ancient doors stirred, as though from a long slumber. Neither door moved to open, but something in them did move.

A gentle wind came from behind and the vines and flowers carved into the doors shifted in the breeze. Her eyes widened; as though the warmth wasn't enough to cause her skin to prickle, now the carvings were moving!

A flower wafted along the surface and Velaria watched it fall on one of the statues' feet. Imperceptible words sounded from above. Her eyes darted up, seeking the owner of the voice, landing on one of the statues carved into the door. "Pardon?"

"I said, most pay little attention to my flowers, cultivated for millennia," the statue replied. "Forgotten High Aelish have we? And here I thought the Eklean Common Tongue would never catch on."

Velaria looked blankly at the statue.

"I wondered if I'd ever wake again," said the statue.

"You can speak?" Velaria asked, realizing the absurdity of the statement, to say nothing of the door knowing two languages, if not more.

"I see the standards for Chairs now lie in the simplest of observations; can't say much has changed. Of course, you're very young to be a Chair. What am I saying, you're young enough to still frolic in the meadows without a care in the world," said the statue.

"Who—*what* are you?" Velaria asked, making sure her mouth wasn't gaping.

"Interesting question. I can't say I've ever had a name, that is, not an individual name." The statue rubbed his chin and looked toward the statue beside him on the adjacent door. "What of you? Were you ever named?"

"What a silly thing," replied the female statue. "What's-a-his-it cursed at me for not letting him pass though; I remember that quite vividly."

Both statues were naked and reminded Velaria of the figures on the Seal of Vyoletryn.

"Would you call us emblems?" The male statue still looked at his companion.

"Well, not *the* emblems," the female statue said. "We'll never hear the end of it if we claim ourselves as such."

"Those two can be quite stuffy. Can't blame them for it, all they do is stand inside on display. I bet they're jealous of us since we get to bask in the sun all day."

"Not as jealous as the Arantiulyn gate statues on the north side of the city; I don't think they've felt the sun since they were wielded into that door."

"Excuse me," Velaria said, interrupting them. "Do all lumaryl statues speak like you?"

"By the Light no! Bunch of dimwits inside if you ask me," said the male statue.

"Aren't I the lucky one then." The female statue grimaced.

I guess that answers my question, Velaria thought, more curious about whether all lumaryl statues spoke or not. "In that case, would you mind if we went in?"

"Do you mind?" the male statue asked the female statue.

"What *I* mind is that they left me well and alone. With *you* as my only companion for fifteen hundred years. To say nothing of that awful mist after we were abandoned."

Just as Velaria was about to ask again, the doors silently opened inward, the gleaming lumaryl surface parting down the middle as the doors fully opened, forcing the two sculptural reliefs to look at each other.

"Fifteen hundred years since I saw you; my word, you're gorgeous!" said the male statue.

"And here I complained that fifteen hundred years was too long but a moment ago—we should go twice as long next time if it means I don't have to look at your sorry face."

"Thank you." Velaria stepped through the door, Yelaris following.

Neither statue responded, continuing to bicker, shifting to High Aelish. Their voices faded the further she went through the large vestibule; it opened to an expansive chamber.

She gaped at the incredible space as her eyes followed the vertical thrust. A translucent dome towered above, bathing the large space in sunlight. A mixture of concave and convex curves dictated the walls, each lined with intricate doors, windows, and balconies, making each side of the large chamber feel like its own building inside the palace-city. The space she stood in felt like a plaza, one protected from the elements. Corridors broad enough to be city streets branched off the main plaza, all with a distinctive curve and lined with ornate buildings.

Directly beneath the center of the dome sat a large bubbling fountain. It filled the space with a tranquil sound that was quickly overwhelmed by the many Azurelles following Velaria inside. A statue with the likeness of a proud elf stood resolutely in the fountain. He had a dignified expression and his robes ruffled in an absent wind. That had to be Cyrelle Azurelle. Of course, the first Chair of Azurelle wasn't an elf, but a draelyn of the Sapphire House.

Velaria approached the fount and rested her hands on its edge. She had never seen water so pure. Her eyes searched the depths of the pool as the light above her shifted.

"Ana lei, Sedeilyn Azurelle," the statue said. Velaria had heard his voice only once before, when she had been captive to the Tenebrae and Cyrelle Azurelle had stripped them of their ei'ana status.

"Forgive me, I do not understand High Aelish," Velaria said, trying to recall what little she remembered from her primitive studies in the language. She knew that 'ana' meant light—every ei'ana did—but was at a complete loss for the rest.

"Light welcome you, Chair of Azurelle." The large statue smiled down at her.

"Thank you, Cyrelle." Velaria pressed her palm to her heart and bowed.

"Only a likeness and a memory; the great draelyn passed to Lu-maeniel long ago." The statue of Cyrelle mimicked Velaria's bow. "But your formalities to a statue are welcome, if unnecessary."

A globe of blue light appeared before Velaria. A soft glow hummed from its core, diminishing at its edges, then fading into the light already present in the space. The globe gently bounced, as though it wanted Velaria to follow it.

She looked from the blue globe to the statue of Cyrelle.

"The globes will escort you to your chambers."

Velaria turned to see hundreds of blue globes, each hovering before a different ei'ana or knight. "Make sure everyone knows to follow the globes," Velaria said to Iraniel and Darnl, the Septyl knight captains among the Azurelles. She turned her attention to the soft blue globe impatiently hovering before her. She took a step and the globe whizzed around, leading her to a grand building along the plaza's perimeter, on axis with the fountain and the city gate.

Following the globe, Velaria came to large double doors at the base of the palatial structure. Hovering above the door hung a monumental balcony; Velaria had seen images of past Chairs of Azurelle woven into tapestries, and they all stood on that very balcony. Velaria rarely had to address a large group, and never imagined she'd be expected to do so from a balcony like the one above her now. She was a Chair, not a queen.

The excited blue globe swirled around the door handle, insisting that Velaria open it.

Not wanting to upset it, she turned the smooth handle. It was warm, just like every other lumaryl object she touched. The carved vines retreated from the center seam and the wooden doors opened easily and silently, gliding inward. Light flooded out from the antechamber. How could this room, this palace inside a palace, be so bright? Was it the lumaryl? Tapestries woven from lierathnil hung on every wall. With a closer look, Velaria saw that the images moved.

The nearest lierathnil tapestry displayed a woman with flowing golden hair aloft in a breeze—even the blades of grass moved! Dazzled by the spectacle, Velaria noticed that the blue globe bobbed impatiently, demanding Velaria follow it deeper into the Azurelle Chair's palace.

Each corridor and chamber beyond held Velaria in awe. None of the statuary resembled anything she had ever seen; each was unique and, like the statues on the gate and the likeness of Cyrelle Azurelle, each spoke with their own personality.

A winding stair carried Velaria up several flights before the globe stopped before another double door featuring intricate vines and flowers. This one was much smaller than the pair leading into the palace—her palace. She passed into the vestibule where columns framed an opening on the far side that let out to a much larger space.

Light spilled into the grand chamber from a shallow glass-like dome; it appeared to be of the same material as the plaza dome. The globe bounced again. Velaria noted several doors leading further into her quarters. None of the doors were open, but each bore the same exquisite detail as the first. Choosing the center door, Velaria crossed the salon, pushed the door ajar, and discovered a study. Half-written letters on faded parchment littered the desk, a seal tumbled to the side.

Picking up the seal, Velaria expected the jeweled figurine to carry weight, but it was surprisingly light. On the underside was the Azurelle emblem. She shuffled through the letters and a name stood out—Nirae Queillis. *Was that the last Chair of Azurelle before Septyl was lost?* she thought, her hand running over the Aelish script. A bright piece of parchment sat near the center of the desk. Even upside down, Velaria recognized the Common Tongue in much fresher ink.

Dear Velaria,

While I might not be the first to formally welcome you to Septyl, I'll at least be the first anacordel. Please find me with the other Chairs at the Sophillium; it's located in the center of Septyl. All roads lead to the Sophillium.

Kevn Weyvien

Velaria's mind buzzed with questions, among others, how had Kevn reached and entered Septyl before the Seven Chairs lifted the seal over the palace-city?

With more questions than Kevn's letter answered, Velaria left the study. The blue globe was gone, leaving Velaria to find the Sophillium on her own. Stepping out into the plaza, she saw that the majority of the ei'ana and knights had dispersed to their quarters. Several knights had already begun patrolling the area, learning more about their new home with every step. For security reasons, the city gate had been sealed after everyone had made it inside. No enemy would sneak into Septyl, especially with Yelaris resting between the fountain and gate.

Scanning the plaza, Velaria chose the broadest corridor, thinking it the most likely to take her deeper into the palace-city. The corridor had a slight bend that became more severe as she went, as though it curled inward.

After walking through what felt like half the city, a second plaza opened before her. It was noticeably smaller than the first yet had the same exquisite features. A voluminous translucent dome sprung above and a fountain with statuary stood beneath it. This fountain featured two elves and a dragon, the emblem of the School of Azurelle sculpted before her eyes. She'd never seen it as a three-dimensional sculpture before.

Tempted to stop and speak with the statues and the ideals contained in their proud forms, Velaria forced herself to continue. She went down the next winding corridor; it had a noticeably sharper curvature. Another plaza appeared, this one only half the distance from the last one.

Standing in this fountain was a statue of herself. Velaria looked at her likeness, lost for words about how it was possible. No one today knew how to manipulate lumaryl as the ancient Luminari elves once had. Walking around her own likeness, Velaria wondered if the forgotten arts of the ancient elves were lost. Unlike the other plazas she had passed through, this felt like an interior chamber. The surrounding walls were lined with hundreds of alcoves, each housing a statue. They had to be past Chairs. The statues spiraled up the space in a spire. Curiously, there weren't any empty alcoves. *Did the spire grow taller with every new Chair?*

The corridor continued at the opposite end of the plaza and terminated at a semicircular plaza. A pointed arch wall towered before Velaria with a dais, seven steps high, arching out. At the top of the dais, monumental double doors were centered on the wall.

Sculpted vines wove across the doors, but instead of flowers or people, small orbs accompanied the winding vines. Velaria climbed the steps and reached for the great handle. Hesitant to push it open, she touched the warm wood as she had done with the lumaryl gate.

Holding her breath, Velaria waited for something to happen. This door felt different than the others had. Whatever authority she held over the palace-city as Chair, she did not think it extended to whatever stood behind this door. Velaria continued to wait without an answer. This had to be the Sophillium, the Great Library of Septyl.

"UNDER WHAT PRETENSE DO YOU BAR US FROM, WELL, WHATEVER IT IS YOU CALLED IT!" Mother Melanie Birkwell's voice thundered through the corridors.

Velaria left the beautiful door and followed Melanie's voice around the colossal building, past small trees, flowers, and shrubs forming gardens along the much narrower path.

"Mother Melanie, please temper yourself," Velaria heard Paurel say, her voice tired.

"This vagrant student dares to deny the Seven Chairs entrance to a part of Septyl," Melanie said, no longer shouting, but still loudly severe. "If I didn't know better, I'd swear he's responsible for barring the Arantiulyns from entering Septyl as well."

A knot formed in Velaria's stomach, no longer interested in why Kevn had invited them to the Sophillium without granting them entrance or how he had gotten into the palace-city.

"Did you not place your palm over the door and declare your identity?" Phendien asked. "Did not the globes of orange light lead you to your quarters in the Arantiulyn Chair's palace?"

Velaria saw the concern etched on Kevn's face; he knew something. Always a bright student, Velaria wondered what conclusion he had come to. He looked at each of the Chairs, settling on Phendien, and spoke in what Velaria could only assume was High Aelish.

Where'd he learn to speak High Aelish? she thought, listening to the indecipherable yet fluid words pass between the two until they stopped and Phendien sighed. Velaria felt the space grow tense, and before she could blink, Melanie Birkwell fell to the floor, unconscious.

Paurel turned on Phendien, eyes flaring in anger. "Explain the meaning of this!"

"Melanie's loyalties did not lie with Arantiulyn nor was she still an ei'ana." Phendien examined the unconscious woman. "Tell me, Kevn, how did you know she was Tenebrae?"

Velaria's breath caught in her chest at the condemnation.

"That's a serious accusation, Phendien." Paurel covered her mouth.

"More curious is how she managed to hide it all this time. We were right to fear there was an imposter among the seven of us." Phendien scratched his chin and turned to Kevn. "It would explain how the Tenebrae knew of our attempt to escape Gwilnor and why she was so opposed to holding trials in the Temple of Ceur."

"It was the only logical conclusion. If she really was the Chair of Arantiulyn, and loyal to her School, she would have had no difficulty entering the Arantiulyn district. I'm amazed Septyl opened at all—the city would have recognized the threat."

"Clearly not a substantial threat," Mother Selenya said calmly, apparently having suspected the betrayal. She turned her attention away from the imposter to the sealed door. "Now that it's resolved, I insist on you granting us entrance; my School has long waited to gain access to the Great Library of Septyl."

"Forgive me, Mother Selenya, I mean no disrespect, but I cannot." Kevn said politely.

"What are you not telling us, Kevn?" Recognizing Kevn's peculiar behavior, quite unlike his usual self, Velaria cut in quickly before Selenya could begin berating him.

"Until a new Grand Librarian is installed over the Sophillium, only I can enter, and I can't permit entrance to anyone until my installation."

"Have you hurt your head?" Selenya asked, suppressing a laugh. "You can't expect us to agree to such a preposterous request. The Albiens are given jurisdiction over Eklean's libraries and records. You're not even an ei'ana, having abandoned Gwilnor for the ei'ceuril. Speaking of which, weren't you elevated as the Ceurtriarch's scribe?"

"I was, Mother Selenya, but I was also called here. I entered Septyl unhindered even as the Shroud still stood. I was greeted by a specter who led me to the Sophillium and showed me many things." Kevn self-consciously rubbed his arm, his features apologetic.

"So, Sophie's chosen her successor," Phendien said.

Selenya rose a skeptical brow. "Who is Sophie?"

"She created the sophilliae along with the Sophillium to house them all. She was rather strict in her policies and has always been involved in the selection of her successors; however, she rarely involves herself to this extent," Phendien said.

"I've never heard of a sophilliae," Selenya said.

"No, you wouldn't have, nor would you have ever seen one," said Phendien, his eyes laughing. "One of her policies was that no sophilliae should ever leave the Sophillium. She freely allowed people to enter and gain the wealth of her and her successors' collected knowledge, but the removal of any sophilliae was resolutely forbidden, as was how to recreate them. Only Sophie's successors know how to create a sophilliae."

VACANT THRONE

Devlyn, Ellendren, and the seven Luminari high aryls sat around a large round table in the aryl's chamber in Aerodhal. Given the delicate situation that required confirmation, the minor aryls also attended today and formed a significantly larger ring around them. Every Luminari aryl had travelled to Arenthyl for this meeting. Luckily, the vaulted chamber was large enough that no one felt cramped.

While Devlyn and Ellendren had chosen Kaela to stand in their place as steward, the aryls still had to agree to it. To Devlyn, this was an easy solution. After all, House Roendryn had served the Luminari as stewards for twelve centuries. Who better to fill that position than the experienced diplomat and heir to that house?

"I don't intend to be counterproductive, but remind me why it is necessary to select a steward?" Toral asked. "The governance of Krysenthiel falls to the collective aryls when the Crystal Throne is vacant."

"As we have not yet taken our place on the Crystal Throne as the Exalted Aryl of Krysenthiel, little will change in the governance of Krysenthiel." Ellendren kept her voice measured and respectful, despite Toral's unsubtle hints that they were not yet the Exalted Aryl and Krysenthiel was being governed just fine without one. "We have full confidence in the aryls' governance in our absence. After all, as you all know, the Exalted Aryl has never ruled in solitude, but simply as the keystone among the aryls. Elven governance does not reflect that of our human counterparts. We are not kings and queens." Ellendren paused for Toral to offer opposition, which he did not.

"Yet you will be High King and High Queen of Eklean," Iridil said.

"Only because the human kingdoms of Eklean so named our fore-bearers in order to bring peace to the war-torn continent," Ellendren said.

"If I might interject," Kyiel said.

"Of course, Ei'denai."

"You're being very modest and careful with your words, Ei'terel," said the older elf. "It's no secret to anyone that you and Devlyn were de-clared wed by the seraph. While the coronation ceremony is necessary, as the Lorenthien heir and bound in marriage, by every right, you two *are* the Exalted Aryl of Krysenthiel in all but name and crown. And you have been acting as such and rightly so. Considering your leadership among us, a steward is necessary in your absence."

Devlyn felt Ellendren beam through their bond. He knew she was fond of Kyiel and his wife Fyona. The Aryl of Verenthyl were a brutally honest, yet kind, couple.

Devlyn's focus sharpened as someone commented on Kaela's un-wed status and the inappropriateness of her serving as a steward and aryl. He had no idea who had said it, but to his complete surprise, Silvia coughed, then rose to Kaela's defense. "I believe Kaela Roendryn will be an exceptional steward. She has all the training and experience we could ever require; recall who her parents are."

"Forgive me, Silvia, but you only say so because your son is cur-rently courting her." Iridil glared at her once fierce ally. The Taerinior and Narielle aryls had thwarted Devlyn and Ellendren at every step from Lucillia to Krysenthiel. "This meeting is not simply whether or not to allow Kaela to stand in the Lorenthien's place in their absence, but to formally recognize House Roendryn or House Lucillia, as Kaela has suggested, as a house of stewards to House Lorenthien for all the days to come."

"And remind me, Iridil, how is that any different from how the Roendryns have already served us? Our ancestors, guided by the anadel, chose Lucillia's children to lead in the absence of the Lorenthiens," Naesiv said.

"I believe that it is entirely appropriate that we recognize Lucillia's descendants and formally recognize them as a house of stewards. Their house deserves a continued place of distinction in our court," Kyiel said.

"Lucillia's descendants will be the next Exalted Aryl, from both branches, Roendryn and Feolyn. What more distinction is needed?" Aegian asked, maintaining the alliance between the Ginielle and Taerinior aryls.

"That's hardly the same, Aegian," Binoral said. "Besides, House Lucillia will become a minor aryldom, joining the countless others who already have that distinction. The only time they will hold any authority over a city is when the Lorenthien aryl are unable to perform their duties. And just as a reminder, such an instance is fast approaching."

"Do you honestly believe that House Lucillia will remain content in that diminished position? The Roendryns served as kings and queens among our people. How long until the formally recognized house strives for more—how long until the Lucillia aryl seeks to implant themselves in one of our cities to wrestle the aryldom away from one of us?" Enoria stood and looked at each of the high aryls, as though to hold them accountable.

The chamber quieted and no one spoke against Enoria; even the minor aryls' rumblings stilled. The ei'terel of House Taerinior had a point. The Roendryns had been monarchs for over a thousand years. Kaela had never dreamt of sitting on her parents' throne, but she had dreamt of ensuring the survival of her house after Ellendren, their house's heir, had become a Lorenthien.

"We should consider the reason why Kaela wants to change the name of House Roendryn to Lucillia." Ellendren did not have to speak loudly, but she did stand, as was customary for whoever was speaking. The high and minor aryls all turned their attention to her, knowing that she would be biased toward the elevation of her former house, if under a new name. "By formally establishing House Lucillia in the place of House Roendryn, there will be little confusion over that house's role in the years to come. There can be no confusion about that house seeking to regain its place as a monarchical power, as House Lucillia never occupied a throne or wore a crown.

"None of us had ever dared to dream that House Lorenthien had survived Erynor's last reign, and in their stead, Roendryn, and his descendants after him, led our people. He followed the customs and traditions the Lorenthiens had practiced here in Krysenthiel and on Luminare before our ancestors were forced to abandon both. Without realizing it, the Roendryns acted as stewards to the Crystal Throne. They did not merely keep it warm, waiting for the Lorenthiens to return, but thrived in that position and our ancestors built a great kingdom, seeing us through our pilgrimage beside the Illumined Wood. Who better to formally recognize as a house of stewards than the same house that has already proven themselves true in that position?"

Murmuring rustled through the chamber once Ellendren took her seat. Following any of the individual conversations among the high and minor aryls proved impossible. Devlyn tried to no avail to focus his hearing on the Ginielle and Taerinior aryls who were most opposed to establishing House Lucillia as a house of stewards.

"I believe we've heard all we need to hear and should proceed to a vote," Naesiv said. Unlike in Lucillia and the chamber tent they had used during their long migration to Krysenthiel, the aryl's chamber had a curious voting mechanism suspended from the center of the shallow groin vault. Dozens of glass-like globes hung there, and depending on the type of vote, whether in support or against, or even a more complex vote, a number of those globes would lower.

Only two of the globes lowered today. Somehow the globes recognized and knew everyone present in the chamber and automatically tallied their votes proportionally, depending on their status as a high or minor aryl. The high aryls' votes counted for much more than the minor aryls' votes, but the collective number of the minor aryls could sway the vote in a certain direction. This was especially true when the minor aryls disagreed with their high aryl. Unlike the high aryls, minor aryls were not bound to a city, but after selecting their place of residence, they answered to the high aryl of whichever city they had settled in. Since Devlyn and Ellendren were not yet the Exalted Aryl, their weighted vote remained equal to the other high aryls'.

The two globes started to brighten; the one supporting a new House Lucillia as a house of stewards lit faster than the other. Given that two of the high aryls did not support the motion, the globe not in favor of the elevation lit the room according to their weighted response. Still, the Aryls of Delmira Wood and Tenyl were in the minority and that globe barely brightened once the minor aryls started to vote. Devlyn had learned that when the minor aryls overwhelmingly supported another position, their high aryl was expected to change their vote.

Ciraenth and Aegian stood after the light in the two globes became stable, signifying that all the votes were in. "As the Aryl of Delmira Wood, we move to change our vote to the affirmative and support Kaela and House Lucilla as a house of stewards." The globe that had had their vote significantly dimmed, but noticeably not by half. Minor aryls had also cast their votes in that direction, likely hoping they would be named as the house of stewards in Kaela's stead. The light cast from the affirmative globe barely changed in luminance as it had already had an overwhelming majority.

The chamber waited to see if Iridil and Enoria would stand to change their vote, but they remained seated and unmoved.

"It is decided then. From this day forward, House Roendryn will be known as House Lucillia and will be a house of stewards to the Exalted Aryl of Krysenthiel," Valerie pronounced. A round of applause followed, and congratulations were offered to Kaela.

The aryls shuffled, ready to be done with the lengthy meeting. Ellendren stood before the aryls had a chance to leave the chamber. "With this meeting concluded, I wish you all the best in our absence. Know that it pains us that we must leave so soon after reclaiming Krysenthiel, but we've been assured by Auriel that there is no other way if we are to be prepared as Phaedryn in the battles to come."

"We don't look forward to your absence either, but you have our full support. If we're to come out of this war victorious, we need you both properly trained as Phaedryn," said Therrin.

The chamber emptied and various aryls extended both their well wishes to Devlyn and Ellendren and their anticipation of their swift return.

Devlyn and Ellendren were finally alone in the chamber. "Shall we find Aren?" he asked.

"I would like to pack a few things in my quarters."

"He said we would not need to bring anything."

"That's unreasonable. We should bring books to study from and clothes to change into."

The door to the chambers opened. "You will not need either," Aren said, Lyren and Pevrel following him. Even without the shadows oozing off his body, he was an imposing figure.

"But what of the Theseryn? Surely, I haven't learned everything I need to know about the Evil One from it. The more I read about him, the more ignorant I feel," Ellendren confessed.

"It is not possible to bring anything but yourself. Nothing but a Phaedryn can go where we go."

"What about a change of clothes? We can't wear the same lierathnil for an entire year."

"You can bring nothing. You will need to disrobe," Aren said.

Ellendren blushed, no longer concerned about books.

"I'm sorry, Ei'terel, but I cannot explain here. Everything will be revealed once we arrive at our destination. If it is any consolation, your lighted form as a Phaedryn will prevent anyone from seeing your nakedness. But understand that this shame of your body is a weakness."

Pevrel moved closer to Ellendren. She didn't ask the men to leave the chamber, but her glare certainly demanded it. Devlyn almost said something about him and Ellendren being married, but neither did he feel like undressing in front of Pevrel, even though it was all but impossible for her to not see him naked when she attended Ellendren while he was bathing.

Devlyn, Lyren, and Aren went into the empty vestibule, closing the door behind them, leaving Ellendren and Pevrel in the aryl's chamber. Aren was always in his Dark Phaedryn form, and Devlyn could tell that he wore no lierathnil. Aren's nudity was not expressly visible, but also not a mystery. Where light concealed Devlyn and Ellendren's naked forms when bonded with their phoenix, shadow cloaked Aren's nudity, his muscles clearly defined beneath the thin membrane.

Devlyn couldn't help being uncomfortable as he began to shed his lierathnil. He'd lost count of how many times Lyren had been present while Devlyn disrobed. Still, he bonded with Aliel as soon as his clothes were off. Lyren barely had the discarded garments gathered in his arms before Devlyn's lighted form cast a thin layer over his body, concealing what should not be publicly displayed to the Luminari court.

The light intensified as Ellendren joined them. Lyren busied himself with folding Devlyn's garments and Pevrel glared again at them to mind their eyes. Devlyn again thought that she was being ridiculous and even if he tried, he couldn't keep his eyes off his wife.

They left the chamber to find Viren and Wyn waiting outside.

"You'll watch over Kaela in our absence?" Ellendren asked.

"Of course. I trust the vote went as expected?" Viren asked.

"It did. House Lucillia will rule as stewards in our place," Ellendren said.

"I'm delighted to hear," Viren said.

"As am I," Wyn said with a smirk. Devlyn had no idea how he had managed to disguise his feelings for Kaela while she garnered Silvia's support. "Will I have to continue as her tutor?"

"You have been a dutiful tutor," Ellendren said, smiling.

"As long as I'm not restricted to that position, I think we'll be just fine."

Aren coughed, ready to leave.

"Right. You must be off. Know that not a day will pass when you are absent from my thoughts. May Auriel and Uriel guide you in Anaweh's light," Viren said.

"Thank you, Viren," Ellendren said.

Devlyn was suddenly sad at the idea of being separated from Viren again, and without any warning, he hugged his sworn protector.

Shocked by the sudden affection, Viren's arms hesitantly wrapped around Devlyn in return. "Take care, Devlyn. I will do everything in my power to keep Krysenthiel secure."

"I know you will."

Devlyn stepped back from Viren and nodded, then hugged Wyn goodbye. There was no need for the three Phaedryn to walk through the entire palace to leave from the main entrance. They walked the length of the corridor outside the chamber to a broad balcony where many of the aryls had lingered, enjoying refreshments and gossip. Aren unfurled his dark wings in a rush of wind, startling the others on the balcony. The Luminari had grown accustomed to Aren since he'd helped them to reclaim Arenthyl by fighting off a Deurghol and shadow elves that had flown on dragons of the Dark Flight. Still, his appearance was like the enemy he had fought. Tenebrys and the Void clung to Aren just as it did to their enemy.

Devlyn and Ellendren unfurled their own wings and before they could even smile at the elves on the balcony, Aren leapt over the edge. His wings held him aloft as he waited for Devlyn and Ellendren to follow.

Devlyn felt the warm air caress his skin and the sun warming him and complimenting the light already radiating from his body as he and Ellendren joined Aren. The elves on the balcony cheered; they all knew what Delyn and Ellendren had to do, even if it meant them leaving Krysenthiel for an unknown period of time.

Devlyn and Ellendren flew behind Aren, circling Arenthyl, gaining altitude in the process as they swirled up and into the clouds. Arenthyl shrank with every flap of their wings, and soon became a tiny speck far below. Devlyn punched through the clouds with Aren and Ellendren close behind. The air grew colder the higher they went. Devlyn's teeth would have clattered if he'd not been bonded with Aliel.

The clouds only cloaked Devlyn briefly as he continued past the lofty moisture. Unable to hide his enthusiasm while bonded with Aliel, Devlyn summersaulted once past the clouds.

Showoff. Ellendren's thoughts passed into Devlyn's mind.

Conserve your energy; it's not a short journey, and we can only rest once. Aren passed his thoughts to Devlyn.

Reprimanded, Devlyn was determined to conserve his strength.

It's for the best; we still don't know how far we're going, Aliel conveyed.

I couldn't help it. A sense of amusement passed between them. Aliel had also enjoyed it.

The sunlit hours soon faded, and the sun dipped behind them as they flew east.

The land below grew indistinguishable and Aren angled downward and into what had to be the Illumined Wood. Devlyn finally understood why they would only be stopping once. Wherever they were going, it was not on Eklean.

THE PRINCE

The small and sovereign island of Jadien stuck out of the sea like a jagged root between the Kinzdol islands and Dagger's Point. It didn't appear that anything green grew on Jadien and where the surface wasn't jagged rose the city that the island and city-state took their name from. Unlike the other city-states along the Erynien Bay, it had never fallen to another's rule and the so-called pirates of Jadien had fiercely maintained their independence.

Rusyl sagged toward a cliff away from the city. They had flown from Teran's estate to the easternmost island's coast, resting only briefly before crossing the waters to Jadien. Rusyl had not overstated how difficult it would be to carry four people. As they thudded onto the rocky cliff, Rusyl's legs gave out and he waited, panting, as his passengers quickly got off. They knew how strenuous the journey had been for the blue dragon, Jaerol sharing that exhaustion through their growing bond.

Rusyl never complained and the only images Jaerol had gleaned during their flight were of determination.

"Thank you, Rusyl." Jaerol rubbed his maw, scratching it to get a cat-like purr from the dragon. "You can rest now."

Rusyl didn't respond but curled his tail around his torso before his rumbling turned into snoring. Jaerol wondered how long Rusyl would need to regain his strength to carry them the rest of the way to Sudern. The most difficult leg of their flight from Cynethol might be over, but the remaining distance from Jadien to Sudern would be just as taxing.

While Jadien's loyalties were in question, they had it in good faith that Sudern's Duke Farneis was a friend of Krysenthiel. They would not have to worry about being turned over to shadow elves once they reached Sudern. That threat was very real here in Jadien though. Jaerol had grown up knowing that the Jadish prince had managed some sort of trade alliance with the Erynien Empire. On an island so remote and barren, they had little choice but to import supplies from the mainland. Jaerol had no evidence that the alliance was anything more than a trade partnership. What did Erynor care about a small island of humans in the sea? Could they supply a military force to supplement Erynor's armies?

Since the Jadish were rumored to be pirates, perhaps they complimented the Erynien navy. The Erynien Empire ruled the Erynien Bay uncontested and had never had the need to display their might on those waters. That had all changed with the arrival of the Daer, who'd swept into Tiel's unprotected coast. The Tieli armada had never recovered from the surprise attack led by the merpeople and Ja'mare seafarers on their way to lift the siege at Myrium. If Jadien was to supplement Erynor's sea power, Jaerol wondered how they would manage it. Jadien didn't exactly have any trees to construct new ships from.

Liam came up beside Jaerol and asked, "Should we investigate the city?"

"I'm sure Devlyn and Ellendren would appreciate us learning where the Jadish stand in this war." Jaerol stretched as he looked over the cliff face and into the stormy ocean.

"It'll be risky. There's a good chance at least one shadow elf is there if they're aligned with Erynor," Teran said, looking toward the city hidden by the rocky terrain. "I'm sure you'd manage, but others would learn which direction we've taken and would know where to track us from here."

Jaerol scratched his chin at the strategic advantages of finding an ally so close to Broid.

"We might not be given the option," Evellyn said.

Before Jaerol could ask what she meant, he heard hooves clopping on the rocky surface shortly followed by five riders coming into view. They had the dark complexion of the Ja'mare seafarers. Hopefully they still maintained a close relationship with each other. That would make striking an alliance easier since the Ja'mare seafarers had no love for the Erynien Empire.

"Declare your intent," said the rider in the center, a big hulking man with a deep voice. Despite his warm dark eyes appearing friendly, his voice carried only a threat.

"We are simply resting before continuing our journey," Jaerol said.

"An interesting group of travellers. Two Cyndinari, a Luminari, and a lethien. How did you come across a dragon? Do you have express permission from the emperor to use one of his dragons?" The large man's questions told Jaerol everything he needed to know about Jadien's loyalties. Fortunately, Jaerol had once been an Erynien emissary and knew how to speak to Erynor's subjects.

"You dare question an elf?" Jaerol clipped his tone impatiently, squared his shoulders, and straightened his spine to make himself taller.

"Forgive this one, I meant no offense to a Cyndinari. Our communication with Broid has been scarce since we received a directive to construct ships for the imperial navy. To say nothing of the lack of support while we had to push back a Daer invasion attempt."

Jaerol smirked to himself. His assumption about the Jadish building more ships had been right. "And what's the state of those ships?" he asked.

"Prince Alkesh has expressed our needs to Broid and our limited resources here."

"Since we're here, we might as well inspect the progress," Jaerol said, sounding bored.

The Jadish man sucked in a breath. "I would not refuse your desire. Prince Alkesh would delight in receiving you. Will you all be joining us?" The Jadish rider appraised the others who had kept quiet while Jaerol spoke for their group.

"I think not. The dragon needs to rest, so it'll just be myself and the lethien."

"As you command."

Jaerol spared a look for his uncle and Evellyn. They both maintained blank expressions for the sake of upholding appearances for the Jadish. The leader and one of the riders extended their hands for Jaerol and Liam to join them on horseback and the small party left for the city. Given the size of the small island, it didn't take long to reach it and if the rocky terrain had not been a factor, they would have arrived even sooner.

Jaerol noted how the city was only fortified along the sea. Given the island's cliffs, the sea was the only means of access. The entire city dipped toward a natural harbor crowded with ships. Their group curved around the north-facing harbor. Jaerol doubted that the harbor would have been adequate for moored ships if it had faced any other direction but north and toward the Erynien Bay. The Tempestien Sea was not known to treat ships kindly. Like the rest of the island, the city had a grey quality about it that was only intensified by thick stormy clouds above. What Jadien lacked in trees and flora it made up with in stone. The structures appeared finely crafted and the masons did not miss the opportunity to express what hewn stone could become.

The people crowding the city streets cleared a path for the riders. Everyone here had the same dark skin, their ancestors having been kissed by the sun over Ja'horan, the large continent far to the south. Like the seafarers of Ja'mare, the Jadish had likely settled here when the Guardian Senate had last assembled.

Jaerol had seen their destination before reaching the city. A great castle loomed over the mouth of the harbor. It clung to its rocky cliff, threatening any unwelcome arrivals passing beneath its shadow. A smaller keep sat on the cliff across the harbor's mouth, but its fortifications would not frighten sailors as Jadien's castle did. It was no wonder that the

Jadish had managed to repel the Daer. By the looks of it, that castle was one of the oldest structures in the city. Jaerol wondered who the original inhabitants of the castle had been. Did it stretch back to the time of Thellion before the elves dared consider abandoning their Skylands?

As they reached the keep, Jaerol saw just how much older it was than the rest of the city. The same grey stone of the island had been used to construct it, but its surfaces and corners were worn from the weather in a way the rest of the city was not.

"Who built the castle?" Jaerol asked, his curiosity getting the better of him.

"The prince knows its history better than any. I'm sure he'd be delighted to answer your questions," the Jadish leader sitting in front of Jaerol said.

"What's the prince like?"

"Irritable. But his son and heir is eager to take his father's place." Jaerol wondered if the son could be persuaded to turn against the Erynien Empire. They went through the castle gate and into the bailey. The tall walls blocked the choppy wind and the company dismounted, handing their reins over to stable hands.

They went into the castle and into a dimly lit entry hall. Most noticeable was how cold it felt, and not because of the temperature. The stark walls didn't display any banners or tapestries. Grey stone blocks sucked the meager lighting from the sparse candles. "I expected more from the prince's residence," Jaerol risked.

"Jadien has been promised riches time and time again for loyalty to the empire. But our halls have no art or other luxuries that the mainland kingdoms enjoy," the Jadish man replied.

Liam glared at Jaerol, knowing that he was playing a dangerous game. They passed through the entry hall and yet another chamber before reaching the throne room. Prince Alkesh, an old man, sat slumped on his throne, the rest of the people in the room keeping their distance. He frowned when he saw the visitors enter.

"Now what do you want? We've already told you that we need more lumber to build your ships," Alkesh spat out. "We can't move forward until you start felling the Illumined Wood."

Jaerol stopped himself from gasping. He knew the Erynien Empire wasn't above chopping down that sacred forest, but he hadn't realized they were considering it.

"They're only passing through. They're curious about the state of the ships," their guide replied.

"Have you also told them how poorly you think I'm governing Jadien? Don't think I don't know what you're plotting, Rezeki. My father would have tossed me from the southern cliffs and into the Tempestien Sea if I had your treacherous tongue," Alkesh said.

"You wound me, father," Rezeki said.

Jaerol blinked. He had thought their guide was just a disgruntled soldier, not the prince's son and heir. Still, who else would have spoken so boldly against their prince? Jaerol's mind spun with possible schemes as he tried to figure out what Rezeki's motives were. Did he want to remain a faithful servant of Erynor? He clearly didn't think Jadien had benefited in any way from their relationship with the Erynien Empire.

"If you don't watch your mouth around a Cyndinari, I won't be the one wounding you. Mark my words, they'll find someone else to sit on this chair after I die if you continue to be ungrateful."

"What do we have to be grateful for? These elves come to our island and demand we build them *our* ships? Our shipwrights have protected that knowledge since we came from Ja'horan. And we're not even being compensated for our labor," Rezeki said.

"You wouldn't know a day of labor if you were strapped to an oar to row like a slave. I've spoiled you beyond redemption," Alkesh said. Jaerol couldn't believe this exchange was happening in front of them. Perhaps there was a way to twist this to his advantage. Not in front of the old prince, but in private with Rezeki.

Rezeki reddened, infuriated. He did not reply though and Alkesh renewed his focus on Jaerol. "As I already told the last elf to visit, we won't have anything worthwhile to show until we receive more timber. And no, we will not be sending our shipwrights to the mainland. Rezeki, make yourself useful and take our guests to the guest wing if they intend to stay the night."

Jaerol and Liam sat together in the quiet of their room in the prince's cold and dreary castle. Neither knew what to say regarding what they had witnessed in the prince's throne room. They would have to return to the others soon. Nothing about the Jadish seemed trustworthy, not even Rezeki who didn't exactly come across as amenable to the Erynien Empire.

The provided candles in the room were insufficient and the narrow windows permitted little natural light. The door was barely closed before Jaerol had wielded a globe of light.

"How long should we stay before returning to the others?" Liam asked.

"We should go soon. They'll be worried if we're delayed and that's not something Rusyl needs right now."

"Now, why would they be worried?" Rezeki had come in unannounced.

"Were you waiting outside the door?" Jaerol asked, curious about what Rezeki was after. Rezeki looked at the wielded globe that Jaerol hadn't bothered to hide.

"I thought men couldn't wield safely."

"Things are changing," Jaerol said.

"You're not who you say you are. I know you're not an Erynien emissary."

"Then why bring us here? Are we your prisoners now?" Liam asked.

"I haven't decided yet. If I were to turn you over to the empire, perhaps we'd be rewarded. It would be a welcome change."

"But that's not what you want, is it?" Jaerol held Rezeki's gaze.

"Who's the elf with the hair spun of gold?"

"Why are you asking?" Liam grew defensive. He was ready to leave to get back to Evellyn and ensure she was safe.

"She's someone special, isn't she?"

"Whatever you're considering, know that she can take care of herself just fine," Jaerol said, more for Liam than for Rezeki.

"You think I want to kidnap her for a ransom?" Rezeki sounded genuinely offended. "No. I want her help. Does she know someone who can free us from beneath Erynor's thumb?"

"You're close to Broid. What success do you think you'll have by pulling away from the empire?" Liam asked.

"Sudern is also in the heart of the Erynien Empire and they've managed without the empire just fine," Rezeki said.

"You realize the empire must not get ahold of your ships, yes?" Jaerol asked.

"We have no way of denying them nor completing them without more supplies."

"What of your father, the prince?" Liam asked.

"He is old and not long for this world."

"You aim to quicken that process." Jaerol held Rezeki's unblinking gaze. "You know patricide isn't the best way to start off an alliance with elves who cherish virtues."

"You would prefer allowing that man to continue selling us out to the empire?"

"Your hands should not have any blood on them is all I'm suggesting. If the Jadish are as upset with the prince as you seem to be, maybe they'll assist you in dethroning your father. If I recall correctly, your people and the Ja'mare seafarers do not care to share your ships with others," Jaerol said.

"What if those same people lump me in with him as a betrayer to our values and culture?" Rezeki asked.

"Then I would suggest making sure they know whose side you are on," Liam said.

PHROENTHYL

From the cliff at the edge of the Illumined Wood, Devlyn watched the night sky soften to violet then to subtle hues of pink and orange painting the clouds as the sun rose from the ocean. He had slept better than expected, but still woke before the sun, and in the brightening dawn, took up a jienzu form, stilling his mind to prepare himself for the journey ahead. Aren still hadn't divulged their destination, but it had become clear when they had landed last night that they would be flying across the Unarian Sea today.

Tempted to break his form to shield his eyes from the sun, Devlyn persevered, arms extended. He breathed deeply, welcoming the day. The Unarian Sea transformed into a golden mirror, with the highest concentration of light creating a wavy line that joined the sun on the horizon to the cliff face. From where he stood, the golden band looked like a belt. Viewing all Teraeniel at once was impossible but Devlyn imagined the band of light wrapping around the globe like a shield. A foolish and impossible thought, but he liked the visual.

The sun had barely risen when Aren and Ellendren joined him. He relaxed his muscles and eased out of the jienzu form. Ellendren smiled at him and he returned it.

"It's time to continue. Prepare yourselves; we have a long journey ahead and will only rest at our destination." Aren stepped to the edge of the cliff and took in the rising sun.

"How do you know where we're going?" Ellendren asked.

"I can feel it within me. After your training is complete, you'll know as well," Aren said.

They had nothing to pack, not even bedrolls. Devlyn had eaten a vaer when he awoke and assumed that Aren and Ellendren had as well. Without warning, Aren dove off the cliff.

"You'd better bond with Aliel; Aren isn't the sort to wait." Ellendren flapped her wings and flew up instead of diving off the cliff. Aren was already a good distance away and Devlyn wondered if the dive had provided an additional thrust of speed.

Bonding fully with Aliel in a brilliant combustion of light, amplifying the already incredible sunrise, Devlyn followed Aren over the cliff. His wings flattened on his back as wind rushed past his body; he drew closer to the water and crags below. Waiting until the last possible moment, he extended his wings, and they caught the air, springing him forward over the water. Sea foam and salt splashed against him as he flew just above the water's surface before angling upward and toward Aren and Ellendren. He zipped past Ellendren and tried to catch up with Aren, but the older Phaedryn kept his pace steady and stayed in front of Devlyn.

They followed him toward the rising sun, maintaining an eastern trajectory after the sun had fully risen, with a slight southern variance. If not for his connection with Aliel, Devlyn would have had no idea of their whereabouts. But Aliel could pinpoint their exact location in Teraeniel, something Devlyn had discovered shortly after they had first bonded in the Illumined Wood. He had been a novice with the ei'ceuril at the time. That felt like a lifetime ago, a life that was no longer his. He had gone from being told that, according to a prophecy, he would never be allowed to marry, to now being Ellendren's husband and the Aryl of Arenthyl.

Devlyn had never learned the exact location of Luminare or the other Skylands, only that Luminare was to the east, Cyndinare to the south, Aldinare to the west, and Eldinare to the north. The only problem with those coordinates was he didn't know their reference points. Eldinare and Cyndinare were easy to approximate, if not necessarily their exact location, for south and north only changed when you reached the northern and southern poles. East and west, however, relied entirely on perspective. What was Luminare east of?

Aren had led them east from Arenthyl, and from what Ellendren had learned through her reading of the Theseryn, Lake Saeryndol was likely the location of the Valley of the Children, the place where the first anacordel, the Children, woke, and later home to the elder ones before they started to venture past the valley. If that was the case, the valley had to be the focal point. The Tree of Life inside Mount Verinien at the lake's center only solidified that logic.

Devlyn grew weary as the sun began to set. He had hoped they would reach their destination today, but Aren gave no indication that they would stop anytime soon. And there was an endless breadth of water beneath them without any land in sight. The only thing that kept Devlyn going was his assumption that they would reach their destination this same day. Now that the sun had sunk below the western horizon, Devlyn's limbs started to weigh him down. His eyelids grew heavy, and he knew Aliel was all that kept him awake. Unlike Aliel, Devlyn was not an anadel and his body required sleep. He assumed it was the same for Ellendren and Tariel.

The stars were exceptionally bright that night. Devlyn looked to the heavens periodically, and each time, he swore they grew brighter. Surely that was impossible. How could they get brighter? His vision through the phoenix's sight illuminated the night as though it was the brightest of days. But the stars sparkled; they appeared brighter when he was bonded with Aliel. Some of them looked like they were dancing. Convinced it was nothing more than exhaustion, he tried to ignore it, but Aliel nudged his fatigued mind back to the stars.

Can you see them sing? Listen and see, Aliel conveyed, elated.

Devlyn had never felt Aliel so excited before. He knew the phoenix shared a kinship with the anadel among the stars, but Devlyn had never learned how to interpret the stars or how to listen to them. Alethea had known how to commune with them, yet she had never explained how she had done it before she had been taken from them. Many others, including Oreniel and all the centaurs, Aewen, and Leilyn, would also know how to listen to the stars. Was it something they had learned by gazing into the starry sky and simply observing the stars until they could understand them? Devlyn had no idea, but he knew his schedule would never permit him to idly watch the stars until he could.

All will be revealed, came Aren's thoughts. *Your thoughts are loud tonight. Probably because they're on the verge of dreaming.*

Only a slight mental chuckle came in response. Devlyn wanted to be frustrated with Aren and his tight lip but too tired to care one way or another, he followed Aren on as starlight lit their backs. Devlyn felt Aliel consoled by their presence and tried to allow it to do the same to him.

While the night appeared bright to Devlyn, he saw the narrowest hint of purple bloom in the eastern sky on the empty horizon.

Suddenly, Aliel grew overwhelmingly excited.

What is it?

You'll see, Aliel conveyed. *Don't blink.*

The sky was cloudless, but Devlyn felt himself pass through a veil of sorts. There was no moisture to it, but Devlyn did feel it wash across his skin and penetrate his heart as he passed. Exerting every effort not to blink, Devlyn looked at something that every part of him had thought impossible. He had heard the stories of the Skylands, and had even seen Luminare in his ancestors' memories, but to see an uncorrupted Skyland with his own eyes was an entirely different experience. He could feel El-lendren's matching awe and astonishment.

Welcome to Phroenthyl. Aren's thoughts filled their minds.

Phroenthyl hung in the sky, as though anadel held it by a string from the stars above. A ridiculous comparison, but what they saw had to be impossible. Lush meadows and streams, flowering trees in perpetual bloom, the golden kryseniels of Luminare and now Krysenthiel blossoming across the landscape filled his vision. Streams flowed from silver lakes and hills, weaving their way across the fruitful land before cascading over the edge to vanish in a mist.

Devlyn could only see a sliver of the underside of the Skyland, and to his amazement, it was not dirt, or any stone found on the land below, but solid, shimmering lumaryl with a light of its own. The glassy golden stone was the Skyland, and somehow vegetation grew on it. He knew lumaryl had been drawn from Luminare, but he had never imagined in his wildest dreams that it *was* the Skyland. He'd always assumed it was a mineral extracted from the Skyland. Was it the same for all the Skylands?

As they drew nearer to Phroenthyl, the sun burst past the horizon in an explosion of light and color flowing in waves across the sky as the sun declared its presence.

Aren led Devlyn and Ellendren through the spectacular sunrise and vibrant rainbows to circle Phroenthyl. Each new scenic view left Devlyn in awe. The kryseniel flowers blossomed and turned toward the sun as it rose to shed its light on the golden flowers. Even the kirenae trees seemed to turn toward the dawning sun.

Devlyn, look at the trees! Ellendren was joyous.

Looking more closely, he blinked. The trees didn't just turn their leaves toward the sun, they moved. Each branch stretched as if stirring from sleep. Curious birds with colorful feathers burst from the trees, flying over the Skyland. Small animals scurried across the meadows and Devlyn had to look twice as creatures moved out from the shaded trees. Dragons and unicorns delighted in the rising sun, just as the living trees and flowers did. Amazed, Devlyn was eager to explore Phroenthyl on foot, keen to interact with the Skyland directly.

Aren finally descended, Devlyn and Ellendren following, their illumined forms adding a sense of wonder to the Skyland. Landing on the plush grass, Devlyn felt his feet sink into the dewfall. A crispness rose through his bare feet; his drowsiness was forgotten.

A unicorn brushed past, nudging her head against his shoulder as he folded his wings. The largest dragon Devlyn had ever seen lounged in the rising sun, warming its golden scales while offering a colorful reflection of its own. The gold dragon lifted its head to gaze at them.

"Aren, welcome back." A feminine voice came from behind, speaking in High Aelish.

"Ei'phaenyl," Aren greeted her, placing his palm on his chest and bowing deeply.

"Elyse will ever serve, dearest Aren." Elyse embraced him, tears visible in her eyes. She had an ageless quality and was miraculously bonded with a phoenix. Her golden form illumined Aren's shadowed body. "How you have suffered." She cupped his face.

"Devlyn lifted most of his Darkness."

"So, he has returned."

"The Evil One's prison has been weakened since we first lost Luminare. His presence on Teraeniel grows as more anacordel act in his name. If he had been securely bound in his prison as we believed, my fate and the fate of the Aldinari elves would never have come to pass. We would never have lost Luminare."

"Has his presence been among us that long?" Elyse asked, troubled.

Aren nodded.

"Why did you not return once the shadow was lifted?" Elyse asked.

"My shame has kept me from you, Ei'phaenyl." Aren dipped his head. "I had no memory of who I was and did as I was bid. I had no control over my actions, but I remember what I did." Aren fell to his knees, tears flowing. "I murdered countless people, enemies of the Evil One. Elyse, I killed one of the miervae. One of the last of her kind, confined to the Illumined Wood, and I destroyed her." Aren openly wept at Elyse's feet, the weight of his crimes heavy.

Elyse lifted Aren's chin to gaze into his eyes. "Dearest Aren, your heart is weighed down by the Darkness of him who we cannot name here, lest he learn our location and claim this Skyland as he has the others. His hold over you is gone. Let not the past and the atrocities he committed through you claim your present and future too."

"How can I forget what I did?" Aren pleaded.

"To forget is a sin; you know this." Elyse rubbed Aren's shoulders, her golden light in stark contrast to Aren's shadowy presence. "While you are not responsible for those actions, you must forgive yourself and allow Anaweh's light to return to your heart."

"I fear for Tyiel."

"Tyiel suffers more in your present state. I cannot say what will happen to the phoenix. But for both your sakes, you cannot continue as you are."

"Will you help me?" Aren's eyes brimmed with tears.

The Dark Phaedryn showed a vulnerability Devlyn had never imagined him capable of. The legends of Aren were one thing but getting to know him over the past month had led Devlyn to assume he was incapable of emotion.

Elyse turned to the great gold dragon. "Lyvenol, would you help me release Aren and Tyiel from their prison?"

The golden dragon stirred and rose. Images of eager agreement accompanied by an ancient fondness for Aren filled Devlyn's mind.

Lyvenol moved to Elyse's side, his golden eyes intent on Aren.

"Devlyn and Ellendren, you will feel a force requesting your help as well; please submit to it for all of Phroenthyl must help to release Aren of this Darkness."

They could only nod in agreement. Devlyn had no idea who the woman was, only that Aren gave her a respect reserved for mentors and elders, making her predate Aren. Devlyn wondered at her age and how long she had dwelt on Phroenthyl. Who was she?

The force Elyse had mentioned stirred instantly. Devlyn felt the entire Skyland thrum, a song he had never heard ringing from the very soil. He imagined the lumaryl glowing beneath their feet as every creature dwelling on Phroenthyl lent their spiritual energy. Devlyn felt his own spirit offer its strength to the song swirling around Aren.

Devlyn distantly recalled when Aren's mind had been freed from the shadow, but he had no idea how it had happened. Part of him thought he had willed it, but whether it was him or Aliel, he could not say.

Only the shift in light told him time was passing although it was difficult to gauge because of the energy swirling about the Skyland. Devlyn felt his eyes strain as the light increased to a luminosity which was unprecedented for Teraeniel. Connected to Phroenthyl and all its creatures, Devlyn sensed another being enter the fold.

Then the light's brilliance multiplied and exploded with the addition of another being.

Devlyn recognized him; Auriel's presence blossomed in that shared energy, but another followed, one much greater than the anadel who shepherded the Luminari. Devlyn had felt the irythil's presence only once before, when Uriel, Lord of the Stars, had been freed from the frozen waters of Lake Saeryndol.

The swirling lights continued around Aren, the song vibrating from Phroenthyl pulsing in Devlyn's bones.

Fading at last, the song settled and the brilliant light dimmed. Elyse, Lyvenol, Auriel, and Uriel surrounded Aren. Devlyn and Ellendren stood at a distance, both spent by their journey and the energy just requested of them.

As his eyes adjusted, he saw Aren, not as he knew him before, but without the Void's taint. His eyes gleamed silver, his hair regrown and golden in the sunlight. The shadowed wings which had carried Aren to Phroenthyl had vanished and Aren no longer had the form of a Phaedryn. Naked, he knelt, a phoenix without light lying motionless in his hands.

"I'm sorry for your loss, Aren; you and Tyiel have been through much together. Sadly, the phoenix has been dead for many years; tenebrys held his mangled corpse in place," said Uriel, his voice humming with power and care. "Be consoled, for Tyiel can now be reborn, and I am sure nothing will keep the phoenix from returning to you." The bird's body turned to ash and scattered in the breeze, transforming to specks of light.

"Thank you, Uriel," said Aren, turning from Uriel to Auriel. "And you, Auriel, you have ever protected me as you were able."

"If only I had foreseen the fate of Aldinare, your misery could have been avoided."

"You know I could not abandon the Aldinari."

"Which is why Uriel, Auriel, Lyvenol, and all Phroenthyl bent our wills to see you restored," Elyse said, warmly.

Aren brushed his fingers across his chest, pausing as he looked down. "It is gone. The corruption of the Void is gone." His voice trembled.

Uriel vanished in a flash of light, leaving Auriel behind.

"Focus and train well, my children; you know what depends on you." Auriel looked at Devlyn and Ellendren, both overwhelmed by the recent experience. Auriel vanished too.

"Aren, you have a choice to make." Elyse folded her arms behind her back. "You have suffered grievous sins against your person, physically, mentally, and spiritually. If you desire, you may remain here. In time, Tyiel will return to you, and your status as a Phaedryn will be restored. Of this I have no doubt, but even if Tyiel cannot find you, you are welcome to stay here."

"Thank you, Ei'phaenyl, but I cannot. My duty will ever belong to the Luminari."

"I thought such would be the case, but do know, you are always welcome here."

"It's good to see this place unchanged, that the Evil One's corruption has not touched it."

"We have taken precautions, and Lyvenol prevents the Void from finding us. One of Lyvenol's flight will return you to Arenthyl, but only when you are ready. I would recommend resting before leaving. As you know, time moves differently here."

"Thank you, Elyse, your kindness is limitless." Aren's shoulders relaxed, the tension of thousands of years releasing with every breath. "Ei'phaenyl, may I introduce you to your new students, Devlyn Lorenthien, son of Evellyn and Dolan Lorenthien, and Ellendren Lorenthien, daughter of Vernal and Harnyl Roendryn. They entered the Empyrean Sphere together and were declared one by the seraph. Devlyn is bonded with Aliel, and Ellendren with Tariel." Aren turned to Devlyn and Ellendren. "This is Elyse Lorenthien, daughter of Kien and Kiara."

Devlyn's jaw dropped and Ellendren's face revealed her own shock.

"Aren, how young have our people grown?" Elyse asked.

"Shamefully young."

Agitated by the comment, Devlyn wanted to argue, but knew he'd only look foolish doing so with an elf dating back to the foundation of wielding.

Even their minds have forgotten much.

Devlyn heard Elyse, fully aware that the mind was not a secret haven to the elves of old.

"Forgive me, Ei'phaenyl," said Devlyn, mimicking Aren's reverence to Elyse.

"Well, you learn quickly. Tell me, Devlyn, now that you and Ellendren are the Aryl of Arenthyl and will become the Exalted Aryl of Krysenthiel, what do you think is most critical to a successful reign?"

Devlyn tried to avoid shifting his gaze to his feet, but suddenly found his toes extremely interesting. Ellendren's anticipation was clear across their bond; she wanted to voice her opinion.

"Must it be only one thing?" he asked, his mind running over every issue Krysenthiel and the rest of Teraeniel faced. It felt like all would be lost if Erynor was not defeated, and the threat of the Evil One returning made the future seem grim.

Even if they managed to defeat Erynor and prevent the Evil One from escaping, if they could not restore the Jewel of Life, life on Teraeniel wouldn't improve. Kingdoms would quickly pick up swords again, seeking more power and wealth. There was no guarantee that immortality would prevent that.

Devlyn also believed that Teraeniel hinged on the success of the Guardian Senate. If the various races and kingdoms could not work toward a common good, Devlyn saw little point in any victory. What would change if another cruel dictator tried to take power and enslave others?

"You have many concerns for one so young," Elyse said. "Before Ceurendol was lost, our offspring were considered children for decades, and spent centuries as adolescents. We would leave adolescence at different times, as every elf is unique of course, but an aryldom, the Exalted Aryldom no less, would never be entrusted to a child breaching adolescence."

Devlyn kept his focus on Elyse but couldn't help but feel belittled.

"I do not say this to embarrass you, but rather to speak to your character; you have been placed in a position that should never have fallen on your shoulders at such a young age. And do understand, that by my standards, none of the current Luminari have grown past adolescence. My parents did not become aryl until they had seen nearly five thousand springs. And even then, they were considered too young. Aren, how many Aurephaens did you celebrate before you and Jacquelyn were elevated as aryl?"

"Almost seven thousand."

"My intent is to reveal to you your situation. You are right in your many concerns. But they branch from a single purpose. I cannot tell you, but you will know it in time." Elyse smiled. "Now, that is not the reason either of you are here. I am not a teacher of aryls; I have taught every Lorenthien aryl who came after me, but that is not my purpose. To those beyond Phroenthyl, it will feel like a year will have passed, but here, it will be seven years. Time fluctuates peculiarly here due to an ancient wield now restricted to the time wardens. However, it was placed long before Desmyn and Valeriel created the Time Key and gifted it to the minums."

AERETHYN

A dragon of the Gold Flight carried Aren back to Arenthyl. The dragon was much smaller than Lyvenol, but still the size of most houses in Cor'lera. It felt wrong to see Aren climb onto a dragon to fly. As long as Devlyn had known him, even when he had thrown bolts of tenebrys at Devlyn, he'd always had black wings that drank in the light. A kernel of insecurity took root in Devlyn now that Aren was no longer a Phaedryn; he dreaded the possibility of losing his connection with Aliel.

"Our time on Teraeniel was never meant to be permanent." Elyse came up to Devlyn. "Many prophets and seers have written how they expect all things to end. But no one truly know what the future holds. Elves were given the gift of Life Immortal, something that I and others not tied to Ceurendol still possess. But our time on Teraeniel is not unending; I trust the Eldinari have revealed this to you."

"They have."

"Some theorize the three realms will merge into one, and Lumaeniel will encompass all that exists."

"Is that what you believe?" Devlyn asked.

Elyse smiled. "What I believe is one thing, what you believe is what you must discover within yourself."

"How am I supposed to learn if you don't tell me?"

"I'll humor you, but you would have been rebuked for that in another age. Before Luminare and the other Skylands were lost, no elf believed there would be an end to all things. Our lives were long, and we did not die painful deaths, but simply transitioned beyond to a different way of living, our body, soul, and spirit intact. Blissful eons passed before any threat reached our oasis in the sky. When the Skylands were lost, our beliefs and philosophies were shaken to the core. I saw how each passing generation of Phaedryn had a dampened perspective of the world. The elves of my youth would not have recognized them. You can only imagine what they thought and believed with the dawning of the Ceurendol War."

Devlyn doubted it was as dire as the world was today. They might have reclaimed Krysenthiel, but the Evil One was still on the precipice of escaping his prison.

"Perhaps," Elyse replied to his thoughts. "I know you have more questions, but they must wait. I've given you and Ellendren a week to rest, and now it is time for your training to begin."

Elyse turned and walked away. He trailed after her, assuming he was to follow. They crossed the Skyland, seemingly without direction since there were no buildings as landmarks. Only the trees delineated the landscape, and they were not reliable markers since they glided across the meadows. Unlike the trees below, these kirenae trees were very much awake.

Cresting a shallow knoll, they went up to a short statuesque plinth of two Phaedryn supporting an orb. The plinth was wielded of lumaryl, but the orb was of a different material entirely.

Ellendren rounded the clearing and alit beside the orb, her wings folding back. Elyse stood beside the plinth, her hands resting on its cloudy surface. "Before my parents were called to Lumaeniel, they had the foresight to create the Aerethyn for future Phaedryn. The Aerethyn is akin to sophilliae, but I do not think you're aware of them yet. You will learn about them when you return to Arenthyl, where the new Grand Librarian of the Sophillium will be awaiting his appointment by the Exalted Aryl."

"The Sophillium?" Ellendren asked.

"It is also known as the Great Library of Septyl, but it has never only belonged to Septyl. But Septyl does protect it. The Aerethyn will reveal much to you, but not all at once. Seven years will pass before you learn everything the Aerethyn can teach you. Your time with the Aerethyn will be supplemented by time with me, but I serve primarily as a protector of the Aerethyn and Phroenthyl. Kien and Kiara are your true teachers."

"How do we use it?" Ellendren eyed the curious orb.

"You must tap your inner sense to breach it. It will do the rest. Your first experience with it will not be brief. Interacting with it will become easier as you grow familiar with it. Please approach the Aerethyn; we only have seven years."

Time might flow differently here on Phroenthyl, but that didn't mean Devlyn had grown accustomed to casually hearing that so much of it would pass. Ellendren couldn't suppress her startled thoughts at the mention of being away from Krysenthiel for so long, even if only a year would pass beyond Phroenthyl. Seven years meant nothing to Elyse though; in fact she seemed to consider it would go by swiftly.

Devlyn and Ellendren drew near the glassy orb and gazed into its depths, which seemed endless. Quieting his mind, Devlyn grew aware of his surroundings, and Elyse's thoughts came to him. She did not direct them to him, but he heard them. Her mind was a mix of quiet excitement and unattainable depths.

The Aerethyn too revealed itself to Devlyn's mind; it felt alive. A cloudy mask fell over his vision, and he no longer saw through his own eyes.

He was suddenly aware that it was the Feast of Aurephaen in the year 7397 of the Second Era. His essence faded, and his perspective melded into someone else's.

———————

Kien gazed into Kiara's eyes, ever longing to love her more fully. It was not the first time they had spent the entire day and night beyond Mar'anathyl, and it would not be the last. A quiet stream of bubbling water swept past them, lumaryl pebbles glistening on the riverbed, and vibrant crystalline kryseniels blossomed endlessly on the shore, making the countryside of Luminare appear golden.

The flowers were beautiful and Kien wanted to gather them into a bouquet for Kiara, but the look in her eyes told him she preferred them where they were, and not withering in her hands, away from their natural nourishment. He didn't think anything could wither at her touch, especially kryseniels, one of the few things that reminded him of Kiara when they were apart.

Strolling along Luminare's edge, Kien watched the water quickening nearer to the cliff, its sound voluminous as it roared along before cascading from the Skyland to the land below.

Observing the water tumble over the edge, Kien wondered about the people living on the land below, the lives they lived, the passions they explored, and the people they loved. How much had their lives veered from the elves since the Great Blessing?

"Lost in your desires again?" Kiara asked, a smile playing at her lips.

"Only if they don't prevent my greatest desire." Kien smirked, delighted when he saw color flow up Kiara's cheeks, then even her pointed ears reddening.

"Will there ever be a day you can't make me blush?"

"I sincerely hope not." His smile faded and his attention returned to the waterfall.

"Do you think we'll ever reconnect with the other anacordel?" Kiara pushed a strand of golden hair from her face; she too watched the water roll past, their minds already synchronized. "I know they're no longer as we are, but they're still anacordel. We're still the same in essence. None of us are elder ones any longer and only two Children remain."

Kien considered her words, imagining how such an endeavor might occur.

"Perhaps we can beseech Auriel; I hear he's particularly keen on granting blessings while praising Anaweh during the rising sun on Aurephaen." Kiara's gaze lingered on the water.

"Auriel and Anaweh already know my heart and desires." Kien tried to sound positive.

As do I. Kiara's thoughts entered the soft privacy of his mind, warming his heart.

My heart is not whole without yours. With the sharing of the thought, Kien held her gaze. They had spoken of joining in permanency before, but they were still young, far too young by the aryl's standards. Neither having seen three hundred springs, they were considered youths.

Kien's heart blossomed at the possibility of spending all his days with the elf before him. Only then did he realize their hands were joined, a physical embrace mirroring their shared minds.

Melodious horns sounded in the distance, their call soft, yet triumphant, mirroring the sun rising to the east. An eastern wind blew past them, caressing skin left exposed by their loose silken garments, the folds billowing in the wind.

"It's to begin soon." Kiara looked north, where the ceremony would take place for those who called Mar'anathyl their home. Luminare's only mountain range stood still further north.

"Is there a better spot to watch the dawning sun than here?" Kien asked, Kiara's fingers still entwined with his.

"You have a request for Auriel." Her fingers tightened in his.

"That's the least of my concerns at the moment," said Kien, blushing as he looked down.

"At least I'm not the only one of us to blush!"

"I can't help it…" Whatever he intended to say, the words melted away as his lips found hers and his heart exploded in his chest, rushing with an eagerness he never wanted to end.

The dawning songs continued, welcoming the morning Light of Anaweh in the middle of spring. The full moon had already faded, and the last visible stars trickled out above, dimming as the sky changed from black to violet, and now a soft orange glow.

Kien did not know when it had happened, but he now sat with Kiara, his arm wrapped around her, her head nestled against his chest.

Their eyes were open as they watched the sky transform into a vibrant gold. Beautiful music filled their ears and hearts as Luminari elves joined their song with Auriel and Uriel, rejoicing in Anaweh, the Creating Light.

The music continued, and they still gazed east, their silver eyes unaffected by the luminous sun. Squinting, Kien thought he saw something coming from the sun—or was it *in* the sun? It appeared as a single figure at first, then divided in two as his eyes adjusted.

"Do you see them?" Kiara asked, sitting up.

"Yes, but…" Kien felt something stir in his heart. Something tried to reach out to him—*someone* reached out to him. The two illumined figures flew from the sun, tails of golden light behind them, weaving whimsical lines drawn in the morning sky.

"They must be anadel," said Kiara, having a better grasp of her emotions as she reconciled the sight. "Have they ever presented themselves during Aurephaen before?"

"Not that I'm aware of." Kien finally remembered how to speak, and for the first time, Kiara was not the cause of that dilemma.

Distant music joined with the rhythm coming from the gathering of the elves celebrating the Feast of Aurephaen, yet it did not come from Mar'anathyl, and Kien listened as he felt it begin within himself as well. Starting slowly in his heart, quiet and still, he felt it reach the pit of his stomach, urging him forward. Soon, his entire being insisted he join that wondrous melody.

Through his shared connection with Kiara, he felt the same sensation in her, yet the music flowed from her lips before his own. Her song extended eastward.

With her encouragement, Kien added his own voice to the song.

Devlyn knew that song—he had always known it. "With an unheard song upon thy heart, might light steps ever mark thy start," he recited.

"So, not everything is forgotten," Elyse said, a smile pulling at her lips.

"How is that possible? How did my mother know that song?" Devlyn asked.

"The heart knows much; one must only remember. I cannot say which of my descendants remembered the Lorenthien hymn, but their heart revealed it, and whoever remembered probably knew much of their ancestry. Each generation contributes, extending its lyrics through the eras."

The sun no longer hung in the same position as Devlyn remembered.

"How much time passes while bound to the Aerethyn?" Ellendren asked, noticing it too.

"Each memory is different, but it takes longer for the inexperienced to interact with the Aerethyn. The more time you spend with it, the quicker you'll take in the memories."

"I have a question about the time wield surrounding the Skyland." Ellendren focused on the sun above. Elyse nodded. "How is it that the days seem no longer than those below? If seven days here are truly a single day below, how can the sun and stars move about the heavens at the pace of a normal day?"

"You saw a true sunrise when you arrived. But the other six were false. A secondary wield lies across Phroenthyl to keep her inhabitants attuned to Teraeniel. By the time you leave, all its mysteries will be revealed to you. Now, what did you learn from the memory?"

"I still can't believe that there is proof of Kien and Kiara existing. I've always believed so, but there has been much doubt cast on events that have since passed to myth and legend among our people," Ellendren said.

"There are other historical accounts of them in the Sophillium, for they were the Aryl of Mar'anathyl after all. But the Aerethyn is only for Phaedryn. My parents kept this special record for the those who would follow them, to serve as a guide after they were called to Lumaeniel. Only Phaedryn can know of the Aerethyn's existence and its teachings. All the wisdom that the Luminari need to reclaim is inside the Sophillium. In time, the Luminari will be restored."

"They truly loved each other, didn't they?" The memory was impressive, but most noticeable to Devlyn had been their shared affection.

"The phoenix were drawn to Kien and Kiara for that very reason; they cared little for their worldly accomplishments. It was the love they shared and could not contain that called the phoenix from Lumaeniel. Phoenix rarely lay eggs. As you know, they are not anacordel, but anadel, and as purely spiritual beings, they do not have a body to reproduce from."

"But Aliel was in an egg," Devlyn said.

"Yes, since the Second Era. The first two phoenix to enter Teraeniel were so moved by the love between Kien and Kiara that their own love produced an egg. There are few recorded accounts of such occurrences, but none of the eggs remained unhatched for as long as Aliel's."

Were you aware how long you were in your egg? Devlyn conveyed to Aliel, mystified by his parentage.

I was, but my mind was often present in Lumaeniel. I was never fully there, but time is different there; there is no past or future. Only the present.

"What happened to Aliel's parents?" asked Devlyn.

"When Kien and Kiara were called to Lumaeniel, their phoenix did not follow; they turned to ash as every phoenix does when the elf they were bonded to leaves Teraeniel behind. They were reborn from the ashes and in time bonded with another Luminari. As for their current state, it is one of perpetual death within the belly of Erynor's dragon, Ythinor."

An ear-piercing, deafening roar filled Phroenthyl; Devlyn and Ellendren covered their ears. Lyvenol sent images of corruption and the need to remove the blemish from Teraeniel.

"Lyvenol is Primus of the Gold Flight, and like all gold dragons, is a physical embodiment of lumenys. He is also the warden of the erendinth he embodies, as are the other primuses. Lyvenol wishes to wash the corruption of Ythinor and his ilk from Teraeniel."

"Does the Dark Flight also have a Primus?" Ellendren asked.

"Tolvenol. No one knows which flight he once belonged to, but like the other early dragons of the Dark Flight, the Evil One twisted him from his original design with tenebrys. The beast's corruption has transformed him to something entirely different; dark dragons are bound to tenebrys and are an abomination to the other flights."

"Empress Qien Wei told me that monks are all that imprison Tolvenol at present."

"Let's hope they can maintain their hold over him," Elyse said.

As curious as he was about how to defeat the dragons bound to the Void and their master, he was more curious about the dragons that did not want to kill him. "Does the Gold Flight here remember Galithinol?" Devlyn asked.

"Fondly, and they sorrow in his first loss and subsequent losses. The gold dragons recognized Kien not only as an elf, but also as a draelyn of the Gold House; a descendant of Galithinol. How else could Kien and Kiara eventually find the rebuilt city of Tenethyl?"

"If the Gold Flight largely lives on Phroenthyl, does that mean the other flights are centrally located in different places?" Ellendren asked.

"You are quick to draw conclusions." Elyse ambled around the orb, seeming to debate how much to tell them. "Before Erynor's transgressions, dragons were a common sight in Eklean and all Teraeniel.

They had colonies large and small, but a Primus' location would ever be their flight's home. Across the ages, few have been granted permission to visit the lair of a Primus. Aside from the draelyn, those few were elves. I trust you know of each elven kin's affinity for a particular erendinth?"

"That was one of the first things I learned when I found out I could wield," Devlyn said, remembering one of his early memories with Velaria in Everin.

"Good, not everything is forgotten; however, I suppose some things are impossible to forget as their evidence is ever present." Elyse's expression was of relief. "As Luminari, we have a special connection with aerys. The white dragons carried our ancestors to Luminare following the Great Blessing, and a number of those dragons stayed with us for a great many years. Blue dragons carried those who would become Aldinari elves, green dragons went to Eldinare, and red dragons went to Cyndinare. While they did not teach us to wield the erendinth, we did grow attuned to their respective erendinth."

"Where is the White Flight now?" Ellendren asked.

"The white dragons had never severed their relationship with the Luminari and along with the Blue Flight, were the most visible dragon flights fighting beside us against the Erynien Empire. Both dragon flights were decimated during the Ceurendol War. They are not extinct, as you know, and their numbers have recovered since, but their pride is wounded by the loss. You'll find the White Flight in Glacien. Their Primus and Warden of aerys, Aerinol, eagerly awaits you.

"The Blue Flight, which you are most familiar with, and its Primus and Warden of aquaeys, Caephenol, has long kept his surviving uncorrupted kin hidden, nestled in the Bay of Nauto in the Illumined Wood, sheltered by the Laudien Mountains and the Unarian Sea. Much of his kin were captured and corrupted by the Erynien Empire, largely because of their connection with Septyl. Few of the dragon flights have suffered as much as the Blue Flight has."

"I didn't think there were many more blue dragons in Tenethyl than dragons of other flights," Devlyn said.

"I did not say they were in Tenethyl, but in the Bay of Nauto. Tenethyl rests on the waterfall precipice above the bay."

"And the others?" Ellendren asked.

"The Red and Green Flights removed themselves from the wars, and they still have multiple colonies, where the White and Blue Flights only have one. Fyrinol, Primus of the Red Flight, had resolutely severed connections with the Cyndinari after learning of their interest in tenebrys. It was too late for many of the red dragons who had already been corrupted by tenebrys though. Fyrinol's lair is hidden away in a volcanic island chain off the coast of Ja'horan. Thereinol, Primus of the Green Flight, is hidden away in Ogren."

"What of the transcendental erendinth? If Lyvenol is here, where are the other two primuses and their flights?" Ellendren asked.

"Intent on recruiting every dragon flight to fight the Evil One?" Elyse raised an eyebrow.

"They'll survive the Evil One being freed of his prison as well as every other anacordel."

"The Gold Flight have always called Phroenthyl their home and welcomed the Phaedryn to dwell among them. The Purple Flight, associated with animys, pass between here and Somnaeniel. Their dwelling belongs to both realms, but places where the veil is thin is where you will find them; their Primus and Warden of animys, Eilynol, is in Kweil Aitch. The Grey Flight, associated with umbrys, prefer places of deep shadows; not caves, but places where the sun casts the darkest shadows. The Grey Primus and Warden of umbrys, Orythnol, dwells in the deep canyons of Daereneth."

"What of the Jade Flight in Qien?" Devlyn asked. "I've never seen dragons quite like them before, even in their current frozen state."

"While their flight is considered young by the other dragon flights, they predate the Great Blessing. Jade dragons are believed to have originated from a series of unions between dragons of the Blue, White, Red, and Green Flights, to combat Tolvenol."

"Do you think the dragon flights will join us? Will they fight the Evil One's forces?"

"That is not a question I can answer. Now, as I've said before, I am not a trainer of aryls and you've asked precious little about your experience in the Aerethyn. Am I to understand that you have no questions concerning what you experienced?"

Devlyn turned to Ellendren. He could tell that she had dozens of questions but was more concerned over the fate of Teraeniel and gaining as many allies as possible. "I do, but they're undefined. I need to reflect first," she answered.

Elyse smiled and left Devlyn and Ellendren by the Aerethyn.

DESERTED TUNNELS

Alex glared at Karl across the map table in Elothkar's Royal Palace. An uneasy Aen chanced glances between the two older men as they stared daggers at each other. Neither could agree on what was more important to focus on during their privy council meeting.

By now, Alex had expected a report from Oliver and the army he was leading to Charren. It would still be some time before they reached their destination to support Sanjin in claiming his late father's throne. Karl, however, was more interested in filling the vacancies on Alex's privy council left by Oliver, Reia, and Sara. Aen would eventually have a seat as an advisor, but he was still too young and inexperienced for the nobles to respect that decision. In fact, they thought Alex was on the young side to be their king. Still, Aen was a constant presence when decisions were made.

Karl again pushed forward his list of candidates. The list was mostly Perrien generals, who all styled themselves as sons of Gneal. Alex didn't have any reservations about them. They had all proven themselves, especially when they had been asked to fight their own countrymen who were sieging Everin and sacking Cyril. The atrocities committed in Cyril still haunted Alex and he was sure his army felt much the same. None of them could imagine that Perriens aligned with Erynor were capable of doing what they had done to the people locked behind Cyril's walls.

"We can't have another Perrien sitting on the privy council without offending Parendior and Evellion," Alex said, pushing the list of names back across the table to Karl.

"You're starting to sound like Sara. I worried about having ei'ana around you for too long," Karl said, gruffly.

"You're an Observant for the Vyoletryn School." Alex was mystified by Karl's qualms about ei'ana. Karl had not only attended Gwilnor, he also belonged to the Vyoletryn School.

"That's not something for you to repeat," Karl growled, giving Aen a threatening look that clearly said to forget what he had just heard.

"Pardon, sir, but I already knew. I won't be repeating it, I promise," Aen squeaked under Karl's heavy gaze.

"What use am I to the Purple Eagle if everyone knows?" Karl asked. "Bother, we're getting off topic. What's next, you'll want an advisor representing the province that's quickly forming around Elothkar?"

"That hardly seems necessary. Everyone here is from one of the other provinces."

"What about Lady Aewen? She's lived here for thousands of years," Aen suggested.

"I doubt she'll want to join our strategy meetings," Karl said dismissively. "Besides, she seems preoccupied with directing the architects and masons from Evellion in rebuilding Elothkar."

"Well, they have been doing a remarkable job. It might be a good idea to offer her a seat on the privy council though. She was a Thellish queen and is my distant ancestor," Alex said.

"Perhaps. I still say Perrien architects and masons would have been just as good as the ones imported from Evellion. Just because most of Elothkar's citizens fled with King Evellion into the Vespien Mountains and found refuge with Belen the dwarf all those years ago doesn't mean Perriens are any less Thellish than they are. Besides, the masons who built Elothkar and Everin were Gestorians!"

"Do you think the Evellions are getting preferential treatment?" Alex asked.

"Their demands in the treaty you signed with their queen dictates that the majority of Elothkar, *our* capital, be of Evellion blood. Need I remind you, they weren't the ones who fought to reforge Thellion. If anyone should make such a claim to Elothkar, it's the Parendians. And if the residents of New Gneal hadn't risen to your support, we wouldn't have ousted the Perrien Council as efficiently as we did."

"Have you forgotten," Diana said as she swept into the room, "that it was Perrien who had aligned with the Erynien Empire and sought to purge my people and kingdom from Eklean? You'll forgive us if we're a tad wary of Perriens making military decisions on our behalf."

"Apologies, Your Highness, I did not intend to offend," Karl said.

"We also know that Perriens came to our defense." Diana smiled and Karl's shoulders slackened somewhat.

"Why not just have an equal number of advisors from each province?" Aen asked, garnering looks from the others.

"And of Elothkar's seat?" Karl asked.

"Easy; give it to Lady Aewen if she wants it and let her pass it to me when I'm old enough and have the required experience," Aen said, grinning.

Alex laughed with the others. "Well, now that that's decided, Karl, please find a Parendian, perhaps one who helped liberate Everin, and an Evellion to join the privy council."

"Only one from each? Do you truly think four people can govern and make the decisions for Thellion? And your advisors can't all be generals," Diana said.

"We are at war," Karl said, earning a glare from Diana.

"What are you suggesting?" Alex asked, worried about what Diana had in mind. The three Thellish provinces were managing just fine on their own. And Karl was right, defending themselves against the Erynien Empire deserved their full attention with a hostile Mindale to the south.

"Thellion is more than just a military operation. We'll need commissions and advisors for every aspect of the kingdom. To say nothing of rebuilding and defending our provinces. Do we even know if our roads are maintained?" Diana asked.

"Do we have the means to support such a bureaucratic endeavor?" Karl asked.

"Perhaps not yet, but it should be a priority if we want Thellion to survive beyond this war with the Erynien Empire. Besides, the roads need to be kept up if our army is to efficiently travel across the kingdom," Diana said.

A tense pause followed and neither he or Karl had a response for the woman who would be his wife and queen. Fortunately, a palace guard announced himself, putting the issue on hold.

"Forgive my intrusion, Your Majesty; an elven messenger has arrived from Krysenthiel."

The room fell into shocked silence at the impossible news. Alex knew that Devlyn and Ellendren intended to destroy the Shroud and reclaim the Luminari elves' lost kingdom, but he had never thought they would manage it. The Shroud had encased Krysenthiel for fourteen hundred years. There had been no news from Devlyn since they parted in Everin. Thellish matters had kept Alex occupied, and ignorant of what was happening south of the Laudien Mountains. He was still dismayed that, under his watch, a Daer colony had formed along the Skrein Sea.

"Take us to her," Alex said.

The palace guard led Alex, Diana, Karl, and the ever-present Aen through the palace to the receiving room where the elven messenger waited. She was immediately identifiable as a Luminari elf by her golden-brown hair. She had a slender figure like every other elf Alex had met, but he knew better than to mistake the lithe frame with weakness. He had learned the hard way by training with Septyl knights.

The messenger smiled at the new arrivals, placing an open palm over her chest as she bowed. "Your Majesty, I bring happy tidings from the Lorenthien aryl. Krysenthiel, in its entirety, belongs once more to the

Luminari."

The words reached Alex's ears. He heard what the messenger said, but what she said was impossible. Nothing could destroy the Shroud, according to what he had learned while studying at Gwilnor. Many attempts had been made by the Luminari elves before Lucillia had faded back to the Illumined Wood.

"But what about the Shroud? How?" he stammered.

"You'll have to ask the Aryl of Arenthyl when you are able to visit, presumably at their coronation when they are to become the Exalted Aryl. The date is yet to be determined. As for the Shroud, all I can say from my own experience is that I felt something pull at me; every Luminari elf did. We were all part of it and Toryn Vicalen used her sword to pierce the Shroud. It is to be known as Shroudsbane for the deciding blow. Beneath the Shroud, the entire kingdom was somehow frozen and Lake Saeryndol remains so. Arenthyl's gates have opened once more."

"Remarkable," Diana said, breathless.

"It truly is." The messenger smiled, still elated at the Luminari elves' victory.

"What of the Erynien Empire? Surely the emperor didn't allow you to simply walk in to take Krysenthiel back once the Shroud was gone," Karl said.

"We were beset by Erynien legions, led by Deurghol and shadow elves."

"Were they defeated?" Karl asked.

"There were too many. They chased us until we reached the protection of our cities."

"And where are they now? Are they sieging your newly reclaimed cities? Does Thellion need to send reinforcements to keep Krysenthiel in Luminari control?" Karl asked.

"Sadly, their location is unknown to us. We haven't had any reports of them travelling back south though, which remains a concern as Erynor is likely planning something foul."

"How does not one, but multiple Erynien legions, encompassing thousands of Cyndinari elves simply vanish?" Diana asked, concerned.

"We know they can cloak themselves and have an enslaved minum, a time warden, at their disposal. For all we know, they are still inside Krysenthiel's borders," the messenger said.

"Sending one of our battalions to Charren might not have been the wisest decision after all. Erynor might still have his gaze set on reclaiming northern Eklean if his legions are unaccounted for and on our doorstep," Karl said.

"There is more. I brought this news to the Queen of Evellion on my journey north and she asked if I might deliver a message on her behalf, since I was already travelling to Elothkar."

"What news from my mother? Is she all right?" Diana asked.

"Lawrence of the Royal House Maroven, King of Mindale, has died. Rumors escaping Binton suggest an assassination."

"Who would kill King Lawrence? He might have had his faults, but surely his adversaries preferred him as their puppet on the Mindalean throne," Diana said.

"Presumably the man who took his throne, a Dwonian chief named Cairn of Tribe Laith. He's calling himself Chief-King of Dwonia and Mindale, Bridger of Dwota's Gap."

"What of Lawrence's son and heir?" Diana asked.

"Cairn challenged the young prince to a duel. The child was said to have died quickly."

"He murdered a child?" Aen said, aghast.

"Allegedly," the messenger replied.

"How have the nobles received this turn of events?" Diana asked.

"Evellion intelligence thinks a resistance is building, although that is only hearsay for now. Cairn has taken one of Lawrence's many daughters as his wife in hopes of solidifying his claim to Mindale. Queen Lara is concerned about the border Evellion shares with Mindale."

"Have the Dwonians been aggressive?" Karl asked.

"Trade caravans crossing the border have gone missing, but nothing more. The queen is mobilizing Evellion's military," she replied.

"Does Queen Lara seek reinforcements?" Alex asked.

"She did not provide any formal requests on my behalf, merely to relay the news."

"Thank you. Will you stay the night? I'm sure your journey was not easy and I would very much like to hear the full story of how Devlyn and Ellendren managed to reclaim Krysenthiel," Alex said.

"That is appreciated and I'd be delighted to tell it all, but know, I am no bard."

"Wonderful; you'll be our guest at our table tonight and a guest room in the castle is yours as long as you intend to stay," Diana said.

"That's very generous of you. Fortunately, my route home will be easier than my passage here," the messenger said.

"How so?" Alex asked.

"Reinyl has been reclaimed and Undol Schtam has opened their tunnels, connecting Reinyl and Parendior."

"Tunnels?" Karl said, alarmed.

"Is something the matter?" Alex asked.

"There are unaccounted Erynien legions, Evellion's borders might become militarized, and we're just learning that those mountains have passages that could be used to sneak into Parendior." Karl rounded on the messenger. "Is the tunnel to Reinyl the only such dwarven tunnel?"

"I trust you know of Harol Schtam's tunnels in eastern Parendior. One was never sealed, and the elves were known to pass through it on occasion. There's also the tunnel linking Ceurenyl and Parendior. It's said to be the first the dwarves constructed for the use of non-dwarves, a deal they brokered with the Aldinari elves when the ei'ceuril were constructing the Temple of Ceur."

"Any tunnels into Perrien?" Karl growled.

"I believe Audun Schtam has tunnels that join the River Arvil to a tributary branch of the River Enduil, and another tunnel to Septyl," the messenger said.

"Have the dwarves opened those tunnels too?" Karl growled.

"I was not informed of that before leaving Arenthyl. I would imagine Undol Schtam would like to rekindle their long-abandoned trade routes though. Especially since their tunnels provide the only river link between the Skrein Sea and the Erynien Bay," the messenger said.

"Conveniently with Irekthia, Alexandria, and Selma on its route." Karl frowned. "We'd best fill those vacancies on your privy council sooner than later."

"We'll also want to arrange meetings with the schtams that control those tunnels. Treaties will have to be drawn up for trade routes and our army's use of them. We'd be a more dependable ally to Sorenthil if we didn't have to go through the Cyrillean Pass," Diana said.

Skimp was tired.

Most of his abilities as a time warden had not been known to the Deurghol who held his leash. Before the battle for Krysenthiel, seguians were believed to be limited in size to a small globe. The other time wardens were aware that Skimp had been enslaved and they also had to know that his enslavers would take advantage of him after they had revealed that they could create massive seguians capable of transporting thousands of people when they had helped save the Luminari elves. The Deurghol had not been kind when he learned Skimp had withheld that information. And now, Skimp had to open those large seguians for the Erynien legions.

The distance mattered little, but the size and duration were a different matter. It was too much for one minum. He had fallen unconscious following every instance he'd had to transport an Erynien legion. While he had taken most of the legions out of Krysenthiel, one remained in a minor fissure in the ice that led to a vast network of long deserted tunnels and shafts below the frozen waters of Lake Saeryndol.

Cold bit through his shoes and it felt like needles stabbed at his feet through the ice. Judging by the extensive network of tunnels, this was not the first time it had been occupied. Oddly enough, it reminded Skimp of a mine. What could the Erynien Empire possibly want to mine from a frozen lake? Legend held that the lakebed had once been the valley where the first anacordel had woken, before the different races had come about.

If Skimp wasn't so drained, he might have risked opening a seguian for himself to warn someone—anyone. But fatigue prevented him from even formulating a plan of action. Escaping the Deurghol was impossible. He'd tried once and that had resulted in his alerting the Deurghol of Devlyn Lorenthien's location, nearly leading to the elf's death. The Deurghol had a means of finding Skimp, regardless of where he went. If he had access to the Time Key, he could escape to some other time. Perhaps before this Deurghol was born. But Skimp knew the Deurghol were much more than the elves they had once been. Ancient anadel allied with Ramiel inhabited the elves who had offered their bodies as vessels for the Evil One's plans. The elves were still alive, but their wills were not their own. Like Skimp, they could do nothing without the Deurghol's consent and were deathless because of that connection.

Skimp didn't understand the link the Deurghol had with him and how the Deurghol could always track him. Even if he had access to the Time Key, which he did not, the Deurghol could possibly feel the link in a different time. He feared his only release from enslavement was death. That might come sooner than anyone thought considering how overworked he was. He would die of exhaustion if he continued at his current pace.

Skimp stumbled across the ice and through the excavated tunnels. He was free to explore if he didn't try to escape. Even if Skimp had the energy, he no longer had the will. He was a defeated minum. He knew it, and the Deurghol knew it. The tunnels all went down; shaft after shaft headed for the lakebed. None of the shafts that reached the lakebed ever went further. Those were all abandoned by the Cyndinari, for whatever they had sought wasn't there.

Was the Erynien Empire hoping to find a lost treasure at the bottom of the frozen lake? Had a ship carrying a weapon sunk before the lake was frozen? The frozen lake might have made reaching the bottom easier, but surely they could have figured out a way to wield air into their lungs before the water had frozen solid. Instead of swimming to the bottom, they had to mine through the ice to reach it.

None of the shafts seemed to follow any logical placement. As Skimp reached what had to be one of the oldest shafts based on its proximity to the others, his stomach flipped, and he turned aside to vomit. Hundreds—thousands of frozen bodies had been tossed down the shaft to pile on top each other. The long-dead elves looked as though they were sleeping. The corpses were well-preserved due to the ice; even their golden-brown hair still framed their dead faces.

The Erynien Empire was known for its slave camps. But why have Luminari excavate the frozen lake? Why send them into the Shroud to die only to dig up ice? Curiously, none of the elves seemed to have been corrupted by the Shroud's poisonous mist. Had they somehow been preserved from it so they might perform their work and not die a quick death?

Was this where Lucillia had been before she became pregnant? Legend claimed she had travelled to Arenthyl and returned pregnant and carrying one of the lucilliae, the jewel of faith. Had she escaped this mine?

The Erynien Empire hadn't bothered to properly entomb the elves. Had the elves even held a funerary rite at that time? Having only recently lost their Life Immortal, they were not accustomed to bodily death. They would have all been familiar with wholly transitioning to Lumaeniel, body, soul, and spirit. These elves had died though, and their bodies had been cast into a mass grave that was never sealed.

Skimp turned away. He couldn't bear the sight. Before trudging back up and through the tunnels, he realized Erynor hadn't brought any slaves to restart the excavation. Instead, the legion Skimp had brought here now dug into the frozen lake. Erynor could easily have acquired more slaves for the task but hadn't.

Skimp was too tired to understand Erynor's reasoning. He turned back to the dead elves in the shaft and closed his eyes.

ENTWINED

Ellendren waited near the edge of Phroenthyl, Devlyn's arm wrapped around her waist. Despite the comforting touch, Eklean's wellbeing preoccupied her. Being removed from the continent's affairs had left her troubled. As the youngest child of the Aryl of Lucillia, she had known her entire life that her duty was to govern and protect the Luminari elves.

"You've already exceeded the Luminari elves' expectations," Devlyn said, squeezing her tighter.

She smiled. "I spent my youngest years fantasizing about abolishing the Shroud and retaking Krysenthiel. I abandoned that idea as a silly dream while at Gwilnor, thinking it impossible." Everything had changed when she met Devlyn and later learned of his ancestry, after he had already captured her heart, and she his.

"My life changed too." He picked up on her thoughts, flowing freely between them. "I never imagined, not in my wildest dreams, that this would be my life and us wed."

"After everything we've been through together, I still can't believe the Shroud is gone."

"But?" Devlyn pried, a twitch of a knowing smirk at the corner of his mouth.

"I wish we could have stayed to help protect our people."

"They're in Kaela's very capable hands."

Ellendren was proud that Kaela had garnered enough support to formally elevate their family's house to a minor aryldom. House Lucillia would ever be a house of stewards. "I still can't believe she outwitted Silvia Narielle and gained her support."

"See? Who better could we have left Krysenthiel with?" Devlyn said, cheerfully.

"I know, and I have complete confidence in my sister's political aptitude, but, Devlyn, I can't shed my fear of Erynor marching his legions and shadow elves and Deurghol back into Krysenthiel. What if the Dark Flight were unleashed to wreak havoc across Teraeniel?" She hugged herself at the thought of fire raining down on their reclaimed and still frozen aryldom.

"I know, Elle." He held her tighter, his golden wing brushing against hers.

"Devlyn, if anything happens, we won't know of it until after we leave Phroenthyl. Couriers won't be able to reach us if Krysenthiel were attacked. Not even Aren can return now that he's no longer a Phaedryn."

They looked silently past the edge, not east as Kien and Kiara often did, but west toward Eklean.

Ellendren had hoped to rekindle the Guardian Senate upon reaching Arenthyl. Instead, she would have to wait a full year before bringing the nations of Teraeniel together. Another year of the world's nations standing separately. Their only chance of thwarting the Erynien Empire and the Evil One was by coming together. For all Ellendren knew, another war could have already begun on the other continents. Not knowing kept her awake at night.

Her wings itched at the thought of returning to Arenthyl. She knew she was meant to be here, but these were unprecedented times. Erynor would be the least of their problems if the Evil One broke free of his prison. Teraeniel had to be united to face him.

Nothing prevented her from leaving. She could leave Phroenthyl, return to Arenthyl, and relieve Kaela of her stewardship. Kaela would be furious if she did though; she thrived in the aryls' political games.

Her mind whirling, Ellendren sensed Elyse approach. They turned to their mentor.

"You spend much time along Phroenthyl's edge." Elyse looked to the distant horizon.

"You know the cause of our anxiety," Ellendren answered.

"I was not intending to feign ignorance. I know it is challenging for you to be here and away from your people, but a year is no more than a breath on the winds. Teraeniel barely registers the passing of a single year. If Ceurendol is restored, you will learn its brevity."

"What if Erynor attacks and lays waste to Krysenthiel? What if the Guardian Senate never has a chance to resurface?" Ellendren repeated her concerns for Elyse.

"As aryl, your responsibility is to protect and govern Krysenthiel, but remember, you are not alone in your obligations. Have faith in the other aryls, the Guardians, the ei'ana, the ei'ceuril, and the other nations. They can manage for a single year. After a year, seven for us here, you will be much more valuable to the people of Teraeniel as aryl and Phaedryn."

"What if it's too late?" Ellendren hugged herself. Devlyn rubbed her back to comfort her.

"Have faith that it is not."

Ellendren's childhood in Lucillia's palace had given her the unique opportunity to visit the lucilliae held there as often as she desired. That lucilliae contained the faith of the Luminari elves, one of a set of seven each containing a different virtue and forming the Jewel of Life—Ceurendol. Even though she had spent her entire childhood looking at the lucilliae, being told to have faith in others was quite difficult.

"Come, it is time to return to the Aerethyn."

Ellendren and Devlyn followed Elyse from the edge of Phroenthyl. It was not a large Skyland, but it was large enough to house an entire dragon flight.

Devlyn smiled at her when they reached the Aerethyn and her

anxiety diminished some.

You have the same effect on me. His mind brushed hers, forcing her to smile as well.

"Are you ready?" Elyse asked.

They approached the Aerethyn. Ellendren's mind refused to settle as she tried to quiet her heart and tap the memories. The stillness did return, and it was no longer 9070 of the Third Era but 7452 of the Second Era.

In the aryl's palace in Mar'anathyl, Kiara sat with the women of her and Kien's families in one chamber, while Kien was with the men of their families in another. Once again, the two families were together. Kien's mother Olien was a wonderful woman, yet she intimidated Kiara. She was, with her husband Penderel, the next Aryl of Mar'anathyl. Kiara sat unusually quietly and still.

The elves of Mar'anathyl had always chosen the Lorenthiens as their aryl. Even though the aryldom was not necessarily passed on through heredity, the elves of Mar'anathyl, in agreement with Auriel and the other anadel who dwelt among the elves, had always chosen the youngest Lorenthien and their spouse, as aryl. It had been that way since Thien and Loren had founded their house as they built Mar'anathyl.

Kiara had studied the history and lore of Mar'anathyl's aryls. Only a wedded couple could become an aryl, as the position was intended to serve all the Luminari elves. It also spoke to the level of maturity of a given elf. She had studied the aryls not only because Kien was a beloved child of Olien and Penderel Lorenthien but also their youngest child. The stars had already sung that his parents would not have any more children, that Kien would be their last.

If chosen, Kien's parents wouldn't become aryl for another fifteen hundred years, but if history was any precedent, Kien and she would follow them.

"Why so still, Kiara?" Olien asked.

"Was it noticeable?"

"Afraid so," Janiel, her mother said. Janiel sat comfortably with the ei'terel and the other Lorenthien women, much more at ease with them than Kiara was.

"This has never been done before," Kiara started nervously. "We have not even bonded yet, and for us to venture beyond the shores of Luminare is unheard of, especially for two so young as ourselves." She wished she had stopped talking before saying half of what she did.

Olien smiled warmly, first at Janiel, and then at Kiara.

She looked as if she was about to speak, but then the door to the chamber where the men were meeting opened, and a disheveled Kien exited, his hair ruffled from repeatedly pushing his hand through it. Kiara had seen him do it countless times before, either when he was frustrated or embarrassed. The two were often connected.

The kirenae wood doors kept sound from passing between the chambers of the aryl's palace, but Kien's red face told Kiara he'd had an exhausting conversation with their fathers and brothers.

Olien and the other women stood, Olien with a flourish, her silken skirts swishing around her. Everyone but Kien and Kiara left the room, Kien's closest sister in age the last to go with a smirk at Kien as the kirenae doors closed solidly behind them as they joined the men.

Kien stood stonily by the door, his arms crossed tightly. In two strides, Kiara had her arms around him, and his own arms were clasped around her lower back. She felt his breath on her neck, making her scalp tingle with the closeness, both physical and emotional. No words came to her; none of consolation nor inspiration.

They remained still, their minds, hearts, and bodies enfolded in an unmoving embrace. She tried to keep herself open to him, but sensed his mind closed off, not entirely, but enough to notice. He did not want her to feel his pain, as though she did not already share it with him.

She could not say how long they remained there, but she felt the door push against them, trying to open despite their bodies weighing against it.

Arms unraveled but spirits still joined, they went into the adjacent chamber to join the others. Bright walls sung from lumaryl rose from the floor and a cool wind swept through the unhindered windows, offering a view of the landscape past the city.

Her mother and father stood next to Kien's parents, with Kien's grandparents, the Aryl of Mar'anathyl, standing nearby. All around were the rest of their families.

Janiel looked from her daughter to Kien. "We cannot permit you to take our daughter away unbound in heart."

Kiara expected this response, but her heart still plummeted. How could they not understand? She had explained to them on countless occasions how the phoenix were their lorendil—their guardian anadel—and how they had come to them. How they had already taught them so much, how they had opened their awareness to the erendinth, how they had invited them to a place beyond Luminare, and how Auriel and Uriel had encouraged them to follow.

"And we," Penderel said, his voice condemning, "cannot allow you to live alone with our son unbound in heart."

The announcement struck Kiara like a punch; her insides wept and shouted in pain. She felt Kien's passions rise next to her; an intensity consumed his mind.

His eyes were alight, no longer a pure silver. They were changing, as were her own. He looked from his parents to her parents, stepping away from her and toward them.

Kiara feared what he might say or do in the situation.

He grabbed their hands and fell to his knees. "I beseech you; bless a union between us."

Kiara's knees began to shake; her fingers trembled.

They had only just celebrated their two hundredth spring a couple decades ago, far too young to make such a commitment, but the fire and determination in Kien's eyes asserted that he was ready for that commitment and had been from the moment they'd met. Even then she knew they'd spend their lives together.

A smile reached her mother's lips, and Kiara prayed it was not out of pity or consolation.

"Do you ask this as well?" Penderel's voice was distant. Kiara's heart felt tattered and weary, her mind unable to comprehend what was being asked of her.

Kien turned toward her, his eyes brimming with tears, not of sadness, but of anguish and the fear of living without her. They had never spoken of joining so soon. Both knew they would do so one day, but not for centuries. She didn't have to sense his emotions to know how he felt.

"Nothing more do I desire." Kiara barely heard herself. She addressed Kien's father, but she could not remove her eyes from Kien.

Every elf present smiled, especially their siblings. Her parents pulled Kien off his knees and into an embrace. "We bless your union with light and joyous hearts," they declared together.

Kiara was surprised to find Kien's parents right before her. She must have walked over to them when she had spoken her desire. Surprised that her wobbly legs could carry her that short distance, she looked up at them and they pulled her into a hug, their arms warm and welcoming.

She knew they were saying something similar to what her parents had said to Kien, but she did not hear it, for her heart sang, unable to contain her elated disbelief.

"All you had to do was ask this of us; the love between you both is evidence enough," said Olien, her eyes alight. "We know what attracted the phoenix to you."

"Every elf on Luminare knows what brought the phoenix to our Skyland," one of Kien's brothers said, half laughing.

Kiara felt Kien turn to her, their hearts already aware of each other. His silver golden eyes danced, before they fell on her, connecting with her own changing eyes.

She looked from his parents to hers, then his arms found her once again, their fingers entwining. His heart opened to her more fully, just as hers did. Her heart sang the words she had heard others sing before, passed down from the time the elves once dwelt in the Valley of Saeryndol, before they were elves now known as the elder ones. Kien's heart melded with hers as they professed the prayer, joining their bodies, souls, and spirits together in love.

It felt very much like she was wielding under the phoenix's guidance; the sensations were all the same, and she began to wonder as she and Kien joined themselves, if wielding was inherent to the elves, and perhaps all anacordel.

Ellendren's eyes were damp when the memory ended. She tried not to look in Devlyn's direction, wanting to keep her tears from showing. She felt his arm wrap around her.

Part of her was a bit frustrated that he knew her so well, but a stronger part wanted his arm to stay there forever. Nestling her head against his chest, Ellendren allowed the tears to spill.

"When were the aryls no longer elected?" Devlyn asked.

"As you saw, the elections always resulted in the youngest Lorenthien for the Aryl of Mar'anathyl. The elections became more of a formality and an affirmation for the youngest child of the previous aryl. And it was not a unique situation for Mar'anathyl. Every Luminari aryldom experienced the same thing. When we began to travel beyond Luminare, we were shocked to discover that the same situations happened in Eldinare, Aldinare, and Cyndinare. Because of its regularity, it eventually became adopted as tradition."

"What happens if an aryl steps down and then has another child? The new aryl is no longer the youngest child. Especially when the elves possessed Life Immortal, having another child several thousand years after the youngest child was probably common." Devlyn brushed his hands through his hair.

"Elven children are a gift of Anaweh. We do not have children as regularly as the mortal races. If we had, the elven population would have overrun Teraeniel," Elyse said.

"I wonder what effect the loss of the Jewel of Life has had," Ellendren said.

"A grave one, I'm sure. A lifespan of only a hundred years at most is not long enough to nourish the type of relationship the elves once shared with Anaweh," Elyse said.

Ellendren's face reddened.

"I don't mean to say that mortals lack a connection to Anaweh, only that the relationship is different. The relationship once common among elves and Anaweh is a prelude to what all anacordel will experience in Lumaeniel. A century is too brief for such a connection to nourish."

"I begin to understand your insistence on our youth," Ellendren said. "Kiara thought them young when they married, and she was three times as old as my father was when he died."

"I hope that with the return of their Life Immortal, the Luminari will regain their forgotten wisdom and maturity," Elyse said.

FORGOTTEN TRUTHS

The door closed behind Kevn as he stepped outside the Sophillium. With no locks or bars, the magical door sealed behind him. Until a Grand Librarian was named, Sophie's policy allowed entrance to the Sophillium only to her nominee, and the self-barring doors enforced it. As Sophie's chosen successor, he spent most of his time among the long undisturbed sophilliae. The orbs were certainly more pleasant company than the Albiens and their resentful glares.

They were furious over the situation and their patience had worn thin. Kevn had expected them to force their way into the library once they had learned that Devlyn and Ellendren would be gone for an undefined amount of time, postponing his installation. Other ei'ana shared the Albiens' irritation, although not as pointedly. Given the current animosity directed at him and his lack of responsibilities, Kevn could spend as much time in the Sophillium as he wanted.

Aware of his over-indulgence and self-imposed solitude, he forced himself to walk through the Vyoletryn district today. He enjoyed walking through Septyl's halls, careful to avoid Selenya or any other Albien. The palace-city shimmered with natural light, filtering through the glass-like lumaryl vaulted ceiling and glowing off the walls.

He tried to make a habit of leaving the Sophillium at least once a day, a rule he frequently neglected. A whole nine days had recently gone by without him realizing it. That was the entrapping and seductive way of the Sophillium. He had not intended to hide himself away for nine days, but he'd kept coming across one intriguing sophilliae after another, each broadening his understanding of the Guardian Senate, something he knew Devlyn and Ellendren would be eager to learn about.

As the Grand Librarian, Kevn knew his future responsibilities would involve providing the Exalted Aryl with any wisdom the Sophillium could offer on specific issues. So far, Kevin had investigated not only the sophilliae containing information on the Guardian Senate, but also sophilliae relating to Arenthyl, Krysenthiel, and the Skylands. Kevn was particularly interested in how Luminare had been lost. The books he had read at Gwilnor had mentioned only the Darkness consuming it without any credible explanation of what the Darkness was. He assumed it was some form of tenebrys or was related to the now defeated Shroud. His research hadn't revealed anything of its origins yet.

Most shocking of Kevn's discoveries was that dragons had carried the elves to the Skylands after the Great Blessing and had stayed with them for a time. That certainly explained why each elven kin had an affinity for a certain elemental erendinth. Neither Gwilnor's nor the Temple of Ceur's libraries had mentioned the dragons' connection with the elves.

Until reaching Septyl, he'd considered himself knowledgeable about the larger world and its hidden secrets. Countless late nights had been devoted to tracking down Aelish scrolls in Gwilnor's library, uncovering knowledge many thought lost or forgotten. He had never imagined that the elves possessed another means of storing information aside from tomes and scrolls.

The scholarship he'd undertaken at Gwilnor now felt rudimentary since he had gained access to the Sophillium. The vast amount of knowledge contained in a single sophilliae would require a ten-volume set of books. He knew bits and pieces of the subjects he delved into, but what he had learned at Gwilnor was comparable to a single finger of the whole body and he'd barely scratched the surface.

Kevn's basic understanding of Aelish, which he'd thought was advanced, was disclosed as laughable after he accessed a sophilliae containing the language in its entirety. He'd known the language was rich and filled with subtleties, but he had never imagined its actual depth. Most of what he had studied prior to learning Aelish more fully now made more sense, as the language itself contained meaning that wasn't easily translatable.

Lost in his thoughts, Kevn didn't hear the approaching footsteps and neither did he see the aged woman walking directly toward him.

"Might I have a word with you?"

Kevn recognized the Chair of Vyoletryn. She had a stern, yet grandmotherly appearance; her hair was entirely white, and like every Luminari elf, her emerald eyes were now silver. As a descendant of Lucillia, Paurel's eyes had been a much more vibrant green than other Luminari elves' eyes, as did anyone who could trace their lineage to the mother of Roendryn and Feolyn.

"*Of course, Mother Paurel,*" Kevn stammered.

"Pardon?" Paurel asked. "I recognize my title in Aelish, but precious little beside that."

He had not realized that he had spoken in Aelish.

"Forgive me, none of the sophilliae use the Common Tongue. How may I help you?" Kevn made certain he spoke in the Common Tongue. He could not help but think how much easier it would be to communicate if others delved into the sophilliae containing the Aelish language. While he couldn't dictate a Chair's education, he would strongly encourage them to absorb the knowledge from the sophilliae that contained Aelish.

"As you might expect, the other Chairs and I have been meeting regularly. And while Selenya is still upset that she can't enter the library, she has made some valid points."

"Mother, it's not within my authority to allow others entrance; even if I wanted to go against the protocols, the doors open only for me—I have no control over them."

"Don't worry child, I am not asking such," Paurel said with a warm smile. "That being the case, we feel blind here. Phendien has told us what he remembers of Septyl, but he was only risen to the Chair of Emradiel when his predecessor was murdered after Septyl had fallen. He knows precious little of the palace-city as he spent most of his time in the Eldin Wood."

Kevn nodded as he listened to Paurel, intuiting what she wanted. "You want me to counsel the Seven Chairs of Septyl *on* Septyl?"

"You've always been a bright student, Kevn. Every Chair hoped you would remain at Gwilnor and choose their own School. But now, we do not know what these sophilliae contain or how they might help us. You've grown wiser than one of your age should be because of them."

"I'd be happy to help. You and the other Chairs cannot be blind in this war."

"Is there anything you can share with me now?" Paurel asked.

Kevn scratched his chin. "Do you know of the pattern of the palace-city?"

"Only that it is irregular and very easy to get lost in." Paurel chuckled.

"Oh no," Kevn said, elated. "It's incredibly logical. It mirrors a celestial pattern above, and not just any, but the conglomeration of stars with Uriel at its core. Auriel, Boriel, Vespiel, and what was once Meridiel's constellation, radiate along its branches. They and other anadel associated with them go beyond that celestial mass."

Paurel's eyebrows rose.

"Sorry; the point is, Septyl derives its strength from Uriel. The energy is inlaid in the very plan of the city, and because of that, that energy can be accessed. Septyl only fell because of betrayal from within. If the enemy had attempted to assault Septyl externally, they would have had better luck trying to push over a mountain with their bare hands."

"How do we tap this resource?"

"Only a single ei'ana devoted to the Light is required. It's how Septyl sealed itself after the betrayal. An ei'ana tapped the palace-city's connection to Uriel and the city went into lockdown. Only the Chairs could unlock the city after that. I assume the only reason I was permitted past the defenses was because of Sophie."

"That is helpful to know."

"I also think that power can be tapped by the Chairs beyond Septyl's walls."

"Like a weapon?" Paurel considered that as she nodded to herself.

"Have you opened the portals yet?"

"What portals?"

"Every Krysenthien city is connected by seguian portals. Did you notice how there weren't any roads connecting the other Krysenthien cities?"

"Their absence certainly made our journey more arduous. We didn't come across a road until we were halfway through the Delmira Wood," Paurel said.

"Right," Kevn said. "Roads certainly led to Krysenthiel, but they all stop at the border cities. Each city has multiple seguian portals that take travellers to any other Krysenthien city."

"Truly?"

"The lumaryl arches at Gwilnor's main entrance are seguian portals and connect Gwilnor to every capital city in Teraeniel. I would have the chancellor open those with caution, though, and not until she has access to the sophilliae that describes how they work. Anyway, the same portals are here in Septyl. When you open them, we'll be connected to Arenthyl, Ceurenyl, and every city in Krysenthiel."

"Will they pose a security threat?"

"Not likely. The ancient Luminari were quite clever. Anyone intending harm to or in the location they were travelling to or to someone dwelling there will find themselves unable to pass. They'll walk through the portal and find themselves on the opposite side."

"How is that possible? It's an inanimate object."

"Not quite; lumaryl and the other substances of the Skylands aren't like any other stone. Our ancestors once sang to lumaryl, as though it was alive, like how the Eldinari and Centaurs still do with trees."

"The other Chairs and I meet every Lerenaen at the eighth hour. Is this convenient for you? I would ask for your counsel throughout the entirety of our meetings."

"What of matters that are strictly reserved for the Seven Chairs?"

"I believe your anticipated station grants you access to any sensitive information we might discuss. As we are unable to learn from the Sophillium ourselves, I would not have us remain in the dark if you can shed light on any matter."

"Of course, Mother Paurel. I would say I am at your service, but in truth, my loyalty belongs firstly to the Exalted Aryl."

"Even though the Sophillium is in Septyl? Until recently, we only knew of it as Septyl's library."

"When Luminare was lost and our ancestors were forced to abandon their home, they left little behind. The Sophillium, as it stands, is unchanged from when it sat on Luminare. The entire structure was transported to the future site of Septyl as it was considered the most appropriate home, since the ei'ana would most benefit from the sophilliae. Seguian portals lead directly from the Sophillium to Arenthyl's and Gwilnor's libraries, but I can't open those until I'm the Grand Librarian."

Paurel's expression brightened. "We'll have to make certain our magisters have access to the sophilliae before our students do. If we don't, our students will undermine the magisters in every lecture! One of you was quite enough."

Kevn and Paurel laughed. He had never heard the older elf joke before.

"You'll have to excuse me now; I've taken up more of your time than a woman my age should of one so young."

"If things are restored, we'll laugh at thinking sixty years was a substantial age gap."

"We can only hope." Paurel's old eyes squinted as she nodded.

"Thank you for your time, Mother Paurel; it was a pleasure speaking with you."

"And for me, Kevn. Enjoy your day." Paurel continued walking in her original direction.

Kevn stood planted, unsure of why he had left the Sophillium in the first place, certain it wasn't just for the sake of stretching his legs. His mind nagged at him about something. He reasoned that if he started to walk again it would come to him.

As he walked aimlessly, Aaron came to mind. Kevn's time as scribe to the Ceurtriarch had been incredibly fulfilling, and he had been torn when he'd known it was time to leave the temple. Since leaving, Kevn had made no attempt to contact Aaron and learn the state of the Temple of Ceur. Dozens of Tenebrae were housed in the temple's cells, and Aaron intended to uproot every steward of Shadow hiding in Eklean.

Quieting his mind, Kevn searched for a distant presence. The entirety of Lake Saeryndol sat between Kevn and Aaron, but that distance mattered little when tapping his inner sense.

Hello Kevn, Aaron sent mentally; he must have sensed Kevn reaching out to him.

Everything going well in the temple?

More or less. I started holding daily rituals in the Chamber of Light. I'm ashamed to admit, but my new scribe has been taking attendance. I don't think anyone has noticed.

That sounds severe. Kevn kept his true feelings on the matter to himself.

I need to uncover the stewards of Shadow, and I have reason to believe some are here in the temple. What I'm going to do about those beyond the temple, I haven't decided yet. We've sent a summons to every ei'ceuril outside the temple for reassignments. Only a quarter of them responded, Kevn—a quarter! Aaron's thoughts thundered across the mental link.

Do you think they know who each other are?

Find one and uncover the rest?

Precisely.

It's worth a try, but we're having difficulty even identifying one. It's not like we can drag every ei'ceuril in the temple from their rooms and into the Chamber of Light.

Perhaps not, but what if you asked to speak with them in your office? Imply that you need their advice on something pivotal to Ceurenyl's wellbeing.

That's awfully close to deceit.

Kevn could hear the disapproval from Aaron in his mind. *But it's also the truth.*

I only said it was close. I believe I'd learn everything I need if I could get the steward who taught Devlyn and Alex at the abbey school of Cor'lera here.

You could send Arlyn.

He is occupied in Arenthyl's cathedral. I've elevated him to Archsteward of Arenthyl. Besides, if Lex Telvin was capable of wielding, I fear what his brother is capable of as a steward of Shadow.

Don't tell me you're thinking of going to Cor'lera yourself. Kevn knew Aaron too well, especially after their risky venture to the Empyrean Sphere. Kevn doubted Aaron would let any obstacle stand in his way. *Well, don't go alone. He could have the entire abbey school barricaded and filled with shadow elves by the time you arrive.*

Have you come across anything relating to the stewards of Shadow and tenebrys?

I haven't been researching them, Kevn shared.

Would you mind doing some digging for me? I wish it were jollier topics, but I'm afraid their numbers are significant.

I'll see if I can find anything.

Thank you. Kevn felt Aaron mentally withdraw.

Having continued his walk through Septyl as he spoke with Aaron, Kevn now entered one of the large plazas. A bubbling fountain rested in the center of the space below a dome of translucent lumaryl. Crisp sunlight spilled across the domed plaza, warming his face. A statue of Vigyl Vyoletryn, carved or sung from lumaryl, stood in the center of the fountain.

Kevn looked up at the proud elf with a sense of awe. Before having access to the Sophillium, he had extensively researched the Founder of the Vyoletryn School. There had never been any logical reason for why Kevn felt drawn to Vigyl, only that he was. Kevn's aptitudes demanded his curiosities research Saeryn Albien, but Kevn had never picked up a single tome or scroll regarding her. He had nothing against Saeryn, but she hadn't inspired him, not like Vigyl had.

"Perhaps if you had known Saeryn, she would attract you more," said the statue of Vigyl. The lumaryl statue twisted toward Kevn.

"What was she like?" Kevn asked, his curiosity piqued by the statue's access to his mind.

"Few who dwelt on Luminare drew my eye as often as Saeryn. She and Sophie liked each other well enough, but I think she also resented Sophie. They were quite competitive."

"How could an Albien, I mean, Saeryn Albien, have any grudge against Sophie and her accomplishments?"

"The Founders were not perfect," said the statue. "Granted, I did make sure others saw me so."

Kevn remembered he was talking to a statue, an idealized representation of the elf. Whoever had sung this statue from the stone had imbued as much as they could of Vigyl's likeness, but it was not actually a person. "Who sung you from the lumaryl?"

"Vigyl's great-granddaughter, Wendiel Vyoletryn," said the statue. "She joined the School of her family and became Chair."

The statue stilled. Kevn was still learning about the vibrant lumaryl statues, mostly by interacting with them. He thought it a waste of time to search out a sophilliae regarding them, especially since his list of promised research had tripled today, and that wouldn't diminish anytime soon. He had now pledged himself as a research aid for the Exalted

Aryl, the Ceurtriarch, and the Seven Chairs.

An Invitation

Low clouds hung over the open plain, shielding Jaerol and the others from the sun. If they had been a smaller party, those clouds would have provided the perfect cover for concealment. Carrying them all at once was too taxing on Rusyl. So, the blue dragon had stayed in his smaller form since they had reached Dagger's Point. Compared to the others, he was still a hulking mass of a man, but at least no one would recognize him as a dragon.

Instead of appreciating the cover the clouds could provide, Jaerol fretted about what they could hide. Any number of dragons carrying shadow elves or Deurghol could be tracking them from above. Now that Dagger's Point was behind them, crossing through Tiel and the Daerinth princedom would prove just as risky as Cynethol had been. Unlike Jadien, there was no doubting the Tieli queen and Daerinth prince's loyalty.

Jaerol had considered having Rusyl fly Evellyn directly to Krysenthiel to get her out of harm's way. While that could remove her from the immediate danger of southern Eklean, it could also place her in the grasp of shadow elves assaulting Krysenthiel. He wanted to believe Krysenthiel was safe, but he had no reassurance the Luminari had reclaimed any of their cities.

Travel worn and hungry, Jaerol spotted a small Tieli village ahead. His stomach rumbled and he wondered if they could risk passing through it. Their journey up Dagger's Point had been arduous. There was a reason the Tieli had never marched an army down that jagged peninsula after the Sudernese declared their independence. If the craggy terrain had exhausted their small group, it would have decimated an army carrying their own bodyweight in supplies and weapons.

The village ahead had to be a satellite village of Nairin. Nairin, and any other Tieli city, sheltered at least one shadow elf. A village was an entirely different matter though. Small, weak villages mattered little to Erynor, so long as they didn't revolt against his empire or hide an enthiel within a family's youngest child. To the emperor, they provided little strategic value.

Jaerol stopped to look at the village and noticed the others looking just as longingly at it. Even Rusyl wanted a respite from the elements. "Should we see if there's an inn that would take us in for the night?" Jaerol offered.

"What happens if they recognize us?" Teran asked.

"It's a small village. I doubt they could distinguish a Cyndinari elf from a Luminari elf, even with us standing in front of them," Jaerol said. No one argued—no one wanted to—and they made their way to the village.

A simple wooden wall surrounded it, more likely to keep out wolves and bears than to defend against an invading army. The gates stood open, without guards to question newcomers so they walked on to the cluster of buildings situated around a village square. The only building open to guests was the squat tavern. The five of them went into the Queen's Breath, garnering glares from the locals. The people inside didn't appear as rough as the Sudernese and none flashed daggers. Still, they didn't look at all happy to see new arrivals.

Jaerol spotted an empty table near the corner; the sooner they weren't standing for everyone to glare at, the better. A portly man with leathery skin and a bushy black mustache came over to their table before they had the opportunity to comment on their welcome.

"We don't get visitors to Groveton often. On your way to Nairin, are you? Most travellers don't bother stopping, us being so close to the city, that is."

"North actually," Jaerol said.

"From here? Think the Brieli will let you cross their bridges and pass through their city, do you? And you a Cyndinari; you'll be lucky if they don't open fire on sight of that cinnamon hair of yours," the man laughed.

"Have the Brieli grown aggressive?" Evellyn asked.

"Ha! Those cowards cower behind their stone walls and rivers. It's been rumored that our queen intends to capture their tiny kingdom for Erynor so she can gain back his favor after that embarrassment up north with the Sorenth several years ago. Not that she has anyone's support, mind you. Most of our lads, the ones that made it home that is, are still licking their wounds from the defeat at Myrium. It'll take more than a few years for our pride to heal from that debacle."

"A shame," Rusyl grunted, having been seriously injured at that very battle.

"Aye. Should've been an easy conquest too, especially with Torsil and those Dwonians involved. No one expected elves, merpeople, and bloody pirates to come to the Sorenth's aid. Our entire navy was gone in a single afternoon when those pirates forced their way through our harbor. Last time I'll trust anyone that calls the sea their home! Mark my words, that rock at the mouth of the Erynien Bay will turn on us before this war is over."

"You think Jadien will betray the Erynien Empire?" Jaerol asked.

"Who's to say? They're certainly remote enough, aren't they? To say nothing about what will happen now that those elven kids up north want to renew the Guardian Senate. Our emperor might be outmatched if other continents get involved in Eklean's affairs. None of their business if you ask me. Especially those Daer! They're worse than the pirates. Pushing their way onto our land and claiming a sliver of Tiel as a colony."

"Did the Luminari invite the Daer here?" Jaerol asked as Liam squeezed his arm, reminding him that they were trying to blend in and not attract attention.

"Why else would they be here? Who's to say who else those Luminari will invite to Eklean, now that it's been rumored that they abolished the Shroud," the man said.

"It's actually gone? The Shroud is gone?" Evellyn asked, less concerned about what the Tieli man believed about the Daer.

"That's what the few traders who take the time to stop in Groveton say. They also say there hasn't been any admittance or proclamation from our queen or the emperor."

Jaerol caught the bartender glancing behind them, a slight gesture, but obviously acknowledging someone. Jaerol's ears twitched as chairs scraped across the wood floor behind him. "What game are you playing at?" His expression hardened.

"I take it you've been avoiding cities and most villages, but the empire did issue one announcement recently. They even provided detailed images of you and the missus here. Fugitives, the post labeled you. And there's a bounty on both of you large enough to build a castle." The bartender grinned greedily.

"And you aim to collect that bounty? You and your friends here?" Jaerol remained seated. He wished the man had done his job first and brought them drinks before threatening them. He was thirsty.

"Don't think we can manage? Hear that, fellas? This scrawny elf doesn't think we can manage the five of them." The bartender's voice rose so the whole tavern could hear and was answered by a low rumble of laughter. There had to be at least ten, maybe fifteen men in on the scheme. How quickly would they regret their actions and would any of the brutes have the presence of mind to run? They couldn't afford someone reaching Nairin to alert a shadow elf.

Jaerol sent images to Rusyl, inquiring how far he could fly them. News would travel quickly after this. Rusyl responded with images showing he would try to get them past the River Reifen but suggested waiting until nightfall. There wasn't any need to let the Erynien Empire know their exact path. They had enough troubles to deal with.

"If you wouldn't mind, I would like that drink now." Jaerol closed his eyes and pressed into ignys. He wasn't particularly concerned about safeguarding a tavern owned by someone who wanted to deliver him to Erynor.

"You won't be getting any service here, elf. I don't serve traitors and fugitives." The man cracked his knuckles.

Fire bloomed in Jaerol's palm and the man's eyes widened with the realization that he wasn't threatening defenseless travellers.

"Violence really isn't necessary," Evellyn said, calmly. She had likely witnessed a fair share of fighting while in the Erynien court. "I don't think this man wants any trouble. It would be a shame if his tavern burned to the ground because of a misunderstanding." Evellyn turned on the man, no shred of concern in her silver eyes. How could anyone wish her harm?

The bartender balked as Evellyn stood to leave. "The only place you're going is Broid." He lifted his hand to smack her, but before he could, a blast of air threw him against the wall.

"That was not advisable." Evellyn didn't turn to look at the unconscious man, but every thug in the tavern did. She hadn't moved a muscle, yet the man ended up crumpled on the floor.

Jaerol could feel the thugs' indecision hanging in the air. They all greedily wanted that bounty. Despite their advantage in numbers, they were realizing they wouldn't be a match for the five travellers. One man did step forward with a glint in his eyes.

Rusyl stood to his full height. "Are you sure you want to make the same mistake?" he growled. The men in the tavern had likely never seen a man as large as Rusyl before. The thug froze where he stood. He cast a nervous look back at his neighbors, looking for support. No one moved forward and the man sank back into his seat and buried himself in his drink.

Evellyn started toward the door, leaving Jaerol, Liam, Rusyl, and Teran no option but to follow. Outside, a handsome elf waited. His cinnamon hair, bronzed skin, and pointed ears marked him as Cyndinari. He handed a piece of parchment to Evellyn, but a flash of recognition crossed his face at seeing Jaerol. Evellyn read the note. "Why should we trust your mistress?"

"Because no one refuses Yloran Eth Gnashar," Jaerol said, a hint of a smile reaching his eyes.

Raelinth had brought them to a delightful mansion just north of the village. While the house was nothing like Yloran's mansion in Broid, it was exactly the sort of house she would have taken for herself in a small and unassuming Tieli village. It likely had belonged to a minor noble before Yloran had moved in, with or without the noble's consent.

They waited in a bright drawing room, where other attendants, all men and all incredibly handsome, lounged about in loose fitting silks. Jaerol knew better than to gawk—these men were Yloran's and she would know if his eyes lingered. As they waited for her, only Jaerol and Teran were comfortable in the new setting. To Liam, Evellyn, and Rusyl, Yloran Eth Gnashar was one of the dreaded Sha'ghol who had lured them all to her house as a trap. While Jaerol and Teran couldn't guarantee that Yloran wouldn't cart them off to Broid, they didn't think it a likely outcome.

Jaerol and Teran had almost finished their drinks—Jaerol was sure the others hadn't taken a sip of theirs—when the door opened and another attendant invited them into the salon.

They went in to find Yloran lounging on a cushioned settee, resplendent in a revealing ruby dress. She didn't acknowledge the newcomers at first but waited for her attendant to usher them further into the room. Yloran's eyes twinkled at Jaerol and Teran.

"Clovis, please bring our guests Teran's finest vintage. I've been waiting for just the right visitors to open it with," Yloran said as she stood.

"Lady Yloran, you are likely the only Cyndinari who has spoken favorably of my wine in the past five years," Teran said, bowing to her.

"Fools. A shame there isn't a cure for idiocy." Clovis returned with a decanter of wine and offered the first glass to his mistress. "I do adore your 9053.3E."

"One of my favorites. That was an uncommonly cold winter. I didn't think the vines would produce any fruit that year, let alone my best vintage to date. If I recall, you purchased a quarter of the casks," Teran said as Jaerol gladly accepted his glass with the others following suit.

"I couldn't let such a fine wine be wasted on those who wouldn't appreciate it. Besides, that was also the year you introduced me to your nephew." Yloran took a sip, allowing the glass to linger by her nose to experience the full effect. "Speaking of fools." Yloran turned on Jaerol. "I never thought you would willingly go back to that nest of snakes. There isn't an elf in Broid who doesn't know your face." She waved a piece of parchment featuring it with a bounty noted beneath.

"At least they captured my good side," Jaerol grinned, uncertain how to defend his actions. Yloran was right; going to Broid was likely the dumbest thing he had ever done.

"Oh, darling, you don't have a bad side." Yloran touched his cheek. "Besides, do you honestly believe that Evellyn Lorenthien needed rescuing?" She held Evellyn's gaze this time.

"I did have some protection, unknown to Erynor. And one of his Deurghol found out when it was too late." Evellyn smiled at the memory of Auriel's power forcing the Deurghol who had inhabited that elf's body back to the Void, killing the elf in the process.

"I must admit, learning that those vile scum aren't as deathless as their name implies is heartening news. I'm quite undecided who I hate more: the Deurghol for bringing about the Shroud and severing us from our immortality or Erynor for commanding it," Yloran said.

"But then, how are you still alive?" Liam asked.

"You do like the inquisitive ones, don't you, Jaerol?" Yloran's gaze fell on Liam. She seemed to know all of who he was through the exchange, including his relationship with Jaerol. "You might not know me yet, Liam, but you would do well to remember that a lady never reveals her secrets. Bold of you to ask though. Kiron would have asked too if he hadn't already figured it out. Oh yes, I know that you two were researching the Sha'ghol while at the Imperium, Jaerol."

Jaerol's heart pinched at Kiron's name. It was a wound that would never fully heal.

"I wish I had had the opportunity to know him." Liam turned him an affectionate smile.

"You are one of a kind, aren't you? You must share your secret, Jaerol—it's not often that one manages to find a compatible companion in so short a life, and you've done it twice now." Yloran took another sip of wine, nostrils flaring as she did. She appeared to be in no rush and either uncaring or unaware that the news of Evellyn passing through Groveton had likely reached Nairin by now.

Shadow elves had to be on the move to track her down and collect her for their emperor. They would hope to gain a favored status with Erynor and be entrusted with one of his dragons. Jaerol sensed Rusyl's uneasiness at the delay. The blue dragon wasn't at all interested in another confrontation with the Dark Flight.

"You are all so impatient. Well, you might as well get comfortable and enjoy the wine while my attendants prepare my belongings for travel," Yloran said.

"Are you going somewhere?" Teran asked.

"I've overstayed my welcome here and the petty lord wishes to feel like the lord of his manor once more and not my errand boy. Fortunately for him, I've grown tired of this small village and would very much like to be surrounded by like-minded elves again. I did tell Devlyn to expect me when he took Arenthyl."

"You've seen Devlyn." Evellyn's head snapped toward the Sha'ghol. Jaerol could tell that Evellyn was still undecided about how she felt about Yloran.

"Oh yes. A kind boy with a kinder heart. It's quite shocking he turned out so compassionate, considering stewards of Shadow had raised him. But he's as pure as they come, annoyingly so in my view. A shame how broken his body was when I found him," Yloran said.

"Broken? What happened? Is he all right now?" Evellyn radiated motherly concern.

"He was well enough when he left me and considering the Shroud is gone, I assume he's managed to untwist himself and reconnect with his phoenix. I'll have to ask him if the Shroud was tied to Erynel, as I suspect it was. Wretched woman. None of the Sha'ghol could believe that she took a dragon's seed, and none other than Tolvenol's at that, knowing that she wouldn't survive giving birth. If she was responsible for the Shroud, the Evil One must have promised her a second life if she agreed to bring forth Erynor, a draelyn of the Dark Flight."

Evellyn's calm returned after learning that her son had healed.

"How do you intend for us all to travel to Krysenthiel? We won't be able to go unnoticed with all your attendants—we'll look like a caravan," Jaerol said. Arguing against her joining them was fruitless.

"The simplest way to hide is to be in plain sight. Have you learned nothing?" Yloran smiled over her glass. "My attendants are quite the athletic group, to say nothing of them being capable wielders. That being the case, what better way to travel than as the Cyndinari Ember Circus, bringing our culture to the mainland?"

"The Ember Circus? I used to go to that as a child. How is it here and not on Cynethol?" Jaerol asked.

"The ringleader is an old friend of mine. I've been close to his family for generations; the men in that family make the best attendants. Raelinth belongs to that family. Forgive me, I digress. The ringleader loaned me a spare tent and costumes. He even provided banners embla-zoned with the circus' emblem. Who would expect Yloran Eth Gnashar, killer of Jaris Iln Desaris, to travel in a circus with the mother of Devlyn Lorenthien, no less?"

UNFURLED WINGS

A band of kirenae trees surrounded Devlyn and Ellendren as they lounged in the afternoon sun. These trees kept shifting and blocking the sun. Devlyn had lost count of how many times they'd moved out of the shade. Ellendren's head rested on his chest, their hands clasped.

Devlyn did not know how much time had passed, but he thought at least a year had come and gone since he and Ellendren had arrived. Each day had been filled with tapping the Aerethyn, followed by reflecting on the events he and Ellendren had witnessed. Elyse regularly led them in jienzu and meditation. There were no bells here to signal the hour Devlyn and Ellendren were to use the Aerethyn; Elyse signaled the appropriate time for them. The hour was inconsistent from day to day. On one occasion, Elyse had called Devlyn and Ellendren to the Aerethyn as they were settling to sleep.

Settled once more with his eyes glazed over, he again felt the familiar chill of unwanted shade. Squinting, he saw the trees surrounding him again. "Can we help you?" he asked, slightly irritated with the meddling trees.

"They're only curious," Ellendren said, unbothered.

"More like nosy." He caressed Ellendren's back, wanting nothing more than for the trees to not spy on him and his wife.

The band of trees shifted, seeming to look at each other.

Remembering that they were trees, Devlyn opened his awareness, focusing his inner sense on them, uninterested in expanding beyond what had been a sunny clearing.

The trees bent toward them, and Devlyn sensed their curiosity. He vaguely remembered observing the Eldinari elves interacting with stellendae trees in Stellantis. Those trees were much larger though, and rarely moved. Extending a hand to the nearest tree, he brushed his fingers against the smooth bark. It warmed at his touch and light bloomed beneath his hand.

Images of acceptance blazed in Devlyn's mind. In the past, he had only seen such images from dragons. Before he could wonder if there was any connection between the trees and dragons, a heavy rumble came from behind. With his interior senses still opened, he sensed Lyvenol approach and turned to see the great gold dragon. The ground shook the closer the Primus of the Gold Flight and Warden of lumenys came. The trees twirled about as though a breeze blew through them. Lyvenol sent images, telling Devlyn and Ellendren the trees liked them, as they scrambled to their feet to greet the dragon.

Bowing, they smiled at Lyvenol. "How can you tell?" Ellendren asked.

Lyvenol transformed to his smaller form. He reminded Devlyn of Galithinol. "The kirenae trees know what Devlyn did in the Illumined Wood during his novitiate. Any tree that hasn't fallen too deep in slumber knows what you did for the miervae and how you subsequently brought forth a sprout of Verakryl." Lyvenol's deep voice reverberated through Devlyn's body.

"How can they know? We're far from the Illumined Wood." Devlyn scratched his head.

"Every tree is connected. Some through a root system beneath the surface, but also through something deeper and stronger than roots. Just as all anacordel are connected, so too is everything created by Anaweh." Lyvenol came further into the clearing then transformed back into his larger draconic form; gold scales rippled across his body and his arms and legs swelled thicker than tree trunks. Lyvenol rotated his massive head on his sinuous neck to look Devlyn in the eyes. Only a single golden eye peered into Devlyn's. The dragon blinked slowly, the double eyelids moving as he did.

Lyvenol stretched his front legs and a mixture of images filled Devlyn and Ellendren's minds; some spoke of terrors to come, while others exuded a sense of trust mingled with hope. The Gold Primus shared that he and the rest of the Gold Flight remained mostly on Phroenthyl, rarely venturing past the enchantment. Devlyn saw gold dragons leaping into the air to soar around Phroenthyl. Devlyn had not seen Lyvenol stretch his wings to join the younger dragons but imagined his wingspan would shade a small village.

Even as he thought it, an image of Lyvenol flying came to their minds, his wingspan engulfing half of Cor'lera. Devlyn thought he saw Lyvenol smile. His teeth remained hidden, but the lines of the dragon's lips turned up at the corners.

Images of invitation flowed from Lyvenol to Devlyn and Ellendren. The great dragon arched his back and strained his legs before unfurling his massive wings.

The trees moved back to create an even larger circular clearing for Lyvenol's wingspan; their roots slithered beneath the ground. Golden petals from their continuously blooming flowers fluttered to the ground leaving behind a golden blanket to encircle Lyvenol. Swaying with excitement, each tree seemed to nudge its neighbor. Sounds of crackling bark filled the clearing.

Wings fully extended, Lyvenol swept them downward. Devlyn's hair blew back in the brush of Lyvenol's wings, and the petals swept past the trees in an expanding swirl. Stepping back to the newly formed tree line, Devlyn and Ellendren watched Lyvenol crouch down.

Despite stepping back, they were nearly blown over by the lateral force as the dragon flapped his wings a second time. Lyvenol bent his legs to launch himself off the ground and Devlyn and Ellendren almost toppled from the force of the leap and the wind. Impossibly aloft in the air, slowly flapping his wings to lift him higher, Lyvenol turned his gaze to Devlyn and Ellendren in invitation. Enticing images filled their minds and they followed the dragon into the air, their wings causing considerably less disruption than Lyvenol's.

Racing to catch up with the dragon, they had to flap at least ten times to match the speed that each of Lyvenol's ever steady flap of wings brought him.

As he roared into the empty sky, a wondrous light mingled with flames exploded from Lyvenol's maw, his own speed carrying him past unscathed, his golden scales awash in fiery light.

Hundreds of similar roars echoed below. Devlyn felt the other gold dragons in his chest before he saw them. Shifting his attention, he saw dozens of dragons flying from what looked like beneath the Skyland to join their Primus. They were all different sizes, but none matched Lyvenol. They quickly reached Devlyn, Ellendren, and Lyvenol. Bursts of fiery light lit the sky.

Careful to avoid the dragons' excitement, Devlyn pressed himself into the erendinth, increasing his awareness of ignys as it appeared with little warning. Only the dragon's roar indicated what was to follow, and that was only half a breath's warning.

Lyvenol maintained his position at the head of the flight with Devlyn and Ellendren close above and to the side. They trailed Lyvenol, not leaving the barrier that kept Phroenthyl hidden and in the time flux. Lyvenol angled his great wings, now steady without a need to flap them to keep him afloat.

Spiraling downward behind Lyvenol, Devlyn's ears whistled with the wind. Below Phroenthyl's surface, Devlyn gazed at the underside of the Skyland. The massive landmass of lumaryl sparkled in the sunlight. Only its thickness prevented Devlyn from seeing through and past the Skyland. The semi-translucent stone had unique qualities that Devlyn was still learning about. Most notable was that it floated in the sky.

He remembered reading in one of the holy tomes that Anaweh had given the Skylands to the elves, but there was no mention of the Creating Light keeping the Skylands afloat. Devlyn doubted dragons kept them from crashing to the ground or water below. With an ever-widening understanding provided by the Aerethyn, Devlyn had learned that each Skyland's foundations was of a mystical stone. Only the Eldinari elves chose dwellings other than buildings sung from their Skyland's foundation, preferring the stellendae trees over the glassy eldaryl.

Leveling his wings, Lyvenol angled toward the lumaryl foundations of Phroenthyl. Water cascaded from above as streams fell to the empty sky, mist washing across Devlyn and Ellendren's bodies as they followed. His eyes widened in wonder as he noticed caverns poking through the Skyland's foundations.

An image of the absurdity of a dragon dwelling anywhere but a cavern entered their minds, and Devlyn knew for certain that Lyvenol was laughing.

Entering a lumaryl cavern, Devlyn waited for his eyes to adjust to the stone's hazy light. The cavern wasn't dark, but the thickness of its lumaryl walls affected the quality of the light, and it was a moment before he noted that the other dragons had come into the cavern too.

Lyvenol's claws scratched the lumaryl ground, yet the stone showed no marks. Lyvenol curled his large wings against his torso then transformed to his smaller form. "Rarely are outsiders welcomed to a dragon's lair; even fewer to a Primus' lair."

"You honor us." Devlyn and Ellendren bowed formally, sharing images of gratitude and humility with all the dragons present.

All had their wings folded against their backs, and some transformed to their smaller forms, mimicking Lyvenol who moved further into the cavern, insisting that Devlyn and Ellendren follow. Most of the dragons who'd accompanied them in the sky went down different tunnels and branches of the cavern, leaving Devlyn and Ellendren alone with Lyvenol.

Enormous tunnels branched in every direction, huge spaces opening unexpectedly, with smaller tunnels opening along the perimeter. Dozens of dragons filled the larger caverns; they showed reverence to Lyvenol, while eyeing Devlyn and Ellendren curiously.

They entered another cavernous space that expanded to an incredible height and breadth. A crystalline tree bloomed in the center. Crystal blossoms resembling diamonds sparkled with a light of their own. Jeweled fruit weighed down its branches.

Images of Kien and Kiara entered Devlyn and Ellendren's minds. They knew their faces well now and were familiar with their younger minds and hearts.

"Your forebears, the noble Kien and Kiara, honored us with a gift that no dragon could ever retrieve: a verathel, a sprout of the Tree of Life. They offered this gift in thanksgiving for my allowing the Phaedryn to forever call Phroenthyl their home, to share with the Gold Flight."

Devlyn turned to Lyvenol, amazed at Kien and Kiara's kind hearts. "I doubt I could ever offer such an incredible gift."

Lyvenol chuckled, the deep sound echoing across the cavern. Nodding at the tree, Lyvenol indicated Devlyn should approach it.

Not wishing to deny a dragon, even in his smaller form, Devlyn hesitantly moved toward the tree, each careful step on the hallowed ground bringing him closer to the crystal bark. A warm light emitted from the tree, thrumming from its core, nearly visible due to the crystalline bark. Laying a hand against the bark, Devlyn felt his mind flood with light. An intimacy lying dormant inside him reverberated through all of who he was. Body, soul, and spirit sang with the connection. His hand pressed against the bark, Devlyn felt his entire being mingle with the tree.

The tree summoned visions of Devlyn's past, most notably the verathel he had called forth in the Illumined Wood over the remains of the murdered miervae. The memory felt like it had been ages ago, but the tree made it feel as though it was in the present; a timeless quality permeated the tree.

Through his connection, Devlyn felt concern in this verathel, a fully gown tree, but still a sprout, linked and dependent on the Tree of Life. A flash of terror passed from the tree to him.

Concerned on the tree's behalf, Devlyn tried to learn what troubled the verathel, but it didn't respond. Lyvenol sent an image of the anxiety he too felt from the tree but could not discover its reason or source.

It is time. Elyse called. There was no need for her to state what for.

Devlyn thanked Lyvenol once again. As he and Ellendren were leaving the cavern, they signed farewells to the gold dragons.

They flew out of the cavern toward the Aerethyn. Despite Elyse's schedule, Devlyn never felt a need to rush to the Aerethyn. Unlike his studies at the abbey school in Cor'lera and then later at Gwilnor and the Temple of Ceur, Devlyn found this relaxed pace invigorating. Even though it was through an entirely different medium, he believed this newfound sense of leisure was the appropriate way to learn.

Elyse waited by the orb for them.

"Lyvenol has taken a liking to you, as have the kirenae trees," Elyse said.

"I've grown quite fond of them myself," Devlyn said, still overwhelmed by the invitation into the caverns below.

"After you leave Phroenthyl, you'll have to visit the Delmira Wood; I sense the kirenae trees still slumbering in their frozen state. Many have grown sick and cold from the Shroud. They will need tending."

Devlyn felt Ellendren's excitement. The possibility of reviving the sick forest seemed beyond their abilities. He wondered if the centaur, Oreniel, could help.

"Oreniel can nurture the forest but only a child of Luminare can wake them. Learn the song from the kirenae here, they will teach you the way. Your sister likely already knows it."

Smiling at the prospect, Devlyn returned his attention to the Aerethyn. Matching Ellendren's pose, he rested his hands on the reflective orb and knew that it was now 8883.2E.

Wings unfurled in the open sky, Kien dove through a misty cloud, wielding aquaeys and aerys to reshape the cloud in the form of Naiel.

I look much better as light than as clouds, Naiel conveyed to Kien, the two bonded together in what he and Kiara had agreed should be called a Phaedryn.

Kiara had chosen the name, but he had proposed dozens of similar variations.

The name sounded appropriate; Kien imagined the words 'elf' and 'phoenix' blended in Aelish, forming the right sounds and filled with meaning. Kiara enjoyed imbuing more meaning into a word than needed. Not that Kien shared that thought with her, but there was little he could hide from her. Considering their bond, she probably knew exactly what he thought about it.

With a final furl, Kien flew out of the clouds to behold what he had sculpted of air and water.

"You forgot the light." Kiara smiled, her eyes playfully alight with mirth as she teased.

Kien sensed Eliel bonded to the love of his life.

"I don't know how to wield lumenys yet," Kien said, a hint of frustration at the limitation.

Only within the Empyrean Sphere may one learn such, Naiel conveyed.

You've said that before.

Naiel sent a hint of amusement across their bond.

Kiara spun around and returned to Phroenthyl, a name chosen long ago by the Gold Flight who lived here.

Kien followed, taking an extra moment to enjoy his temporary cloud art. Returning to Phroenthyl's surface, Kien and Naiel withdrew from each other, his form returning to a normal wingless elf. The entire landscape shifted from the brightness seen through light itself. Kiara had already withdrawn from Eliel, and her beautiful figure walked delicately along a narrow lake.

They hadn't brought anything with them to Phroenthyl; how could they since their clothes disintegrated whenever they bonded with their phoenix? The elves knew their bodies and were unashamed of them, but he still recalled the shock of those on the land below and humans gaping and shaming them as they withdrew from the phoenix, revealing their naked bodies.

"Planning our next travel?" Kiara asked, turning from the still water.

"A few ideas." Kien gazed past the lake, his eyes settling on a rolling hill, covered with kryseniels, the lumaryl stone shining from beneath.

"I did enjoy our visit to Aldinare. It's exciting to see what Theseryn is doing," Kiara said.

"I hope he has the story right. Could you imagine the ramifications if it was recorded incorrectly? After all, he was only a toddler when he was taken from Tenethyl."

"I'm sure the other aldarchs are assisting him in the matter. The draelyn are among the few races from that time who haven't been called to Lumaeniel," Kiara said.

"If anyone remembers all of it, it'll be the aldarchs. I wish I had had the opportunity to ask Thien about the Fall of Tenethyl and the Great Blessing before he had transitioned to the World-Beyond."

Pressing into terys, Kien wielded a chunk of lumaryl out of its place and caught it in his palm. His fingers wrapped around the smooth stone, examining the crevices and properties. He discovered more intimate properties, invisible to the eye, as he continued to wield.

Kiara observed him, intrigued as he fell into his methodical rhythm. She had grown accustomed to his attention shifting without warning when creativity struck. He was relieved that she never grew angry with him when his attention drifted from her.

Why would I grow angry; especially when all your artistic creations are given to me? Her thoughts filled his mind, mingling with his own. His thoughts drifted as he set himself on a task he did not fully understand.

And who said I was making something to give to you?

Are you not?

Kien smiled at the lumaryl, delving further into it. Pressing more fully into terys, he began molding it, then condensed it under incredible pressure. Weaving the other elemental erendinth, Kien pressed into them, imbuing their properties into the lumaryl as its mass shrank.

A great wind billowed about him; his hair whipped about his face. Unaffected by the disturbance, he continued, wielding all four elemental erendinth. A tug inside him wanted to imbue more of the erendinth into it, so he submitted his will and brought animys into himself before wielding it into what was taking on the likeness of a jewel. He wanted to intensify the already present light imbued in the lumaryl, annoyed once again that he couldn't wield lumenys.

The wind gentled and his golden hair fell to his shoulders, and he looked at what was now visibly the most beautiful jewel he had ever seen.

Looking from the jewel to Kiara, he stretched his palm out, offering her the new creation.

"What a beautiful lucilliae." Kiara's eyes sparkled in the seemingly infinite depths and facets of the jewel as she received it.

"Since when is it called a lucilliae?" Kien's naming privileges had again been denied.

"Is it not a jewel of light?"

Kien followed her logic and the roots she had taken from Aelish to name his creation.

"Have you decided on our next destination?" Kiara smiled, the lucilliae still caught in her gaze, but not her attention.

"Why so eager to travel again?"

"Soon, we'll have to return to Luminare and remain there for many years."

"Why so soon? My parents won't become aryl for another two

hundred years."

"Those aren't the parents of my concern at present."

Kien raised an eyebrow.

"Have you not felt him yet?" Kiara lowered her hands to her belly.

Kien's eyes lit up in shock as he understood what Kiara was insinuating. "Are you sure? Isn't it too early to tell?"

Kiara smiled, and Kien felt her beckon through their bond, pulling his awareness into herself. Nestled deep within her, almost unreachable, as if between two different realms, grew a body and soul for a new spirit.

DWONIAN LION

Tye of Tribe Fendur perched on a mound of arid rock and surveyed the land before him. Without vegetation or surface water, Dwonia had baked under the hot sun for the past eighteen hundred years. The land east of Dwota's Gap had always been lusher, but the elders claimed Dwonia had had trees and grasses before the blight. Some of the elders even spoke of lakes.

The elders said many things. Tye believed most of their stories, but a lake in a land that didn't have puddles was difficult to swallow.

The wind blowing from the south—the winds rarely came from anywhere else—picked up strength. As a sand warrior, more commonly known east of the Gap as desert bandits, Tye could travel as far south as he wanted and had even gone to the edge once. The southern lands rose and fell in deep ravines, carving and segmenting the landscape into plateaus. It looked as though someone had scooped a serving of fulp from the middle of a dish. The mashed and starchy staple of Dwonian diet was a perfect medium to depict the landscape.

The ravines eventually leveled off, and Tye remembered the first time he had seen the endless expanse. It reminded him of the flats, where only a dusty haze obscured the otherwise unobstructed horizon. That southern thing was different though, for it was a vast body of water. The desert fell in a cliff at the edge and into the water, where violent waves crashed against the side of the rock. The sand warrior who had taken Tye there had called it the Tempestien Sea and said the water was poisonous to drink.

Like all Dwonians, Tye had had an instant distrust of this large body of water. He never heard an elder or anyone in his tribe speak ill of the ocean, but there was an edge to their voices and a warning whenever the poisonous water was mentioned. Knowing that the deserters lived near an ocean always made him happy. Only two tribes remained in Dwonia when there had once been twelve. Ten tribes had joined the Erynien Empire, and only one of them had regretted that choice. They had become the Sojourners, doomed to travel the land east of Dwota's Gap until they found the song that would bring the seeds back to Dwonia.

He felt the southern wind strengthen; stinging sand caught up in the gale, and he wrapped the urda woven especially for him by his grandmother about his face. Tye had to focus on his approaching meeting with the chiefs.

Turning away from the sandy wind, he ducked down into a shallow fissure. The crevice dropped after ten paces, forcing him to crawl as he felt for the carved ladder. The tribes had to take care that the enemy never found their home. One had to know the ladder was there to find it. Throwing his leg over the edge, he found the first rung. He descended into the darkening gap, the natural light from above dimming with every rung down.

Darkness bathed the bottom. Extending his hand to the wall, he found the latch he sought easily enough. Putting his strength to the heavy door, he pushed it open just enough to squeeze through, as light from beyond flooded one of the secret entrances into Nynev. There was nothing bright about the light, but the contrast did make it seem so at first.

Tye pushed the door closed behind him then unwrapped his urda. Hiding one's face was forbidden in Nynev. As a child, he had thought it was a means to prevent deserters with nefarious intentions from hiding in plain sight. An elder had later told him that it was a tradition predating the deserters' betrayal, but for the same reason.

Indiscriminate rays of light filtered down to the streets from strategically placed holes that had long ago been carved into the sandstone ceiling above Nynev. The cavernous city set in the canyons was originally intended only as a place of meeting for the Twelve Tribes of Dwonia, offering shade from the oppressive heat. But after the Desertion, the remaining two, Tribe Vadir and Tribe Fendur, had agreed to band together, knowing they would have to defend themselves from the deserters and the larger Erynien Empire.

Dwonians were not meant to hide beneath the ground like cowards though, cut off from the sun. The sunlight that did reach Nynev's streets could do nothing to warm them. Few living in Nynev were happy with the arrangement. Their place was on the surface, with the sun warming their skin, and their spears pushing back skirmishes from the Shadow Mountains.

Tye suppressed his thoughts on Dwonia's current predicament; he had to concentrate on what he was going to say and thinking of Dwonians hiding underground only frustrated him. His grandmother, an elder, had urged him to focus on his meeting with the chiefs and elders.

Heading toward the Hall of Ancestors, he ignored the merchants lining the streets, shouting their wares. Unlike in the cities east of the Gap, Dwonians bought and sold only the necessities. Most of the merchants sold food, which largely consisted of ingredients for fulp. The only reason there were merchants in Nynev was because the farmers who managed to cultivate plant life underground were required to devote all their time to those plants. With merchants to sell the wares, the farmers could stay near their work. A few merchants sold clothing, but Dwonians rarely needed to purchase any; they mended their own until it was past repair.

The number of shops diminished as Tye approached the Hall of Ancestors. It had once served as the meeting place for the chiefs of the twelve tribes, and the city had expanded around it. Like the city, the Hall of Ancestors was carved into the canyon. Unlike the other buildings though, the Hall had no door. Tye stopped before the simple sandstone post and lintel entry. Long-dead chiefs had declared that since they represented their people, no door should stand between them during a gathering. When one took place, the ancestors guided those that followed.

A series of crypts had been dug beneath, each tribe entitled to one. Tye had gone down once but had quickly discovered that only chiefs were given the privilege of being buried below the Hall of Ancestors. Despite spending a fair amount of time in the Fendur crypt, Tye had never reached the end of it, giving witness to how long the Dwonians had followed their way of life.

While the chiefs' role remained central to Dwonia, the Desertion had forced the remaining two tribes to alter their ways. They had decided long ago that it was foolish to leave deliberations on Dwonia's fate in the hands of only two chiefs. Elders were now invited to the Hall of Ancestors to speak at gatherings, serving as advisors to their chief. The final decision remained with the two chiefs, each deciding what was best for their tribe. Any Dwonian over the age of sixty belonging to one of the two remaining tribes was considered an elder.

Passing through the doorway, Tye walked down a long hypostyle hall before crossing into a large chamber lined with people on either side of a central walkway. Sitting on a simple sandstone bench on the right was Chief Genin of Tribe Vadir. Chief Roen of Tribe Fendur sat opposite Genin; also on a sandstone bench. The elders sat on more benches behind their chief, filling the rectangular chamber in neat lines.

The purpose of the meeting glowed from a plinth in the center of the walkway. A warm, yet oddly crisp orange light separated the two tribes as it rested between them, just in front of the two chiefs. Both tribes benefited from the curious jewel the elders called a lucilliae.

The orange jewel caught Tye's focus. His courage and confidence had been shaken when he had first seen the chiefs and elders, but as he gazed upon the jewel, determination fueled him. Fortitude returned to his bones and he straightened his spine, squared his shoulders, and walked forward to stand before the chiefs and the lucilliae.

"Tye of Tribe Fendur, son of Japhin, place your request before our ancestors." Chief Roen remained seated as he spoke. It was customary for a petitioner's own chief to speak first and ask the supplicant to state the reason for summoning the chiefs and elders, even though everyone in the chamber already knew Tye's request.

"I believe it is time we returned the lucilliae to the Luminari elves." The request was simple, his grandmother's recommendation, as long-winded entreaties were often ignored.

"The lucilliae was a gift from those elves shortly after the Desertion, given to us for rejecting Erynor and his evil ways," said a newly designated elder, no older than sixty-three.

"There are whispers that the elves have returned to Krysenthiel," another elder said. That was news to Tye; he had assumed they were still in Lucillia behind their barrier.

"What does that change? A gift is still a gift."

Elders were allowed to offer a single comment during these meetings; chiefs could speak as much as needed. The intent was to keep the meetings brief, without stirring heated debates.

"It changes everything; this lucilliae is linked to a greater one located in Arenthyl."

Tye knew very little about the lucilliae, only that it belonged to the Luminari elves, regardless of its status as a gift. If not for his curious dream, Tye would never have made this request, but a young woman named Abbie Wintyr had entered many of his dreams over a period of time. He had only met her in person once when he had ventured past Dwota's Gap to warn the leadership of the Lucillian Alliance of the giants marching toward the Gap.

He had assumed they were only dreams, but Abbie had once slapped him. Tye would have disregarded the slap, but when he woke the following day, he could still feel its sting.

Abbie made no secret about her knowledge of what lay hidden in Nynev and who it belonged to. She had told him Devlyn and Ellendren would soon be the Exalted Aryl of Krysenthiel, and they needed what the Dwonians hid in Nynev. She shared little else, and all but demanded Tye return the lucilliae to the Luminari elves. Curiously, Abbie never mentioned it by name. Granted, there was little need to; it was the only elven artifact Nynev possessed.

"Forfeiting the lucilliae is a sign of weakness—we cannot."

"We ought to pull every sand warrior back to Nynev to ensure it remains secure."

"We can't ignore the skirmishes along the Shadow Mountains; what would happen if they discovered Nynev's location? We'd be over-run. It wouldn't matter what treasures we hold."

"Our greatest treasure has already been destroyed, cut down by Erynor when he offered every chief twelve weapons, cultivated from that verathel. Ten of our tribes accepted those gifts. Only our two tribes did not. If not for Erynor and the deserters, our land would still live; our treasures would not lie hidden in caves but would be the land we once roamed and dwelt on. It nourished us as we nourished it."

"The lucilliae and the felled tree are unrelated."

"Not so! This lucilliae was said to be sung from the Tree of Life itself. It is our last surviving connection. Without it, we have no hope of returning the seeds to Dwonia."

Tye listened attentively to the elders' deliberations. He expected the chiefs to speak more, but Roen had only introduced Tye, and Genin remained silent. Tye's grandmother had made it clear that he was only permitted to voice his request before the ancestors and say nothing fur-ther. The rest of the session was reserved for the elders and the chiefs. As different elders used their speaking privileges, the lines shifted as they whispered to one another, asking others to voice their continued opinions for them.

Weary of the discussion, Tye stifled a yawn just as Genin stood, ready to make his declaration.

"I've heard the elders of both Tribe Vadir and Tribe Fendur." Genin had once been a strong sand warrior, leaving his post only after the elders of his tribe had named him their chief. He had been willing, but Tye knew he missed his days in the Purged Desert, fighting off skirmishes and protecting Dwonia more directly. "Relinquishing the lucilliae is unwise—I do not support the request." Genin sat as a mix of sighs of relief overwhelmed the minority who supported returning the jewel.

Roen rose from his bench and cleared his throat. "I've heard the elders of Tribe Fendur, and those of Tribe Vadir. I agree, now is not the time to return the lucilliae. Our focus must be on staying hidden and secret. If the outside learns that Nynev still stands, albeit buried in the sand, our survival will be short. We've learned distressing news that the deserters have conquered Mindale and that he who pretends to be chief of the disgraced Tribe Laith now also calls himself a chief-king. He intends to control the Gap and take Nynev from us if he can find it."

Tye felt disappointment and anger at the declaration. He was frustrated that they had refused his request, but Roen's reasoning infuriated him more. His chief wanted outsiders to believe they had all died, buried and forgotten in the sand.

The same chorus of relief followed Roen's declaration as he also resumed his seat. Neither Roen nor Genin looked at Tye. He was expected to accept their judgement since it was guided by the ancestors.

But their ancestors would not have stood for hiding. They would never have agreed to bury themselves alive in Nynev, abandoning their way of life among the plateaus of Dwonia. It might now be a full-fledged desert, but even before the land wilted at Erynor's touch, it had never been a plentiful country. The land had made Dwonians strong. Hiding had made them forget who they were.

Dwonian lions would never hide in caves. Tye was sickened at how his tribe no longer emulated the animal they claimed to revere above any other. Their prides stalked the lands, providing security and shelter while confronting threats. Every Dwonian claimed to admire the lion. Tye wondered when the last time had been that any Dwonian had seen one with their own eyes, and whether the elders even remembered how lions lived and survived.

He turned away from the chiefs and elders and left the way he had entered.

His anger was reflected in his stalking pace through the streets as he made his way to his quarters first and prepared to leave Nynev. He retrieved his pack and stuffed enough fulp and dried meat into a container to last him several weeks. Finding food would not be a problem once he passed Dwota's Gap, for Eklean was abundant in vegetation and wildlife.

He scanned his room and grabbed a change of clothing and his cloak before closing the door behind him. Tye could not steal the lucilliae, but there were other ways of making sure he did the right thing. Pressing forward, Tye was soon through the heavy door and up the ladder under the baking sun. He wrapped his urda about his face, shielding himself from the sand-filled winds, and turned east, leaving Nynev behind.

THE DUCHESS

After a brief respite in Overen, the Thellish entourage rode south, following the road west of the River Eindol, headed for the Duke of Overen's celebrated lodge. There, they were to meet with Lord and Lady Ashton. Alex rode his winged horse, Dennion, and Diana and her mother, Queen Lara of Evellion were beside him on a pair of Evellion's prized white mares. Aen rode close behind on a grey courser. He was about the same age Alex and Devlyn had been when they first rode the large horses that Velaria had miraculously procured when they had fled Cor'lera.

Their entourage also included enough soldiers to make the so-called chief-king of Dwonia and Mindale think twice about crossing Evellion's border. The Thellish army, composed of soldiers from Evellion, Parendior, and Perrien, was unquestionably a display of power. Alex's petty council had agreed it would be best to remind the chief-king that to attack Evellion was to attack Thellion. Even the dwarves had come out of their mountain halls to remind those loyal to the Erynien Empire that Evellion would not quietly entertain another invasion.

Northern Eklean had expunged the Erynien Empire from its lands and intended to keep it that way.

Sending a message to Cairn wasn't the only reason Alex had personally travelled to Overen though. Lara had recommended the duke's lodge as an appropriate location to meet Lord and Lady Ashton. They had long opposed Mindale's alliance to the Erynien Empire and now led the resistance against the new Mindalean rule.

Alex didn't quite know what to expect, and was impressed at the double row of trees, perfectly spaced, lining the road to the anything-but-modest house. The entourage rode into the lodge's grand three-sided stone courtyard where an elderly woman, accompanied by many well-dressed nobles, waited on the steps of the entry to the lodge. Dark burgundy velvet covered her frail body; her hair was hidden beneath a veil of the same fabric.

"Has Duchess Ursula called in every noble in her territory to greet us?" Alex whispered to Diana as he took in the number of nobles.

"The duchess is known for her large family," Diana explained. "It's rumored that she raised her children here away from the city to prevent them from getting into the same trouble that her late husband and his brothers were known to have caused Overen in their younger years. Ursula didn't think it appropriate for House Corvin."

Their immediate entourage dismounted and the duke's stable hands relieved them of their mounts, allowing them to be greeted by the awaiting nobles.

"Your Majesty," Ursula curtsied to Alex, then offered the same greeting to Lara. Her children approached and offered greetings as well, and the two groups melded in pleasantries.

"We appreciate you welcoming us to your lodge and the risk in which you place yourself and your house for our sake," Alex said.

"The Erynien Empire and its dogs require little encouragement to trespass on our lands. We stand loyal to Evellion and Thellion," Ursula said, turning toward the man next to her. "But you should be thanking my son, Todrick. He might still listen to his mother, but he's been the Duke of Overen for at least a decade, ever since we lost my husband."

Alex nodded at Todrick, a man no longer in his prime. He looked nearly the same age as Alex's grandfather. He appeared healthy enough, but Alex doubted he would ever step onto a battlefield and survive. Alex also knew, thanks to Diana, that Todrick did nothing without first consulting his mother. Todrick might be the Duke of Overen because of Evellion's archaic laws of succession, but Ursula was the real authority in Overen.

"Should we retreat indoors? Lord and Lady Ashton arrived late yesterday and await you inside. They had to cross the border under the cover of night," Todrick said.

"Let's not keep them waiting," Lara said. "How have they fared?"

"They have received every comfort, I assure you; they will not leave our lodge cold and hungry," Todrick said thinly, taking Lara's comment as doubt that the Ashtons had been properly seen to. He impatiently waved an arm to indicate they should go on in. Most of the Thellish soldiers stayed in the courtyard tending to the mounts; only those who held strategic positions in court went inside.

Todrick walked beside Alex, offering more pleasantries, although his speech revealed his advancing years and possibly ailing health. He asked about their journey and the wintry weather they had ridden through. He seemed particularly interested in the rebuilding of Elothkar and what ancient treasures had been found there. Alex engaged the duke as much as he was able, but the duke's monotone only made Alex yearn for a warm bed as he stifled a yawn. He'd noted some of the younger members of House Corvin, but they stayed behind the duke and his mother, keeping their distance, as though they'd been instructed to stay away from Alex.

Passing through the grand house, Alex was delighted to find that it appeared to have suffered no touch of war. His uncle's army must have been too focused on Everin to journey this far south. Although built of stone, the house would not survive a siege.

The lodge's interior halls were in stark contrast to its cold stone facades. Warm wooden paneling lined the walls, further softened with fabric panels and ceiling coffers. The Ashtons waited in a cozy room, not due to its size, for the hall was quite large and had two fireplaces at either end facing each other, but to its decor. The chosen colors reminded Alex little of Evellion. House Corvin had decorated the lodge in their ducal colors rather than Evellion's blue and white. Rich burgundy dominated the fabrics and notes of gold shimmered throughout. Lord and Lady Ashton were seated at a long wooden table, accompanied by several others—knights and generals most likely—all examining a much folded map set before them.

Lady Daphne Ashton was the first to see the new arrivals and rose to embrace her longtime friend, Lara. Diana had told Alex they had studied at Gwilnor with Velaria, so Alex half expected Velaria to make an appearance. He well remembered his first visit to Everin under her protection.

"I didn't expect you would make the journey yourself," Daphne said, hugging Lara.

"And miss the opportunity to greet you in my own kingdom, Daphne?"

"What about little Amryian? Surely, he's too young to be without you," Daphne replied.

"His nursemaids are well-equipped. And I'm overdue for a tour of southern Evellion. Our less-than-amicable neighbors need reminding that Evellion stands strong," Lara said.

More greetings and pleasantries were shared and Alex quickly tired of the formalities. His patience had its limits when it came to Evellion's stuffy decorum. Lara and Diana were blessedly exempt from that, no thanks to Lara's cheery disposition. Even in her grief following the loss of her husband, she had maintained a positive demeanor for her people. She was a good queen, and all Eklean knew it. Dismissing Evellion's archaic laws of succession and allowing Lara to keep her crown was one of Alex's proudest moments as King of Thellion.

Once everyone had been introduced, Todrick excused himself, leaving his mother to participate in the strategy meeting. Lord Ashton— Henry—pointed to the map of Mindale. It showed the entire kingdom, and slivers of territory past its borders. The map's edges were worn, and thick creases from repeated folds lined the middle. Alex recognized it as a map that belonged in a military camp on a folding table.

"Has your resistance received any support from other Mindalean houses?" Lara asked.

"Less than we had hoped for. The nobles who first sought an alliance with the Erynien Empire in hopes of growing their fortunes have found the opposite happening after Cairn took Lawrence's throne. Their coffers will be dry if they pay the chief-king's new tax," Henry said.

"Do you need their support?" Ursula sat on a cushioned armchair, studying the map.

"Their support would lead to a unified transition. The kingdom has been divided under weak leadership for too long," Daphne said.

"Do we know what Cairn has done with Lawrence's son?" Diana asked.

"One of his sisters took him out of the city when the Dwonians attacked. They made it as far as the crossing at Wexly, but none of the ferries were on the eastern shore of the river. Cairn's men reached them. The princess was bound and tossed in the River Eindol while the prince, only a boy, was returned to Binton, where Cairn challenged him to a duel. Needless to say the prince did not survive," Henry said.

"How barbaric," Lara gasped. Henry nodded in agreement.

"Is there a natural succession in line? What are Mindale's laws of succession? Could any of Lawrence's daughters take the crown?" Alex asked.

"They are much like Evellion's former laws. The Mindalean nobles will expect a man to occupy the throne and they'll tear the kingdom asunder to take it for themselves," Daphne said.

"If I recall, there was a time when you were to inherit the throne," the duchess said.

"I was only a child when my father died. His younger brother quickly claimed the throne, pointing out that my father had left behind a mourning queen and a daughter," Daphne said.

"Ironic that Lawrence himself had so many daughters as well. I do mourn the young prince, though," Henry said.

Alex began visualizing the Ashtons on Mindale's throne, his mind a flurry of possibilities as to how they could wrench Mindale's support from Erynor and oust the Dwonians, further securing Thellion's borders.

A scream and a commotion in the nearby corridor interrupted his thoughts and the room erupted into motion. The knights accompanying the Ashtons unsheathed their swords and placed themselves in front of their lord and lady, even as Henry drew his own sword. Evellion and Thellish knights took up defensive and protective places around the table, all attention directed to the entrance. Guards wearing the duchess's house colors barged into the hall.

"I knew I should have brought my bow." Diana glared at her mother who had discouraged it. Lara and Daphne remained calm, but they seemed to be concentrating on something as Ursula struggled to stand. Only the duchess and Diana weren't equipped to fight.

"What's the meaning of this?" Ursula demanded, as the guards charged toward the clustered group, swords raised. The quiet and cozy hall erupted into a battle scene as the two sides fought. Lara and Daphne drew fire from the large hearths and launched fiery balls at their assailants. One turned and fled, clearly not having expected ei'ana among the group.

From the corner of his eye as he clashed swords with one of the Corvin guards, Alex saw Aen fighting a man twice his age and twice as wide. The man could have snapped Aen in half. Then the man's sword found its target and Diana screamed as Aen fell to the floor.

Enraged, Alex struck down his own assailant and rushed at the man who had stabbed Aen. Alex's sword was in the man's belly before he realized he had to defend himself.

"Who sent you?" Alex yelled, pushing his sword deeper into the man.

"The duke," the man confessed in a near whisper, about to die.

The other guards soon fell, only one dropping his sword to submit. The brief, yet serious conflict ended as quickly as it had begun. The attacking guards lay on the floor where they had fallen. Henry questioned the sole survivor, but Alex couldn't focus on that.

"Light, don't let it be too late," he prayed, tears falling down his cheeks as Lara wielded a healing spell over a deathly pale Aen. Blood pooled around the boy's body and Alex knelt close to take his hand. He was too young to hold a sword. Alex had only given him one as a gesture for his squire. Even though they were at war, Alex had never imagined that Aen would have to use it, not yet. He'd barely started the change—his voice hadn't even deepened.

Alex felt Lara wielding, felt the various erendinth pouring into Aen to mend his small body. Alex prayed, willing that Aen would survive. He poured every emotion into it and felt the small hand tighten around his own. Relief flooded through him, and he allowed the emotions to wash over him as he wrapped his arms around Aen.

"He'll be fine, but he'll need to rest," Lara said, her hand on Alex's shoulder. "You're a good king, Alexander. And I imagine you'll be an even better husband and father when the time comes." Alex hadn't thought of that. He cared for Aen and felt responsible for him. But how would he cope if something like this happened to Diana or one of his future children?

The duchess said, "Bring him to the couch; he'll rest easier than on the cold, hard floor."

Alex didn't question her and didn't care that the couch would be ruined by the blood saturating Aen's clothes. He carefully placed the pillow Diana brought under Aen's head.

"If I had known you could wield, I would have asked you to stop using that silly sword and help Daphne and me wield ignys," Lara said.

"I can't wield," Alex said, taken aback. He'd seen Devlyn wield, the first kien wielder to safely wield at Gwilnor Academy in a millennium. He'd witnessed what the ei'ana were capable of and he didn't want anything to do with it. He didn't care about Aewen's subtle words referring to his capabilities. He was not, nor would he be, a kien wielder. What would the ei'ana demand of him if they knew he could wield? He certainly couldn't return to Ceurenyl and sit in a classroom again. He had a kingdom to lead and a war to fight.

"You can and are remarkably strong too. Not to the extent that Devlyn is, but Aen only lives because of you," Lara said.

Alex didn't know what to say, but managed, "Thank you for helping him. Wielder or not, I wouldn't have known how to wield a healing spell." Lara smiled in return.

The elderly duchess, seeing that none of the Thellish entourage had died, marched toward her house's—her son's—guard. "Explain yourself." Her voice sliced through the quiet hall.

"The duke…he didn't say you'd be here. He ordered us to kill everyone in the hall," the man stuttered, rightfully fearful for his life.

"And how does that justify attacking our queen, and our Thellish king? How does that justify murdering guests under our roof?"

"I…I don't know," he stammered. "We weren't permitted to ask any questions."

"Are you saying my son doesn't let his soldiers think? How will you survive a battle if you can't think? You would have avoided treason if you'd taken a moment to do so. No wonder you lot fell as quickly as you did." Ursula sucked in her breath, furious. "Where is my son now?"

"I don't know. He rode south just after he gave us our orders."

"Coward," Ursula said, disgusted. Two of the Thellish knights had already left in pursuit. They rode winged horses and would catch the duke before he reached wherever he intended to flee. The duchess looked mournfully at Alex, then Lara. "My house has betrayed you. I will not beg forgiveness on my son's behalf. Who do you wish to name to the Duchy of Overen?"

"We won't know the full scope of your son's offense until he is questioned. I think it wise to withhold judgment until then. Do you agree, Alexander?" Lara said. He nodded.

"Thank you, Your Majesties. Please know you have my full support to search the premises for anything that might help in your investigation."

"Thank you, Ursula." Lara turned to one of her knights. "We need to learn if this was an isolated incident. Confine the ranking members of House Corvin and have them questioned. Find out if they knew about Todrick's treason," Lara said. The knight bowed and turned to leave.

"Please be gentle with Antony. He adores his father, the duke, but is a gentle boy. If he wasn't his father's heir, he would have become an ei'ceuril," Ursula said as the knight walked out, less worried about the fate of her house and more so for her family.

"As his father's heir, joining the ei'ceuril might be his only option now," Henry said.

Alex decided he liked the duchess. He imagined his mother in her role and how she would handle this situation. Vine would tear the hunting lodge apart to defend her children, although perhaps not their spouses.

Henry coughed, looking back at the map of Mindale. He had travelled from the Ashton Wood to determine a strategy to deal with Mindale's stolen throne. Alex recognized that they still had a strategy to plan and returned to the long table and their original purpose. An alliance between House Ashton and the Kingdom of Thellion, while never in question, was solidified. Thellion would supplement their resistance and support Lady Ashton's claim to the throne over the late king's daughters. Daphne had voiced her lack of interest for the throne, but when pressed as to who she felt was the better option to repel the Erynien Empire, could name no one.

Time passed during which various letters and missives taken from the duke's desk were brought into the hall, all further incriminating the duke. The duke had been in correspondence with Mindalean nobles and even their late king. The fool had kept everything. A smarter traitor would have burned any evidence of treason, especially when inviting his queen under his roof. The most recent letter had been sent from Mindale's new chief-king. Its contents condemned the duke more than his own actions had. Cairn had learned of the meeting at the hunting lodge from Todrick. In response, Cairn offered an alliance, something the duke had apparently long sought with Mindale, on one condition. Todrick had to deliver the heads of the Ashtons, Alex, and Lara.

Todrick would never see his alliance. He would be lucky if Lara permitted him to keep his own head after she'd read that letter.

Alex's knights returned with the duke, hands bound behind his back. By the look of his battered body and bruised eye, he hadn't come quietly. Aen had almost died because of him. Alex wished he had been the one to punch him in the face. He still thought he might. Todrick was barely in the hall before his mother strode over and slapped him hard across one cheek.

"Your father would be disgusted with you. You shame his memory and our house."

"My father wouldn't have allowed our house to stand by and watch a woman forfeit Evellion to another crown."

"Your father was an honorable man," Lara said, cutting Ursula's tirade short. "He knew every Thellish legend and longed to see Thellion restored. He often recounted the stories in my late husband's court. I'm sure you learned some of them from him. I also believe that your father would have explained the penalty for treason."

"You are unworthy to wear that crown," Todrick spat.

"And you are a traitor to the crown, unworthy to represent it. I strip you of your titles, rights, and lands. I will not have you killed, the traditional punishment for treason against the crown. Our kingdom has seen enough blood in recent years. Instead, you will live at the mercy of your mother. Ursula will resume her position and authority as Duchess of Overen. The crown rescinds the laws of succession from House Corvin. Duchess Ursula will present an heir, and the crown will judge whether he or she is acceptable to the crown."

"As though she ever truly allowed me to rule in my own right," Todrick said, scowling.

"You managed to commit treason well enough on your own," Alex said.

"You should know that we had a successful meeting after your planned interruption. A pity you won't be able to relay the news to Cairn," Henry said.

"Your guards were quick to fall. What did you imagine would happen if you were successful? An entire Thellish battalion currently occupies the Duchy of Overen. Did you think Cairn would give you reinforcements to take back what was your duchy after having me killed?" Alex eyed the former duke. "Did you truly expect to succeed?"

"I expected to be rid of those who shackled me."

"Take him away. I want him locked away in the dungeons and the key lost," Ursula said.

LIVING MEMORIES

29 Estlenth 9,789.2E

Three dozen excited Luminari elves crowded around Kien and Kiara's table in the private quarters of the aryl's palace in Mar'anathyl, squeezed into the room which comfortably sat twenty. They had all come with the express desire to learn to wield the erendinth. This was not the first meeting of its kind and Kiara was sure it would not be the last. While Kiara was relieved Kien's parents had offered them their own quarters in the aryl's expansive home, days like this made her long for the solitude of Phroenthyl.

She had spent fourteen centuries with only Kien, their phoenix Naiel and Eliel, and the Gold Dragon Flight on the small Skyland. She understood the necessity of returning to Luminare and living in Mar'anathyl, but part of her wished their small family could live in Luminare's countryside. Mar'anathyl was a beautiful city, but that had only drawn more elves to call it home, and it felt crowded to her.

Though its splendor hadn't stopped Kien from making improvements when they had returned. He had wielded incredible sculptures from the lumaryl that their songs had never managed to produce. The stone seemed to come alive when Kien had sung to it, simultaneously wielding it.

Kiara brought her attention back to the meeting. Kyrendal, their first born and so like his father, sat next to Kien, his bright silver eyes admiring him. Their youngest child, Elyse, was sound asleep against Kiara's side. Kiara wrapped her arm around her daughter, hoping their guests would not wake her. Before the guests had arrived and Kiara had allowed her to stay, Elyse had promised to stay awake although Kiara had known she would not. Their three other children didn't care to attend this meeting.

"You've said it yourself; a phoenix's bond is not required to wield the erendinth," Moendil said.

"We want to learn," Wenthol said, an echo of agreements supporting his request.

Kien looked over at her. There was determination in his eyes, and only Kiara, and their phoenix Naiel and Eliel, knew the intent behind that determination. Kyrendal looked anxious. She remembered the day Kien had begun to teach him. He had been so young, but he had pressed into the erendinth just as naturally as his father had. She was not convinced at first that the erendinth were meant to be wielded by everyone, but after witnessing how quickly her son had mastered it, she thought otherwise. There was so much they didn't know about the erendinth and what they were capable of. But it felt natural, as though they were meant to wield them.

"I believe that wielding the erendinth is intrinsic to our nature as anacordel," said Kien, mimicking her own thoughts.

Stealing my words, are we?

Intrinsic fits better. He smiled at her as his conversation with the gathered elves continued.

"Will you teach us?" Vigyl shifted in his violet cloak.

Kiara felt the excitement in Kien's heart. She was surprised he was able to sit still. Ever since he had first become aware of the erendinth, he had hoped the Luminari elves would want to learn to wield them; he wanted others to share in that gift.

Kien and Kiara had learned through the phoenix, and believed it was their responsibility to share that gift with others who were willing to learn. The most striking observation they had made, was how she and Kien wielded the erendinth differently. To wield, she had to embrace the elemental erendinth within herself, while Kien had to press himself into them. The transcendental erendinth were different, and they had both struggled with those at first, but eventually learned to wield them with each other's help. Kiara also noted that the more she wielded with Kien, the stronger her wielding became, while Kien learned to better control his wielding with her.

There was a balance between the two types of wielding, much as there was between herself and Kien.

The giver who receives and the receiver who gives. Kiara sent her thought to Kien, not wanting to wake her sleeping daughter by speaking aloud. She brushed her hand through Elyse's golden hair.

Are you sure? I mean, that's exactly what it is, but those are our names.

The phoenix came to us for a reason, and we were named in the Light. I wonder if our parents knew what would become of us.

"For a man to wield, he must give of himself, in order to receive. For a woman to wield…" Kien started but looked to his wife to finish.

"…she must receive within herself, in order to give."

Feast of Aurephaen — 15 Aurenth 10,948.2E

Kien and Kiara held hands, their fingers intertwined as they watched dozens of phoenix soar before the rising sun. The morning songs filled Kien's ears, Auriel's whimsical voice joined with the Luminari elves and phoenix alike. He felt weightless as he listened, as though he could float from the surface of Luminare without being bonded with Naiel.

Their five children surrounded him, but only one had bonded with a phoenix. Elyse was still young, barely considered a youth, but a phoenix had come to her.

Kien had had no idea that this would happen. As the phoenix had unexpectedly arrived that Aurephaen, Kien began imagining their next challenge: training Phaedryn. He and Kiara had learned a great deal over the past three thousand years, much of which they had only come to with each other's help.

Kien and Kiara had learned how to communicate without words or images after they'd learned the names of the phoenix that had come to them. Kien still thought it odd how he could speak Naiel's name vocally, despite having never heard the phoenix say it aloud.

Dozens of phoenix flew across the rolling hills of Luminare, and Kien struggled to keep his feet planted on the ground. Kiara must have felt similarly, for she had already bonded with Eliel, her bright wings carrying her upward.

Unable to hold out any longer, Kien launched into the sky, his clothing an ashen heap left behind. Kien pressed fully into aerys and aquaeys, while embracing lumenys. Wielding the transcendental erendinth was so very different from the others. He knew it was similar to how Kiara wielded the elemental erendinth, but he had never expected such an electrifying sensation from pulling the erendinth inside himself.

Weaving the clouds together and apart, changing their forms and purpose, Kien wielded them into an image of how he imagined Anaweh would appear in a physical likeness, watching over the Luminari elves on their feast day. Guided by an interior sense, Kien wove the clouds in various directions, pulling misty threads behind him.

The newly arrived phoenix trailed after him, adding their own luminous touch to the artistic clouds.

Grateful to have had the privilege to enter the Empyrean Sphere with Kiara after Elyse had been born, Kien wielded lumenys into the clouds, giving a likeness to Anaweh beyond anything physical. He felt Kiara smile through their bond.

There are more to teach now. He smiled in return.

We already had more students than we could handle; elves of every Skyland are travelling to Luminare; even a draelyn has come to us. So many elves wish to awaken their awareness to the erendinth. Kiara's thoughts were calm, but noticeably troubled. *How long do you think we'll be able to keep up with these numbers?*

Kien's thoughts quieted; he knew Kiara was alluding to them succeeding his parents as the Aryl of Mar'anathyl.

Our earliest students are prepared to teach.

Are they ready? Kiara asked.

They've already spread across Luminare, sharing what they know with others, but each is very different; even their ideologies are unique.

Do you think their differences will strengthen or divide them?

Only time will tell.

---

21 Lierenth 11,790.2E

Kiara and Kien strolled along the lumaryl streets of Mar'anathyl, holding hands as their lierathnil garments blew about them in the wind. Kiara had long ago altered the garments' design slightly; the typical Luminari fashion had an elf's back mostly covered. Her alterations had allowed the fabric to drape loosely over their shoulders and down their backs, allowing their wings to freely spring without getting snagged. Granted, that was after Elyse had discovered how to weave lierathnil garments capable of withstanding their transformation.

Two millennia had passed since she and Kien had first begun to teach other elves how to wield the erendinth. The interest had grown steadily and elves of every Skyland had made the journey to Mar'anathyl to learn from Kiara and Kien. She was relieved that those days had ended. It was a special time in her life and she looked forward to new adventures with the education of new Phaedryn. Elyse wanted to visit Phroenthyl, but Kiara and Kien couldn't leisurely leave Luminare. The current aryl had Kiara and Kien attend many of their chamber sessions, requiring more time than either of them had.

Seven of their earliest students had banded together and formed Septyl, after they had already established their own schools across the Skyland. They called themselves the Seven Chairs, and each had gathered a sizeable following before founding Septyl. They had even designated a specific color and creature to symbolize each of the schools. Kiara hadn't decided how she felt about the intrinsic philosophical differences between the seven Schools. Despite their unique stances, she hoped they would learn to work together, but also feared division among them. Still, she was excited to see the new order of Ei'ana. She liked the name but feared its institutional tendencies.

Kien's parents had allotted a portion of Mar'anathyl to Septyl, which in turn was quickly renamed the Septyl Quarter. Kiara had never had reason to visit that area before, as it sat along the western outskirts of the city. While much of Luminare expanded westward, she was always drawn east to the rising sun, as were Kien and many other Luminari elves.

Waiting for his parents at the edge of the Septyl Quarter was their eldest son. Kyrendal was among the first not connected to one of the seven Schools to move to the Septyl Quarter. Although he had learned to wield from his parents, Kyrendal had still felt drawn to the newly founded institution. Because of his unique upbringing, all Seven Chairs had competed for him to join their own School. Kiara had not been the least bit surprised when he had opted for his childhood friend's School. Vigyl Vyoletryn had gladly welcomed Kyrendal and quickly named him a Vyoletryn ei'ana.

Kyrendal rushed across the plaza and hugged his parents.

"How do you like living outside the palace?" Kien asked, hugging his son back.

"It's wonderful here! Vigyl gave me a teaching position once I became an ei'ana." Kyrendal beamed a smile before lowering his voice. "I think he was afraid I might join another School if he did not accept me as swiftly as he did."

"What of Lanielle?" Kiara asked.

"She's fine. Spends a lot of time with the kirenae trees."

Kiara smirked at Kien. They both knew how their son felt about

Lanielle Emradiel.

"In all honesty, I think she's part dryad. Can lorendil mate with anacordel? I've never heard of an anadel doing so before, but I doubt there are centaurs that care about trees and fauna as much as she does." Kyrendal led his parents through the streets. Annexes had been added to the older buildings, sung into existence from the ground beneath their feet.

"Where are the Chairs now?" Kiara looked at her son.

"They're expecting you in what they're calling the Chamber of the Seven Chairs. I doubt the name will stick. Every time I go in there, I feel like I've been summoned for punishment."

The chamber was in an older building, renovated to suit its new residents and their very different needs. A circular table of kirenae wood occupied the center, with ten chairs surrounding it. Kiara imagined that the extra seats were added or removed as needed.

Kiara smiled at each of the gathered elves, fondly remembering her time as their teacher, if in a less formal setting, and noted that each one was dressed in a different color. Each Chair stood to greet Kiara and Kien, warmly embracing them before returning to their seats.

Kiara was eager to learn of their intentions for Septyl and their broader visions, but most importantly, how they intended to educate young wielders.

Lyon Arantiulyn looked to the other ei'ana. "Let me start by saying, on behalf of the other Chairs and the ei'ana here in the Septyl Quarter, welcome to our home. Our doors will never be barred to you, or anyone bonded to a phoenix."

"Our respect and admiration of our first teachers and their order will always have a place in our halls, and we are always willing to learn more from you as new discoveries are made by the Phaedryn." Saeryn Albien spoke as though she was not accustomed to speaking to people. Her head was often buried in a scroll or book.

"Thank you for your kind welcome." Kien smiled at his former students, and Kiara could see how proud he was of them, as though he saw them as his own children. "Kiara and I would first like to learn the manner in which you will pass on your teaching to young wielders."

"Student wielders will begin on a more general level, learning from every School of Septyl, along with a general education we expect all our students to have," Cyrelle Azurelle said. Cyrelle was the only Chair who was not a Luminari elf. He had travelled to Luminare from Tenethyl and was a draelyn of the Sapphire House. "A novitiate will follow when a student is ready, and they will spend a time in seclusion, preferably no less than a year, but it will depend on the individual. After their novitiate, they will return to Septyl for a Choosing ceremony, where they will decide which School they would like to join.

"The School retains every right to refuse the student if they do not deem them an appropriate fit, but only the Chair of said School can refuse a student. Following the Choosing, the student will attend classes strictly from that School. They can attend lessons from ei'ana of other Schools if a topic is of particular interest, but it will be the exception. We have not attached a time frame but have begun writing up examinations that will determine when a student is ready to profess the Counsels and become an ei'ana of Septyl."

"What do these examinations entail?" Kiara held Cyrelle's attention.

"The examinations will have various wielding exercises. Student wielders who desire to profess the Counsels will be required to wield complicated wields consisting of all the elemental erendinth, along with animys and umbrys. Ideally, lumenys would be involved, but there is no consistent way to ensure a student wielder is brought into the Empyrean Sphere to receive the ability from the seraph," Cyrelle said.

Remembering the seraph fondly, Kiara's thoughts drifted to the brief span she had spent outside of time. Everything she had been told before then was wrong. It should not have been possible for them to enter; crossing the threshold into Lumaeniel should have been permanent, and neither she nor Kien should have been able to return to Teraeniel.

"Are your required accommodations met here?" Kien asked.

"For Septyl, yes. For student wielders, no." Caelyn Crimsyn looked to the other Chairs.

"Mar'anathyl is a remarkable city, but it is set apart from the other races. We intend, once properly established, to open an academy on the surface below. We are currently looking into which continent to settle on, but in truth, we could use the help of the Phaedryn in this matter. Your knowledge of the lands below is without compare," Saeryn said.

"Our presence is known of below, but we fear the repercussions of continuous interaction." Kiara was still troubled by the last time she had travelled to Eklean, and the humans there. They had forgotten much since the Great Blessing, when the different races were created in the First Era. While they could no longer speak Aelish, she had been aware of their thoughts. She knew humans could only live for a century or so, and not even the elves knew how long ago the Great Blessing had occurred, as it was before they had a need to record the passing of years. The elves had begun recording time at the start of the Second Era, calling everything before that the First Era. Still, for humans in Eklean to identify her and Kien as gods was deeply troubling.

She had spoken with Theseryn about the interaction, and he too was troubled. The aldarch had begun to consider missions from Aldinare to the surface below. While she knew there was no stopping future Phaedryn from travelling and seeing the lands below, she feared the results of their interactions.

---

1 Marenth 12,000.2E

Kien and Kiara bowed before the assembled Luminari elves of Mar'anathyl. Kien's parents stood before them, each extending a circlet, the same circlets Kien had seen his parents wear upon their brows for three thousand years, and his grandparents before them.

The circlets had originally been crafted of lumaryl, but as his prowess with the erendinth increased, he had managed to transform them into diadems of lucilliae. They had been intended as a gift for his parents, the Aryl of Mar'anathyl, but now, they were being passed on, and Kien and Kiara would wear them.

Kien and Kiara had been officially selected as the next Aryl of Mar'anathyl the previous night. No elf in Mar'anathyl expected otherwise. The Lorenthien's youngest child had served as the aryl for as long as Mar'anathyl had had an aryl. The first aryl had been Loren and Thien, and from them came House Lorenthien.

Auriel was present today. While the anadel did not have a physical body, he took on the appearance of an elf, only more luminous.

Kien felt his mother place his father's weightless diadem on his brow, as his father placed his mother's diadem on Kiara's, officially transitioning them to the Aryl of Mar'anathyl. He had never disagreed with his parents' decisions as aryl, but there were things he wished had happened.

Visiting the other Skylands had inspired him; while they had a similar form of government to Luminare's, there was a unity among their aryls that Luminare lacked. From their sanctuaries, the Aldarchs of Aldinare, all draelyn, kept the aryls aligned and the four major aryls of Eldinare worked with the minor aryls. Eldinare was much smaller than Luminare and could more easily govern their population. Aldinare was a vast Skyland though and its population was equal to every other Skyland's put together. Cyndinare was similar in size and population to Luminare, but the Cyndinari aryls didn't appear divided, at least not from a visitor's perspective. Unlike the other Skylands, much of the Red Dragon Flight had remained with the Cyndinari, while a smaller percentage of white dragons had remained on Luminare.

Splintered city-states were scattered across Luminare. Kien knew that he and Kiara were the source of that division but hoped they might also become a source of unity. He dreamt of Mar'anathyl and all the elves living there becoming a beacon of dialogue and unity.

For reasons he could not understand, some of the aryls were fierce-ly opposed to wielding the erendinth, as though they were breaking an unknown accord with Anaweh, as happened when the Children started to age.

Sympathetic to their reasoning, Kien wanted to work with the oth-er Luminari aryls and show them that they weren't doing anything to an-ger Anaweh. He and Kiara would have to clear up any misconceptions during their time as Aryl of Mar'anathyl. After all, the phoenix were anadel associated with Uriel, and had opened their awareness to the erendinth. They had learned that awareness was intrinsic to every ana-cordel. There might be differing talents and strengths with the erendinth, but every anacordel was connected to them.

TWILIGHT

This land was strange to Thaerwn. Her skin loathed the arid heat and her mouth was dry from breathing it in. She missed Zarathyl. This land might not corrupt its people like Aldinare had, but her purple skin and its blue markings appreciated the change in temperature and humidity as little as she did. The skin exposed to the sun had darkened, and parts had become scaly.

She had never seen the sun or felt its effect until the aldarchs had wrenched Aldinare from the sky and out of the Darkness. Her first glimpse of that globe had been wonderous but after travelling across Dwonia, she preferred the subtle lights of night over the harsh sun.

Once the sun vanished behind the horizon, so too did the heat. Thaerwn didn't understand it, but something about the lack of humidity in the air made the desert's temperature shift dramatically between day and night. Aldinare did not have deserts, so she had not known that odd occurrence between sweating and barely able to breathe to that moment of relief at twilight.

As she sat in the cool of night looking up at the stars, she again wondered who her god was. She had prayed her entire life to Lerathel, thinking the aldarchs were divine. Even as she had travelled to her goddess' Sanctum of Val'quin, Thaerwn had believed she was going to meet her goddess. Lerathel was everything that Thaerwn had imagined she would be upon meeting her. Her hair was a velvety violet and her eyes were the color of amethyst, each with a light of their own. Lerathel was resplendent and magnificent. She was divine.

But, Thaerwn's view had crumbled when Lerathel had informed her that she was no god. She was an anacordel, just as Thaerwn and all the Aldinari elves were. Lerathel had spoken about Vespiel and Uriel, and many other anadel. She had told Thaerwn about the Creating Light, and how Anaweh had woven the realms out of the Void. Anaweh was the font of all existence.

So now, Thaerwn looked up at the stars, once again conflicted. Not only had her goddess denied her divinity, but anadel and the Creating Light were superior to her. The priests had told Thaerwn the gods required devotion and offerings, that it was their sustenance. They clearly didn't require Thaerwn to worship them or any other Aldinari, as they had managed without the vast population of Aldinare's devotion since the Darkness had severed the Skyland from the rest of Teraeniel. The Aldinari had forgotten them.

These questions plagued her as she struggled through the desert. She sat in the stillness of night, waiting for the answers to come to her— for someone to answer her.

"Who are you?" She looked up to the stars, demanding answers. "Why do you hide?" Thaerwn's frustration grew daily and the desert's harsh conditions had only made it worse.

As she sat, her breath quickened and something changed inside her. She recognized that feeling, that sensation deep in her being that the priests had always told her to suppress. Well, they weren't priests—they didn't serve a god. They worshipped anacordel, wrongly believing them gods. If they were wrong about that, they could be wrong about suppressing the sensation.

Tired, Thaerwn gave in to the magical feeling she had always known was just out of reach. She always believed she could grasp it, if only she had permission to do so. She had never thought she could give herself that permission, believing it had to come from someone else.

Following her instincts, she embraced the feeling inside her she didn't have a name for. It felt alive and filled her being. It was vibrant and wanted to be interacted with. Her hesitancy only kept her from fully embracing it for a moment.

She swirled whatever was inside her, shaping it into what she wanted. Now, she not only felt it inside herself but could feel it on the outside as well. The sand around her responded as though it had been called into service or given an order. Before she knew it, the sand swept up and twirled around her. Miraculously, *she* was making it happen.

What else could she do? Her time was limited; she couldn't waste an entire night making sand spin. The sun would soon rise. While the sun was still a magical globe to her, it was also dangerous. The thought of hiding from the sun crossed her mind.

The sand shifted and a hole opened. The sand solidified into a hard glassy surface, forming a tunnel. Wary about stepping into the hollow, she touched the nearest glassy wall. Would it hold against the weight of the sand? She travelled alone; no one would know if the desert buried her.

She took a hesitant step down into the hollow, following the tunnel until it opened to a domed cave. The sand beyond the dome hid the stars outside; would it hide the sun as well? Her shelter could keep the heat off her when the sun rose. The thought of resting after what had been an exhausting journey enticed her. She could sleep during the day and travel at night while the sun slept. She liked how that sounded. Perhaps the rest of her journey to what Lerathel had called Krysenthiel and a golden crystal city named Arenthyl, wouldn't be so bad.

"It's called the erendinth, what you just wielded. There are seven of them, and the one you just wielded is called terys."

Thaerwn spun to face the voice. She had been alone. Now, a woman wearing a pearly gown with silver hair and skin of starlight stood in the cavern with Thaerwn. "Who are you?"

"You called out to me." The woman seemed sad, as though she

had spent many years weeping. "My children have forgotten me. I failed to protect them—I failed to protect you. In my failure, not only were you lost in the Darkness, but you also forgot Anaweh. Your voices were silenced on Aldinare and I feared the Darkness had taken you entirely, body, soul, and spirit. I should have had more faith in my aldarchs. They have never failed me or you. Aldinare became the greatest Skyland, rivaling empires, given its breadth. We—I—believed nothing could hinder us. I was wrong. Aldinare could not stand against the Darkness—the Void." The angelic woman began to cry. She didn't sob or wail, but tears flowed unhindered down her cheeks, as though she had been weeping since the Darkness had descended on Aldinare.

"I spoke to Aldarch Lerathel. She does not believe you failed us, Vespiel." Thaerwn didn't know how she knew that this woman was the enthiel who guided the Aldinari elves, but she did. She knew it just as surely that despite her purple skin and bare scalp marking her an aelith, she was still an Aldinari elf. She was the same as the beautiful elves in Zarathyl's many tapestries and statues—the same as the beautifully sublime elves who had been spared the change in the sanctums. The Darkness—the Void had corrupted the Aldinari. It had left its taint on them and those who had been directly exposed had lost their minds to it, forgetting who they were and adopting baser, more violent natures.

"Lerathel and the other aldarchs did what I could not. I should have found a way to work with them—I should have pressed through Ramiel's domain to be with and protect you. In my despair, I believed you were lost forever." Vespiel approached Thaerwn and cupped her cheek.

Light blossomed in Thaerwn's chest at the connection, infectious and warm as it spread, tingling through her body, no part untouched. As Vespiel's light poured through her, she vividly felt all three parts of who she was; each part nestled inside the other, but curiously not confined. Her body wasn't a container for her soul, but her soul dwelt in her physical frame, capable of reaching beyond her body, just as her spirit was not confined in the recesses of her soul.

"If you desire, I can restore you—as though the Darkness had never touched you."

Thaerwn saw a vision of herself. Silver hair spun from her scalp like a waterfall and her purple skin and blue markings glowed with light until all that remained was pearly skin, just like the elves in Lerathel's Sanctum of Val'quin. The only thing in the vision that did not change was her eyes. They remained the same silver, maintaining their constant inner light. She wanted this. She had wanted it all her life, to shed the Void's corruption and become like her ancestors.

"What of the others? Those who have lost their minds and are now more beast than elf?"

"I am not powerful enough to cure everyone." The vision faded and Thaerwn pushed back her sleeve to see her purple forearm remained unchanged.

"I do not wish to stand apart from my people."

"I see why Lerathel chose you. Your will is strong, but your love and loyalty to Aldinare is stronger yet. You are more perfect for this quest than you know."

"How do you mean?"

"Do not kill the one who approaches." Without explanation, Vespiel vanished. Thaerwn thought Vespiel had regained a measure of confidence during their meeting. And did she have a glint in her eye that wasn't from a tear? Confused by Vespiel's message, she turned and saw a veiled person swing a spear at her from the tunnel opening. Alarmed by the violent intruder, Thaerwn managed to dodge the spear and twist backward as she drew her sword.

She swung it and caught the spear as it flew back at her. She could see her attacker's eyes but they gave nothing away. She had no idea whether this was an elf, a human, or some other race. She couldn't even tell if this was a man or a woman. The eyes remained passive; they weren't angry as she had come to anticipate from the neridu who had lost their minds. Whoever this was had no disdain for Thaerwn. This was the action of someone defending their home and that's when she recognized the emotion in the attacker's eyes. Duty.

She parried another spear thrust and said, "I mean you no harm."

The veiled person kept the spear pointed at her. A deeper masculine voice responded in a language she did not understand. One mystery solved; but their inability to verbally communicate made it clear that they would learn little about each other.

Attempting to show that she did not mean any harm to him or his home, she made a display of placing her sword down, careful not to let it clatter and alarm him. She'd hoped that he would do the same, but he maintained his grip, if not more firmly. Was he expecting her to spring a trap of some sort? Whoever this man was, this desert was clearly his home. Thaerwn couldn't imagine someone defending a land with nothing but sand for any other reason.

Cognizant of their communication barrier, she slowly pointed to her chest. "Thaerwn." She had hoped that the people of Eklean had remembered Aelish. She knew they had their own languages but had assumed the elves of the other three Skylands would have maintained and shared their language and culture.

"Tye." He pointed to himself, then gestured outward. "Dwonia."

She understood that. She knew she was in Dwonia. She pointed to herself again then made a walking motion with her fingers and said, "Krysenthiel—Arenthyl." There was no reason to speak in full sentences. Tye might miss the pieces she wanted to express. All that mattered was the destination. She hoped those places had the same name in Aelish as Tye's language.

He nodded and made the same walking motion with his fingers and repeated her words. "Krysenthiel. Arenthyl." He pointed to himself again and said, "Dwonian."

Thaerwn had already made that assumption, but she realized that she had not offered the same information. "Aldinari." She pointed to her chest.

His eyes widened in understanding. She let out a breath of relief; her people had not been forgotten. Tye didn't seem capable of reconciling her appearance with what he thought an Aldinari elf should look like. Surely there weren't other elves on this land below who looked like her. They might share the same pointed ears and Life Immortal, but that was where the similarities would have ended. Perhaps Thaerwn should have let Vespiel remove the Void's taint from her, if only to be recognizable as an Aldinari elf.

Whatever Tye knew or thought he knew of the Aldinari, he did not see her or her people as enemies. He unwrapped his veil to reveal his tanned leathery skin and darker hair. He pointed to himself, then to Thaerwn, then made their agreed walking symbol. "Tye. Thaerwn. Arenthyl."

Thaerwn nodded and repeated his words. Her isolated journey had come to an end. She placed her palm over her heart and bowed to Tye, a sign of respect among the elves, that Tye seemed to recognize as he mimicked it, if not as fluidly.

Tye and Thaerwn left the glassy cave the following evening. In all his years travelling the Purged Desert of Dwonia, he had never come across such a cave and was sure it wasn't a natural one. He could say the same of Thaerwn though; there was nothing natural about her or her purple skin and the markings she tried to hide.

Were all Aldinari elves like that? His experience with elves was limited, but he knew that Aldinare and its elves were lost in the Darkness. All Eklean knew that. Had the Darkness changed their appearance? If so, how had Thaerwn managed to escape? Too many questions sprang to mind and their inability to properly communicate ensured they would remain unanswered.

Instead, he devoted his attention to finding Dwota's Gap. The Gap was several leagues long but finding it along the stretch of mountains was not an easy task. They could easily go too far north and run into the Vespien Mountains, or not travel far enough north. Travelling too far north was preferable to drawing too near the Shadow Mountains—those were to be avoided at all costs. The Shadow Mountains were also the reason the mountain range wasn't in sight. Those borders were constantly watched and Tye and Thaerwn would be seen if they drew too close.

Moving under the cover of darkness only made determining their destination more difficult. Tye knew which stars would lead them north and which stars not to trust, since some stars moved irregularly about the night sky. Curiously though, one of the stars that had reliantly stayed in place now moved. In all of Tye's years, he had never seen it move and his grandmother had told him as a child that he could depend on that star to stay in its western spot in the sky.

If not for the other stars, Tye would have allowed that western one to guide them. Tye wondered what it meant. All he knew about that star was that it was important to the elves.

"Vespiel," Thaerwn said, having noticed the star Tye was looking at.

"Why has she moved?" Tye asked, despite knowing Thaerwn wouldn't understand him. She returned a blank stare and Tye wondered how he could express his question. He tried pointing to where the star typically floated in the sky, then made a motion to indicate movement.

Thaerwn frowned at his gestures. Their language barrier was going to be a problem. He had no idea what they were going to do if they ran into any trouble east of the Gap.

EVER BOUND

19 Meridenth 12,145.2E

Kiara looked into her daughter's eyes. Elyse had grown so much since her spirit had first brushed against hers. She knew the strength of will her youngest daughter held, and when a phoenix had chosen her on that memorable Aurephaen, Kiara knew her daughter's future would very much resemble her own. Though she looked at her daughter with joyful eyes, it was a moment that she hoped would never come.

Kien sat next to her, his heart just as heavy. Their effort to establish ties with the other Luminari aryls was proving more difficult than expected and they found themselves continually away from the Phaedryn, the very people they had vowed to instruct. Just as they had to relinquish their responsibilities with wielders, now too, they had to relinquish their role with the Phaedryn.

Their replacement was an easy choice; Kiara had been considering it since she first received the lucilliae diadem. In their early days as the new aryl, Kien had insisted they would not have to relinquish their roles.

It only took ninety-three years before he entertained the possibility, and fifty-two more before he conceded to the necessity of passing on their formational role among the Phaedryn.

"Are you certain?" Elyse looked at her mother.

"None other would we entrust this to," Kiara said, her mind running over possible candidates. None were near Elyse's caliber. They were certainly gifted Phaedryn, but Kiara had no confidence in their ability to educate.

"What of the leadership of the Phaedryn? As of now, we are only Luminari elves, and most are from Mar'anathyl. But there is no saying whether that will endure," Elyse said.

Kien looked at Kiara, for neither had considered themselves as the definitive leader of the Phaedryn, but that was a view only shared by themselves. Every elf saw them as the leader of both Mar'anathyl and the Phaedryn and even Septyl would bow to them.

"Another reason Luminare must unite," Kien said. "It will appear that we, the Aryl of Mar'anathyl, will hold strength over the other aryls with the Phaedryn and Septyl at our disposal. We cannot permit fear and jealousy to divide us. The Luminari elves must be one."

"And there is the possibility of Phaedryn rising among other elves, or the mortal races." Kiara considered the downside to other elves or races reporting to the Aryl of Mar'anathyl. She was happy with her choice of Elyse to guide the Phaedryn. So many new phoenix had entered Teraeniel, Elyse would ensure the new Phaedryn received proper instruction.

"What if we take our formation back to Phroenthyl?" Elyse asked.

Kiara longed to return to Phroenthyl, but to have others claim the small Skyland was difficult to accept. She felt Kien share the same anxiety. Phroenthyl had been their home, so much of who they were was connected to Phroenthyl. Yet Elyse's request made logical sense. It would create a separation between them and the Phaedryn, allowing the other aryls to approach them on a more level ground, despite Kien and Kiara being Phaedryn.

"If you take them to Phroenthyl, it will not remain just the place for formation, but will become a hub for Phaedryn—their home—bound to a place not of their origin as they are transformed into something other than what they were born," Kien said, his voice prophetic.

Kiara saw the truth in his words, and, accepted that Phroenthyl no longer belonged to only her and Kien, but to the Phaedryn, and every Phaedryn yet to come. She hoped the Gold Flight would not begrudge that decision. What sort of gift could they offer in exchange?

---

13 Meridenth 12,392.2E

Kien strode back and forth, furious following his recent interaction with the humans of Eklean. He felt Kiara's concern for him, but she was equally disturbed by the interaction.

Pausing, he turned before continuing to pace. His thoughts were undefined; his emotions strained. Kiara brushed against his spirit, as though rubbing his back to soothe him.

"I'm sorry my love, forgive my anger," he said.

"Your anger is justified, as is mine."

"How could they address us in that way?"

"Much has been forgotten; remember, their lives are not as long as ours."

"It's only been a hundred and fifty or so years."

"Closer to three hundred." Kiara's eyes were sad. "None of the people we knew still live. Humans have the shortest lifespan of all ana-cordel. They do not pass on to Lumaeniel with Anaweh's Calling as we elves do, departing this World-Below of our own accord. They die, often painfully, at an age when we are still considered children."

"But to address us and worship us as gods!"

Kiara remained silent. She had seen the two gold statues and the altar before them. Every villager had been present, and they had prostrated themselves when Kien and Kiara had arrived. She remembered Kien's anger as he destroyed the statues and altar with terys and ignys.

"Theseryn might be right; the time might have finally come for some elves to live among the mortal races."

"There are more ei'ceuril every day to remind the humans, mostly Aldinari elves. They've already begun constructing their temple on the lands below."

Kien no longer paced but planted his feet on the lumaryl flooring.

"What of the anadel? Do we know how they address them?"

"Most have withdrawn, ever watching but not interfering, hoping that their absence will allow humans to focus on Anaweh, and not them," Kiara said.

---

9 Estlenth 12,507.2E

Stone from every land defined the enormous temple, offering a cloudy iridescent quality. Through her inner sense, Kiara felt that her eyes only saw a fraction of the building. An entire substructure was concealed beneath much of the mountain, its rear foundations exposed to the cliff behind.

Tall doors stood unguarded and dozens of Aldinari elves went in and out of the Temple of Ceur. Many of the ei'ceuril here were young, far too young, in her opinion, to make such a life altering decision; the youngest had seen no more than two hundred autumns.

A gentle stream rolled before the temple, then divided. One branch rushed down the mountainside to join a mightier river, while the other wove along at a slight decline, following the less severe elevation, before it too joined the larger river that hugged the mountain.

She and Kien crossed the bridge of the same cloudy stone over the narrow stream before it forked, their phoenix hovering about. Neither Kien nor she remained fully bonded with the phoenix longer than necessary, especially when travelling to the lands below the Skylands, concerned by how mortals might acknowledge them.

Bright-eyed ei'ceuril walked swiftly about carrying out their tasks. Standing at the entrance was one of the few older elves that Kiara had seen. He smiled widely as he approached. "Welcome Aryl of Mar'anathyl to the Temple of Ceur," Ceurtriarch Waelyn greeted them. Shimmering yet simply designed white robes draped his body.

"Thank you, Waelyn. It's wonderful to see you again; your invitation was very much appreciated." Kiara embraced the Ceurtriarch, a kiss on either cheek.

"You have ever been a friend and sister to us."

Kien embraced the Ceurtriarch in a similar fashion. "Did Theseryn give any notice before he transitioned to Lumaeniel?"

"Afraid not. I don't think he anticipated it when he set about his work with the temple. I understand that you are distantly related to him, yes?"

"Yes; a relation as old as our house."

"We shall celebrate his life and joyous transition to Lumaeniel. Please, you'll have to see what's become of this place; there are wonders inside beyond our ability and dare I say, beyond your own as well. I believe Theseryn sparked something before he transitioned." Waelyn's excitement bubbled over as he ushered Kien and Kiara through the doors and into a dark corridor.

"Ominous," Kien said.

"Only to those who fear solitude."

"I take it Thalia assisted Aldarch Lerathel with the architecture." Kiara's eyes followed the dark lines. Thick columns rose on either side.

"I've never met an erendinth architect so gifted," Waelyn said. "The entire temple spews symbolism; even I don't understand all of its subtlety."

"We should have warned you. Did she take over the project? The architecture is still noticeably Aldinari," Kien said.

"It's meant for *all* anacordel, and Thalia was quite capable of wielding it to our designs. Besides, Aldarch Lerathel of Val'quin ensured the design met her architectural standards."

Another pair of doors stood at the end of the corridor, opening easily to let the light from beyond flood the entire space, transforming it. Moved by the hidden meaning, Kiara made a note to compliment Thalia and Lerathel next she saw them, hoping it would be on this visit.

Kiara passed through the doors into the Chamber of Light. Her eyes were drawn to the center, where a beam of light filled the space. It appeared as though the beam fell from the temple's crest, but her lighted eyes couldn't see its source. The light lessened along the edges but was still brighter than the sunniest of days. "I am not worthy to enter into such splendor, but by the will of Anaweh, the Creating Light," Kiara said, marveling at the sight. "Waelyn…" she could not keep from gasping. "How is this possible?"

"You gaze upon a drop of Lumaeniel in Teraeniel."

"But, how?" Kien was equally bewildered and amazed.

"Theseryn was adored by Anaweh, but this was not accomplished by elven hands if that is what you wonder, nor did Vespiel or Uriel intervene with its opening here. We intended this space as a place of worship, where anacordel could gather in large numbers and praise Anaweh, the Creating Light, together. When the temple was completed, and we withdrew from the erendinth, Theseryn entered alone. He never came out. Curious, we followed him in and found the Chamber of Light as this. It is not of our design; it is a gift from Anaweh, blessing our endeavor."

As she walked across the chamber, she felt weightlessness enter her body, and her feet left the tiled floor. She felt Kien's amazement when he, too, rose off the floor.

"Those of pure hearts are lifted in the Light; those with malice are weighed down."

"What of the mortal races?" The elves would appreciate this but Kiara wondered how other races might react.

---

20 Delenth 13,985.2E

Hand in hand, heart in heart, Kien walked with Kiara through the streets of Mar'anathyl. The sun had already set, and he looked forward to an evening walk. Elyse had returned from Phroenthyl and was with her brother in the Septyl Quarter. Kien looked forward to seeing them together again; they had always been close, even if Kyrendal was nearly a thousand years her senior.

The Septyl Quarter came into view as Kien and Kiara rounded a corner, and they crossed the expansive plaza to Kyrendal's home. Kien knocked on the door; there was movement inside.

With a bright smile, Kyrendal welcomed his parents, ushering them to the sitting room where Elyse spoke intently with a young elf, presumably an ei'ana. She held an illumined orb in her hand, and on the table were several others, all different sizes and colors.

"Oh, it's so good to see you," said Elyse, jumping up from the couch to greet her parents.

"Welcome home, Elyse." Kien pulled his daughter into a hug, kissing both cheeks after Kiara had done so.

"Thank you. Have you met Sophie yet? She's an Albien ei'ana."

"Pleased to meet you."

"Sophie's been working on something most inventive; they're incredible."

"It's a pleasure to meet you, Ei'denai, Ei'terel. I'm only modifying something I've come across in my travels. Are you familiar with the Ja'horan Chronicle Stones?"

Kien had heard of the curious objects developed in the southern continent but had never come across one. "Are these them?"

"Don't be silly." Elyse laughed and pulled her parents closer. "*These* are sophilliae!"

"I've not agreed to that name."

"What name have you settled on?" Elyse crossed her arms, holding her friend in her eyes.

Sophie's expression was thoughtful and they felt the waves of her churning thoughts across their minds.

"Exactly," said Elyse after a long pause, beaming triumphantly.

"The *sophilliae* hold not just memories, as the Chronicle Stones do, but wisdom and knowledge."

"In concept, they're similar to scrolls, containing written information and stories, but the entirety of a topic is imbued on the beholder as they encounter these orbs."

"As they encounter the *sophilliae*." Elyse smirked as she corrected her friend. "This will revolutionize how we educate! Imagine the possibilities."

"Well, creating them is not a simple task, and I've yet to find someone capable of replicating the process."

"Now that you've started, I doubt Saeryn will reassign you to anything else, for surely she understands the potential," Elyse said.

"We've spoken, and she does appear excited, but…"

"It's the closest I've ever seen her to smiling," Kyrendal said. "There's more news with Septyl as well."

"Is there?" Kiara asked.

"We're finally establishing an academy on the land below, and they're considering me as chancellor!"

"That's wonderful, Kyrendal." Kien clapped a hand on his son's shoulder. "Has a location been decided yet?"

"Most likely near the Temple of Ceur. I just wish it wasn't so inaccessible, being up in the mountains and all."

"True, but it's safe there; all I hear about the lands below is war between themselves, each vying for power or wealth." Elyse crossed her arms, concerned.

"True, but how are students to reach us? It's not like they have dragons, alicorns, or griffins to carry them up the mountain. Not that dragons would ever agree to carting students to a school."

Elyse turned to her parents. "There is another way."

"Have you discovered how to stabilize one?" asked Kien, excitement bubbling.

"Not consistently, but there has to be a way to anchor them."

"What are you talking about?" Sophie asked, curious eyes darting to each Lorenthien.

"I'm calling them seguians."

Kien chuckled to himself. *Remind you of anyone?*

You know very well where she gets it from. Kiara's thoughts reached his own.

"Have you tried using lumaryl?"

---

14 Borenth 15,247.2E

Kiara watched Luminari elves pass through the seguian to the entrance of Gwilnor Academy. The portals set within the lumaryl arches could take the traveller anywhere, but these were tied to specific locations. The aryls of the four Skylands had agreed to permitting seguians, but only to the newly established Gwilnor Academy.

Kyrendal, as discussed, had been named the chancellor and reported directly to the Seven Chairs in Mar'anathyl, but the academy was entirely under his direction.

Kien walked beside her. "Magnificent, isn't it?"

"You knew lumaryl would work."

"This is her contribution, not mine." Kien smiled as more elves approached the seguian.

"But you knew."

"I might have tried it once or twice…" Light danced in his eyes as he watched the elves disappear. "I still think her passing on becoming the next aryl was a mistake. Imagine what she and Ehlen could have accomplished as Aryl of Mar'anathyl."

"They are both still young; a consequence of her parents falling in love so young. Besides, she wasn't ready to leave Phroenthyl, and the elves who call Mar'anathyl home weren't ready for us to step down."

"I still can't believe she put our names forward, breaking tradition."

"I doubt Thien and Loren were only aryl for three thousand years," Kiara said, patting Kien's arm.

"If only we knew. At least the other Luminari aryls are finally seeing the virtue in cooperating as a unified people. It only took us three thousand years. Imagine what we'll manage with the next three thousand."

"Wonders beyond wonders." Kiara looked carefully at Kien. "Were you looking forward to stepping down?"

"Some days. I wanted to resume our travels. I still want to see the Bowl of Theniel. Do you think the Meridean Conclave will permit us?"

Moving Kien to safer waters, she stepped toward the seguian and gently tugged him into it. They stepped onto a stone plaza with large doors set in the stone. Seven lumaryl arches surrounded the plaza, each containing a seguian to a different part of Teraeniel. Elyse had worked with the ei'ana to set a rotating schedule for the seguians to open and close at certain intervals. The schedule was artistically carved into the stone near each portal.

Ei'ana and Phaedryn had travelled far and wide during Gwilnor's construction to bring news of the school to teach wielding the erendinth. Few had agreed to leave their homes for Gwilnor Academy. Wielding was still new to the people on the land below, and the elves who had come to their homes had been met with suspicion. Some human leaders saw the benefits and had insisted on some of their people attending, resulting in a few non-eleven students.

Turning away from the arches, Kiara walked into the castle built from the stone of the mountain it rested on, rooting it to its location. An expansive hall stretched past the door, and seven pillars of woven stone rose upward like vines. Two winding stairs were set in those pillars, leading to the lofty tower above.

"His quarters are at the top, right?" Kien's gaze followed the stair.

Kiara nodded as she made her way to the stair. She craned her head back, hoping to glimpse the top before reaching the first step. The first landing had a balcony looking over the entry hall, balustrades on either side, before leading away into corridors and classrooms.

"We could always fly up."

Kiara saw the twinkle in his eyes, and knew he was a heartbeat from bonding with Naiel; she even felt the phoenix's presence blossom inside him.

"It's not that much further." Kiara held his hand to keep him on the ground.

A door waited at the top of the highest landing. It had a pointed arch like all the other doors she had seen at Gwilnor, reflecting the pointed arches of the castle's steep roofline. Intricate swirling lines wove a pattern in the door and its surrounding casing. "Come in," Kyrendal called from inside before they could knock.

"He's becoming more attuned with every passing day," Kien said, following Kiara inside.

"It's natural—it shocks me we neglected our interior senses for so long," Kyrendal said.

"Presupposing that it's something to forget, and not acquired as one ages." Kiara crossed the vestibule toward her son waiting just beyond. The seven-sided room was at the top of one of the seven towers of the castle. Large circular windows were set in every dormer. Each window displayed a different crest, associated with a different color, painting the room a colorful prism as light washed through it.

"Do you mean to say there are elves who remembered their interior sense when they left the Valley of Saeryndol, before it was flooded and became the lake?"

"I remember one of my forefathers peering into my mind. His generation consistently had their minds open to others."

"Why did it fall out of practice?"

"It hasn't for everyone, and the older generations tend to prefer it over speaking, not wanting to break the silence."

"Interesting." Kyrendal mused for a moment, his mind drifting before he scrunched his brow. "I'll have to look more into that later."

"You seem troubled?" Kiara said.

"Gwilnor has been a challenge from the start," Kyrendal admitted, frustrated. "The schools are already competing for students and rivalries between students are springing up like wildfire."

"Do the students have any recreational activities?" Kien asked.

"Like games?" Kyrendal scoffed. "They're here to study and become ei'ana, not play games like children."

"Perhaps the game can be informative." Kiara said.

"Like logic puzzles?" Kyrendal suggested.

"I recall you and a young Vigyl playing a game with a ball and hoops when you both first started to wield," Kiara said.

"The erendinth aren't something to be played with."

"Perhaps they should be," Kien said, a twinkle in his eyes.

"I'll put some thought into it. Granted, it would have been better if Elyse hadn't nominated you as Aryl of Mar'anathyl. I still can't believe she did that. You could have had a more active role here as magisters."

"Neither of us are ei'ana, Kyrendal," Kiara said.

"Well, considering you first taught the elves, including the Seven Chairs, how to wield the erendinth, I hardly think that's a requirement."

"Not the first," said Kiara, catching a smirk on Kien's face.

NOBLES AWAIT

Wyn winced and took a deep breath as the sword reverberated in his grip following Viren's counterattack. Since Devlyn and Ellendren had left Arenthyl, he had spent much of his time training with Viren. He had never considered his own swordsmanship as lacking, but Viren's was flawless by comparison.

The Guardian knights, especially Viren, were happy to have returned to their citadel in Arenthyl. It had been built on Arenthyl's fifth tier and its soaring walls and spires were joined to the Guardian Senate Chamber on the sixth tier. While the two structures were identifiably distinct, they were undeniably connected.

The training yard at the citadel was like every other training yard Wyn had seen since leaving the Eldin Wood, only this one was surrounded by walls of lumaryl. He was still getting accustomed to the remarkable stone that seemed to sing in the morning light. Every elven kin used the stone of their Skylands in different ways. There was certainly overlap in their uses, but the Eldinari were alone in not using eldaryl for buildings.

Distracted, Wyn missed the slight shift in Viren's grip and posture and froze when Viren's sword abruptly stopped half a handspan from Wyn's neck.

"You are more distracted than Devlyn usually is," Viren said, letting his sword drop.

Wyn heaved a sigh and let his own sword drop. "I suppose so."

"Anything you would like to talk about?"

Wyn sighed. The winter solstice had come and gone and Wyn couldn't bring himself to walk outside to celebrate Boriel, Auriel, and Anaweh on that darkest of nights when the stars were brightest. All he could see was Alethea being swallowed by the Void. As much as he tried to avoid reliving that night, he found himself incapable of purging it from his memory. "I'm anxious about Alethea. She's been in the Void for over a year now."

"You had hoped to find answers in Arenthyl."

"I hoped Arenthyl would attract the one who has the answers." Wyn glanced over the training yard's walls.

"The Sha'ghol."

"I have never mentioned Yloran to you."

"No. Devlyn did. He asked me to watch out for her arrival and to intercede on her behalf if she reached the city before his return."

"Did he say whether she was actually coming here?"

"I doubt anyone knows what Yloran Eth Gnashar intends. She'll have her own agenda; you can be certain of that."

"Do you think she'll help me reach the Void to rescue Alethea?"

"She might, but only if it serves her own interest." Viren scratched a pattern on the dirt with his practice sword. "I'm not suggesting the risk isn't worth it, especially when the person in question is Alethea Lenwyn, but think carefully before you approach Yloran."

"I will." He glanced at his own sword, debating Viren's readiness for another bout.

"I think we've trained enough for one day." They returned the practice swords to the training rack and left the citadel to make their way back to the palace. Both Wyn and Viren had their own rooms there, but Viren seemed to spend most of his time at the citadel, training new recruits for the Guardian knights while Devlyn and Ellendren were away.

"Are you happy with how Kaela has been executing her role as steward?" Wyn asked, trying to fill the silence that so often surrounded

Viren.

"There was never anything to worry about with that one. She was born to navigate politics. Truly, I haven't seen the aryls so relaxed since before Harnyl passed. She's even managed to appease the diplomats who've started to arrive."

"She is quite talented, isn't she?" Wyn said, wondering if he had waited long enough to see her more regularly. Kaela had to be careful not to raise Silvia's suspicions about her and Trethien's faked courtship to secure her position as steward.

"That's not all you wanted to ask though, is it?"

Wyn's breath caught in the back of his throat. "I'm tired of the charade," he said honestly. "I miss spending time with her, not as her tutor, but as something more. We've had to be so careful this past year."

"I can understand that. But hasn't Trethien already ended the courtship and gone back to Gwilnor?" Viren asked.

"He has, but Silvia still comes to Arenthyl too frequently for Kaela to let down her guard." Wyn would have continued, but they had reached the palace and strode up the ramp to the gates. Kaela stood on the terrace that overlooked the city and lake, resplendent in her subdued clothing as she spoke with an Aldinari elf. Her smile immediately brightened his disposition, and for a moment, his worries about Yloran melted away.

The trees and shrubs had been restored and flowers waited for the spring to bloom after sleeping too long under the Shroud's frozen mist. Wyn imagined Kaela always standing in a garden, surrounded by flowering trees with blossoms in her hair.

She spotted them as they reached the terrace and waved them over. "Hello there, Wyn, Viren. I trust you know Etrien. He's largely responsible for training the gardeners on how to care for the city's flora."

"They only needed reminding; this flora is part of them. As you know, it's all native to Luminare," Etrien said.

"And *you* are too humble," Kaela said, her musical voice warming

Wyn. "How was training today? Are there many more recruits for the Guardian knights?"

"Our numbers are increasing, but slowly. As Jeanne informed your sister, it's unlikely that anyone will be knighted a Guardian during this present conflict."

"Not Byron or Toryn? Toryn carries Shroudsbane, doesn't she?" She arched an eyebrow.

"I did say unlikely, not impossible."

"I see," she said. Wyn could see her mind working, already trying to figure out a way to speed up the process. "Well, if either of you are interested, I received a message from Prya not too long ago. A dragon was spotted flying from the south. She and Liara went to investigate and were delighted to share that Rusyl was surveying the area for danger. It appears that Jaerol, Liam, and Rusyl were successful in their quest to rescue Evellyn Lorenthien from Erynor's grasp and have been travelling under the guise of a circus."

"When will they arrive?" Wyn asked, sorry that Devlyn was not here to greet his mother.

"Within the hour. It's why Etrien and I are here on the terrace, seeing to final preparations. Winter doesn't mean we have to go without flowers for the occasion."

"They can bloom for a short time, but they will not like the chill," Etrien added.

"And neither do I, but here we all are." Kaela laughed. "Well, if you'll excuse me, I must finish getting ready for Evellyn's arrival. If Enithil and Binoral Clarion don't insist on her staying in Eandyl that is. I've asked some of the Guardian knights to go there to serve as an escort and all the other aryls, high and minor, have been informed. I've already received notes in return about the suddenness of the occasion. As though I had any control over Evellyn's arrival!"

"If you'll allow me to counteract those negative messages with a compliment, I think you look perfect as is." Wyn blushed as he said it. It was true though. Her elegant lavender gown had clean lines that complimented her.

"Wyn Lierafen, are you courting me?" Kaela batted her eyelashes, knowing exactly what she was doing.

"Only if you'd welcome such a courting." They had rehearsed this public interaction.

"Perhaps you'll find out if you escort me along the terraced gardens sometime."

Wyn caught a parting smirk from Viren, mentally nudging Wyn to do precisely what the former princess suggested.

Evellyn looked up at Eandyl's remarkable golden lumaryl walls. She could see a small party waiting outside the city gate. It felt right coming to Eandyl first. Not only was it on their route north, but it was the first city the Luminari had reclaimed. The Shroud was miraculously gone. Although Evellyn had never seen the Shroud, Auriel had. While Uriel had been frozen in Lake Saeryndol, Auriel had hidden from Meridiel and Ramiel in the heart of the youngest Lorenthiens to ensure House Lorenthien's survival. It was no accident that Gwendolyn Lorenthien's parents had survived Erynor's enslavement before Lucillia gave birth to the twins.

Since the Shroud had been destroyed and Uriel freed from his frozen prison, Auriel had left Evellyn. She had grown so accustomed to the anadel's presence in her heart that his absence left her feeling hollow. That emptiness was only intensified when she looked at Liam—he looked so much like his father. His kind and cheerful eyes, marred by tragedy and suffering, were so much like her late husband's. The news that Dolan's murderer, Lex, who Dolan had believed to be his brother, had also met his end had done little to appease her long suffering.

As they neared Eandyl, Evellyn fretted about their welcome. Only one Cyndinari was expected to return to Krysenthiel. Teran might have been easy to explain since he was Jaerol's uncle, but Yloran Eth Gnashar, one of the Sha'ghol, and her many attendants posing as circus performers were another matter entirely. Because of the Sha'ghol, tenebrys had been introduced to Teraeniel and the elves had lost their Skylands.

Yloran's attendants were convincing entertainers but somersaulting and flipping through the air mattered little—they were still Cyndinari elves crossing into Krysenthiel. Friendly or not, the free people of Eklean assumed that every cinnamon-haired elf belonged to Erynor. Because of that lack of trust, the pretend Ember Circus had not erected its large tent for performances north of Torsil. That was just fine with Evellyn, as every performance slowed their journey, although it had been a necessary precaution during their travel through the Erynien Empire.

The circus ended up being the perfect cover for her escape from imperial controlled lands. Rusyl had stayed in his smaller form until they neared Krysenthiel in northern Sorenthil. The blue dragon seemed delighted to return to his larger form and stretch his wings fully again. The Erynien Empire knew that a blue dragon had been involved in her escape. If they heard of any sightings of him or even the rumor of a dragon, they would have surely hunted them down. Erynor's wrath upon learning of her escape was a sight she hoped she'd never witness. The elves responsible for her confinement likely didn't survive telling their emperor that news.

Even now, she couldn't quite believe that she was free of Erynor. Not only free, but in Krysenthiel. The Shroud was gone and before the day ended, she would miraculously be in Arenthyl. Her father had told her stories of the portals that connected every Krysenthien city, and she was eager to see if they were real. *What other wonders have been lost since Krysenthiel fell?*

At Eandyl's city gates, twenty armored knights clad in shimmering armor stood to either side of richly dressed elves, all wearing silks in subtle pastel colors. The gathering watched the circus caravan, shadowed by a dragon above, approach the city. Evellyn wished she could have a moment to freshen herself before meeting the Luminari nobles. She wondered how the gathering would receive their curious caravan. Focused on Evellyn, they smiled kindly enough, knowing precisely who she was. She had never had any sort of interaction with elven nobility before being stolen away to Broid as Erynor's slave and prisoner. There was nothing noble about the rulers of the Erynien Empire and all she had learned while in Broid was to avoid speaking around them.

She hoped the Luminari aryls would be different. Her father had told her about Lucillia and the fair elves who lived there. But the last Roendryn monarch had died and the city woven from the trees had faded with him.

"Ei'lythel Evellyn Lorenthien," the woman near the center of the gathered elves said. "I am Binoral Clarion, and this is my husband, Enithil Clarion. As the Aryl of Eandyl we gladly welcome you."

"Thank you for your warm reception," Evellyn said.

"We are honored to serve your House in this small way. You must be weary from your travels. Come, we'll escort you to the palace where you might rest before going on to Arenthyl."

"Kaela was hoping to welcome her to Arenthyl within the hour," said one of the knights.

"After such a long and perilous journey? I'm sure our steward would understand a brief respite," Binoral said.

"I would appreciate a bath before another reception. But if you don't mind my asking, what need is there for a steward?" Evellyn asked, noting that this was also news to Jaerol and Liam, as they too wore a curious expression.

"Of course, you wouldn't know. Forgive me, Ei'lythel, but Aren took Devlyn and Ellendren somewhere for some sort of Phaedryn training. They wouldn't tell any of the aryls where they were going, only that they would be gone for a considerable span of time," Binoral said.

"They're with Aren?" Evellyn's voice cracked. She remembered Aren well and the occasions Erynor had given him orders to commit atrocities in Ramiel's name.

"Oh, not to worry," Enithil said at Evellyn's alarm. "He's changed, or rather, has remembered who he is. He helped the young Lorenthien aryl fight the Shroud, even fought that nasty Deurghol."

"How's that possible?" Evellyn asked.

"You'll have many questions. Let's get out of the cold and I'll answer as many as I can at the palace." Binoral smiled warmly and looked past Evellyn to the Cyndinari elves behind her. "As for your companions…" Binoral trailed off as Yloran stepped forward.

"What of us?" she asked proudly.

"You cannot expect us to allow such a large host of Cyndinari into our city. We know nothing of you and as the Aryl of Eandyl, it is our responsibility to protect this city and the gateways to other Krysenthien cities," Binoral said.

"Are you aware that I nursed your young Lorenthien back to health in Lankor? He would have been good as dead if anyone else had found him after his broken body fell from the sky. Would you like to inform your soon-to-be Exalted Aryl that you turned me, Yloran Eth Gnashar, away?" Her voice held power that Evellyn had previously heard only from Erynor. Shocked murmurs arose. The gathered elves had not forgotten the name.

While Evellyn was still leery about Yloran, the Sha'ghol had saved her son and nursed him back to health. As far as Evellyn was concerned, that forgave her past transgressions, even her part in bringing tenebrys into Teraeniel.

Binoral shrank at Yloran's tone and before she or Enithil could respond, Evellyn said, "I vouch for Yloran and her attendants. She is no more a servant of Shadow than I am."

AUREPHAEN

Abird called from the nearby hills. The shrill voice penetrated Kien's ears and reached into his spirit, beckoning him. He had long felt the early stages of the Calling and knew Kiara had begun to feel it as well. They had seen over twenty thousand springs of bliss in the world Anaweh had given them to dwell in.

Other than a couple of hundred years, they had spent their entire lives bonded, and with them, their phoenix. Thousands of years had passed before Kien discovered why the phoenix had come to them rather than to other elves, let alone another race, but Kiara had always known. She had told him that the love they shared had beckoned the phoenix from Lumaeniel to Teraeniel, passing through Somnaeniel to connect with that which they were so familiar with—love. Their shared love was in turn shared between their phoenix, a love that had produced an egg yet unhatched.

Kien's eyes watered the first time Kiara had told him, and they still did whenever he thought of it. Brushing a tear away, he followed Kiara along a quiet path on Phroenthyl.

The summer heat made him think of Ja'horan.

"I hope they've healed. The people and the land," Kiara said.

"They'll never forget, especially with their Chronicle Stones documenting it all."

"Do you think the Cyndinari elves had malicious intent in their interactions?"

"There's no reason to believe that, but it cannot be ruled out."

"A task for the younger aryl." Kiara smiled; her hair had turned to a silvery white from the golden threads of her youth.

His hair resembled hers. He wondered what form they would take in the World-Beyond. Would they take a physical form in Lumaeniel? "And here I thought we had accomplished everything in our seven thousand years as aryl."

"Elyse and Ehlen could have begun their reign at the end of our second three thousand years as aryl."

"Yet they and every Luminari elf insisted on an additional thousand years, to bring our reign as Aryl of Mar'anathyl to a blessed seven thousand years," Kien said.

"And naming us as the first Exalted Aryl of Luminare," Kiara reminded. Kien hadn't forgotten. His mouth twitched into a smile at what he considered one of his greatest accomplishments: uniting the Luminari. "Do you think the Schtamite will ever reconcile with the Nuntol and Zorik Schtams?"

"I've never known a dwarf to change their mind, let alone their hearts," Kien said, agony pinching him over the reasons for the estrangement.

"How could they have come across a gateway to the Void?"

"I think Uriel knew it would not remain isolated. Why else would he have beseeched Theniel, Sariel, and Tariel to form Mount Cyngol in Eklean? There are likely more mountains of fire elsewhere, intent to ward off anyone from finding those paths to the Void."

"I hope it's not too late for Nuntol and Zorik. I so enjoyed their company when we were young. Nuntol especially; he was such a lively and determined dwarf, it's a shame his descendants have met this challenge."

Naiel and Eliel floated nearby.

You'll watch over the future Phaedryn, yes? Kien conveyed to Naiel.

When you pass into the World-Beyond, we will turn to ash, and in time, bond with another.

Kien smiled at that. Knowing that their phoenix would remain in Teraeniel brought him peace. Despite that tranquility, he feared what would happen if the Phaedryn lost their direction—if the elves lost their direction.

Keep them from thinking themselves gods among others, Kien conveyed.

You and Kiara must tell them.

A smirk came to Kien's lips.

Sophie never showed us how to craft her sophilliae, Kiara conveyed to Naiel and Eliel.

The four of us can manage it, Eliel conveyed to Kien and Kiara.

Kien found that quiet place within his heart, the place where a gentle song ever sang. As he delved into it, the song rolled into a chorus, growing more powerful the further within he went, reaching that quiet light, followed by an explosion of light. His eyes no longer saw the world as his elven eyes saw; it was a world wrought of light. Every tree and blade of grass, every cloud and breath of wind, every stone and drop of water. Yet, brightest of all was Kiara bound to Eliel, her entire body wrought of light.

Their minds and hearts forever connected, they reached back to their earliest memories, not yet together, and poured their thoughts into form. Kien wielded the lumaryl to contain their memories, adding the other erendinth to transform it into a lucilliae.

But this one would not be a typical lucilliae.

Kien's mind and heart travelled with Kiara's, and Naiel and Eliel wrapped their own history into theirs, preserving their entire legacy for future generations.

As he poured more lumaryl into the sophilliae, it continued to grow. Kien hoped future Phaedryn would do the same, passing on their wisdom and memories to those that followed.

When his memory returned to the present, Kien and Kiara pulled away from the sophilliae. Stepping away, Kien saw two lumaryl statues, capturing his and Kiara's likeness while bonded as Phaedryn. A pair of clasped hands supported the sophilliae above. Their likenesses did not look at the sophilliae, but rather gazed into each other's eyes.

Kien's eyes sparkled as he looked at the representation of his love for Kiara from a different perspective, only ever needing to see her eyes looking into his own. Turning from the statues and the sophilliae to Kiara, he asked, "What should we call it?"

"Aerethyn."

Devlyn blinked as he withdrew from the orb on its slow rotation. His fingers lingered on its smooth surface, but the vision ended. He felt Ellendren through their bond, her heart brushing against his.

"My parents left this World-Below on the same day they entered it together, and indeed, the same day they were first greeted by Naiel and Eliel, in the year 27,759 of the Second Era. I wept for them, as did my siblings, and all Luminare. But those tears were not of sadness, but of joy. Anaweh had called them to Lumaeniel and they answered.

"I watched as the morning light filled my eyes and the bright songs of Auriel, other anadel, and a plethora of Luminari elves could be heard throughout Luminare. Phaedryn and ei'ana joined in the triumphant hymn to welcome the dawning light that memorable Feast of Aurephaen.

"My parents faded into the light, listening to Anaweh's Call, beckoning them toward Lumaeniel. As I watched them pass, I felt a new era begin. There was no need to call a session or document it; every Luminari elf had felt it, as did every elf of Cyndinare, Eldinare, and Aldinare. The Second Era had ended, and the Third Era begun."

"I never knew two elves could be so extraordinary," Ellendren breathed, her voice weak.

"That they were," Elyse said, gazing east.

"How have we forgotten them?" Devlyn asked. Now knowing their story, it seemed impossible that Kien and Kiara could have been forgotten.

"Their names are still remembered by all, if not for what they accomplished. With the Sophillium soon to open to the world again, the world will remember my parents; not as Phaedryn would know them from the Aerethyn, but from sophilliae documenting their achievements."

Devlyn quietly looked across the landscape. It was time to leave. He felt it in his bones. It was time to return to Arenthyl. Neither he nor Ellendren had wanted to leave Arenthyl in the first place but leaving Phroenthyl would prove difficult after spending seven years here, what was only a year to the rest of Teraeniel. There was a rightness about the Skyland. His heart sang as his feet pressed against the ground while his lungs filled with air. The elves who were forced to leave Luminare might have brought as much of the Skyland to the land below as possible, but the Skyland remained distinct in every way.

Spending seven years on Phroenthyl had made Devlyn realize how difficult it had been for those ancient elves to leave their home. He had never truly understood what his ancestors were giving up.

"You now understand why the Aldinari could not bear to leave," Elyse said. "It was not their pride that kept them planted, but that they could not abandon Aldinare."

"Is there no hope for them?" Ellendren asked, her eyes pleading. "What you did to Aren—can it be done for them?"

"Aren was a Phaedryn. Whether or not the Aldinari survived as Aren did is unknown," Elyse replied.

Ellendren turned west; somewhere there, Aldinare remained enshrouded by the Evil One's meddling. A part of her belonged to Aldinare. Devlyn reached for her hand, a physical touch that mirrored their deeper connection.

"Know that your training will never fully end, but your time here has. When you return to Arenthyl, it will be the Feast of Aurephaen in the year 9071 of the Third Era."

"That's barely eight months," Ellendren said. "Does that mean we weren't here for the full time?"

"Seven years still passed here. Teraeniel grows cold and the dead linger. Time is not on our side. With Auriel's help, I've managed to alter the time wield slightly. I won't be able to correct the original wield for quite some time and because of that, it will fade once you leave."

"All that time—was only eight months to the outside world?" The question died on Devlyn's breath as another surfaced. "Has something happened for you to risk doing that?"

"The threat that has always loomed over the living grows stronger. Somnaeniel is lost to us," Elyse said. Devlyn's wings rustled against his back, showing his eagerness to return to Arenthyl.

"The time has indeed come." Elyse raised her hand to her heart and bowed.

"Ei'phaenyl," Devlyn and Ellendren said, mirroring Elyse's posture. The reverent gesture felt deeper than it had before; Devlyn felt as though he saw all of whom Elyse was in doing so.

"You continue to grow and learn," Elyse said. "Our expressions and gestures were never meant for pageantry. Our spirits touch those around us, and our ancient custom is a recognition of the anacordel we greet, acknowledging all of who they are."

"Thank you, Ei'phaenyl." Devlyn glanced at Ellendren and saw the readiness in her eyes. Unfolding their wings, they leapt into the air. They were only above the tree line of Phroenthyl when a roar reverberated through the sky.

Lyvenol's golden body shimmered in the light, his wings rising and falling slowly.

Images of farewell entered Devlyn's mind, which he returned fondly to Lyvenol. Leaving the Gold Primus was difficult; Devlyn had grown familiar with his presence and constant images in his mind.

Ready to return to Krysenthiel? Devlyn conveyed to Aliel.

This place is as Krysenthiel should and will be, Aliel conveyed. *Awake.*

Devlyn and Ellendren passed through the thin barrier of light surrounding Phroenthyl, leaving the altered time wield that had permitted them to train for seven years in only eight months. Devlyn did not feel seven years older, and he knew he did not look it, for he had aged as the elves with Life Immortal had in the time wield. For those who still possessed it, seven years was but a single breath in their long lives.

Should we shift to Arenthyl immediately? Devlyn heard Ellendren in his mind.

I want to get back as soon as possible but shifting doesn't seem appropriate after our time on Phroenthyl. Devlyn shared, fearing the sudden return would be too jarring.

Ellendren agreed.

Continuing their long flight home, Devlyn watched the sky and land at the horizon as it transitioned between day and night, and returned to day again.

He watched the stars fade as the first signs of dawn showed Mount Verinien in the distance. Nearing Arenthyl, Devlyn felt the sun rise behind him and a song stir in his heart. He knew it was Aurephaen, and he now knew how the elves of Luminare had once celebrated that feast. Parting his lips, he began to sing the hymn he had heard Kien and Kiara sing in that first memory and all the others following.

Ellendren sang with him. The beginning of Aurephaen and the knowledge of what it meant beckoned them. With the rising sun at their backs, they flew toward Arenthyl. Circling the city with Ellendren in a dance among the dawning light, Devlyn heard other elves singing the ancient hymn, beseeching Auriel to guide them in Anaweh's Light. Every Luminari held that hymn in their hearts as their voices filled the city.

Assembled in the plaza in front of the palace were hundreds of Luminari elves. There were others assembled, dignitaries and monarchs, but the majority were golden-brown haired Luminari. The plaza and ramps were overcrowded, and only a small space was reserved for Devlyn and Ellendren to land. On the furthest point from the palace's entry, Devlyn's feet touched the ground beside Ellendren's.

As he looked at everyone assembled, he recognized faces. Family and friends filled the front lines, as did every Luminari, Eldinari, and Aldinari aryl. Every monarch opposed to Erynor was present, including an unprecedented attendance of the Dwarven Schtamite. Leaders among every race in Eklean and beyond united in the Light were present: elves, humans, dwarves, centaurs, minums, and even some goblins. The Seven Chairs of Septyl stood together, accompanied by their wise ones. Archstewards of the ei'ceuril were present, with Aaron, the Ceurtriarch, standing toward the front of the assembled ei'ceuril.

A bright light bloomed behind Devlyn and Ellendren, Auriel appearing before the gathered mass. The enthiel of the Luminari appeared as an elf with a body of ethereal golden light. Even bonded to their phoenix, Devlyn and Ellendren were but dim candles beside Auriel.

"The six-winged anadel declared you one. May all present today give witness to that union," Aaron declared, grinning broadly at his sister. "May your union as the Aryl of Arenthyl and the Exalted Aryl of Krysenthiel, High King and High Queen of Eklean, and Prelate of the Guardian Senate lead us all into a bright future."

Devlyn smiled at Ellendren. It felt silly, since their union had occurred nearly eight years ago for them, but in real time, they had been married a year ago today. Yet as Ellendren looked back into his own eyes, he stopped thinking. Teraeniel's leaders had gathered to witness their declaration of love and their formal coronation as the Exalted Aryl of Krysenthiel. Devlyn felt a pull from within, and memories from the Aerethyn surfaced. The words of union spoken by Kien and Kiara all those years ago filled his mind, not in the Common Tongue, but High Aelish.

"All of who I am is woven to you," Devlyn said, eyes only for Ellendren.

"No longer two, but one," she continued.

"May the winds never tear us apart."

"But ever hold us together."

The words wove something in their hearts, their very spirits, already linked and bonded together. There was no need to wield animys. Devlyn's spirit mingled with hers, reaffirming their union. Devlyn felt his entire being sing; he wanted to leap from his skin and soar through the skies with Ellendren. The exhilaration demanded an outward sign but Devlyn didn't think flying was the appropriate action.

His lips found hers and he pulled her closer as she returned the kiss. The words brought a joy he had not expected. When they had stood before the seraph in the Empyrean Sphere, neither had declared anything vocally. They knew how they had felt about each other, but without voicing those words of union, he'd felt he had forgotten something.

Everyone assembled, both on the palace plaza and the overflow in the next tier beyond the palace walls, exploded into applause as songs and bells and wind instruments echoed throughout the city. Devlyn saw Alex clapping wildly, Wyn leaning in to tell him something privately. Devlyn knew he would turn crimson if he heard what was said.

Two elves walked out from the broad palace entry and Devlyn felt his knees give out. Each elf carried a crystal crown. The diadems were unlike anything he had ever seen before. Lumaryl created jewels that were entirely different—only some of the jewels were lucilliae. Woven into the crystal crowns were jewels of lumaryl, eldaryl, cyndaryl, and aldaryl. The incredible combination of jewels from every Skyland displayed on the crystal crowns was mesmerizing.

As wondrous as the crowns were, Devlyn's heart stopped in his chest as he saw who carried them. One he easily recognized as Aren, and he extended the crown toward Ellendren. But the other, the woman, Devlyn only knew from a faint dream and a wrinkled portrait. His eyes brimmed over with tears as did his mother's when they saw each other for the first time since that wretched night when Dolan had been killed.

Their eyes locked; she closed the gap between them and placed the crown on his head, as Aren placed the other on Ellendren's.

A greater light materialized after the crowns were placed as another being of light appeared, one of the irythil—Uriel, Lord of the Stars, one of the seven anadel who had brought the erendinth into the Void to create Teraeniel.

"Devlyn Lorenthien, you were born of every elven kin, and descend from the draelyn of the Gold House. When the first elves divided into four at the Great Blessing, Anaweh saw only unity in the elves, and indeed in all anacordel. As such, the assembled aryls of every Skyland have named you and Ellendren Lorenthien as their Exalted Aryl. These crowns are not the ones of your ancestors, wielded and sung by the Luminari elves, but of my very will were they wrought and sung from Verakryl, the Tree of Life."

The crystal diadem had a light of its own, complimenting the other jewels. Devlyn felt the weight of the crown on his brow.

"Embrace the people of Eklean as their High King and High Queen." The exuberant light faded, and Uriel no longer appeared before them. Auriel remained slightly longer, and Devlyn felt the enthiel brush against his shoulder before also fading.

He smiled as he turned to Ellendren. Their fingers had been entwined the entire time.

A quiet song in High Aelish lifted; the child's beatific voice filled Devlyn's ears. No one dared to interrupt the unknown child. Devlyn's familiarity with the unused language had greatly improved after his time on Phroenthyl and the words were just as beautiful as the child's voice. Devlyn knew this song. He had always known it; he had learned it from his mother, kept safe and guarded in his deepest memories.

With an unheard song upon thy heart,
Might Light steps ever mark thy start...

ROYAL SCEPTERS

Devlyn and Ellendren Lorenthien, the Exalted Aryl of Krysenthiel, High King and High Queen of Eklean, and Prelate of the Guardian Senate sat on the Crystal Throne in Aerodhal's throne room. Their throne had been sung from a single piece of lumaryl, its two chairs joined in a grand sculptural expression. The gathered elves and representatives from across Teraeniel filed into the room, in order of their stations, to proclaim their loyalty. The role of High King and High Queen was only ever meant as a stabilizing force on the continent, to mediate when civility dissolved.

The Luminari aryls came first, both high and minor pledging their obeisance to Devlyn and Ellendren, followed by the Eldinari and Aldinari aryls. Human monarchs who recognized the new High King and High Queen of Eklean followed the elves.

The final group to recognize the Lorenthien aryl were dignitaries of the Guardian Senate. Peoples of every race, largely limited to Eklean at present, who had agreed to be part of the Guardian Senate came forth. Elven aryls, human monarchs, dwarven patriarchs and matriarchs, as well as centaurs and fauns and goblins and minums came forward to present their chosen representatives for the Guardian Senate. Only merpeople, giants, ogres, and humans from Ja'horan, Ogren, and Qien were absent. A lone representative from Daer had come, likely from one of their established Eklean colonies.

Messages had to be sent to them all, beseeching their involvement in the Guardian Senate. The entirety of Teraeniel had to join together and act as one to confront the threat of Ramiel escaping the Void. Eklean could not do it on its own. Erynor, at the head of the Erynien Empire, while a servant of Ramiel, was only a pawn.

Devlyn's eyes bulged when Angennia and her husband, Enrico Desillio, stood before him and Ellendren. While Angennia was a Judge of Yanil who had always opposed the Erynien Empire and her nation's involvement in it, Enrico was a prominent noble, rumored to be the Yanilean's favored and heir. How much confidence did Erynor's subjects have in his rule, if even the Yanilean had sent delegates to Arenthyl? Devlyn remembered Ange fondly as she had helped him escape the Tieli queen's cage.

One last pair approached the Crystal Throne as the formal ceremony neared its end. Two centaurs. Devlyn recognized Oreniel easily enough but not the other. Both carried an elongated parcel wrapped in leaves and vines. The wrappings would have been collected after falling naturally from trees in the Illumined Wood; no centaur would have plucked them. Devlyn knew how sacred the trees were and the sad state of those that had fallen asleep in the rest of the world.

Extending the parcel forward, Oreniel placed it in Devlyn's hands, Ellendren receiving the second parcel from the other centaur. Even when concealed, he could feel the power emanating from the contents. Kyrendal had insisted their coming about was impossible. And he would have been right if the draelyn had not provided the seeds and if Saecrien had refused to allow them to nourish in her waters. Despite his vow to never again create a verathn, Kyrendal himself had tended the seeds every elven feast day over the past year, bringing forth two verathn. They were made especially for Devlyn and Ellendren, and only they would be able to wield them.

The leaves fell away from the slender scepters to the floor when they accepted the parcels. Oreniel gathered each leaf, as though he intended to return them to where they had originally fallen. "I expect your court would not be pleased if ivy swept across the entire palace."

"It would take root outside the Illumined Wood?" Devlyn asked.

"It is not the Illumined Wood which makes those trees who they are, but the trees that make the Illumined Wood what it is."

Power from the translucent scepter thrummed through Devlyn's fingers. The verathn was smooth in his hands and shone with hues of gold, silver, bronze, and clear crystal, the polished material feeling like warm glass. Devlyn knew the verathn had weight, but it felt as though he held air in his grasp, weighing no more than the leaves which had contained it. The erendinth hummed from the verathn, flowing continuously to focus a wielder's strength and control.

Devlyn had heard wondrous tales of verathn wielded by Phaedryn, but he had never imagined he'd one day hold his own.

"Thank you for bringing these," Ellendren said. Like Devlyn, she too had difficulty removing her attention from her verathn.

"Kyrendal stressed the importance of finalizing the bond between you and your verathn. Once the bond is complete, none will be able to even lift the verathn without your express intent, let alone tap its power, as long as you live. As a Phaedryn, you amplify its potential and when you pass from this World-Below, it will be linked to your phoenix, and whoever your phoenix bonds with will be able to claim this verathn as their own and use it in the same manner as you."

Devlyn looked up from his verathn to Oreniel. "How do we complete the bond?"

"You both must bond fully with your phoenix and reveal yourselves to the verathn."

Without a second thought, Devlyn and Ellendren did so; golden light bathed the domed throne room, washing it in brilliance that not even the brightest sun could replicate.

The many anacordel in the room looked at the Lorenthien aryl in awe.

Devlyn mingled his consciousness with Aliel, and exerted it outward and into the verathn, similarly to how he and Ellendren had unsealed Arenthyl. The experience was like tapping his inner sense while interacting with the different life forces around him. He intimately felt the erendinth thrum from the staff as his consciousness wove through and melded with it. The quiet hymn he had ever known sprang within his heart. The verathn's thrum shifted, reflecting the tune of Devlyn's heartbeat.

The glow that Devlyn saw around everything while bonded with Aliel intensified around himself and his verathn. The verathn grew familiar to him, becoming an extension of himself, his very spirit imbued with it, linking it to his body, soul, and spirit.

"Thank you, Oreniel." Devlyn felt the bond complete, as he and Ellendren remained in their Phaedryn form, golden wings folded against their backs, brushing the floor.

"You are welcome, children of Luminare. Know that much depends on how you wield the verathn. You are not exempt from the temptations of power and the downfall of others."

"I know—it frightens me as I compose myself to sleep. May Anaweh preserve and strengthen us," Ellendren said.

"Perhaps Teraeniel will not be lost."

Devlyn raised an eyebrow, curious whether Oreniel expected Erynor to be victorious.

"It is not Erynor you should fear, but the one he serves." Oreniel looked beyond Devlyn, not specifically toward the doors, but beyond.

"Can the Evil One truly return?" Devlyn repeated the question that continuously taunted him. Even after the time spent on Phroenthyl and everything he had learned while there, he did not want to believe it possible. The assembled crowd hushed at the mention; they had all been listening attentively. They knew of the threat, but like Devlyn, did not want to consider it a possibility, despite that being the original reason for the establishment of the Guardian Senate.

"His prison was created like any other, and his taint has been corroding its seals since he was first locked away. To pass that barrier should not be possible, but we were once all Children before time entered and we began to age against the original design, and we later divided into distinct races. That which is and is not possible has no limit."

Devlyn's heart ached at the thought of someone more dangerous than Erynor coming forward. He knew he was not a match for Erynor. How was he supposed to confront the crazed Cyndinari elf who had toppled Krysenthiel and murdered every Phaedryn alive at the time?

"Thank you for the warning, but for all our sakes, I hope that will never occur." Shifting his mind from those thoughts to the banquet to follow, Devlyn asked, "How long will you remain in Arenthyl?"

"For a time; but I believe we will be more wanted to help awaken the Delmira Wood. You should reach out to you sister, Leilyn. The trees will hear her song better than our own," Oreniel said. "The stars sing of what is to come."

Twilight settled over Arenthyl when the ceremonial oaths had concluded after a long day. The gathered dignitaries were all ushered from the throne room into Aerodhal's grandest banquet hall, a room large enough to fit the entire population of Cor'lera.

Devlyn had escaped the crowds to a balcony that looked over the room. His eyes followed the vertical lines of the massive arboriform column, interrupted briefly as it wove into the balcony he stood on. The sculpted lines left the column to meld into the balustrade, returning to the sinuous column of lumaryl before those lines wove with other columns and arches to form a magnificent dome of translucent lumaryl. Devlyn had no trouble seeing past the glass-like dome and into the stars twinkling above. Were Auriel and Uriel among the starry multitude, or had they shifted to Lumaeniel, the World-Beyond?

A single star blinked brightly in the night, dancing softly in the east; it had to be Auriel. Devlyn made a mental note to thank the anadel and turned away to return to the guests below. He went into a large corridor then down a decorative staircase. Every architectural element in the palace had an ornate grandeur yet was also incredibly simple. His eyes were constantly deceived.

A light melody, muffled by conversation, filled the banquet hall. Long-standing feuds were evident even tonight as groups huddled with their backs to other groups. Devlyn was still baffled by the presence of dignitaries from Yanil and Torsil. Perhaps the Guardian Senate would have a chance to succeed with well-intentioned senators from across the world.

Distrustful Sudernese nobles kept to themselves, their eyes scanning the room, their brightly colored cloaks concealing their arms and hands, and undoubtedly hidden knives. Despite wanting the diplomats to interact with one another in a civil manner, Devlyn grinned when he saw the vehement distrust as the Sudernese dignitaries scowled at their Yanilean counterparts.

"Ah, Ei'denai Devlyn Lorenthien." Aorinol, a Daer senator, patted Devlyn's back, too friendly for Devlyn to believe authentic. The Daer stood a head taller than everyone else in the room and his shock of white hair contrasted with his ebony skin, making him stand out. "Fine banquet you've thrown us all. You must come to Daereneth so we can return the favor."

"In time; as you know, we've only just returned here."

"Oh, yes. I confess I did not expect Eklean to be in shambles. After you elves came from the sky and became high kings and high queens, Eklean was said to be the epicenter of order and prosperity."

"Several events took place which altered that." Devlyn grimaced.

"History never was my strong point," Aorinol said. "Economics captured my fancy. Speaking of which, if you wouldn't mind, my bankers wish to weigh these lumols, narols, and kenols against our own currency; a necessary process if we're to establish international trade."

"The Goblin Guild has already measured and weighed them against the Eklean currency; I'm sure they'd be more than happy to answer any of your questions," Devlyn replied.

"I'm sure they would, but from what I've learned their senior members are somewhat under a house arrest. Surely that's not possible…"

Aorinol's tone irked Devlyn. Across the room, he saw Alex speaking with someone wearing a checkered yellow and black seal, with a heron at the center. "You'll have to excuse me." Devlyn left Aorinol and crossed the lumaryl flooring, extending a hand to the Brieli noble. "Welcome to Arenthyl, my lady. I hope your accommodations are comfortable."

"You're rather polite for one of your position," said the dark brown-haired, middle-aged woman finely dressed in black and yellow.

"No fine greeting for me?" Alex raised a brow as he held back a laugh.

Devlyn cleared his throat and forced a formal, yet light tone, "Not satisfied, Alexander?"

"Not you too." Alex groaned at his full name, something Devlyn knew he despised.

Returning his attention to the woman, Devlyn took her hand in greeting. "I am Devlyn…"

"Oh, I'm quite aware of your name and titles," the woman laughed. "I doubt you're aware of mine though. I can only imagine how many squabbling Brieli nobles shoved their names down your throat when you passed through Briel. Quite a stir you made. The moment it reached our ears that the Luminari elves marched on Krysenthiel, with Lucillia impossibly returned to the forest, every house offered itself to Irvienne as a candidate for the Guardian Senate. Less concerned about appeasing his own people, Irvienne insisted that I make the trek north. I do hope you do something about those frozen waters. I would have preferred to sail the entire journey up the rivers and along the lake. Light knows how deep it is."

"With time, we hope the sun will melt the waters so boats might return to our shores and ports," Devlyn said, delighted by her candor. "Forgive me, I still don't know your name."

"Oh, how foolish of me. I am Bernadette Haert of Briel, the king's sister."

"Please, Princess Bernadette, tell me you've been treated with proper respect."

"Oh, not to worry. Kaela knew precisely who I was the moment I arrived. Very little gets past that one. The late Roendryn aryl were clearly diligent about their children's education. I doubt Ellendren learned half as much at Gwilnor as her own mother imparted to her and Kaela. Poor thing; her sacrifice only bought time for her people. Those were unfortunate circumstances; still Erynor would have undoubtedly unleashed havoc if the barrier was not lifted."

"Yes, Vernal was a spectacular woman and queen. Apart from Harnyl, I believe I was one of the last people to see her before the Protection of the Wood was raised."

"Another tragedy; I still find it difficult to believe that they're both gone from us. I always enjoyed their visits when I was young. Of course, with instability gripping Eklean, their visits ceased and Briel became isolated. I would have so liked to have seen them once more." Bernadette's gaze drifted from Devlyn. "Was that the Daer senator you were speaking with earlier? Has he told you whether they intend to enslave Tiel? If they wouldn't mind, they should start with their queen." Bernadette shared a mischievous smile.

"He hasn't mentioned it, although if you would like, I could introduce you."

"Don't trouble yourself, I'm quite capable. This is not my first banquet, after all." Bernadette glided across the room toward Aorinol.

Devlyn watched her briefly, digesting his conversation with the Brieli princess. Nothing in her reminded him of King Irvienne. Alex elbowed him. "It's good to see you again."

"You too, Alex." They hugged, knowing they wouldn't have any time for themselves.

"Be careful with the Daer; they have something called a sorcery."

"Sorcery?" Devlyn asked, having never heard of it.

"As far as I know, they trap anadel and siphon their powers. Sanjin knew more about it, but he's gone back to Charren to claim his throne. He said the Daer still practice it."

"Great, something else to worry about."

"I'd prefer that over planning a wedding. My mother has been insufferable and the Evellion nobles are all losing their patience with me. If I'm not careful, they'll force Diana and me into the nearest chapel and have whatever ei'ceuril is present declare us wed. All the while expecting an heir to be born the day after the wedding!"

"And all this time I had thought Evellions were prudish."

"None more so! Diana and I can't even be alone in the same room until we're wed."

"Has a date been announced?"

"Once Mindale is dealt with and Evellion's borders are secured. Can't come too soon if you ask me, since no one mentioned that I'd be sleeping alone throughout our entire betrothal," Alex growled.

Devlyn patted Alex's back, suddenly grateful for the seven years he and Ellendren had had together on Phroenthyl. He and Alex moved toward a laughing crowd near the center of the hall. Winding his way past, Devlyn heard Ellendren's voice carry over the laughter.

"…not a second after it touched his skin, it disintegrated."

A blushing Devlyn knew this story far too intimately. *Why are you telling them this?*

"Was it true? Did you really fight off shadow elves in the buff?" a Torsillian noble asked, balancing his drink as he held his sides from laughing.

They need to see that you're a real person, especially after all that pomp of the coronation. Ellendren's thoughts sang in his mind.

Surely there are other stories that make me seem plenty real while still dressed,

Devlyn shared. *Like that time we practiced wielding in the main courtyard at Gwilnor.*

And how you accidentally fell on top of me?

That was your wield that tripped me.

Was it?

"Unfortunately, it was before I knew anything about lierathnil." Devlyn braved a smile.

"If memory serves," Wyn said with a wry smirk, "There were a few other occasions."

"Oh, you must tell us!" cried a Sorenth noble, brushing tears from her eyes.

"I think Devlyn's been embarrassed more than enough on our behalf today," said Ellendren, her eyes still laughing.

"We've hardly breached the surface," Alex hollered, lighting up the crowd.

"Finally, we can agree on something." Abbie smirked, Andrew at her side grinning knowingly.

UNSPOKEN

D evlyn collapsed on his bed, exhausted by coronation festivities and reunions with friends and family. He had half hoped for an easy transition from Phroenthyl. That optimistic view had been shattered when he realized the coronation ceremony was to occur the moment they returned to Arenthyl. As though the day had not been long enough, advisors and secretaries had stolen every moment between the various rituals and festivities to brief Ellendren and him on what had happened since they had left.

Unsurprisingly, Kaela had been efficient. Whatever reservations the aryls had had regarding the establishment of House Lucillia as an aryldom of stewards had evaporated during Devlyn and Ellendren's absence. Silvia had appeared so pleased in fact, that she didn't even bat an eye when she saw Kaela and Wyn escape for a quiet walk during the banquet. Devlyn had expected the opposite reaction once Silvia discovered she'd been duped.

Ellendren was still with Kaela, Myranda, Danielle, and Fiona. Despite her pleasure at seeing them, he knew she longed to resume her delayed research regarding the Evil One.

Heavy eye lids closed to the dark room again, his mind forgetting the events of the day as the welcome embrace of sleep neared. Just as he was about to lose consciousness, a knock came at the door. He ignored it, discounting it as a part of a dream. A second knock followed, and a slit of light poked through the slightly opened doors.

"Ei'denai?" Lyren whispered.

"Just Devlyn, Lyren."

"Yes, Ei'denai. I apologize for the hour, but there's someone here to see you."

Rolling over, Devlyn pulled himself upright to sit on the edge of the bed. Lyren brought Devlyn a simple robe to cover himself. Judging by its simplicity, this was an informal meeting. Granted, Lyren had never before disturbed him in the middle of the night for a casual encounter and normally forbade him from wearing his robe outside his quarters.

Covered, Devlyn followed Lyren through the lumaryl-screened corridors and stairways that offered a sense of privacy from the currently empty main living area.

How much more crowded would the residence become after he and Ellendren started to have children? *Not yet*, he thought. He didn't fully understand how to account for his age anymore. By most standards, he and Ellendren were now eighteen. But they had spent seven years in a time wield on Phroenthyl. For them, they had seen twenty-five springs. His own mother had been younger when she had given birth to Leilyn.

He pushed those thoughts aside as Lyren eventually brought him to a comfortable salon that opened onto a southern balcony. The balcony wrapped partly around the slender spire, offering a stunning panorama. Devlyn had grown fond of that balcony as it had one of the best views of the city and surrounding lake. A light breeze pushed the curtains apart, revealing an elf standing alone on the balcony.

The salon glowed softly with the lumaryl, but not sufficiently to illumine the room without added lamps. Devlyn didn't need a lamp to recognize the elf on the balcony though, nor did he have to tap his interior sense.

"Mother."

"Devlyn." Evellyn spun slowly; her golden-brown hair caught the moonlight.

He quickly closed the distance between them to embrace her; he hadn't had a chance to speak with his mother yet. "I saw you walk away at the banquet, and I tried to come after you."

"You were busy with the dignitaries and your friends. I didn't want to interrupt. Besides, Vine and I had a long talk."

"I never thought she'd change, but she actually cried when I last saw her in Cor'lera."

"She is still very much Vine Vaerin, but a redeemed Vine Vaerin."

"I dreamt so often of you when I was at the abbey school. They told me terrible lies about you and Da—I believed them. I had convinced myself that my dreams of you were a fantasy."

Evellyn rubbed his back as she held him, undisturbed by his sudden show of emotion as he convulsed in her arms. He had never forgiven himself for believing the lies all those years.

"The dreams were a gift. I could not speak, lest it be discovered that I could touch your dreams through Somnaeniel, but I never abandoned you. I was with you the entire time, but I could only visualize you as the toddler who had been ripped away from me."

"Dreaming of myself as a toddler was pretty awkward." Devlyn laughed into her shoulder as he gathered himself.

"I'm sure it was. And here you are. The toddler I sang to every night before I was taken is now grown and married."

"The song," Devlyn said, acknowledging the one he'd always known.

"You were so young when you heard the words; I could only hum in the dream. Our family's history was written into that song, as was a promise for our future. For twelve hundred years we lived peacefully in Cor'lera, and the youngest child would pass the song to their youngest child. The song stretches back to before our ancestors left Luminare. I feared the song would end with me."

"I remembered the words when I saw the statue of Lucillia holding the jewel of faith."

"Feolyn and Gwendolyn's youngest child added to the song. She knew her line stretched from Lucillia and House Lorenthien. She sang it only to her parents and her youngest child. She sang it so we might have a future. A future, Liam has told me, you've been working hard to achieve. During our trek north, he told me much of what I'd missed over the past sixteen years. And Arlyn told me even more after I reached Arenthyl. I even learned a great deal from Yloran."

"Yloran? How did you come across her?" Devlyn asked, shocked that his mother knew a Sha'ghol.

"We travelled with her from Tiel, under the guise of a circus. She's here in Arenthyl. I'm sure she'll present herself to you and Ellendren once she's ready."

"She's here? In Arenthyl?" Devlyn asked, startled. If she hadn't been given a proper palace to reside in with her attendants, their meeting would occur sooner rather than later.

"Yes. I was wary at first, knowing who she was. I grew quite fond of her after learning she had healed you in Lankor, all the while shielding you from those who wished you ill."

Devlyn felt a bit dazed. He had known that Yloran would eventually make her way to Arenthyl but never imagined she'd arrive with his mother. Still fixated on the song, he set that aside to say, "I still don't understand how I could remember the song by looking at a statue."

"Many gifts come when one is bonded with a phoenix. Lorendil, like all anadel, are not bound by the restrictions of time. They experience time passing when they are here in Teraeniel, but the passage of time is not found in Lumaeniel. Aliel would have known much, even if he was in an egg and only hatched when you were born."

"You speak of the lorendil as though you have experience with your own guardian anadel."

Evellyn smiled. "My experience with the lorendil is only because of another."

"I don't understand."

Evellyn stepped toward the balustrade and looked across the lumaryl city glowing under the full moon. "While the prophesies all pointed to you, the weapon Erynor feared had indeed been hiding in Cor'lera. More than the song passed to the next Lorenthien child."

"I don't understand. What else did you pass to me?"

"Not what, but who. And I never had the chance to pass the bond. You were too young when I was taken—as a toddler, the bond would have consumed you. And as you were too young then, so too is it too late now to pass the bond, for it is no longer mine to give."

Confused, Devlyn frowned. His mother spun mysteries just as cleverly as any ei'ana.

"You've already met him. Because of our past bond, I can still feel him, but only as a shadow, a tremor in a pond. There is no need for him to hide in a bond with the youngest Lorenthien in a small village any longer. Now that Uriel is freed from the frozen waters of Lake Saeryndol, Auriel has returned to his rightful place among the stars, to shepherd our people in the dark days ahead."

"Auriel—you were bonded with the guardian of the Luminari elves?"

"Auriel never abandoned the Luminari, nor Teraeniel. He did not turn an uncaring eye away from this realm as so many had believed."

Devlyn couldn't believe his mother had concealed Auriel within herself—even as Erynor's prisoner in Broid. Sharing a bond with a phoenix had been thought a miracle. But this—Auriel was one of the enthiel! A bond like that was unimaginable. "So, all this time, there really was a weapon in Cor'lera."

"Not a weapon; it was perceived as such by Erynor who only understands power and violence and death. Erynor fears death—he fears the transition should he fail. He has chosen Ramiel as his Master and is actively trying to free him from his prison. If they succeed..."

"The Void—the Darkness—will claim us all." Devlyn looked into the sky, remembering the vicious storm clouds that had consumed Somnaeniel and occasionally showed in Teraeniel.

Devlyn's braided crown weighed little, but the gathered aryls reminded him of its true weight. When Uriel had named him and Ellendren the Exalted Aryl of every elven kin, Devlyn had been unsure as to what exactly that encompassed. The aryls, even the Luminari aryls, were largely independent. Lorenthien aryls had never dictated how other aryls lived or governed their cities, yet they were part of Krysenthiel. It was a single unified nation of aryldoms without any territorial breaks. The Aldinari elves had recovered some of their numbers, but they were still a diminished people, and the Cyndinari loyal to Krysenthiel were even fewer.

The Eldinari were chief among Devlyn's concerns. They were an entire civilization. The Eldin Wood was almost the same size as Krysenthiel, and the Eldinari elves were quite capable of governing themselves. Devlyn didn't understand why they had agreed to bow to the Lorenthien aryl for all the years to come.

"Your thoughts remain loud," said Fendryl Lierafen. The chamber where the aryls gathered was much more crowded now, as it was not limited to the Luminari aryls.

"I'm sorry," Devlyn said. "It's still confusing to me."

"Please elaborate; some mysteries of the past are not yet revealed to us," Enithil said, blessedly unaware of Devlyn's thoughts.

"What is the role of the Exalted Aryl to be among the Eldinari, Aldinari, and Cyndinari elves?" Devlyn asked.

"Suzerainty, of course," Valerie replied, without missing a beat. "The same as it has always been with the Luminari elves. As our Exalted Aryl, we are subject to you, but we govern in our own right."

Devlyn nodded. He had no desire to tell immortal elves who were thousands of years his senior how to conduct their lives. "What of their military? Aside from city guards, Krysenthiel does not have an independent army."

"We cannot force anyone into the Guardian knights, but I imagine many of our star wardens will join the resurfaced order in time. Many will retain their posts in the Eldin Wood, the same as Krysenthien cities maintain their own guards," said Indryn Allandis.

"With the seguian portals opened once more, we'll be able to ensure the safety of our lands, while cooperating fully with you and the Guardian Senate."

Devlyn's mind was soothed. "Has the Erynien Empire made any movement?"

"Eklean has been quiet. Eandyl and Verenthyl are beset by occasional skirmishes, but not by an Erynien legion. As you know, every legion simply vanished after we reclaimed Arenthyl. It's likely the captured minum returned them to Broid. But we have no way of confirming that. Our scouts haven't had any sightings of additional forces marching north, and Yanil, Tiel, and Torsil have remained within their borders. Mindale, as you know, is now under the reign of a Dwonian chief named Cairn, with King Lawrence cold in a grave," Binoral said.

"Do we know how Cairn has responded to the Ashtons and their resistance?" Devlyn asked, having only learned of it from Alex.

"Only by observing their actions. There hasn't been any formal condemnation from the chief-king regarding the resistance, but skirmishes are quite common around Binton. As you already know, Cairn arranged to have the Ashtons and the King of Thellion and the Queen of Evellion assassinated but failed in that endeavor." Binoral looked back at his agenda, ticking his tongue until he found where he had left off. "Ah, here we are; the Daer have been provoking the Erynien Empire along Eklean's southern coast. Only Thellion seems to have arrived at some sort of arrangement with the Daer, permitting their colony to remain on the Skrein Sea."

"What of the fleet near Eddle Port?" Ellendren asked.

"Eddle Port does not have the strength to engage the Daer invaders and neither would they ask Tiel for help. Tiel is busy enough with their own Daer colony, to say nothing of the Tieli not being able to replenish their navy. From what we've learned, Eddle Port has barricaded themselves inside their walls; they're masons, farmers, and fishermen, not soldiers," Naesiv said.

"Can we send any assistance?" Devlyn asked.

"Things have been relatively quiet here, but the strength required to repel the Daer is more than we can spare," Jeanne provided.

"But enough to ensure the Daer won't obliterate Eddle Port and enslave its people," Ellendren said.

"Yes, I'll arrange a contingent to travel south," Jeanne said, her mind already working out the logistics. "I would recommend asking Sorenthil to contribute forces to this maneuver. Briel is their closest ally, but they are busy securing their borders against Tiel, Torsil, and Daerinth. Sorenthil is their next closest ally, and the fallen kingdom of Gestoria was once Sorenthil's greatest ally and friend. The two kingdoms ever acted as one, as twins would."

"A shame Myranda has returned to Myrium. I'll send word immediately," Ellendren said.

"Why not go to her personally?" Devlyn asked.

"We've only just returned to Arenthyl."

Devlyn turned to Ellendren, attempting to convey that he could handle Arenthyl for a day. *It's not like you're travelling in a conventional manner.*

I could return by tomorrow, Ellendren's thoughts passed to Devlyn. "Very well, I'll ask the Sorenth queen personally."

"I'll prepare an escort for you, Ei'terel," Jeanne said.

"That won't be necessary; they won't be able to keep up."

"Ei'terel, I must insist. We are at war. Assassins with daggers or arrows can be hidden in any shadow." Jeanne wore a stern, resolute expression.

"I won't leave Myrium's palace, I promise."

"Eandyl is not far from Myrium, I'll send an honor guard ahead of you. I ask that you await their arrival; they can be there in a week."

"Does Eddle Port have an additional week to spare?"

"The contingent I'll send to Eddle Port will leave once they are informed. The Sorenth will bolster our strength, while reconnecting them to their ally."

"Very well."

"Thank you, Ei'terel." Jeanne let out a relieved breath. Through their bond, Devlyn felt Ellendren's frustration at having to wait a whole week until she could travel to Myrium. Devlyn was secretly relieved but tried to keep that sentiment private. He looked around the table. "Is there anything else on the agenda?"

CHIEF-KING

Thaerwn and Tye crouched in the tall meadow grass. They were somewhere in the Plains of Mindale, east of the kingdom's capital city of Binton. Several days earlier, Tye had pointed out the city's towers rising in the distance. They had kept their distance but were close enough to recognize that two flags flew over the gates and towers. The Mindalean flag had a brown ox on a green field. A larger one flew above, dwarfing it. That one had five black spears, four encasing a larger central spear on an orange and red checkered field.

Tye had recognized it but didn't share what he knew about it with Thaerwn. How could he possibly describe the deserters to Thaerwn through hand gestures and symbols? Although their communication was improving, it didn't mean they could understand each other's language.

Binton was a couple of days behind them now and Tye continued to wrestle with the idea of how to communicate who the deserters were. As he tried to think of what gestures could possibly define someone who betrayed their own people, the ground trembled ever so slightly. He gripped her wrist and yanked her to the ground, surprising and infuriating her.

She was about to protest the brusque handling as Tye lifted a finger to his lips, imploring her to be quiet. He thought she might ignore him, but she must have recognized the terrified look in his eyes. Tye hated how vulnerable he had to make himself to express their current danger.

He typically maintained a sense of surety and confidence, at least on the outside for others to see. But with Thaerwn and their difficulty in communicating, expressing his emotions through facial expressions was the easiest way to communicate. She understood that better than any gestures.

"Deserters," he whispered. He didn't think she knew the word, so he pointed toward the direction the horses were coming from, unsure whether she felt the vibrations of the ground from the horses' hooves. All she needed to know was that they were dangerous. Tye didn't have to explain what they were to Dwonians or how they had once been Dwonians themselves.

As the horses and riders drew near, Thaerwn and Tye remained perfectly still in the tall grass, crouched low so they might go unseen. The ground vibrated more as the riders neared, the pulsing increasing with every passing breath that Tye tried to muffle. Thaerwn and Tye had stayed clear of the road and had hoped to avoid crossing paths with anyone, especially scouts. But as the horses closed in, Tye became convinced that the riders knew exactly where they were hiding. He already gripped his spear but couldn't see past his crouched position. Then the vibrations lessened and he let out a breath he hadn't realized he was holding.

The horses had passed them.

Tye wanted to believe they were in the clear—wanted to let his guard down, release the rigidity of his muscles, and run as fast as he could for Krysenthiel. They weren't far from where the Shroud had been. He had seen that sickening fog cling to the land like a fungal infection, hungrily stretching outward to consume more of the land.

Waiting for the riders to be far enough past so he and Thaerwn could run for the border, his heart froze when he heard the horses circling back. He tightened his grip on his spear, hoping that Thaerwn would recognize the danger and at least reach for her dagger. Not that they would prove capable against what sounded like twenty deserters on horseback.

Tye hoped his rage and hatred toward them would give him an edge. He was not the one whose tribe had abandoned Dwonia for Erynor or had forsaken their way of life and left Dwonia a wasteland, bereft of her seeds. The elders claimed that the one born of the east, south, west, and north would find the song that would return the seeds. Aside from believing that Devlyn should retrieve the lucilliae in Nynev, Tye had a second reason to bring him to Dwonia. Devlyn was born of all four elven kindred, each from a Skyland floating at a specific cardinal direction. And if that wasn't enough, he was a Phaedryn—bonded with a phoenix. Tye had heard the bird's song when he had last been with Devlyn. The elders might be more willing to release the lucilliae if Devlyn could return the seeds to Dwonia.

The horses drew near again and rushed past, too close for Tye's liking. He cursed under his breath as the riders fell into formation around them. They knew someone was hiding in the grass. A bead of sweat dripped down Tye's neck as the horses rounded about.

"Come out. In the name of Cairn, son of Suin of Tribe Laith, the one to bring back the seeds, Chief-king of Dwonia and Mindale, I demand you come out from hiding."

These deserters had lost their way. No true Dwonian would claim land east of Dwota's Gap and Cairn had no claim over Dwonia. Tye doubted this chief-king had ever crossed the Gap into the desert. The grass reached Tye's waist as he stood, Thaerwn rising beside him. The riders were not only the descendants of those who had betrayed Dwonia to serve Erynor, worse, they had completely forsaken their traditions and bowed to a chief-king whose stolen kingdom began east of Dwota's Gap, a chief-king who had never felt the harsh desert wind against his flesh.

Disgusted at seeing the deserters face to face, Tye spat on the ground beneath the speaker's horse. "Dwonia does not embrace you. You will die outside her comfort. You will never know Dwonia—you will never breathe her air, feel her sun kiss your skin, or tread one step across her sands." Tye spoke in the desert tongue, wondering if the deserters recognized it.

"How dare you speak so to an emissary of our chief-king? Who do you imagine you are, speaking to me so? You're nothing but a runaway, likely trying to escape his pitiful place among his tribe. And what is this you flee away with?" The deserter scowled at Thaerwn.

"I am no runaway and I will not bow to your chief-king. My tribe has never forsaken Dwonia." Tye gripped his spear tighter, knowing precisely where this was headed.

"So, you've finally crossed the Gap, have you? Whether or not that was brave or foolish is yet to be seen. Our meeting was inevitable. Cairn will bring an army across the Gap to claim Dwonia and return the seeds," the emissary said.

"Your chief-king is born of a disgraced tribe. The elders do not speak of him and neither do the ancestors recognize him."

"Your elders and the traditions they cling so tightly to will burn. We have not forsaken Dwonia—Dwonia has forsaken you. You and those who remained are weak and unworthy of her. Why else would Dwonia deny her seeds? Did you never wonder why the seeds left when our ancestors joined Erynor? Dwonia favors the strong and abandoned the weak who remained. The strong weren't the ones who were punished and had to suffer," the emissary spat.

Thaerwn couldn't understand what they were saying. It was odd that there weren't any women among the riders. Dwonia was the only word she recognized. Why anyone would argue about a desert was beyond her. She hoped to never experience those harsh conditions again.

Tye's stance became defensive; he was done talking. Thaerwn knew the riders wouldn't be friendly, but she had hoped they wouldn't delay them. She did not have time to dally, or worse, be taken prisoner. The rider who had been doing most of the talking yelled something, and Thaerwn couldn't tell if he was yelling at Tye or to his companions.

Then the riders reached for their spears, different from Tye's more nat-
ural-looking spear. Instead of having a wooden shaft with a metal head,
the weapon was a single piece of metal, from shaft butt to spear head.
They were a simple design that had to be unnecessarily heavy due to
being entirely metal.

The riders moved forward, tightening the ring. The leader spoke
again, laughed, and stabbed his spear toward Tye. Tye swept his spear
in an arc and deflected the attempt, but more riders were ready to take
their own stabs. That was enough for Thaerwn; she reached for aquaeys
and terys, embracing the erendinth. For whatever reason, she felt most
comfortable wielding aquaeys, something deep inside resonating with it,
even though she didn't understand it.

She couldn't think of that just now. She had to focus on staying
alive. None of the men knew she had embraced the erendinth. Having
had limited opportunities to practice wielding, she didn't have the slightest idea what she was capable of, but she had to do something.

As another spear hurtled toward Tye, Thaerwn wielded terys to lift
a boulder just in time to collide with the spear. Tye's eyes widened slightly at the revelation that she could wield, more in relief than anything
else, since their odds had now improved significantly. Even as she tried to
figure out what to do next, she realized that she should have revealed her
ability to Tye earlier so she could have practiced openly, rather than trying to hide it until it was her turn to keep watch and Tye slept. Still, she
had no idea how he would have responded. The Aldinari priests would
have exiled her if they had discovered she could wield, forcing her to live
outside her city's protection. Her mind would have deteriorated, and she
would have become one of the neridu.

The deserters now saw her as a threat, and one shouted something,
shifting their focus entirely to her. Tye's spear swirled at an incredible
speed to deflect some of the attacks aimed at her, but she embraced
aquaeys and terys more fully, pulling them deeper into herself to move
the ground to her will. The horses reacted, whinnying nervously and sev-

eral tossing their riders when they bolted.

One of the tossed men recovered quickly then sprang for her. Unprepared, she launched the closest thing she could find, a pebble, at the man's forehead and knocked him unconscious. She smiled at that. Wielding a pebble required much less effort than shaking the ground or throwing a boulder and had a much better result. Distracted by her success, she didn't see the spear headed toward her neck. The clang of a spear intercepting it, closer than she liked, made her ears ring. Furious at herself for not paying attention and irritated by the ringing in her ears, Thaerwn wielded the ground beneath her attacker to launch him up into the air. Her ears were still ringing when he hit the ground. She hoped that would discourage the others, half of whom were currently nursing wounds after being thrown by their frightened horses.

Still surrounded, Thaerwn caught the remaining assailants making eye contact with each other. She didn't have to be a warrior to understand they were planning a synchronized attack. Knowing she and Tye couldn't repel six spears at once, Thaerwn pulled the ground up and around her and Tye, cocooning them in hardened dirt just as the spears were thrown at them. The men outside cursed, unable to dislodge the deeply imbedded spears. She could have snapped off the spearheads caught in her wielded dirt if they hadn't been formed of solid metal.

Choosing the next best option, she sank the cocoon into the ground, burying the weapons, but leaving Tye and her exposed again. Enraged at the loss of their spears, the deserters unsheathed daggers, some seeming to appear out of thin air.

Tye smiled. He had the advantage now with the longer reach of his spear. That was the first confident smile Thaerwn had seen on him since they first heard the horses. He whipped his spear up, slamming the butt into one rider's face and smacking the side of it against another's. Thaerwn was impressed by the advantage Tye now had as he quickly dealt with the rest.

Looking about, Thaerwn couldn't tell whether the men on the

ground were dead. Some moaned, but most were still. Tye picked up a spear from one of the silent men. Clearly impressed, he attached it next to his own on his back.

Thaerwn and Tye caught one of the horses and rode for Krysenthiel. They had been much closer to the elven border than Thaerwn had imagined. How could such a powerful realm have enemies so close? Perhaps the Luminari weren't as powerful as the aldarchs had envisioned.

The horse carried them within sight of Verenthyl and Thaerwn's breath caught at the sight of the city's outer wall rising before her, glistening in the sun. She had seen the regal splendor of Val'quin, for Lerathel's sanctum was built entirely of aldaryl, but Val'quin was not a city. Even from a distance, it looked as though every surface of Verenthyl had been constructed of lumaryl. The buildings couldn't have been gilded in the substance either, for they glowed in the sunlight, as though a flame was set within. Aldinari cities were not as extravagant as Verenthyl. The buildings she had grown up around had certainly employed aldaryl, but it was rarely ever used for the whole structure.

What caught her attention was that this was not Arenthyl. As spectacular as this city appeared from a distance, there was another even more majestic city. She wondered how much more amazing Arenthyl could be. She let that thought slip as Tye tried to communicate his plan.

She tried to follow his hand gestures as he spoke unrecognizable words. She was starting to understand some of those words, but not enough to form a sentence. Still, what she was gleaning from Tye now did not seem like a good plan. He pointed to the city and then made a climbing motion, as though he intended to scale the outer walls and enter the city in secret.

She didn't understand why he wouldn't just go through the city gates. Surely, he could see that scaling the walls would appear suspect if he was caught. Despite this current folly, Tye had safely navigated them through Dwota's Gap, keeping them from being seen until they were close to Krysenthiel. Judging by his insistence that they remain hidden and how he had fought the deserters, Thaerwn had assumed that he was allied with Krysenthiel. But now, she wondered if Tye's loyalties were more complex than she had first thought. Were those deserters enemies to Dwonia or to Krysenthiel? For all she knew about Eklean, Tye and Dwonia could have nefarious intentions toward Krysenthiel.

While Thaerwn trusted Tye, his intent to enter Verenthyl in secret was suspicious. She considered following his lead and scaling the walls with him, but she had been sent on behalf of Aldarch Lerathel. What need did she have to creep into the city? Surely the Luminari would welcome someone on a dignitary's mission.

When Thaerwn did not follow as Tye made to move, he grew frustrated and left her. He was in as much of a hurry as she was and didn't have the time to convince someone he couldn't communicate with. If they could have talked it over, perhaps she might have convinced him that there was no need to sneak into the city or understood why he felt that was the only way.

Nothing was to be done about it. Tye disappeared, impressing Thaerwn by how easily he managed to meld into the landscape. Perhaps he would reach Arenthyl with his method. Turning away, Thaerwn led the horse toward the road that linked Binton and Verenthyl.

Dark Passage

Wyn passed beneath the shade of the blossoming kirenae trees in the park. Even they were expressing delight that not only had Devlyn and Ellendren returned to Arenthyl, but they'd been crowned the Exalted Aryl of Krysenthiel, a title which now encompassed all four elven kindred.

Erynor was likely furious at Uriel's declaration although Wyn didn't think anything would change in how the elves actually governed themselves. Devlyn and Ellendren would never force Fendryl and Dalenya to do anything. If anything, it was a clear message to Erynor who had been promised the same authority by Ramiel. Uriel intended to show that Ramiel had no authority among anacordel and no right to make such promises. Still, whether the Evil One's authority was recognized mattered little if he managed to escape his prison to wreak havoc and spread chaos once again.

Despite knowing how detrimental Ramiel's freedom would be, Wyn was actively seeking a way to enter the Evil One's domain. Unlike the Luminari, whose memories had shortened as an ill effect of the loss of their Life Immortal, the Eldinari had never forgotten about the Void. They knew of that realm's scattered access points and how they were all impassable, or rather, that they were supposed to be impassable. The most well-known path was beneath the Tree of Life's roots; those crystalline roots were all that kept Ramiel from escaping. Wyn didn't want to tamper with that passage, lest he accidentally quicken the Evil One's escape.

The second most well-known entrance was theorized to be beneath Mount Cyngol. While the Sha'ghol had never acknowledged entering the Void, the larger world had condemned them of doing so. There wasn't an elf alive at the time of Erynor's first rise to power who was not convinced of it. And today, those events were irrefutable. The Sha'ghol had gained access to the Void and had taught their fellow Cyndinari elves how to wield tenebrys. That breach of sacred law had led to dwarven schtams falling into Darkness as their mountain homes were corrupted by the polluted effects of the Void, leaking out through Mount Cyngol.

The Shadow Mountains, Mount Cyngol in particular, were to be avoided at all costs. His earliest lessons with Alethea had touched on the perils of those places and the strict instruction to avoid the foothills of those mountains. If he could taste the hints of sulfur in the air from Mount Cyngol, he had already drawn too close.

Just thinking of what he intended to do brought a foul taste to his mouth. He tried to ignore it, but he knew what he had to do. First, he would have to speak with one of the few elves who had willingly gone into the Void and returned—a choice that had cost the elves their Skylands.

Yloran Eth Gnashar basked in the sunlight of a rare opening in the otherwise shaded gardens. A few of her attendants surrounded her. Wyn recognized Clovis and Raelinth from when he had rescued Devlyn in Lankor. Even the way Yloran lounged on the grass made it look as though it was a plush carpet that had been specifically laid out for her pleasure. This was a woman accustomed to the world responding to her every whim. The foolish few who dared refuse Yloran likely never saw the sun rise again. She might have scorned her alliance with Erynor and the Evil One, but that had little to do with her being a virtuous follower of the Light.

Wyn tried not to get distracted by her. Not only was she a stunningly beautiful elf, but even the way she bit into the strawberries she was eating was seductive.

"Wyn Lierafen, child of Eldinare, a pleasure to see you again," Yloran greeted him.

"Yloran Eth Gnashar, you honor me." Wyn bowed. He had no idea how to act around her; his palms were already sweaty.

"So formal. Is it because you are well mannered and genuinely have an esteem for me or…" Yloran bit into another strawberry. "Is it because you desire something of me?" She didn't bother looking at him but took another strawberry from the bowl Raelinth held for her.

"I believe you already know the answer," Wyn replied.

"Hmm," Yloran purred, still lounging on the grass. "I haven't decided whether you are smart or stupid. Judging by what you seek from me, I would say the latter. Others would call you brave or heroic, but frankly, I've never seen a difference between heroes and fools."

"Someone dear to me is trapped in the Void. I can't stand by and let her stay there."

"Dear to you, but not a lover. Most would only risk such an endeavor for their beloved. Love makes people do idiotic things. If I heard correctly, your lover is already here in Arenthyl. She must not be that special if you so willingly try to escape her to enter the Void of all places." Yloran offered a wicked smile.

"I would not have waited to seek your guidance if Kaela was in Alethea's position. As you said, I would have likely acted without thinking." Wyn chose his words carefully. He needed Yloran's help. He couldn't afford to offend her.

"It's still a fool's errand. Does the steward know what you intend? How will the smartly lipped Kaela Lucillia react when she learns that you make for the Void? A realm where the souls lost there are too many to count and its cities large enough to swallow any of Teraeniel's. You realize that by entering the Void you risk joining its inhabitants, yes? By wanting to go there to save another, you might never return."

Wyn sucked in a breath. Kaela knew Alethea had been swallowed by the Void on that fateful Borephaen. She'd comforted him on his return to the Luminari with Devlyn and Rusyl. Still, they had yet to talk of his intent to follow Alethea there. Since being reunited, they spoke only of happy things. Kaela had a way of making his burdens slip off his shoulders. He rarely thought of Alethea's imprisonment when around Kaela.

"Conflicted? Perhaps you should discuss what you intend to do with her before diving blindly into the Void," Yloran said as she turned her head away.

"I'll talk to her before I leave, but I have to know how to go about getting into the Void, and more importantly how to escape it."

"Because of the love you bear for Alethea, yes? Love makes fools of us all. We allow others to dictate our paths simply because we love them or did at one time. It was that foolish emotion which saw me enter the Void all those years ago. I might have been power hungry and ambitious, yes, but I would have never followed the others into the Void if Jaris hadn't been one of them. I grew to resent and despise him in the years after. We weren't the same elves who had gone into the Void. Perhaps if we had known the consequences of embracing that forbidden power, we would have never sought it. Well, some of us. Some would have paid an even higher cost for power. Do you know what I miss most?"

Wyn shook his head. "I didn't realize that the Sha'ghol had to pay a price."

"The Evil One claimed it was not a price, but that it would make us more like him and that we would grow in power if not blinded and distracted as we were. He didn't explain what he meant, only that a piece of us—a weakness in his eyes—would be stripped of us and remain locked away in the Void. A piece, that if I agree to help you, you will retrieve for me."

"And what piece is that?" Wyn risked.

"A piece that you never realize how precious it is until it is gone. A piece that you can never imagine could be taken from you."

"And that is?" he asked again.

"Delight from our senses. I can still see, smell, taste, touch, and hear." She spoke as though each contained untold pleasures that Wyn could hardly fathom. "But not as you do. Any sense of pleasure from my senses was stripped away. Each of us lost something different."

Wyn glanced at the lush fruit and the seductively dressed men around Yloran. This was not a woman who appeared to be without delight. Pleasure clung to her like honey to a beehive.

"Yes, I can see how my lifestyle appears to contradict my account. You could say that they are filling a void. So, what say you, Wyn Lierafen, child of Eldinare? Will you agree to retrieve what was taken from me in exchange for me telling you how to enter and escape the Void? Don't be confused though, you'll only know how to escape after you've collected what is rightfully mine. I wouldn't exactly say I'm a trusting person."

"How will I know how to escape if you don't tell me?"

"Whoever said I wasn't going to tell you? You simply won't remember until you've collected what was taken from me."

Wyn felt Yloran wield animys and his guard instinctively went up as it interacted with him. Every fiber of his being warned against trusting Yloran. And now she was placing a wield over him that would make him forget how the Sha'ghol had escaped the Void all those millennia ago. It settled over him and Wyn felt its chilling effect, as though he had stuck his head in a freezing lake.

"To enter the Void, you must travel to Mount Cyngol. This you've already surmised, I'm sure. But be warned, the Shadow Mountains were once the Evil One's fortress. They have ever been known by that name, for they were where umbrys first materialized in what would become Teraeniel. The Evil One relished in those mountains, especially after Uriel brought lumenys to Teraeniel. It was there that my former Master first began to twist his power, fusing umbrys with the Void and eventually controlling an entirely different power: tenebrys. As the anadel continued Anaweh's creation, the Void became smaller. Favoring it over the three realms, my Master secreted away the remaining Void, scattering portals to pass through across Teraeniel.

"When Anaweh sealed my Master away in the Void, not all my Master's minions had been swept away. The deepest recesses of the Shadow Mountains remained as nests for those beasts as they slept, awaiting their Master's return. It is where most of the Dark Flight hid when more gruesome monsters were sent to the Void with their Master. Make no mistake, Mount Cyngol is being prepared for my Master's return. If that happens, that is where he will launch his revenge against the living. We will be pawns in his war against Anaweh. His fortress will be filled with his supporters and more will arrive each day until their Master is freed and can issue commands directly. Are you positive you want to go there?"

Wyn's mouth went dry. Every thread of his essence revolted against going anywhere near the Shadow Mountains, but he heard himself squeak a barely audible and unconvincing, "Yes." He had heard of the horrors that still called the Shadow Mountains their home and the even worse beasts that had been banished from Teraeniel during the Great Blessing.

"I wonder if you are more fool than brave—that will be decided if you return. To enter the Void, you must pass through Mount Cyngol undetected. Getting to the Void will be the easiest leg of your journey. Deep within the volcano, where it is nearly too hot from the molten rock to breathe, lies a dorthl cavern that is impossibly cold. Only the small in frame can pass through—most anacordel can manage it. But just because we can, doesn't mean we should. Even now, the dwarves of those mountains refuse to approach it, unless forced to mine there.

"From the dorthl cavern, you will have to crawl on your belly before passing over into the Void and into the city called Tosk. I do not know where your Alethea will be kept, but she will likely be in Vasknir, the Evil One's fortress, the same place my senses are kept. But she might not be. The Evil One cares little about anyone escaping the Void, for none have done so without his consent."

Yloran went on, describing how to escape the Void, but Wyn couldn't register her words.

Wyn had known Yloran would demand a price from him; he had known that even before he had left Stellantis. Not knowing how to escape the Void until after retrieving Yloran's senses troubled him. He didn't think she was trying to deceive him, but what if she had made a deal with the Evil One? What if Wyn was to be part of an arrangement for Yloran's freedom?

Wyn wrestled with his thoughts after leaving Yloran. He knew she wasn't being flippant about the possibility of never returning. As far as he knew, only the Sha'ghol had entered the Void and escaped. And in doing so, they had left with a new power and were loyal to the Evil One. Wyn wouldn't be able to leave in the same way they did.

He had considered leaving Kaela a letter, telling her what he intended. He feared she would never speak to him again if he did though, not wanting to risk that in the chance he did return. No, he had to tell her in person. He had to tell her directly that he might never return.

"What's wrong?" Kaela asked as she entered the drawing room in her apartment. Wyn's head snapped up in surprise. "You do realize I've been learning to tap my inner senses and broaden my awareness of others? Your anxiety is thick enough to slice and serve on a platter."

"You must have found a good tutor to have learned so quickly." Wyn had spent too many hours to count here in Kaela's drawing room as her tutor. Some of that time had even been dedicated to its intended purpose.

"Don't pretend like you've had nothing to do with it. Now, what has you so troubled?" She crossed the room and took his hand in her own. Her light skin contrasted with his much darker skin.

Sweat beaded his brow. He hadn't been this nervous since he was a child and had broken one of his mother's favorite vases. Inhaling a steadying breath, he said, "I'm going to follow Alethea into the Void and bring her home."

"And you intend to do this alone?" Kaela's voice was unreadable. Wyn couldn't tell if she was mad, hurt, or worried.

"I can't ask Devlyn to come with me; he and Ellendren are needed here."

"They aren't the only capable elves at your disposal, you know."

"Surely you're not recommending yourself?" Wyn didn't have it in him to describe how dangerous the task he was setting himself on was. He feared if he spoke it aloud, even to convince Kaela to not follow him, he would shy away from the task.

"Don't be ridiculous," Kaela said. Wyn exhaled in relief. "Not that I wouldn't be useful. I'm hardly defenseless." She flashed the hidden dagger Duke Farneis had given her in Sudern.

"I doubt daggers—any weapon—would prove useful where I'm going." The fear rose in his throat, and he forced the bile down. "Who were you considering?"

"Who better to go to the Void with you than one who has already experienced the Void? Aren, of course."

"Would he agree to it? He's largely secluded himself in Parenhal since returning."

"I suppose you'd have to draw him out, as the only way in is to fly over its walls. I'm sure Devlyn would be happy to ask on your behalf. I assure you, I am not the only elf who would prefer that you return whole." She reached for his cheek; their lips touched a breath later.

INTRUDERS

Devlyn woke to Lyren rushing about the bedchamber. Ellendren's attendants had brought them a bowl of fruit so they could have a leisurely morning, a wish that seemed all but dashed now. Lyren was supposed to wait at least another hour before reminding Devlyn of his responsibilities for the day. Despite what was already promising to be a busy day, Devlyn defiantly remained in bed with Ellendren.

Lyren rustled through Devlyn's wardrobe as Ellendren's attendants presented the gown they thought appropriate for the day. The dress reminded him of sunshine with flower petals bunched at the hem. Ellendren nodded her consent to the outfit, knowing that her attendants would return with further options to accompany it.

Lyren pulled out a darker ensemble. While Devlyn's outfit did not have to match Ellendren's garments, it did have to complement hers. They were the Exalted Aryl of Krysenthiel and were expected to always be seen as a single aryl, not an individual ei'denai or ei'terel. They spoke with one voice. Even when separated, they spoke collectively as the aryl.

While it wasn't uncommon for Ellendren's attendants to show Ellendren her outfit for the day this early, it was for Lyren. Devlyn had hoped to lie in bed with his wife and lazily eat fruit as the sun rose, perhaps even banish their attendants for an hour or so. The mornings were one of the few opportunities that they had to spend with only each other—and their attendants. They didn't have to worry about political engagements in their bedchamber. Their time alone in the morning was their haven, giving them the strength for the rest of the day.

Devlyn glared at Lyren.

"Don't give him that look." Ellendren shoved Devlyn as he wrapped his arms around her to keep her from pushing him off the bed.

"Is there at least a good reason for us to be getting dressed so early?" Devlyn grunted, not at all interested in moving.

"Afraid so, Ei'denai." Lyren shuffled forward, letting the dark blue, almost black outfit he held dip a bit. "You've heard that the Dwonians have taken Binton and one of their chiefs has placed himself on the Mindalean throne, yes?"

"I have. I don't understand how that's our concern this morning though. That crown passed from one Erynien puppet to another. What difference does it make this morning?"

"Well, one of them, a Dwonian that is, managed to sneak into Verenthyl last night. He won't say how he managed it; scaling the walls should be impossible, especially for someone with ill intent. The sewers are of course another option, but that sounds vile."

"The Aryl of Verenthyl is more than capable of dealing with an intruder," Devlyn said.

"They intended to. They were going to hold a trial and execute the young man but he claimed he knew you both personally. And he was quite offended at the suggestion that he was a deserter, one of the Dwonians aligned with Erynor, claiming they were no longer Dwonians." Lyren lifted the dark garment again for Devlyn's approval.

"Devlyn, could it be Tye of Tribe Fendur or one of the Sojourners?" Ellendren asked.

"He's the only other Dwonian we've met that wasn't trying to kill us."

"Where are Kyiel and Fyona keeping him now?" Devlyn considered the logistics of travelling to Verenthyl. Being a border city, it would be well defended with a contingent of Guardian knights. He would only have to give Viren a moment's notice before shifting to the edge of Krysenthiel.

"He was brought here to Arenthyl and is waiting in the palace dungeons. The guards who'd brought him would not risk a potential threat in the palace by offering him more comfortable quarters." Lyren shook the garments gently, intent on getting Devlyn's approval.

"Very well." Devlyn stretched, his joints cracking as his body rebelled against starting the day. Finally forcing himself out of bed, he went to the wash basin and splashed water on his face, brushed his teeth, and disappeared behind a door to the lavatory.

After returning to the larger bedchamber, he took the trousers Lyren held and pulled them up as Ellendren's attendants averted their eyes while he dressed. Devlyn saw that Ellendren had yet to move from their warm bed.

"You're not getting ready?" Devlyn asked.

"Not yet. We have a meeting with the Seven Chairs today and I need to be prepared in other ways. They did not provide the purpose of the meeting. I also have a meeting with Etrien. He sounded frazzled."

"Odd. I wonder what about."

"I intend to find out." Ellendren smiled.

"Do you think Therril will want to see his kin again?" Devlyn asked, reflecting on the Aldinari elf who had fallen in love with Lucillia.

"I'm sure he would. Gwilnor must be keeping him busy if he hasn't made the trip to see his family yet." Ellendren's attendants returned with more selections to accompany her outfit.

"He's probably grumbling about starting from scratch after Hannah canceled his theoreticals class."

"I still can't believe Hannah was Tenebrae."

"Myrah must have her hands full as the new chancellor," Devlyn said, pulling the selected shirt over his head.

"Few are as capable and devoted to Gwilnor as she. Well, you should be off; you don't want to keep poor Tye locked up in a cell longer than necessary."

Devlyn kissed Ellendren goodbye and found Viren waiting outside the bedchamber. In a rare occurrence, Viren lounged on a sofa. He stood the moment Devlyn came into the antechamber that served as a buffer between their bedchamber and the rest of the residence.

"Good morning, Viren."

"Devlyn." Viren nodded with a wry smile.

Devlyn wondered what that was about, but neither did he want to ask. Viren, like every other elf who had survived the Fall of Krysenthiel, was sensitive to others' thoughts. The elves didn't intentionally eavesdrop, but it was part of the way they had once communicated—they'd thought it natural. Closing one's mind off had been considered rude and uncouth. Still, Devlyn didn't want to comment on what was going through his subconscious.

"There's always tonight," Viren said, more aware than Devlyn preferred.

"It was supposed to be last night," Devlyn grumbled.

"You'll survive." Viren chuckled softly as they walked through the aryl's living quarters and down the highest spire, continuing through the palace to the dungeons.

A number of elves greeted them as they walked through the public portion of the palace. Devlyn nodded in return, hoping to not come off as haughty.

He was aware that he was sulking as he went down to the belly of the castle, despite trying to hide it. He didn't think there was anything funny about his sexual frustration. He missed Phroenthyl. Their phoenix, attuned with their deepest thoughts and desires, had known when to fly off. Finding solitude for intimacy had been easy there. He and Ellendren only had to avoid a single elf, not a palace overflowing with them. Phroenthyl didn't have any attendants pestering them in the morning or aryls keeping them up late with the world's troubles. While their training had certainly kept them busy, they had had more than adequate time for each other.

The adjustment back to Arenthyl was harder than expected. After the months following their wedding leading up to the removal of the Shroud, the time on Phroenthyl had felt like a gift.

Devlyn's thoughts settled as they reached the dungeons. Even though this part of the palace was intended to contain prisoners and criminals, it had to be the most pleasant dungeon in all Eklean—in all Teraeniel. The space was certainly more welcoming than the old room he had once shared with Alex at the abbey school in Cor'lera.

What Devlyn did not expect was to find Abbie waiting at the dungeon's entry. "Abbie?"

"Hello," she replied.

"What are you doing down here?"

"Presumably waiting to visit the same captive as you are."

"How do you know Tye is here?"

"Because I told him to come."

There was something she wasn't saying, but he knew better than to press Abbie Wintyr. The guards led them further into the dungeon to one of the holding cells and opened the door for them. Devlyn immediately recognized Tye. Despite the years that had passed since they had last seen each other, Tye looked the same. His black hair, dark leathery skin, and currently irritated brown eyes acknowledged them. Tye recognized them just as easily.

"You're no longer a boy, I see." Tye stood and approached Devlyn. The guards made to rush forward to restrain him, but Viren motioned them away; Tye was not their enemy. They reluctantly stepped aside.

"Sorry for all this. Dwonians have been quite aggressive since we last saw each other," Devlyn said.

"You mean deserters. Their ancestors were Dwonians, but never them. They've never felt the Dwonian sun on their back or sand beneath their feet." Tye crossed his arms, disgusted to be confused with deserters.

"Yes, the deserters. But I must ask, why did you sneak into Verenthyl? You could have easily gone through the gates," Devlyn said.

"I assumed the guards would mistake me for a deserter—and rightly so." He glared past Viren and toward the guards. Devlyn wondered if they were the same guards who had brought Tye from Verenthyl and if they'd been kind to him.

"You were scaling the walls," Abbie quipped.

"I didn't see another way into the city."

"I'll reach out to the aryl there and set things straight. You can go back whenever you're ready," Devlyn said.

"I went there because it was the nearest Krysenthien city to Dwota's Gap. But I came to find you."

"Me—what for?"

For the first time, Tye looked uncertain of himself, then glanced at Abbie. "Is there somewhere private we might speak?"

"With the exception of the aryl's bedchamber, this is likely the most private location in the whole palace," Viren said. Devlyn blanched at the reference.

"Right." Tye didn't seem to notice or care about the insinuation. Devlyn reminded himself that it was perfectly natural. People would know and expect him and Ellendren to have sex. If anything, they expected the young aryl to produce an heir to continue the Lorenthien line. "Can you ask the guards to not listen in then?"

Viren glowered at the guards and they stepped out of the cell, their footsteps echoing down the curved corridor.

"My people have been holding a secret for many centuries. Likely since before Krysenthiel fell." Tye paused then and shuffled his feet. "My tribe does not know I am here."

"What are you not saying?" Devlyn asked.

"They will exile me for this—I might have a place among the Sojourners, but Tribe Fendur will not welcome me back to Nynev. They will not let the sand hold my bones after I breathe my last breath. Even if I found the one to bring the seeds back to Dwonia, I doubt I'd be forgiven."

"Surely the punishment for revealing the secret can't be that severe."

Tye took a deep breath, then said, "We have one of the lucilliae. It has given us strength and courage to endure over the years, the fortitude to withstand the deserters and to remain loyal to Dwonia. I would have never come here if not for her." He pointed at Abbie.

"And I told you to bring it here, not to merely tell Devlyn about it. I could have done that myself without troubling you or getting you banished."

Devlyn's lips parted to speak, but he stood in a daze. The orange jewel was the only one not accounted for. Even if the red lucilliae, the heart of the Jewel of Life, was inaccessible, it was still inside the palace—it was still here in Arenthyl and out of Erynor's clutches.

"Take me to it."

Wait. Ellendren chimed in Devlyn's mind. Hearing her in his mind did not bother him, nor that she had known what he would do had she not intervened. What irritated him was that she wanted him to wait. What could be more important than retrieving a lucilliae? Ceurendol could be whole again and Life Immortal returned to the Luminari elves and any who sought it.

We can't wait, Devlyn sent back.

We have a meeting with the Seven Chairs. We must wait.

Devlyn had completely forgotten about their appointment. "We can't leave yet. Ellendren and I have a meeting with the Seven Chairs. Until then, Tye, can you tell me what I should know about Dwonia? And there's no reason for us to remain here in the dungeons. We'll find you more accommodating rooms in the palace."

Viren nodded and made to leave the cell. Tye took a step out of the cell to follow them but the guards returned with their swords drawn, directed at Tye.

"We can't allow the prisoner to be free," the head guard said.

"Do not point your swords at my guest. Tye has done nothing wrong; he's brought us sensitive information, risking much to do so," Devlyn said.

"Ei'denai, he was caught scaling Verenthyl's walls."

"Yes, fearing he'd be turned away from the gate. He is as much aligned to Erynor as I am." A tense exchange followed as Devlyn stared down the two guards before they parted to let Devlyn, Viren, Abbie, and Tye through. The guards might have a captain who would be angry with them for letting their prisoner free but refusing the Exalted Aryl's request would have put a quick end to their careers and possibly result in them standing on the inside of that cell.

The four of them were quick to leave the dungeons and followed the gentle curve of the palace walls. Devlyn was still acquainting himself with the palace's floorplan; he couldn't identify or locate all the rooms, but he knew how to find the spaces he needed to get to. He knew this particular corridor would eventually open to the throne room.

THE SOPHILLIUM

Ellendren waited outside the throne room for Devlyn, speaking with the palace guard standing at the entry. The large double doors towered over them, reminding Devlyn of a golden tree. Intricate silver designs were inlaid in the panels, exemplifying the craftmanship and artistry of the elves. So much of the palace told a story and these doors were no different.

Greeting Ellendren with a kiss, Devlyn nodded at the palace guard who promptly pushed the doors open. They looked large enough to require ten people to operate, but despite their appearance, they slid open easily and Ellendren walked straight to the Crystal Throne in the otherwise vacant room. She took her seat with an elegant twirl. The doors closed behind Devlyn, and she looked at him curiously, wondering why he hadn't yet joined her.

The enormity of what was about to happen weighed on his mind. While the reason for the audience requested by the Seven Chairs still eluded him, that it was happening at all showed his changed status. He well remembered standing before them like a supplicant, hoping to be admitted to Gwilnor Academy as the first kien wielder since the Balance had been broken.

Devlyn could hardly recognize the boy he had been when he had first met the Seven Chairs—he could hardly recognize the world from what he had known of it then. He'd barely understood what an aryl was, and now he and Ellendren were the Exalted Aryl of Krysenthiel!

Reminding himself of who he was, he joined Ellendren on the Crystal Throne.

Once they were both seated, the doors opposite the throne opened, this time to allow entrance to the Seven Chairs of Septyl. He recognized Velaria at once. Exquisite blue fabric clung to her but allowed the vines to breathe more than her previous clothing had ever done. Her cinnamon hair was growing back and curled around her pointed ears.

As he took in the others, he saw that the Chair of Arantiulyn was a different woman. Had a second Chair of Arantiulyn been killed? If so, that was quickly becoming the most dangerous role in Eklean. The Arantiulyns would have to beg their next nominee to take up that mantle if anything happened to this one. He made a mental note to ask Velaria later about Melanie.

Behind the Seven Chairs walked Kevn. *What was he doing here?*

Excited to see his friend once more, Devlyn nearly leapt forward to greet him. Kevn had been his first friend at Gwilnor Academy and they'd briefly lived together before Devlyn had been kidnapped. It was only Ellendren's forceful thoughts that kept him seated before she spoke.

"Welcome to Arenthyl, Chairs of Septyl. Arenthyl's gates will ever be open to you." Ellendren echoed what the Founders of Septyl had told Kien and Kiara.

"Thank you Ei'terel," Paurel said. "We have requested this audience in regard to an official appointment."

"One that has sat empty for far too long," Selenya said.

"What sort of appointment in Septyl requires our consent?" Devlyn asked.

"The Grand Librarian of the Sophillium," Paurel said. "The appointment is made jointly by the Exalted Aryl and the Seven Chairs."

Again, Devlyn wanted to ask why Kevn was present; he must have translated an ancient Aelish manuscript and knew the words of appointment.

"Is there a list of recommendations?" Ellendren asked.

"A single nominee, selected by a memory of Sophie, the founder of the Sophillium." Paurel turned to Kevn, and the Seven Chairs parted for him to come forward. Sophie's face bloomed in Devlyn's mind, a vision from the Aerethyn. Kien and Kiara had viewed Sophie as a highly intelligent and capable elf; Devlyn saw Kevn much the same.

"The last we spoke, I mentioned that something was calling me to Septyl. I had no way of knowing at the time, but Sophie, or a remnant of her, had reached out to me. She beckoned me to Septyl; the calling became too great to ignore. Your alicorn, Laureniel, graciously carried me around the Shroud before diving into it, seeking Septyl. We were attacked by shadow elves and dragons; doubtless Erynor sought to claim the palace-city before the ei'ana could, perhaps even at Ramiel's directive.

"In fleeing our pursuers, Septyl opened to us when we drew near. No one else could enter the sealed city, but I could. I was led to its core, where a sophilliae, with a specter of Sophie within, revealed much to me. Even after the ei'ana arrived, only I could enter the Sophillium, as Sophie's nominee. The Sophillium will only fully open when the next Grand Librarian is installed," Kevn said.

Devlyn tried to conceal his shock even as he felt Ellendren's surprise. He knew Kevn had fantasized about visiting that library, but he had never become an ei'ana. In fact, for the longest time, he had tried to avoid learning to wield, afraid what would be expected of him if he did. As though Kevn being nominated by an elf who had long transitioned to Lumaeniel wasn't enough to swallow, surely the Albiens would demand leadership of Septyl's library.

With a quick glance toward Selenya, Devlyn saw that she clearly held a similar view—by right, the Sophillium belonged under the Albien's care. It didn't matter whether Kevn was most qualified for the position, he was neither an ei'ana nor an Albien. All that considered, no one possessed Kevn's command of Aelish. Despite Kevn's qualifications,

Devlyn remained uncertain why the Exalted Aryl was involved. The library was at Septyl—it belonged to Septyl.

"I might be able to explain that last part," Kevn said. "Sorry, it's impossible to close my awareness to others' thoughts now."

Devlyn chuckled, remembering all too well the brief time he and Kevn had lived together at Gwilnor. Kevn had learned to tap and control his inner sense quickly and had joined in that chorus of elves who reminded Devlyn that he needed to learn to gentle his thoughts. Devlyn again wondered how his thoughts sounded to others.

"The Sophillium does not *just* belong to Septyl, but to all Krysenthiel. Sophie was an ei'ana, so it had always been part of Septyl and was originally constructed in the Septyl Quarter of Mar'anathyl, but the treasure of knowledge stored there ever belonged to the entirety of Luminare. When our ancestors migrated to what became Krysenthiel, the whole Sophillium had been transported to its current location and the ei'ana had built their palace-city around it. Because the library belongs to both Septyl and the Luminari elves, the appointment must be recognized and confirmed by the Seven Chairs of Septyl and the Exalted Aryl of Krysenthiel." Kevn's tone had changed, as though his youth had washed away from his vocal cords, despite his age.

"Do the Seven Chairs of Septyl approve this appointment?" Ellendren asked.

"We do," Paurel said.

Ellendren turned to Selenya.

"It's difficult to object when the founder of the Sophillium names her successor. He will be recognized as an honorary member of Albien. Besides we cannot afford the Sophillium being closed to us any longer," Selenya said.

"Very well. What must we do to finalize the appointment?" Ellendren asked.

Velaria excused herself, returning a moment later with three ei'ana. Two each carried a pillow, one with a scroll, the other with an orb on it while the third carried a bundle of lierathnil.

The ei'ana walked around the Seven Chairs and stood on either side of the Crystal Throne, between the Chairs and Devlyn and Ellendren. The two carrying pillows lifted them. The third ei'ana stood behind Kevn then unraveled her bundle and placed it over Kevn's shoulders. Kevn pushed his arms through the sleeves and wrapped the layered lierathnil robes about his body.

Newly dressed, Kevn stood in the middle of the enclosure, the Chairs behind him, and the Exalted Aryl in front.

Rising from their Crystal Throne, Devlyn and Ellendren closed the circle around Kevn, joining the two ei'ana beside them. Devlyn recalled this ceremony from the Aerethyn. Elyse had warned Ellendren and him not to reveal what they had learned on Phroenthyl, and especially how they had learned it. Feigning ignorance, Devlyn looked to the scroll and raised a questioning eyebrow to Kevn. The Exalted Aryl was supposed to give Kevn the orb, while the Seven Chairs were to present the scroll.

Kevn explained everyone's role in the ritual and provided the words they had to recite in High Aelish. Devlyn and Ellendren both nodded, each perhaps too comfortable with their role in the ceremony. They held the orb while each of the Chairs had a finger touching the scroll.

"Protect and share the knowledge held in the Sophillium. Might that treasure grant wisdom to all who seek it," Devlyn and Ellendren spoke together in High Aelish, offering the orb to Kevn.

"Your halls are welcome in Septyl. May your recorded gifts ever enhance the Ei'ana of Septyl. Might we never grow blind to the wisdom of our past," the Seven Chairs said in unison.

Kevn took the scroll in his free hand. "The Sophillium's treasure will remain open to any friend without malice."

Devlyn had no trouble understanding Kevn's High Aelish; in fact, it was only while using the Aerethyn that he had heard the accent Kevn now used. Based on it, Kevn had been spending every waking moment digesting sophilliae from when the Luminari elves lived on the Skylands.

Kevn had always been a bright student with a seemingly endless font of knowledge, but his younger self wouldn't be able to hold a candle up to what he now knew and was still learning.

"With the Sophillium finally open, is there anything that you would like to request?" Kevn asked. "I've already looked into several matters that might benefit you. I can prepare a formal report."

Ellendren's eyes lit. "Is there anything that references the Evil One and his Void beasts?"

"Dangerous research," Selenya said.

"We must be prepared if he manages to escape his prison and unleashes the Void on Teraeniel. And based on what we have learned, we have no reason to doubt his likely success in that endeavor. Truly, I think the Guardian Senate was envisioned by our ancestors for this very purpose. Teraeniel will only survive Ramiel's return if we collectively resist him and I fear we're running out of time," Ellendren said.

Selenya sucked in her breath and clicked her tongue. "The Albiens will devote ourselves to this. We will study everything we can to keep him locked in his prison and how to defeat him if he escapes the Void." Selenya's concern was clear as she retreated into her mind.

Devlyn hoped they weren't too late, and while he did not want to admit it, he feared they could not stop Ramiel's return to Teraeniel. With few options in preventing Ramiel's escape from the Void, there were still other matters that required his attention. "What about Dwonia? Are there any sophilliae concerning their city, Nynev?" Devlyn asked as Ellendren glared at him. She knew what he intended before the thought was clear to himself.

"What do you wish to learn of the Lost City of Nynev?" Kevn asked.

"It's only lost to some of us." Devlyn took in those gathered here and believed he could trust them with what Tye had told him. These were the Seven Chairs after all. Velaria was one of the first to know about him hunting down the lucilliae that formed Ceurendol. As for the others, the new Chair of Arantiulyn being the exception, they too knew he was seeking the lucillae. "I've learned that the two remaining Dwonian tribes have the unaccounted-for orange lucilliae, the jewel of fortitude."

Velaria understood immediately. "How have you come to this knowledge?"

"Tye is here."

"Is it Nynev that you wish to learn about or Dwonians so that you do not offend them?" Velaria asked, knowing Devlyn all too well.

"Do you think they will prevent us from reclaiming it?" Devlyn asked.

"Hard to say. Dwonians are a proud and protective people. They would've had the jewel for at least fourteen centuries. How many generations would have come and gone with that jewel as their heirloom? It's important to note Tye did not bring the lucilliae with him." Velaria held her chin, thinking to herself.

"In case the Dwonians end up being hostile, I would like to learn as much as possible before travelling there. Are there any maps?" Devlyn asked.

"They aren't exactly maps, but I could show them to you," Kevn said.

"Where are they?"

"In the Sophillium but removing sophilliae is prohibited; not even you can take them out."

"When can we leave?" Devlyn asked, giving Ellendren a pleading look. If not for the Seven Chairs being present, she would have rolled her eyes.

You are very predictable, she shared with him.

"Well, the seguian portal to Septyl is on Arenthyl's lowest tier; in the western crescent port," Kevn said. "When I open the seguian portal directly to the Sophillium, it will be inside this palace. I think it's in the library here."

Devlyn only heard the first half of what Kevn said, a sense of urgency overwhelming him. After Tye's revelation about the lucilliae, he didn't want to waste any more time. In a flash, he bonded with Aliel, reached for Kevn's hand, and shifted, leaving the others behind, including what would be a very agitated Viren in the corridor. The eastern and western crescent ports were closest to the palace but had the least direct paths up the terraces. The slope fell in steep cliffs from the upper tiers, while the southern portion of the city had a more gradual slope into the lake.

Lumaryl walls rose behind them in the western crescent, protecting Arenthyl as the docks opened their arms to the melting lake that had once served as a bustling trade hub.

"I said, all I had to do was open the portal in your palace." Kevn glared at Devlyn, straightening his robes.

"Well, we can't go back; Viren will be furious with me for not waiting."

"Fine." Kevn headed to a single pointed arch of lumaryl and walked through.

Devlyn followed and Arenthyl was replaced by a relatively low city. Not that the buildings were short, only that it was not a tiered city built on the face of a mountainside. Devlyn withdrew from Aliel and walked beside Kevn into the unfamiliar city. The swirling pattern of Septyl's roads or corridors baffled him. He recognized that there was a pattern but tracing their path was disorienting. They passed one plaza after another, each with a fountain and statue.

Reaching the Sophillium, Kevn opened the doors to let Devlyn in and led him into the darkened hall with glowing orbs as the only light. The orbs bobbed up and down in the air, but Kevn walked directly to a specific yet nondescript orb, and encouraged Devlyn to touch it.

Curious about how similar the sophilliae were to the Aerethyn, Devlyn grasped it and his mind was transplanted to Nynev. The city floated in his mind. Most notable was that the city wasn't situated in a desert, but rather, a lush oasis set in a deep canyon. This had to be a memory of the city before Erynor had ravaged Dwonia.

Removing himself from the sophilliae, Devlyn looked around. "Are there more?"

"That should have taken longer." Kevn eyed him skeptically. "The sophilliae take time to understand and maneuver in them. I can't take in an entire sophilliae as quickly as you just did."

"Must have something to do with me being a Phaedryn." Devlyn guarded his memories of Phroenthyl and the Aerethyn.

"Doubtful. Here's another. I'll bring more since you can somehow gather information from them so quickly. And don't think I didn't notice your improved Aelish—High Aelish for that matter! Your pronunciation was near perfect."

Devlyn shrugged his shoulders and entered the next sophilliae.

OLD ALLIANCES

Warm rays of sun fell on Ellendren as she sat on a broad southern balcony overlooking Myrium. The island city sloped gently until the walls cascaded into the River Meyien on either side. Despite the warm spring sun, she felt a chill in the air.

Her honor guard of Guardian knights had arrived the day before, giving Myranda ample notice of her arrival. Ellendren's visit was unexpected though, and she knew the Sorenth queen would have prior commitments, so she was prepared to bide her time in the sun.

"Sorry to keep you waiting," Myranda said, pushing aside the heavy draperies to join Ellendren on the balcony.

"It's good to see you." Ellendren stood and embraced Myranda.

"We just saw each other at your coronation."

"Well, yes, but it was far too short a visit. The ceremony and the feast had me on my feet the entire night, greeting diplomats and nobles, foreign and local alike."

"And that's after returning from who knows where eight months later." Myranda's look was prying.

"Don't be silly." Ellendren knew that look all too well. Whenever they had talked and shared secrets with each other at Gwilnor, Myranda always had the same energetic and secretive expression when she wanted more details. The last time Ellendren had seen it was when Myranda had noticed Ellendren's reaction when she first met Devlyn in the streets of Ceurenyl. In retrospect, Ellendren had never been so bold before. "You know I can't tell you."

"Oh, very well." The expression remained. "I've been briefed to a certain degree as to the reason for your visit. It involves Eddle Port, yes?"

"It does, but more specifically the Daer threat to the people of Eddle Port. We're sending a contingent of Guardians to bolster the city's defenses, and thought Sorenth involvement would be beneficial, particularly because of the ancient friendship that once existed between the Sorenth and Gestorian crowns."

Myranda's blank expression as Ellendren spoke was another tell. Now Ellendren wore the prying look. What was Myranda not saying?

"You know I cannot possibly say," Myranda mocked.

"I sincerely hope you do. What's this about?"

"Donovan, dear." Myranda called from the balcony and to the adjacent room.

An attractive man, wavy brown hair curling behind his ears, strode out onto the balcony, his icy blue eyes piercing Ellendren.

"Ei'terel Ellendren Lorenthien, might I introduce you to His Highness, Donovan Orithil."

Donovan extended his hand to Ellendren and bowed his head. "It is a pleasure to make your acquaintance, Ei'terel."

"Erynor killed the Orithils." Ellendren's mouth gaped in shock that the Royal House of Orithil, Gestoria's monarchy, had survived.

"Just as he killed the Lorenthiens." Donovan smirked, and his hand found Myranda's. "My family suspects that the Erynien Emperor is more interested in slaves and pets than death. After all, what good is a dead monarch to an emperor? Even a rose with thorns is still beautiful."

"Forgive me, but how have we not known? The Erynien Empire last fell twelve hundred years ago. Why has your family not revealed itself? Surely, you know you would have been welcome in Lucillia and now Arenthyl." Ellendren had many questions but limited them.

"Our kingdom was utterly destroyed and our capital of Quellion

reduced to rubble; every Gestorian's pride was shattered. Revealing ourselves before we were ready would have made us vulnerable as we picked
up the debris the Erynien Empire left scattered across the plains."

"And what have you managed in that time?" Ellendren asked in a
whisper.

"As you know, there are no major rivers flowing through Gestoria,
nor do the roads which once connected Gestoria lead anywhere but our
cities. The Plains of Orithil have remained out of Eklean's eye, as there
has been no reason for anyone to look upon the dead kingdom and its
salted ruins." Donovan smiled grimly as he looked south.

"Gestoria's wealth did not come by means of a river, but rather
its coastline. Precisely, the cliffs along the coastline, the finest and purest
limestone Eklean has ever known; only stone from the Skylands is a more
preferable building material. Every Thellish palace south of the Laudi-
en Mountains used our limestone. Even the nascent Evellion found it
worthwhile to import.

"When my family secretly returned to Gestoria, we went to Eddle
Port and found the people there had not forgotten their forbears' craft,
but out-of-work masons were everywhere. Eddle Port was the Gestorians' last haven. The economy slowly recovered as our quarries reopened,
but we were careful to make it seem to be Eddle Port's success, not
Gestoria's. Tiel was our main concern.

"In time, we felt confident enough in our economy and people that
we believed it was time to rebuild Quellion. Our population was stable
again, and the number of masons increased with our growing numbers.
It was not just our confidence that carried us back to Quellion, but the
salted plains began to show life once more. Our finest masons and architects travelled north to the ruins. None of the buildings or walls stood,
but the foundations were whole and strong.

"Any reusable stone was used as the core of the outer city walls.
The castle followed, meant to stand as a beacon across the plains for
Gestorians, as well as a fortress to protect the people we had failed in the

past. Our masons ensured that no one would ever again be trapped in the city during a siege. Quellion is near complete and whole once more, and many of our masons' children have devoted themselves to our military, while our best masons have reestablished their guild. That Elothkar is also being rebuilt is a boon to our quarries and masons, as both have been supporting its reconstruction."

Ellendren listened in awe. The similarities between Gestorians and the Luminari were incredible. In fact, they seemed too amazing. *Can you confirm this story? Go to Quellion,* she conveyed to Tariel. She found the prince believable, but she had to see it for herself. She imagined how a resurrected Gestoria might tilt this war in their favor. Gestoria was a southern kingdom, and currently the only threat to the Erynien Empire came from the north.

Ellendren felt Tariel's bond in the glow in her eyes and knew Myranda and Donovan would see it. Amid the vast grasslands speckled with farms and tiny villages stood a city of shimmering white on the Plains of Orithil. Every watch tower rising above the city culminated in a gilded dome. The entire city was built of the limestone of Thoril's Cliffs. In the center of the city was the castle, speckled with domes and turrets, reminding Ellendren of Myrium.

Watch towers were anchored to robust foundations along the city's defensive walls which in turn ballooned outward, each serving as a fortress. Waving in the open wind above every domed spire, short or tall, flew a winged, white gold lion on a blue field. As Ellendren prepared to withdraw from Tariel, her doubts appeased, a rush of white gold feathers soared past Tariel.

Tariel swooped upward, the creature hovering aloft before her. Through Tariel's eyes, Ellendren saw a creature that should have been as extinct as Gestoria and House Orithil should be. The lion's mane framed its great head and feathered wings held the creature aloft. A knight in shining metal sat on the winged lion's back, her visor up. The winged, white gold lion was painted on the polished metal of her armor, appearing silver in the sunlight.

Ellendren saw the woman's confusion as she looked at Tariel.

Fear not, this is a phoenix. And it is bound to me, High Queen Ellendren Lo-renthien of Krysenthiel. Ellendren shared her thoughts with the woman who didn't seem disturbed by the intrusion into her mind. *I am currently with Prince Donovan and Queen Myranda in Myrium.*

None of this is possible, the woman replied mentally.

What is your name?

Princess Victoria, Donovan's older sister.

If you can manage it, I would like to arrange an audience with your king and queen. It can be in Arenthyl, or we can meet in Quellion. I just learned that Gestoria has risen from the ashes, and it is vital that your kingdom be involved in Eklean's stand against the Erynien Empire's aggression. Ellendren's thoughts poured from her to the skeptical Victoria.

I'll ask my father, King Leonard, about arranging an audience. But I expect to learn from my brother the details of your meeting before anything is agreed. This is not possible.

Ellendren sent affirmation across the mental connection, filled with understanding. Withdrawing from Tariel, Ellendren returned wholly to the balcony.

Myranda and Donovan looked worried.

Her eyes returned to normal; they were still golden, but they no longer shone with a light of their own. "Forgive me, I had to see for myself. I met your sister. You need to tell her that she and I did speak and accepting my invitation to Arenthyl is vital for our survival."

"I don't understand; what exactly did you do?" Donovan asked, bewildered.

"It's too difficult to explain, as it has to do with me being a Phaedryn. But Gestoria must resume its place on the Guardian Senate. It's our best chance to unify Eklean, and the rest of Teraeniel against the Erynien Empire." She didn't mention Ramiel. There was no need to terrify Myranda and Donovan further.

Donovan was thoughtful. "I suppose avoiding the conflict is not possible going forward. Naturally, I can't speak for my father; the decision belongs to him. That being said, he did send me here to get to know the Sorenth queen." Myranda blushed at Donovan's smile.

"Are you..." Ellendren trailed off, expecting Myranda to know her question.

"We've only just met." Myranda's cheeks darkened briefly before the blush subsided. "On a different note, that was quite the coronation ceremony. An irythil and an enthiel in attendance."

Donovan's mouth gaped. "You're still in touch with anadel?"

"Uriel was frozen in Lake Saeryndol, the Shroud acting as an extra lock to contain the enthiel. Since we've returned to Krysenthiel and the Shroud is destroyed, Auriel has returned to us." Ellendren looked from her folded hands to Donovan, expecting him to ask more.

Donovan sat still, his face turned to slate, unreadable.

Bells chimed somewhere. Ellendren mentally counted them off, the final gong numbering thirteen. "I'm sorry, but I must be leaving. I promised I'd return at the thirteenth hour."

"Who demands Eklean's high queen return at a specified hour? Surely, it's not Devlyn; I expected more from him," Myranda said, almost scolding.

Ellendren stood and tapped that quiet space within her heart. Tariel still soared over Gestoria, but only for a moment longer as Ellendren felt her body transform with light.

Startled, Donovan pushed himself away from the table, his chair falling back. Myranda remained sitting; a smile crept to her lips as she looked from the corner of her eyes at Donovan.

"He would not dare, but Jeanne Darkel, First of the Guardians, would and does. The other aryls also expect me to return safely to Arenthyl at the agreed-upon time."

"Funny to think Arenthyl is considered safe once more," Myranda said.

"If only your last visit hadn't been so brief. There is so much to see," Ellendren said.

"I arrived a week before you did, not that we had much warning of your return and coronation. My own guard took every precaution in reaching Krysenthiel without any trouble. Admittedly, I was hoping to spend more time with you. They didn't even let you brush your hair before the ceremony began! Granted you looked gorgeous despite your journey."

"You are too kind. It was wonderful to meet you, Donovan; be sure to tell your sister she's not losing her mind." With a final smile at them both, Ellendren saw in her mind's eye the great doors leading into Aerodhal. The shift was abrupt, and her eyes stung from the light, something that had become rare since she first bonded with Tariel.

Withdrawing from Tariel, Ellendren's vision returned to normal, and her bright surroundings dimmed. She had grown accustomed to seeing in that brightness for seven years, and admittedly, found it odd to look at Teraeniel from a different perspective.

Preferring to soak in the sun's rays, she walked to the far end of the great plaza in front of the palace. She found its shape interesting; it was modeled after the front-most façade of the palace with a wide pointed arch and its elevated dais mimicked the lines of the entry portal.

Looking over the city, Ellendren watched as elves carried out their business in the lower tiers. They walked through streets shaped by the lumaryl buildings and crossed intricate arched bridges. The long deceased Luminari elves who had sung Arenthyl into existence had created beautiful statues and palaces from lumaryl. Noticing where the art stopped and the architecture began was impossible—a common feature in elven architecture.

Closing her eyes, Ellendren heard the soft rumble of the city, but the lack of any sound from the lake was disturbing, especially after just visiting Myrium where the River Meyien rushed along either side of the island city. Lake Saeryndol was still mostly frozen. If she walked into the lake, the melted waters might reach her waist now. Ellendren looked forward to the waters fully melting; the frozen lake felt unnatural.

Her head tilted westward toward where she assumed Aldinare soared. She refused to accept that an entire population was lost. Aren had done a valiant thing all those years ago when he led the Phaedryn to rescue as many elves from Aldinare as possible, but so few had managed to escape the Skyland's fate. Aldinare had supported the largest elven population, a population still trapped there and possibly twisted after the Darkness had fallen on them.

"Ei'terel?" came a voice from behind.

"Etrien, how can I help you?" Ellendren asked, opening her eyes to find the Aldinari elf.

"Aldinare."

"The Skyland has weighed heavily on my mind as well," Ellendren admitted.

"In what way?"

"It's hard to describe. The Darkness that consumed the Skylands is related to tenebrys and the Void, stemming from the Evil One. We know his chains weaken, but not why." Ellendren accompanied Etrien to one of the gardens.

"You are not alone; Aldinare has weighed heavily on all our minds, and even more so recently. Our people have not perished, but they suffer," Etrien said.

"How could they survive the Darkness? Wouldn't the Void have suffocated them?"

"I cannot say, but they are refused Anaweh's Call because of it. I fear the Evil One's influence is much stronger than we had assumed and has been for a long time."

Ellendren made a mental note to visit the Sophillium to learn everything she could about Ramiel. His name and influence on Teraeniel were worrisome. How could anyone prevent someone from transitioning to Lumaeniel?

Ellendren and Etrien left the seventh tier and walked toward a park with an exposed root of the Tree of Life. Beautiful stonework joined buildings and arched bridges spanned the streets. Everything in Arenthyl had a statuesque quality, and the concave and convex lines of the architecture provided a fluid character to the urban fabric. Ellendren's favorite aspect was that as one ascended or descended the various tiers, the workmanship and attention to detail of the buildings was consistent. While Aerodhal was recognizably extravagant and massive, visible from any point in the city, the same process of wielding the palace into existence had been used in the lower tiers.

As they walked into the park, Ellendren saw that a large gathering of Aldinari filled much of the open space. Turning from the gathered elves to Etrien, Ellendren asked, "How do you know the elves on Aldin-are still live?"

WESTWARD CALLING

Devlyn hunched over the map table in Aerodhal. It was unlike any he had ever used, including the woven lierathnil maps. Sculpted of lumaryl and like the lierathnil maps, it could be altered to view any location in Teraeniel. Devlyn currently had it set to the area around Nynev, as they had to find the safest route there to retrieve the lucilliae. Jeanne and Viren were with him, as was Tye who looked just as shocked as Devlyn had been when he first used the map table.

"If we were to shift there, how far outside the city should we appear without causing any alarm?" Devlyn asked.

"Sand warriors will confront us the moment we enter this perimeter." Tye drew a circle with his finger around what looked like a large sand dune.

"And there's no way to give them notice of our arrival?" Viren asked.

"Doing so will only put more sand warriors between us and the entrance. No outsider has entered Nynev; not even before the deserters joined the Erynien Empire."

"What's stopping us from shifting to an entrance then? I'd rather avoid a fight with our allies." Devlyn stared at the map, hoping a solution would present itself. The remaining tribes of Dwonia had yet to send representatives for the Guardian Senate to Arenthyl and Tye had come here without his people's permission. If the Dwonians had sent a representative, they could have a more formal discussion. Surely the Dwonians would want Ceurendol made whole again. They would benefit from the Jewel of Life just as any other people would if they so wished.

"Sneaking into Nynev will be viewed as cowardly. My people won't forgive it."

"How else are we supposed to open dialogue then? If not for returning the lucilliae, surely they're aware one of the deserters now calls himself a chief-king and has an army in Dwota's Gap. Are the remaining tribes just going to ignore the threat?" Devlyn didn't mean to let his frustration bubble over, but now that it had, it was too late.

"It is not our way." Tye glared at Devlyn. "Nor can we abandon Nynev. If left undefended, the deserters will take it—we do not have the numbers to defend Nynev and confront them."

"If there's little else we can plan for, we ought just go there now," Devlyn said, frustrated.

Devlyn, Ellendren's voice bloomed in his mind. *I'm with Etrien. Come join us, it's urgent.*

Devlyn grumbled under his breath. "Perhaps not yet. Ellendren requests our presence."

"Is it more important than retrieving the jewel?" Tye asked.

"I suppose we'll find out." Devlyn turned from the map table and made to leave, Viren, Jeanne, and Tye following.

Devlyn felt that she wasn't inside the palace, but in one of the upper tiers where the Aldinari resided. Devlyn thought she might be in a park with one of Verakryl's exposed roots.

As they made their way out of the palace, Devlyn noticed human and dwarven diplomats among the elves going about their business. They were here as representatives for their people, intending to serve on the Guardian Senate. Informal sessions had taken place, but Devlyn and Ellendren had yet to properly open the Senate Chambers. Only some of the original representatives had made the journey to Arenthyl. There were far too many absent human representatives from other continents.

The merpeople had yet to send their delegates and Devlyn didn't know if the giants ever would. He had to remind himself that only some of the giant clans had attacked Everin. There were many more giants scattered across the frozen north and there were likely more aligned with human kingdoms than to the Erynien Empire.

Fortunately, as he passed through the throngs, he did not see Aorinol. He did not want to deal with the Daer senator now. Devlyn had accepted that not every Daer wanted to colonize Eklean and enslave her inhabitants, but that didn't mean he had the will to listen to the long-winded Aorinol trying to get him to visit Daereneth, something that Devlyn knew was inevitable.

Rounding another bend in Arenthyl, they came to a park filled with kirenae trees. Devlyn felt Ellendren before seeing her. Many Aldinari were there, gathered around the Verakryl root where two elves were speaking. Excited whispers abounded, many speaking hopefully of Aldinare.

That didn't make any sense. Aldinare was lost to the Darkness—it had been lost since all the Skylands were consumed and the elves forced to leave. The elves that had escaped Aldinare's fate, and their descendants crowded the garden, listening to Ellendren and Etrien speak. Even Therril had made the journey to Arenthyl, happy to be rejoined with the family he had left behind. He too was anxious to meet other Aldinari elves again. The crowd listened excitedly to their conversation. Some of the younger elves sprinted away to tell others what was happening.

The crowd parted for Devlyn and his small entourage. Aliel and Tariel soared above, winding downward toward him and Ellendren. Ellendren smiled as he arrived; she could barely contain her excitement. What could be more exciting than possibly recovering another lucilliae?

Etrien and Therril greeted Devlyn, but neither held his attention, as another elf stood there. She looked unlike any elf he had ever seen, although she had pointed ears much like his own. She was bald, and her skin was dark purple with blue markings flowing across like marbled veins. She stepped forward. "Ei'denai Devlyn Lorenthien, I am Thaerwn of Zarathyl. I was summoned by Lerathel of Val'quin and instructed to come to Arenthyl."

"It is an honor to meet you, Thaerwn of Zarathyl." Devlyn pressed his palm to his right chest and bowed. He barely registered that they were speaking High Aelish.

"Thaerwn has brought the most incredible, the most wondrous news, Devlyn!" Ellendren bounced in elation as Devlyn tried to figure out where Zarathyl was and who Lerathel of Val'quin was. He recognized the latter's name, but he had no idea where Zarathyl was located. "Devlyn, Thaerwn is an Aldinari elf—she came here from Aldinare, from the Sanctum of Val'quin, Aldarch Lerathel's sanctum!"

"Forgive me, Ei'terel. Those of us who live in Aldinare's cities and were touched by the Void are aelith now. It has not touched every elf on Aldinare, as the sanctums were fully protected when that foul fate befell us. The aldarchs expanded their protection to Aldinare's cities when they were able to, to keep the madness from eating away at our minds. But those who lived beyond the aldarchs' protection have deteriorated and become neridu. They are lost to us."

"How did you manage to leave Aldinare? We thought that anyone who tried to leave would be struck down by tenebrys lighting." Devlyn's mind whirled. Thaerwn's presence here should not be possible. Aren and a hundred Phaedryn had helped get as many Aldinari elves away from the doomed Skyland as possible, but even the Phaedryn could not save them all. Only a small percentage had managed to escape from a single city near the edge of the Skyland.

"Lerathel explained that she and the other aldarchs have been biding their time. While the aldarchs are all incredibly powerful, they could not manage to free Aldinare or its inhabitants from the Void on their own. When you destroyed the Shroud with all the Luminari and Auriel and Uriel, a cosmic wave reached every corner of Teraeniel. The aldarchs have waited thousands of years for such an event to free their home and people from the Darkness."

"What did they do?"

"The aldarchs could not banish the Darkness, so they wrenched our Skyland from its place in the clouds and for the first time in thousands of years, we saw the sun and stars twinkling after twilight. Vespiel, the evening star and our guardian, shone bright that night."

"Vespiel's long lamentation has ended; her song will be of joy once more," Etrien said, delighted.

Thaerwn nodded. "Aldinare no longer soars among the clouds. But we are not as we once were, and not just in appearance. Before Lerathel summoned me to Val'quin, I worshipped her. We aelith had mistaken the Aldarchs' Chamber in our various cities for shrines and devoted ourselves to them. We had forgotten Anaweh and the anadel and took the aldarchs as gods instead. The priests of the dead god, Theseryn, will be difficult to sway. Even though Vespiel has revealed herself to me, I too find it difficult to believe that Aldarch Lerathel is not a god."

Devlyn knew Thaerwn was saying something crucial, but the only thing that had resonated was that Aldinare was no longer in the sky. Before Etrien could comment on the aelith, Devlyn asked, "If not in the sky, where is Aldinare now?"

"I don't know the names of the places on this land below. Aldinare fell into a large body of water, salty and deadly to drink from. From there, an alicorn carried me across that water and left me in a desert to cross alone, with the setting sun at my back. It was there that I met the man standing beside you." She nodded at Tye. "Together, we crossed Dwota's Gap and the mountains gave way to a lush and vibrant land in stark contrast to the desert. Tye tried entering the city, but I continued and found the lake surrounding the mountain that holds Verakryl." Thaerwn looked from Devlyn to Ellendren, hoping they would know Aldinare's current location.

"The ocean you landed in, was it coated in fog?" Ellendren asked, referring to the narrow Misty Sea that separated the continents of

Eklean and Qien.

"No, the waves were large and treacherous. I don't think any vessel could manage those."

"The Tempestien Sea then." Ellendren nodded to herself.

"Thaerwn, to what end did Lerathel send you to us?" Devlyn asked.

"She and the other aldarchs desire your presence on Aldinare. Lerathel would not say what they wished to discuss with you, only that you must travel with haste."

"What of the Aldinari here in Arenthyl? Are we permitted to come as well?" Etrien asked, longing resounding in his voice.

"Lerathel did not mention others, just the Lorenthien aryl. Perhaps representatives can accompany the aryl," Thaerwn said. Tears glistened in Etrien's eyes. His people here in Arenthyl had believed that they would never see the land they had fled or the people they had left.

"Thank you," he managed, dabbing at his eyes with a piece of cloth.

Tye stood quietly behind Devlyn. "Forgive me for interrupting, I wasn't able to follow your conversation—I know the elves had their language before, but I didn't think anyone still spoke it—not until I met Thaerwn, of course."

Devlyn turned to Ellendren. "Were we speaking Aelish just then?"

"High Aelish."

"I didn't realize it."

"It likely has something to do with our time away."

Devlyn nodded. The Common Tongue had not yet been formed in the time of Kien and Kiara; the elves had exclusively spoken what was now called High Aelish and would have only recognized it as Aelish in their day. All the memories they had left behind for the Phaedryn were in that language. Turning to Tye, Devlyn forced himself to speak in the Common Tongue. "Aldinare is now in the Tempestien Sea, west of Dwonia. We must go there."

"West? Why not stop in Nynev on the way?" Tye asked.

Ellendren looked at Devlyn. She knew the importance of retrieving the lucilliae as much as he did. "I suppose we should. Tye, would your people welcome Devlyn and me, Thaerwn, Viren, and Etrien to Nynev?"

"They won't be pleased about it. As I told Devlyn, I'm risking banishment for telling you that we have it. I'd rather not consider my punishment for revealing Nynev's location as well."

"There's not much to be done about it then. Were you able to devise a strategy to reach Nynev?" Ellendren asked, aware of some of their earlier meeting.

"It sounds like all we can do is simply show up uninvited. To send any delegation or message in advance of our arrival would have the Dwonians even more on guard," Devlyn said as a shadow darkened the park and the sounds of horns and bells alerted the city of an unexpected arrival. Looking up, he saw the underside of a dragon—the sun made it difficult to determine who it was or what flight they belonged to. All he could see was a darkened mass and extended wings. A second dragon joined the first, and assuming it wasn't an attack, the two dragons had to be Liara and Rusyl. Prya was likely riding Liara while Jaerol and Liam rode Rusyl. The three of them, dragon, elf, and lethien, had become inseparable.

The park didn't have a clearing large enough for the dragons, so they headed for the broad street outside the park, then came back to meet with Devlyn and Ellendren. The gathered elves parted for the new arrivals, the dragons now in their smaller forms, and the horns stopped.

Prya bowed to Devlyn and Ellendren, "The Ealyn of Tenethyl have sent a message."

Devlyn had not heard anything from the ealyn since they had given him the seeds that had become his and Ellendren's verathn. They had promised to help in the battles to come, but never specified when or how they would lend their strength. "What message do they send?"

"Remember who the aldarchs are and from whence they came," Prya said.

Devlyn did. He nearly said that they were draelyn and that Aldarch Gael of Quel'anir would have become queen if she had stayed to rebuild Tenethyl. "What does this change?"

"You will not be travelling to Aldinare alone." More horns and bells pealed before Prya could finish speaking. "Ealyn Niron of the Sapphire House and Ealyn Allister of the Opal House, as well as Caephenol, Primus of the Blue Flight, and Aerinol, Primus of the White Flight have sent the bulk of those who will be joining you, but every dragon flight and house has sent a force to accompany you to Aldinare. Do know that they will not take part in Erynor's war. You already know of the conflict that we prepare for."

It only took a moment before dozens of dragons of various colors soared over Arenthyl, flying around the city's lofty spires. Devlyn had only seen so many dragons flying together at Tenethyl. The dragons had largely fallen into myths and legends across Eklean, and few knew that the draelyn had ever existed. "Well, if there's one way to remind Ramiel that we won't easily bend to his will, this should do it."

———

The dragons gathered on the banks of Mount Verinien as close to Arenthyl as their size allowed. While dragons could transform to a smaller size, Devlyn had yet to meet one who preferred it. Instead, they warmed their scales on the mountain's southern slopes, soaking in the sun.

Hundreds of images of dragon greetings filled Devlyn and Ellendren's minds. Many of the older dragons had been here before, when elves last called Krysenthiel home, and some even before that. Devlyn and Ellendren walked among them, sending out their own images of welcome. Viren accompanied them as always, as did Jaerol, Liam, Rusyl, Prya, and Liara. Rusyl and Prya stayed in their larger forms among their dragon kin.

While there were dragons of many different flights, there were noticeably more white and blue dragons. As Devlyn took in the sight, two dragons stood out. He'd only seen one dragon equal to their size. The two, one white and one blue, shared similar images of greeting, but theirs were deeper, ancient, and conveyed who they were. They transformed to their smaller sizes, the blue dragon, Caephenol, was male and the white dragon, Aerinol, was female. Like all dragons, their smaller forms were still much larger than elves.

Devlyn and Ellendren bowed to the Primuses of the Blue and White Dragon Flights. "You honor us in leaving your lairs and coming to us," Devlyn said, remembering the etiquette he had learned from Lyvenol.

"We are not the first primuses you have met." Aerinol tilted her head, intrigued. "How has Lyvenol been?"

"The Primus of the Gold Flight is well. He gave us the impression that we would have to seek you out in your lairs for an audience," Ellendren said.

"Time is not on our side and already you must journey to far off lands," Caephenol said.

"The dragon flights will aid you in this war, but know, it will only get worse before a sliver of light returns," Aerinol said, prophetic.

"Thank you." Devlyn didn't want to think of how things could get worse. The threat of Ramiel ever looming over their heads was likely the reason.

As Devlyn and Ellendren spoke with the two primuses, a white dragon approached Viren. Devlyn didn't pick up on the images passing between them, but there seemed to be an established familiarity between them.

"Falthion had hoped you would return to Glacien, Viren," Aerinol said.

"I longed to return, especially after Reinyn was killed at Septyl,"

Viren said, revealing another sliver of his history. "I can't help but think we could have made a difference if we had bonded before the war started."

"You were young; too young for such a bond," Aerinol said.

The white dragon, Falthion, nudged Viren with his head. "But not anymore it seems," Viren said, climbing onto the dragon.

"Not anymore." Aerinol agreed. "Complete your bond and may the White Dragon Flight be Guardians once more."

"Not only the White Flight," Caephenol said.

Devlyn tried to catch up. "The dragons were Guardians and were bonded with Guardian knights?"

"How else did you imagine we reached every corner of Teraeniel?" Viren asked before Falthion stretched out his wings and carried them up into the sky.

SHADOWS OF THE PAST

Elves, draelyn, and dragons gathered at Arenthyl's lowest tier. News of the expedition to Aldinare had spread like wildfire. There wasn't a child who didn't know about it. The Aldinari had gathered in force, despite only Etrien and Therril among their people making the journey.

Devlyn could hardly believe that the Skyland had been wrenched out of the clouds and now floated in the Tempestien Sea as would any island. But Aldinare's underside would not stretch to the bottom of the ocean. The Skyland's foundation might delve far below the waves, for Aldinare was known to be vast, but surely it didn't have the depth to reach the ocean bed.

Jeanne stood beside Devlyn and Ellendren, giving them both another scrutiny. "I understand that you must go but know that your leaving troubles me greatly."

"I too feel uneasy about leaving so soon after returning to Arenthyl," Ellendren said. She glanced behind her and up at the majestic city of golden spires.

"We'll be surrounded by dragons and draelyn, to say nothing of Viren." Devlyn winked at the Guardian knight.

"Don't expect flattery to work if you try to sneak off without me," Viren said, reminding Devlyn of the far too many occasions he had already done so. Toryn stifled a laugh. As Jeanne's squire, she too would remain in Arenthyl. Her sword's reputation, Shroudsbane, had increased since Devlyn and Ellendren had returned and every monarch in Eklean had all but demanded to see the sword that had destroyed the Shroud.

"You'll answer to both Viren and Falthion if you try again," Toryn said, admiring the white dragon who had bonded with Viren. Viren scratched the dragon's chin; a delightful rumble arose.

"Still, the Erynien Empire's sporadic skirmishes near Eandyl and Verenthyl are peculiar. Erynor has never been known to rein in his aggressive tactics. I fear he's biding his time and planning something big," Jeanne said.

"We've looked at this from every angle," Ellendren said, with a hint of tired frustration. "What aren't we seeing?"

"Whatever it is, we're in the dark. There haven't been any reports of Deurghol or shadow elves. Their whereabouts are entirely unknown, as are the Erynien legions that mysteriously vanished after we reclaimed Arenthyl." Jeanne frowned as more dragons flew above the port.

Wyn, Kaela, and Aren came forward with Eolwn, Wyn's griffin and Leithel, Alethea's griffin. Devlyn's insides twisted, knowing what Wyn intended to do.

"Don't look at me like that," Wyn said, forcing a smile.

"We're allowed to worry about you," Kaela said, holding his hand as she turned to Aren. "You'll keep him safe?"

"We'll keep each other safe." Even with the Void's corruption stripped from him, Aren remained stony, mourning the loss of his phoenix and dealing with the weight of his memories.

"Is there no other way?" Ellendren asked.

"Alethea needs our help. I can't do nothing while she suffers. Even Boriel cannot bear Alethea suffering; she came to me, encouraging my decision to find a way into the Void."

"What path will you take?" Jeanne asked, already having made her displeasure known at his decision.

"We'll fly with the others to Dwota's Gap, then we'll go south along the western ridge until we reach Mount Cyngol," Wyn said.

"Won't Mount Cyngol be heavily guarded?" Ellendren asked.

"Parts are but not all of it. There's little reason to guard a way into the Void," Aren said.

"Are we positive flying through Dwota's Gap is the best route?" Devlyn asked.

"We won't land or rest in Mindale. We'll camp in Evellion before passing through Dwota's Gap. Flying over the mountains is of course an option, but the dragons discouraged doing so. They say it's an unnecessary risk," Viren said.

"At least the deserters have been reasonably content in Mindale, their agreement with the former Duke of Overen to assassinate Lara and Alex notwithstanding," Ellendren said.

"They won't remain so," Tye said, arms crossed. "They have forsaken our ways and trample on our traditions. If not dealt with, they will try to expand their domain. Their control over the Gap is troubling."

Jaerol and Liam shared a private look. "He's right. Cairn is too cruel and ambitious to stay peaceably in Mindale. Erynor will expect him to launch a campaign from there," Jaerol said.

Devlyn knew now wasn't the time to ask Jaerol and Liam how they knew about Cairn's motives. Had something happened between them and the chief-king? That would have to wait though, as they'd wasted enough time on the docks. He took Ellendren's hand, and she squeezed his in return. She had been ready to leave for Aldinare the moment she'd learned it was accessible. They bonded with Aliel and Tariel and the gathered crowds blossomed in light.

"Are you okay with us leaving again so soon?" Devlyn asked Kaela.

"I'll manage to survive the aryls somehow." Kaela batted her eyelashes.

"Don't pretend you're not thrilled about it." Ellendren turned on her sister, eyes alight. "You wouldn't admit it when we came back from Phroenthyl, but you would not have complained if we had been gone longer. And to no one's surprise, you thrived as our steward."

"The other aryls didn't mind?" Devlyn asked.

"Of course, they did. That's part of the reason I love it so much," Kaela said.

"Farewell, sister. Don't drive any of the aryls or dignitaries away."

"I wouldn't dream of it."

Ellendren's smile was infectious as she leapt into the sky. Dragons of various flights dotted the sky in a glittering array of colors, many of them carrying draelyn to assess the situation on Aldinare. The Skyland was the only thing to have had any direct contact with the Void. Only the Sha'ghol had ever had the opportunity to directly study the effects of the Void.

Knowing that he had dawdled too long, Devlyn leapt to join the others aloft. With every flap of his wings, he flew higher, and soon, Arenthyl was below and behind him. He joined Ellendren beside the great throng of dragons, Falthion carrying Viren and Tye close behind them.

Fog and mist covered Lake Saeryndol, rising from the ice. The Laudien Mountains seemed to cup the frozen lake, as though it was something precious with Mount Verinien and Verakryl as its prized jewels.

As the sun dipped and twilight took hold, the expedition angled downward toward a valley in southwestern Evellion. The most direct route would have taken them through Mindale and right over Binton, but no one wanted to risk an encounter with the Erynien Empire. Even as they set up camp, the dragons stayed in their larger forms. While they didn't anticipate uninvited visitors, neither did they want to encourage it.

Ellendren had barely landed before joining some of the draelyn to practice jienzu. She had learned much from Prya, but she had so much more to ask the draelyn of the other houses.

Before leaving Arenthyl they had agreed that only Devlyn, Tye, and Viren would go to Nynev, while Ellendren and the others would continue toward Aldinare. Dozens of dragons descending on a hidden city would not keep it hidden for long. Tye had sacrificed enough—he didn't want to also be responsible for leading the deserters to the Lost City of Nynev. Hopefully their time in Nynev would be brief and the two parties could rejoin before reaching Aldinare.

The dragons and draelyn mystified Tye. "You'll get used to it," Devlyn assured him.

"We believed the dragons all bowed to Erynor, and these draelyn...I never knew they existed," Tye said.

"They guarded their existence from much of the world. Truly, I didn't know House Lorenthien originated with a draelyn of the Gold House," Devlyn said.

"Neither was it ever common knowledge," Viren said.

Devlyn looked around the camp. Wyn and Aren were speaking quietly, and Devlyn knew better than to interrupt them; their mission promised to be far more perilous than his own.

"How do your brother and the Cyndinari know Cairn?" Tye asked, clearly wondering about it since before they left Arenthyl.

"I honestly don't know; they never told me. I didn't realize they'd had any interaction with the deserters," Devlyn said.

"Do you suspect them of having befriended them? They spoke of Cairn too familiarly," Tye asked, suspicious.

"Unlikely, but I'm also curious about it. Should we ask them?" Devlyn glanced at Viren.

"Unless you want to practice jienzu, there's little else to do tonight except rest," he said.

Devlyn cast a last look toward Wyn and Aren, then went with Viren and Tye to find Jaerol and Liam. They were usually easy to find, given Rusyl's added presence, but not with dozens of other dragons in the same camp. Fortunately, the draelyn had a sense of Rusyl's whereabouts and pointed Devlyn in the right direction.

Across the camp, many draelyn were already moving into jienzu forms. Some practiced together in large groups, others fell into the agile poses on their own. Devlyn found Jaerol, Liam, and Rusyl in his smaller form.

The three moved in a sinuous unity, not a finger unsynchronized. Rusyl had already begun to sweat, but that could have been due to the flight from Arenthyl rather than the jienzu forms. Devlyn watched for a moment, their forms too beautiful to interrupt. Their entire beings had to be aligned to be so well synchronized.

As though we are not? Ellendren hummed, making him think of how distracted he often was whenever he and Ellendren performed jienzu together. Aliel sent an image of Devlyn and Ellendren in the forms and they looked just as unified as Jaerol, Liam, and Rusyl did now.

Rusyl saw Devlyn watching. He completed the form then relaxed out of it, getting a rise out of Jaerol and Liam. They followed his lead, finished their final form and went over to Devlyn, Viren, and Tye.

"You should have joined us," Rusyl said.

"I didn't want to interrupt," Devlyn admitted.

"A tad late for that now," Jaerol said, stretching.

"I suppose so." Devlyn scratched his head.

"What can we do for the High King of Eklean?" Jaerol asked with a wry grin.

"Well for one, I haven't had the opportunity to thank you for rescuing my mother."

"No need to thank us—if ever there was someone worth saving from Erynor's slimy fingers, it's Evellyn," Jaerol said. "Besides, she's the one who saved us at the end. I'm not sure if she mentioned it to you, but the whole thing was a trap, particularly for me."

"A trap?" Devlyn frowned.

"Apparently, I'm less forgettable than I imagined."

"And more modest than I imagined. We never would've found Evellyn if not for Jaerol," Liam said.

"She was easy to find—the other servants did lead me to her, didn't they?"

"You wielded yourself invisible and made it so no one could detect you wielding, after being taken as a palace servant. That's difficult enough when you're only trying to hide from one person, let alone the entirety of the imperial palace." Liam crossed his arms.

"It wasn't all that bad; you didn't see what all the servants were wearing or rather, weren't wearing." Jaerol winked before Liam whacked him on the back of the head. "Ow!"

Devlyn and Rusyl laughed and Viren shook his head. "Didn't you want to ask them about Cairn?" Tye reminded.

"What about him?" Jaerol's mood darkened, and Liam's smile quickly disappeared.

"How do you know him?" Devlyn asked.

"To put it lightly, if he had had it his way, we wouldn't be alive today," Liam said. Tye's shoulders eased a bit at learning they weren't allied with Cairn.

"I don't understand—neither of you fought against Dwonian deserters before. Why would he have wanted to kill you?" Devlyn asked.

"You were in the Illumined Wood during your novitiate at the time. Jaerol and I snuck out of the temple for some, um, fresh air," Liam said, avoiding eye contact with Devlyn.

"The fresh air isn't what got us into trouble," Jaerol interrupted, making Liam blush.

"You don't have to explain everything," Liam said.

"I'm sure he can figure it out; he is married now. Anyway, as Liam was saying, Cairn and the other deserters in that camp wanted us dead because of who we are—for what we are."

"Why would they want to kill you for being a Cyndinari?" Devlyn asked.

"No, not that," Liam said.

"Those bastards caught us lying together by the river," Jaerol said.

"That's terrible," Devlyn said, stricken. How could anyone want to harm, let alone kill, someone just for who they loved? He almost asked for more details but decided against it. Jaerol and Liam were still sensitive about it, and Devlyn could sense their walls going up.

"I still can't believe he took Lawrence's crown. It won't be long until he tries to invade Dwonia. The fool believes he can bring the seeds back to the desert," Jaerol said.

"I've heard that too. How have you learned this?" Tye asked.

"When we were his captives, Cairn was quite chatty. He thinks he can enact some prophecy by taking four wives, one from the east, south, west, and north," Liam said.

"He had already impregnated a Sorenth noblewoman at the time, and I've heard he's taken a Mindalean princess as another wife," Jaerol said.

"The deserters have forgotten much if that's how they're interpreting that prophecy. It has nothing to do with someone fathering children with a woman from those locations, but someone being *born* from the east, south, west, and north." Tye and the others looked at Devlyn.

"Don't look at me—I'm not even Dwonian, or human for that matter," Devlyn said, uncomfortable with another prophesy looming over his head.

"None of the elders have ever said anything about that person being Dwonian, or human. I had thought Velaria would be the one to bring the seeds back to Dwonia when I first met her. How could she not with that leafy dress of hers?" Tye frowned and looked at Devlyn. "After finding out you were born of all four elven kindred, though, it's hard to imagine anyone else bringing the seeds back to Dwonia."

"We have a sister, too; Leilyn was also born of all four elven kins," Liam said.

"She's more likely to bring the seeds back to Dwonia than me. She's spent most of her life in the Illumined Wood," Devlyn said, just as Prya and Liara joined them.

"We might have trouble," Prya announced, her ruby eyes severe.

"What sort of trouble?" Viren asked.

"Some of the older dragons sense the presence of other dragons. It's too subtle for me and the other dragons," Liara said, still imposing despite being in her smaller form.

Devlyn arched a brow. The camp was filled with dragons, and he didn't see the problem.

"Do they suspect the Dark Flight?" Rusyl asked.

"They do," Liara said.

"Is it safe for us to camp here?" Devlyn asked, aware of the severity of the situation.

"They're not nearby now; the older dragons can only sense their lingering presence. The Dark Flight has passed through here; they could be stationed as close as Mindale," Liara said.

"What could they possibly be doing in Mindale?" Devlyn asked.

"Before we left Broid, a great many dragons of the Dark Flight flew north. Evellyn mentioned that Erynor planned for them to travel north, but I'd thought that was to stop the Luminari from reclaiming Arenthyl," Liam said.

"I wonder if that's where the legions have been," Devlyn said, frowning in thought.

"The Dark Flight can't be left unchecked this close to Krysenthiel. Liara and I volunteer to stay behind to observe their movements," Prya said.

Jaerol, Liam, and Rusyl shared a private look, then Rusyl said, "We'll stay too."

"Monitor only. Under no circumstances are you to engage them," Devlyn said, his voice authoritative. Jaerol, Liam, and Rusyl had suffered enough. He didn't want them falling into the Erynien Empire's hands again.

STUBBORN FORTITUDE

Devlyn gripped his verathn as he peered at the great sand dune that hid Nynev. As planned, Ellendren was with the larger group of dragons and draelyn flying west, while Devlyn, with Viren and Tye on Falthion, had left them after passing Dwota's Gap. Wyn and Aren had been with them briefly before they separated.

Seeing nothing on the surface, Devlyn tapped his interior senses and located a network of canyons hidden beneath the sand. Nynev was just as Devlyn had perceived from the sophilliae that had been created before the city had been hidden away.

Curious about the large dune, Devlyn pressed into terys. He expected to feel a hardened shell of stone around the city with a layer of sand on top, but the only stone was the canyons themselves. Rather, the whole sand structure was supported and maintained by some ancient wield. By its feeling, the wield had existed for as long as the Shroud had, perhaps even longer.

He considered asking Tye what he knew about the wield but saved it for later. Tye had been adamant about silence. Sand warriors were likely to find them even if they did everything right; even though Falthion was in his smaller form now, the dragon would have been noted when they landed hours ago. They had to make sure the right sand warriors found them first.

Sneaking into Nynev would have disastrous consequences. They had to avoid being viewed as hostiles to Dwonia at every cost. Ellendren had made it clear he was to build an alliance with the remaining two tribes of Dwonia. Sneaking into the city to retrieve the lucilliae would undoubtedly ruin any chances at an alliance. Tye had made that clear from the onset.

Still, they all very much wanted to avoid getting caught by the wrong sand warriors and being turned away. In Devlyn's mind, the ideal plan was to reach the city gates and request a meeting with the chiefs. But Nynev didn't have any discernible gates. He couldn't stroll up to an agreed-upon location and declare himself and his intent. Pressed into the erendinth, he sensed the various entries into the city; none were meant to welcome an outsider. They were slender tunnels leading into the city beneath the sand. They had considered using them, then abandoned the idea.

"This is as close as we should go," Tye said.

"Thank you, Tye." Devlyn knew how much Tye was risking by bringing them here. Not only had he told Devlyn about the lucilliae, he had broken a long-standing custom and brought outsiders to Nynev's doorstep. He might not have shown them into the city, but Devlyn and Viren could have forced their way in if they wished.

Aliel had been soaring above, dancing among the stars while Devlyn and the others reached the agreed-upon location. Aware of Devlyn's mind and heart, the phoenix plummeted like a falling star. Aliel did not crash though and his light did not diminish as he reached the surface. Instead, Devlyn and Aliel bonded and washed the sand in a brilliant light.

The light from the stars above did not diminish with Devlyn's illumined form; to him, it intensified a hundredfold. He saw the stars as they truly were, very much alive—all of them anadel who carried out Uriel's desires and revealed Anaweh's Light in Teraeniel, a constant reminder, especially at night when those who preferred to live in the shadows would cause harm.

Devlyn's display did not go unnoticed. Twenty sand warriors, their faces covered, surrounded him, Viren, Tye, and Falthion, their spears pointing at them. "I am Ei'denai Devlyn Lorenthien, Exalted Aryl of Krysenthiel, High King of Eklean, and Prelate of the Guardian Senate. Would you do me the honor of escorting me to Chief Kodin of Tribe Fendur and Chief Genin of Tribe Vadir?"

The sand warriors shifted, uncomfortable with the request. "We do not have the authority to show you into the city," one of the sand warriors said.

"Teraeniel lies on the precipice of ruin. I must speak with the chiefs of the two tribes who have remained true to their ways and have not abandoned Dwonia," Devlyn said patiently.

"You would have us break our ways to admit you to Nynev?" the sand warrior asked.

"I am not the first Lorenthien to seek entrance. Your city is hidden in the dune only to safeguard the jewel hidden inside. Ei'denai Faerndryn Lorenthien brought the lucilliae to your people, and after he was killed, his wife, Ithendryl, returned to place the wield over your city to keep it hidden," Devlyn had no idea how he knew all this, only that he did and knew it to be true.

"And neither were they the only two." An old woman stepped forward.

"Grandmother," Tye breathed.

"You have wronged us, Tye. I cannot shield you from the consequences," she said.

"You understand why we had to come, yes?" Devlyn asked.

"I am not the chief of Tribe Fendur; I'm only an elder. Tura. Tye not only ignored our chief's order, he contravened it. He will answer for it."

"Will you take us into Nynev? I must speak with the chiefs," Devlyn said. "You could blindfold Viren, Falthion, and me if that would make you more comfortable."

"As though that would do any good. Your elven ways are not unknown to us here in the desert. As you've already pointed out, you are not the first Lorenthiens to come here. Others, from what might now seem like an age of myths and legends, would have known this land to be quite different—before Dwonia's seeds abandoned us and when every Dwonian tribe was united. Before Erynor drove a spear between us." Tura turned and shuffled toward the large sand dune. The sand warriors repositioned their spears and pointed them toward the sky, allowing Devlyn, Viren, Falthion, and Tye to follow the older woman.

"I hope this does not end in peril, Tye," one of the sand warriors said.

"We'll know before the sun rises, I'm certain, Aisa." Tye replied.

Tura led them along an invisible path in the shifting sands that the Dwonians seemed familiar with, as though the route into Nynev was etched in their minds. Devlyn almost missed the outcropping of rocks and the deep shadow in the stone ledge. The older woman, as nimble as the younger sand warriors, ducked beneath the ledge and into the shadows. Devlyn followed, finding himself in a cramped space. Dallying here was impossible—they couldn't squeeze everyone in if they'd wanted to. Tura waited only long enough for Devlyn to pass through before continuing, Viren, Falthion, and Tye squeezing into the space behind him.

The passageway beyond wasn't much better. He had to hunch over, and he still bumped his head on the irregular rocky ceiling. After passing down and through what felt like a maze of catacombs, they reached the city. Devlyn had expected to see the wielded sand dome above, but he had not anticipated being so far below it. Nynev had been built into a series of narrow canyons and its buildings were carved out of the natural cliff faces. While much of the canyon walls were undisturbed, buildings climbed halfway up the canyons at the densest locations. Narrower canyons splintered off from the one they walked down and Dwonians were quick to take note of the newcomers and their escort. Most of the people here would never have seen an outsider before and certainly not any elves.

As more spectators came out to observe the informal procession, a larger gathering formed in what had to be the center of Nynev. Devlyn wondered if they had expected him or if Tura had acted on her own. The crowd grew as Devlyn, Viren, and Falthion stopped before them like supplicants. Tura moved away and would not permit Tye to join the crowd, but had him remain with his guests, as though he too were now an outsider.

"Chief Kodin of Tribe Fendur, Chief Genin of Tribe Vadir, and elders of Tribes Fendur and Vadir, we are not alone or secluded this day. Our way of living sequestered from the rest of Eklean—the rest of Teraeniel—has always been a guise, no more real than the seeds remaining to our desert home," Tura ignored the scandalized gasps of the other elders who pressed in close.

The two chiefs barely stood out from the rest. Their clothing was not embellished in any way; if anything, the only difference was that they were younger than the elders. Devlyn only recognized them for who they were because Tura had addressed them. Kodin and Genin both remained silent and still, showing no reaction to the outsiders or to Tura's introduction.

"Your grandson was forbidden from going to the elves and giving them any information. Yet, he has showed them the way to Nynev, and you brought them in. We've only survived because of our seclusion—Nynev remains standing because it was presumed lost by those who would destroy it," one of the enraged elders shouted.

"Tye was not forbidden. The chiefs stated that their decision was that we would not return the gift. As for revealing our location, that has become a custom built from our own fear—never a law. Tye has done nothing wrong. That jewel has done little for us but keep us hidden. Since when did the Dwonian Lion hide away and let the rest of the world fight? Our accursed kin wreak havoc across Dwota's Gap and what have we ever done about them but hide?"

"How dare you accuse us and our ancestors of hiding," said another elder.

"We are but a shadow of who we once were. The seeds might not have left us because of our actions, but we have done nothing to show that we are worthy of their return," Tura said.

"And what would you have us do? Call in our sand warriors scattered across the desert and march east to confront the degenerate who calls himself a chief-king?"

"What would *you* have us do? Should we allow him to dishonor Dwonia? Every action he takes does so. Our inaction is nothing more than cowardice and it is inexcusable." The elders and gathered crowd gasped at Tura's accusation. While Devlyn wasn't overly familiar with Dwonian customs, it was clear that calling them cowardly was a great insult.

"If you were not an elder, I would recommend you attempt defending what little honor you have left in the pits, and if you were to survive, you would be exiled for the rest of your days, letting Dwonia determine your worthiness," one of the elders said.

"Enough," Chief Kodin said, stilling any more argument. "Since when do elders fight among themselves? The tension rising among us will be enough to burst the dune and leave us exposed for this so-called chief-king to bring his army down on us."

In the silence following Kodin's pronouncement, Devlyn saw it as a moment to insert himself. "Chief Kodin, Chief Genin, my ancestor, High Queen Ithendryl Lorenthien was the last elf to pass through Nynev's canyons. Her visit was also the last time the sun reached this city."

"If you know of the wield, then you must also know that it only stays in place because of the jewel," Kodin said. "We know why you've come; our decision, as Tye knows, was already made. Removing the jewel from Nynev would see the wield collapse on itself, leaving us exposed. Your ancestor might have been a kind and magnanimous queen, but we are not deceived. She only wielded our protection to safeguard the lucilliae. We know that elves care little for humans. All that matters to you is your lost immortality."

"Our immortality means nothing if Erynor succeeds and Ramiel is freed," Devlyn yelled, enraged. He couldn't believe how poorly the Dwonian chief viewed the elves.

"Erynor also came to our people, promising us much. Only two clans did not heed his silver tongue. The seeds left Dwonia as our people splintered; the rivers ran dry and only sand remained. We will not be joining your elven war. We remaining Dwonians will abide in Dwonia as we always have. We will protect our own from your senseless war," Genin said.

"Senseless? The Luminari didn't start this war. Krysenthiel has only just been freed from the Shroud. The Erynien Empire is actively seeking a means to free the Evil One who will ensnare every anacordel still alive in Teraeniel. This dune won't protect you," Devlyn said.

"Our decision has been made," Kodin said.

"What if I could find a way to maintain the wield without the lucilliae being here?" Devlyn asked, desperate. He tried his best to keep his anger in check.

"And how would you manage it?" Genin asked.

Weighing his options, he wondered what Ellendren would do. Taking the lucilliae by force would shatter any diplomatic relationship with the two remaining Dwonian tribes. She would never permit that to happen. She'd find a way to sustain the wield.

Devlyn again felt the wield. It was massive. Even as he pressed into it, he could feel it being sustained only by the lucilliae. He followed the wield to its source, hidden away in a dark chamber. He could almost see its orange glow. A portion of the Luminari's vitality was all that kept the wretched sand dome from collapsing. He considered going to the chamber and simply taking it and shifting away. The lucilliae weren't mere baubles or treasures to be hoarded and bartered for. They each contained a piece of the Luminari elves' essence. Each was embedded with a prized virtue, cherished by the Luminari. They were not another kingdom's heirloom.

He had no feasible way to sustain the wield himself. But dozens of dragons and draelyn were flying west to Aldinare. Dragons of the Green Flight and draelyn of the Emerald Houses were among them. Few could claim to have as intimate an understanding of terys than they had. While they were heading to Aldinare to assess the effects the Void had had on the Skyland and its people, creatures, and vegetation, perhaps they could help on their way home to Tenethyl.

Removing himself from the erendinth and the wield that sustained the sand dune, Devlyn said, "I cannot manage it on my own. But I know others who might know a way. Would you allow me to return with them?"

"And reveal Nynev's location to more elves who only care for themselves and never dying?" an elder said.

"I could take the lucilliae now and never return." Devlyn didn't turn to the elder who had spoken but kept his focus on the chiefs. They were quiet and Devlyn wondered if they knew how to communicate mentally.

"We will allow it. If you betray us, know that Dwonia's wrath will come for Arenthyl and you too will know what it is to lose your seeds," Kodin said.

Satisfied with the outcome and eager to leave Nynev, Devlyn extended his hand to Viren and Falthion. "Will you be joining us, Tye?"

"Tye is of Tribe Fendur no more. He is to be exiled and sentenced to death for betraying us," Kodin said, as Tye bowed his head. Devlyn was shocked by the severity of the sentence, despite Tye having told him so all along.

"Is that your ruling?" Tura asked.

"It is decided."

"Then I too turn away from Tribe Fendur. Dwonia would not approve of this cowardice and neither do I."

"Grandmother, you can't. Chief Kodin, please don't let her do this," Tye pleaded.

"Chief Kodin is no longer my chief," Tura said, definitively. "As Fendur fathered his tribe ages ago, so will I mother my own tribe."

"You cannot," an elder said, echoed by others.

"As chief of Tribe Tura, I welcome Tye into my protection." Tura ignored the growing chorus of elders. "Aggression against someone of my tribe is war. If a single spear reaches my grandson, you will receive a hundredfold in return."

"You are a tribe of two people; what threat do you imagine you carry?" an elder asked.

"Tribe Tura has strength," said one of the sand warriors who had accompanied them, supported by others in the group. Chief Kodin and Chief Genin looked at Tura, furious with her.

"We do not welcome you to Nynev," Kodin said.

"With the majority of Dwonia's tribes in accord, you are not welcome in Nynev," Genin echoed.

"So be it," Tura said. She looked sternly at Tye, demanding he follow her, and before he could say anything she said, "Your actions and strength have brought pride to Tribe Tura and to Dwonia."

Devlyn and Viren followed the newly formed Tribe Tura out of Nynev, unsure whether Devlyn would be invited back. They returned to the surface, where sand whipped their faces.

"Grandmother, why did you do that?" Tye asked, once they were away from the city.

"I did as Dwonia demanded."

Inner Sanctum

Turbulent waves crashed against the Dwonian cliffs, stretching as far as the eye could see. Devlyn stood on the edge of the precipice taking in the impossible. Where the Purged Desert of Dwonia normally ended in cliffs plummeting into the Tempestien Sea with nothing but an empty horizon, the vast Skyland of Aldinare now floated a few leagues off the coast.

Devlyn had heard stories of Aldinare's enormous size, but had struggled to fully grasp its breadth, even now as he peered at it from across the narrow sea separating it from Eklean. Even its furthest extents were hidden from his enhanced sight. Aldinare's edges faded into the horizon. He didn't need to tap into his inner senses to perceive that Aldinare dwarfed the other Skylands. It could very well equal the size of all three other Skylands combined!

How had such a large land mass hovered in the sky and why had it fallen now and not before? Fortunately, when it had fallen, it was into the sea. Anywhere else would have been catastrophic. What sort of effect had it had by crashing into the ocean? Had tidal waves followed and were coastal towns now drowned?

Thaerwn stood beside Devlyn, taking in the Skyland. "Until recently, I had never seen the sun touch Aldinare. We lived in a grey haze. We could see color, but everything was muted. My eyes didn't quite know how to adjust after the aldarchs pulled us out of the Void."

"Zarathyl must be that much more beautiful now," Devlyn said, looking at the distant coast.

"There's a cult that worships people like you and Ellendren. Elves with wings came from the sky and saved a great many Aldinari, preserving them as we once were." Thaerwn rotated her forearm, her purple skin drinking in the sunlight.

"This cult—should I be concerned about them?" Devlyn asked.

"Its followers are all neridu. They worship someone like you and call him a living god. Lerathel told me he lived among them for thousands of years."

"Aren." Devlyn knew that Aren had been ensnared by the Void, sacrificing himself so his companions could flee the doomed Skylands. The Luminari had wondered what had become of him, until he had suddenly appeared and killed a miervae and Queen Karena of Sorenthil, his mind utterly lost and his body and will enslaved to the Evil One.

"I saw Aren in Arenthyl. He is not as our stories said. He appeared as any other elf."

"He has changed; his mind has been restored from the madness, his phoenix freed to be reborn, and the corruption of the Void cleansed from him. He would have appeared as I am now when he came to Aldinare to help," Devlyn said as Etrien and Therril joined them.

"I remember that day as though it happened yesterday," Etrien said, musing on the past. "We felt fortunate to be saved from the Darkness, but the longing to return ached within us all."

"Even those of us born in Arenthyl felt so," Therril said, his eyes glassy as he looked across the narrow sea.

"And when we thought we'd escaped the Darkness forever, the Shroud fell on us," Etrien said.

"It seems our entire kin was doomed to be swallowed by the Void, at least for a time. I'm happy the Shroud was different from what claimed the Skylands."

"I would prefer your colorful skin to my wrinkles any day," Therril said cheerfully. "Not that I regret walking through the Shroud after I felt Lucillia pass, mind you. Feolyn and Roendryn were a gift I never expected. As for the Evil One's obsession with Aldinari elves, you have to remember what our civilization was. We did not view ourselves as an empire, but under the aldarchs' watch, we built the largest civilization Teraeniel knew before the humans formed their own empires. But where the humans wrought them through blood and conquest, we were ever unified. War never touched Aldinare."

"Until the neridu," Thaerwn said.

"They are Aldinari just as the aelith are," Etrien said, gaining a pause from Thaerwn.

"Ei'denai," a green-haired draelyn of the emerald house addressed him. "We are ready. Gael has answered us and awaits our arrival at her Sanctum of Quel'anir."

"The Reverend Mother." Thaerwn covered her mouth and bowed slightly.

"She would have been our queen if she had remained with us," the draelyn said.

"The aldarchs never claimed one is above another, but they all defer to her," Etrien said.

"She is eager for our arrival," the draelyn said, a green dragon jostling him as he pushed his head past the draelyn.

Reaching out to Ellendren, Devlyn found her already up in the clouds with many of the dragons. She might very well be more excited than Etrien and Therril. *Are you going to make us wait all day?* She asked, aware he had reached out to her.

Already bonded with Aliel, he leapt, his wings carrying him higher than he could have jumped. He flung himself toward Ellendren once he was close enough and chased her through the clouds. Wisps of mists clung to their bodies, streaming behind them like banners.

Seeing the Phaedryn in the sky was the only confirmation the others needed as they began to cross the narrow sea separating Eklean from

Aldinare. The Tempestien Sea was known to be a violent body of water, but even the sky above it had strong winds. The dragons flew at a slower pace but remained steady while the much smaller Devlyn and Ellendren navigated the winds as best they could. Devlyn swore the wind enjoyed tossing them through the sky, as though some part of Aldinare remembered that Phaedryn had long ago stolen some of its elves.

Nearing the Skyland, he had hoped his vision would sharpen and he'd be able to see the distant edges of Aldinare. Still, no matter how much he squinted, he simply could not—Aldinare was too vast for even his eyesight. What he hadn't been able to see from the cliffs of Dwonia, that he could now clearly see as he flew just over the water, was that Aldinare had not actually crashed into the ocean. The Skyland had not plunged into the Tempestien Sea as he had thought, but rather floated just above the water's surface. The ocean wasn't stormy with tall swells because of the intrusion, that's simply how it always was.

Devlyn sped up to rejoin the rest of the expedition and they flew over the first sliver of land. They would be the first outsiders to fly over Aldinare since the Void had claimed it. Much of Aldinare's wilderness had a diseased look. Thaerwn had said the neridu lived in the wilds. They didn't live as nomads, traversing Aldinare without a home, but rather were the unlucky elves who the aldarchs had been unable to shield from the Void. Except for the sanctuaries, the Void had corrupted the entire Skyland. Eventually, Aldinare's cities and later generations of elves were shielded and protected. While newborn elves inherited the physical changes, their minds remained whole. They did not share in the neridu's madness.

Curious, Devlyn tapped into and broadened his inner sense to the land below, all of it hidden beneath a diseased, gnarled tree canopy. He first sensed the legendary ilithae trees and was glad so many of the species had been preserved in the Wooded Hills of Thellion, perpetually flowering in silver petals.

The forest below did not sing nor slumber; the trees sent up a dirge, calling out their agony, remembering a time before the Void had twisted them. In that twisting, they had grown bitter and angry. Devlyn feared the trees would be just as dangerous as the neridu, although he did not sense any of them below. From Thaerwn's description, he had expected they would be everywhere in the wilderness. Either they could conceal themselves or they had all gone to a different part of the Skyland.

The myriad of dragons and draelyn flew over forests, streams, and hills. Devlyn could see the occasional city in the distance, but they did not divert their course to explore. Just as the sun started to set after a full day of flying, Devlyn spotted their destination.

A low mountain rose in the center of the Skyland and on its peak stood a silvery jeweled beacon, wrought entirely from aldaryl. It looked as though it should glow with an incredible light but it only shimmered in the setting sun.

The spire was not their destination though. At the base of the mountain was a grove of uncorrupted ilithae trees. Their silver flowers swayed in the wind and Devlyn caught a glimpse of how Aldinare must have once appeared. Nestled in the grove, as though frozen in a perpetual dance with the trees and land, was a palatial complex—Quel'anir. Devlyn now understood why the Aldinari had mistaken their aldarchs for gods. Quel'anir looked more like a temple complex than the seat of a ruler.

The aerial party descended toward a wide clearing near what appeared to be the entrance to the sanctum. What Devlyn had had difficulty sensing earlier on Aldinare was in abundance in the sanctum—life! Elves filled the sanctum and the trees sang in crystal tones, seeming to implore their sickened brethren to remember themselves and shed their rot.

Dozens of elves adorned with lacy aldaryl circled the grassy clearing. After landing and with the draelyn dismounted, the dragons shifted to their smaller forms, to allow other dragons to land in the freed space. Devlyn and Ellendren both withdrew from their phoenix, who flew off into the ilithae trees where their song joined the song of the uncorrupted trees.

Silver-haired elves came out from the trees to greet the newcomers and another elf came out from the portal that led into the sanctum. Her hair was spun of emeralds, matching her deep green eyes. The elves in the clearing quieted as Devlyn and Ellendren approached her.

"I am Meadil, daughter of Gael and Muirol. My mother welcomes you, Devlyn and Ellendren Lorenthien, Exalted Aryl of Krysenthiel and all the Skylands, High King and High Queen of Eklean, and Prelate of the Guardian Senate," Meadil said, her voice like crystal.

"We thank you, Lady Meadil, for your warm reception," Ellendren said, stepping forward to embrace her.

"You are all very welcome here at Quel'anir."

Etrien came forward and bowed to Meadil. "I am Etrien, part of a small community of Aldinari who live in Arenthyl."

"What do you seek?" Meadil asked.

"We long to return to Aldinare."

"Even in its corrupted state? The wilds are controlled by the violent and maddened neridu, and the Void's effects linger."

"What would you recommend?" Etrien asked, worried that he'd be refused.

"Our Skyland did not fall to this location by accident. How long the Skyland remains here is not known to us, but Aldinare will always be open to its children," Meadil said.

"Thank you, my lady," Etrien said, bowing gratefully.

Meadil looked at Devlyn and Ellendren. "My mother awaits; if you would, follow me." Meadil turned, her bejeweled gown glimmering as she walked back through the portal.

Taking Ellendren's arm as they followed Meadil through a vaulted entry hall, Devlyn had difficulty determining whether it was sung from the trees or from aldaryl, for the columns and arches and vaults did not resemble any architecture he was familiar with. Rather, the entire sanctum seemed to glorify the ilithae trees by enshrining them in sculptural aldaryl. Quite unlike walking through a forest though, Quel'anir followed an ordered symmetry and the tree-like columns were equally spaced. Even the vaults above echoed the ilithae trees, as carved leaves and flowers filled the spaces between the arches.

Devlyn felt the space shift as they entered the next chamber. The ceiling was lowered to about half the lofty height of the previous hall. There were no doors here at Quel'anir—each space transitioned to another through an exquisite carved portal. This smaller, more intimate chamber had another portal opposite where they had entered. Passing from that chamber to the next hall, Devlyn realized that the chamber was like a breath; a pause between one great movement that was the entry hall, to the masterful composition which they had just stepped into.

This hall was even taller than the last. The columns here threaded upward in a lacework braid, thinning the higher they went, like branches. Silver light gleamed off the aldaryl, reflecting off a still pool with lotuses floating on lily pads and silver fish swimming beneath. An island rose in its center, with its own smaller ring of columns and a vined dome above, mirroring the larger chamber it sat in. Meadil led them to the edge of a glass-like bridge that spanned the pool. Stepping aside, she gestured for Devlyn and Ellendren to cross.

"The inner sanctum is reserved for my mother. None but she has ever set foot on her island—not I, not my father, nor any of her devotees. I cannot impress enough upon you the honor that she is extending to you."

"Thank you, Meadil. Truly, we will cherish this moment as the beginning of a sincere and renewed friendship." Ellendren held her hand out for Devlyn, and together they stepped on the glassy bridge. It reminded Devlyn of Aewen's Bridge in Thellion. The fish and flowers were drawn to the Exalted Aryl, following them from beneath as they crossed.

The aldaryl of the inner sanctum was different from the rest of

Quel'anir, as though it was more refined, crafted in such a way that it was more jewel than stone. Devlyn and Ellendren took their first step onto the small island, somehow larger than it appeared. It was as though they had been transported to a lush meadow, blanketed with soft grass and flowers of every sort.

Amid the improbable beauty of Gael's inner sanctum, Devlyn tried to figure out how this place was possible. He had just seen the extent of the small island and its aldaryl tholos. It shouldn't take ten steps to cross its length. But now, they were somehow in a vast, empty valley, with only the sky above them.

Lounging in the grass and flowers on the edge of a crystal lake was a stunning woman with green hair and emerald eyes. A gown of green silk flowed along her body, sweeping past and swirling on the grass like a blanket. Gael barely seemed to register their arrival.

Torn between asking how this place was possible and greeting the aldarch who would have been the Queen of Tenethyl, Devlyn tried not to fidget. As his inner debate intensified and he wondered whether he and Ellendren should disturb Gael, her face turned toward them, the movement slow and deliberate, her eyes taking in more than what was on the surface.

"This is not the first place you have entered hand in hand." Memories of the Empyrean Sphere swirled through Devlyn's mind and heart, as though Gael had summoned them to the surface, which he wasn't entirely confident she hadn't. "My words do not hold the same weight as the seraph, at least, not for you. To most Aldinari, the aldarchs are now viewed as gods. To the others in the wilderness, we are viewed as demons, enemies of their proclaimed living god who was twisted by the Void. It gladdens me to learn that Aren is free from that prison. Tyiel will be reborn and find him in time. Unless Aren is ready to pass from this world, of course. He must be weary—so many of us are. If not for the Void encasing Aldinare, there were times when I, too, thought about transitioning. But no one here on Aldinare could accomplish it because of the Void encasing us. Our bodies might perish, but we would have lingered. So many are lingering now."

Devlyn didn't know how to respond. He had been prepared to thank Gael for bringing them into her inner sanctum and for asking them to come to Aldinare. But Gael had wasted no time with niceties or the formalities of introduction. She had no attendants to see that she followed protocols. Here in her sanctum, she defined what was custom and tradition. Unlike the other Skylands whose aryls would only serve for a generation, the aldarchs had ever led the Aldinari elves from their sanctums and the Aldinari aryls ever bowed to their judgment. So great was their devotion to their aldarchs, they now worshipped them as gods.

"Reverend Mother," Ellendren started, "we've seen how the Void has affected the Aldinari in the cities, and it seems to have affected only their appearance. We've been told that those who were not in the cities have grown mad. Is there any way to help them remember who they are?"

"There were a few unlucky elves living in the wilderness when the Void descended on us. Most had reached the cities by then. But those who didn't make it reproduced, spreading their affliction to their offspring. Their numbers steadily grew and now there are as many neridu as there are aelith. If we could clear their minds and remind them of who they are, as was done for Aren, there would be nothing in their own minds to remember. They were born in the Darkness and have known nothing but. I fear Ramiel will use them against us. We aldarchs can maintain our protective shields for now, but by pulling out of the Void and bringing our Skyland to this land below, we have opened ourselves to a series of threats. The Deurghol and Sha'ghol will come, if they have not already, intent on making thralls of the neridu. Nor will they be pleased to learn that we have managed to protect a great many more Aldinari from Ramiel's twisting. War will scar Aldinare. Unless he is stopped, Aldinari will murder Aldinari at his behest."

"Can nothing be done?" Devlyn asked. Teraeniel had enough war to deal with. They needed allies to fight the Erynien Empire, not a whole new battlefront beyond Eklean's borders. "I did not know who I was, but Alethea led me to discover my identity and the history of my ancestors written on my heart. I was able to see Luminare as my ancestors had known it. Surely, there must be a way to wipe away the madness."

"Thien loved Luminare." Gael smiled, reflecting on a time long gone. "He loved Loren even more, of course, and together they founded your house. He warned me and the other draelyn who had mixed with the Aldinari elves, fearing the elves would one day see us as god-kings and god-queens. I never allowed myself to be concerned by his warnings. Aldinare was as fair as it was strong and wise. The Aldinari sang their past, studied philosophy, and created prose and poetry to make any listener weep. We had never planned for the Darkness though. We had never planned to be cut off from our people and them forgetting who we were.

"Thien knew, even before we were given the Skylands, that he would one day transition to Lumaeniel with Loren when Anaweh called her. As a draelyn of the Gold House, he could have ruled Luminare as we aldarchs have done here. But he chose a different path. He trusted the Luminari to rule and make their own decisions. I wept when Thien transitioned. When Kien and Kiara came here, they barely remembered his name, only that he and Loren had founded their house. Theseryn told them much and more about his brother and sister-in-law. In case you were not aware, he was the first and only aldarch to transition to the World-Beyond, and he only did so after meeting Kien and Kiara Lorenthien and founding the Temple of Ceur. His absence among the aldarchs is felt to this very day and his priests and followers call him the dead god now. If one of our number could reach into the neridu's minds and hearts to remind them of who they are, it would have been Theseryn."

"What of Vespiel and Uriel? Surely, the anadel haven't forgotten you," Devlyn said.

"Vespiel has long wept for your people," Ellendren added.

"And for good cause. The neridu would have to be open to them. A closed heart will not hear Vespiel's song." Gael seemed to be seeing something far off. Troubled, her eyes closed.

"What's happened?" Ellendren asked.

"You aren't the only visitors to Aldinare. As I feared, a Deurghol has reached us and is at a neridu colony—one of the largest of its kind. If he sways them to join Ramiel, this war will grow even more complicated," Gael said.

"Is there anything we can do? Thaerwn said the neridu worshipped Aren; what if we intervened? What if we could convince them that the Deurghol only wants to use them?" Devlyn asked, worried about Ramiel's armies growing even more powerful with neridu.

"You can try but be careful. As you know, the Deurghol are ancient beings—anadel who sided with Ramiel from the beginning and have taken over anacordel as hosts to manifest themselves in Teraeniel, using their hosts like puppets," Gael said.

"Where is this neridu camp?" Devlyn asked, determined.

Gael rested a hand on Devlyn and Ellendren's temples, filling their mind with an image of a twisted grove far to the south. "Be warned. The neridu have likely already chosen their path. For all that I and the other aldarchs know, Ramiel could have won them over from the moment the first Aldinari were lost to their madness. You might not be able to reason with them."

"We understand. But we will try," Ellendren said.

34

NERIDU

Devlyn and Ellendren left the inner sanctum, Gael following them out and across the glassy bridge. The Aldinari bowed to their aldarch, and she inclined her head, acknowledging them each in turn. Viren spoke with Meadil, his guard over Devlyn lessened here inside Quel'anir. His shoulders tightened as Devlyn's intentions reached him.

Before Viren could advise against going to a neridu colony, Devlyn said, "If there's any chance of us breaking through their madness, we have to try."

"You're not going alone," Viren didn't give Devlyn a chance to argue. "This isn't just a hostile camp you're set on going to; a Deurghol's there."

"We can devote some of the sanctum guard to join you," Meadil said. She seemed eager to journey past Quel'anir. "Is there enough time to fly to the colony?"

"A small group must shift there at once. The Deurghol cannot be left alone with the neridu. The rest can fly to the colony once ready."

"I'll come with you," Meadil said, turning to her mother. "I feel like I need to be there."

"Very well."

"I'll come too. I've always feared the neridu, but they're Aldinari just as I am. I need to start seeing them like that," Thaerwn said.

Devlyn nodded, then he and Ellendren bonded with Aliel and

Tariel. Quel'anir bloomed in light. They held their hands out to Viren, Meadil, and Thaerwn then shifted to the neridu camp Gael had shown them.

The change between the Sanctum of Quel'anir and the wilderness was stark. Here, twisted ilithae trees covered the land like a disease. Primitive huts hewn from the trees housed the camp, but Devlyn didn't see any neridu. Had they abandoned their belongings and simply left? That scared Devlyn. Had the Deurghol brought Skimp here to teleport thousands of neridu to Eklean as fresh recruits in Erynor's war? Or worse, to serve Ramiel directly?

"Keep your eyes peeled," Viren warned, his sword unsheathed. "If anything happens, shift back to the sanctum at once; do not concern yourself about us."

"We can't simply leave you," Ellendren said, gripping her verathn tighter.

"He's right, you must flee if necessary. Your role in the struggle ahead is only just beginning," Meadil said, as she too unsheathed her sword. "We, however, have neglected the neridu for far too long."

Arguing would prove futile, so Devlyn channeled his energy to his inner senses.

They moved carefully through the large colony. The corrupted ilithae trees seemed to watch them, and Devlyn swore some of their branches and roots reached out for them. He and Ellendren remained bonded with their phoenix, which seemed to elicit longing in the ilithae trees. Devlyn couldn't say whether the trees wanted to consume their light or whether their brilliance reminded them of the time before the Darkness. Either way, he felt their being press against him.

Devlyn couldn't help gasping when he heard a twig snap. Their group froze, scanning their surroundings. "Reveal yourself," Meadil ordered.

A frail child stepped out from behind a tree that seemed to pay her no mind.

"Who are you?" Meadil asked.

"Graza. Who are you?"

"Meadil, daughter of Aldarch Gael, and this is Devlyn and Ellendren Lorenthien, and their protector, Viren, and this is Thaerwn."

Graza looked no different than Thaerwn; she had the same purple skin tone with sinuous blue markings. "We're the same," Thaerwn breathed.

"Where are the others?" Devlyn asked.

"A stranger came and ordered them to attend him in the basin. He scared me, so I hid."

"Where is this basin?" Devlyn asked, wondering whether going there was the wisest idea.

"It's just outside our home; there's a dip in the forest and the speaker can be heard by anyone in the basin."

"Do you think he's trying to convince the neridu to join him?" Ellendren asked.

"We'd better get there before he succeeds," Devlyn said, then turned to Graza. "Can you take us there?"

She nodded shyly. "Can I stand behind you when we get there? The stranger scares me."

"Deurghol scare me too," Devlyn said.

Graza led them down a path into the trees, closer than Devlyn wanted to be to them. Their eerie dirge and shifting roots were the only sounds other than their footsteps. Devlyn felt the land dip before he saw the basin. The voice of whoever was talking reached them as they stepped near the basin's rim. Hundreds—no, thousands of neridu filled the basin as though at an arena spectacle; at the bottom and center was a Deurghol atop a dragon. They immediately saw the new arrivals and hungrily eyed the Phaedryn, as though they had been waiting for them.

"And here are those who would deceive you," the Deurghol said in High Aelish, his drawl thick and slow and ancient.

"What lies have you promised?" Devlyn asked, the many neridu looking their way now.

"Something which you can never provide. You must understand, not all wish to live in Anaweh's Light; there are those who prefer the Dark. And there are those here who long for the Void. They crave its return."

"The Void has twisted them—us. They don't even know who they once were or what they've lost—what was stolen from us," Thaerwn said.

"Because you aelith barred us from your precious cities," a neridu called out.

"You have the Master's touch. Do you not long for the Void's return? Do you not miss the quiet and emptiness? Do you not yearn for our Master's continued touch?"

"Ramiel has enough slaves," Devlyn said.

"Brave to speak the Master's name." The Deurghol sneered, concealing something in his expression. "Or foolish. Nothing has been stolen from them. They've been given so much more. It was not the Master who kept them from their cities and sanctuaries. Their own people—their aldarchs and aryls carry that blame. They will fall and the cowards hiding away in their cities will be enslaved and Aldinare will belong to the neridu."

"And who will the neridu belong to?" Devlyn challenged, loud enough for the crowds to hear. "Ramiel only offers twisted promises and empty rewards. It's not who you are—you are so much more." Devlyn heard himself shouting, trying to push past the neridu's alleged madness.

"They care not for your twisted promises. You can give them nothing. You were even foolish enough to bring one from a city that rejected them and the daughter of an aldarch who refused to shelter them. But they need no shelter or protection from the Void; they desire its return and to wrench Aldinare from their oppressors."

The crowd's temperament shifted, feeding off the Deurghol's enticement.

"We should leave before this turns violent; there are too many of them," Viren said, just as a stone flew at them.

Thaerwn stopped it in midair with a wield. Another stone followed, and more neridu joined the first to throw yet more stones.

"Devlyn," Viren pressed.

"Not yet." Devlyn pressed into terys, assisting Thaerwn in halting the projectiles. "We are not your enemy," he yelled.

"They will overrun you." The Deurghol laughed as the neridu began moving toward the small group. They didn't have any sophisticated weapons, only clubs and rocks, but their numbers would quickly overwhelm Devlyn and the others.

Realizing that nothing he said would sway the neridu, Devlyn tapped his inner sense and reached far into the depths of his spirit. Ellendren understood what he intended and joined him so their spirits danced together, unseen by anyone unable to sense the invisible reality. Broadening himself, he sensed Viren, Thaerwn, and Meadil join them, and through Meadil, Gael lent her own strength, already bonded with the elves at Quel'anir. Gael's light blossomed as Devlyn felt the other aldarchs waiting for his touch, expanding even further to all the elves on Aldinare.

More rocks flew at them. Viren punched one of the neridu who had come too close and Meadil wielded a barrier just in time before a mass of bodies pressed against it as it rippled under pounding fists. The neridu clambered over each other, forming a dome of bodies. Devlyn hoped Meadil's shield would hold. Focused on his own task, he couldn't lend her any of his strength.

As the violent neridu pressed against them from without, all Aldinare pressed back from within Devlyn. The two forces clashed. Devlyn had thought his studies had provided him with an accurate understanding of Aldinare, but he now felt the lived history of the Aldinari pressing into him. He saw how they had once lived and the pride they had held for their Skyland and culture.

They had seen their home as an incorruptible jewel of civilization—a beacon for the entire world to emulate. But Devlyn knew that even the brightest jewels could be corrupted. Despair now overshadowed that pride. No one on Aldinare had been healed of the Void, even those who had been protected from it. The trees reflected the dirge of their twisted kin in the wilderness and the aldarchs felt a failure. They had tried to stave off the Darkness as best they could, but they were all changed, some worse than others. Most sorrowful was Vespiel.

"What are you doing?" the Deurghol asked. His voice quavered.

Entranced, Devlyn didn't hear Ellendren scream as a bolt of tenebrys lashed through the neridu, killing them to create an opening for the Deurghol to launch more tenebrys bolts. The neridu didn't have a chance to scream before death came. Wield after wield, more bodies fell as the Deurghol carelessly slaughtered the neridu.

A brilliant light exploded in front of them, consuming the next tenebrys bolt. "How dare you harm my children!" Vespiel cried, standing between the neridu and the Deurghol, shielding them. "You and the one you serve have terrorized Aldinare long enough!" A wash of light unfolded from her, barreling toward the Deurghol and his dragon. "Begone from this realm!"

"They are no longer yours. The Master's Void will consume all that you anadel sung into existence. Even Lumaeniel will be swallowed by it. Anaweh will be the one to suffer, imprisoned this time, as will all those who have already chosen that fate," the Deurghol spat.

"Leave my children." Vespiel issued another eruption of light, drawing on the combined power of all the Aldinari that Devlyn had been channeling. It did not strike the Deurghol, but mushroomed over the neridu, reaching deep into their beings, in a way that Devlyn could not. Vespiel was trying to illumine the deep well within their spirit to reveal who they were. They were the elves of the setting sun—guardians of the west wind. They had stood behind the aldarchs and built the largest elven civilization that had ever existed. The songs of their past were not only playing silently on their hearts, but now audibly blossomed. All

Aldinare reached out to the twisted elves, pushing past their madness. Even the corrupted ilithae trees tried to sing past their own gnarled and twisted disease to reach the elves.

"You cannot reach them all," the Deurghol yelled. "You are a fool if you think our Master hasn't been taking these wretches off this cursed rock over the millennia." The dragon roared and launched into the sky. "And you, the greatest fool of all!" The Deurghol pointed to Devlyn. "You should have taken your precious jewel with force when you had the chance. Oh yes. We know you went to Nynev, and in your anger, let slip our Master's name. Now you shall have neither the Dwonians as an ally nor your precious lucilliae. You will never regain the Life Immortal that your ancestors sacrificed. Our Master is pleased with the chief-king and grants Dwonia and Mindale to him. He might even permit the release of the seeds to that desert again." The Deurghol took a final look down on Aldinare, knowing its loss would be his greatest failure.

Devlyn and Ellendren were still bonded with Aliel and Tariel, but the light that had first emanated off them, and then been plucked away by Vespiel, had yet to diminish. Vespiel turned to them as a tear rolled down her cheek. "Thank you. Uriel was right in naming you two as the Exalted Aryl of all the elves. You have returned hope and light to Aldinare."

"Devlyn," Ellendren breathed. She wasn't looking at him, but at the Aldinari and their Skyland. No one was maintaining any wield of lumenys. Rather, Aldinare itself gleamed in a brilliant silvery light. The ilithae trees had shaken off their twisted disease and silver flowers bloomed endlessly from them as silver pollen filled the air, holding that light. The silver light was now reflected in some of the neridu's eyes, brilliant and possessing a degree of knowing and self-awareness. Like Devlyn had so long ago, these Aldinari had remembered who they were.

No longer neridu, they were washed clean of the Void's taint. Their silver blond hair had regrown in voluminous loops and their skin returned to the color of pearls. Their markings and the madness had left them. Even Thaerwn had shed the Void's grasp over her body.

"We have to leave for Nynev...the lucilliae." Devlyn began to formulate a plan to retrieve it. From everything he knew of Cairn, he would likely keep the lucilliae as a trophy.

Before Devlyn could apologize to Meadil for having to leave so abruptly, she said. "Go. The dragons and draelyn will remain and help prepare us for the coming struggle."

The restored elves shared looks of confusion, mixed with admiration, as though waking from a long slumber. Though the Deurghol had been right. Not all the neridu had been open to Vespiel. While they were now the minority, there were still some bald and purple-skinned neridu. Gael had feared that would be the case. Seeing what had happened to their brethren, they now fled into the wilderness, although the trees were no longer wild and twisted. If those neridu remained on Aldinare, they would find it difficult to adapt to the restored surroundings. Light softly glimmered throughout the entire Skyland now, not only reflecting the sunlight, but from the aldaryl. Even Aldinare's deepest caves would not be in complete darkness.

The restored Aldinari gazed in bewilderment at the small group, Meadil's protective wield long vanished.

"We worshipped someone like you—we thought him a god. He disappeared several years ago; the Deurghol promised us his return if we went with him," an Aldinari said in High Aelish.

"Aren has been restored just as you have been. Now, Ramiel has just as much hold on his mind as he does yours," Devlyn said as a ruffle of wings filled the air. Expecting dragons, he had to blink as dozens of alicorn flew overhead, feathers wafting down, then the creatures themselves landed to join the gathering, bringing the sanctum guard that Gael had promised. Fortunately, they no longer needed to fight their brethren.

Devlyn searched for a dragon among them, hoping Falthion was among the arrivals. If the lucilliae truly had been stolen away from Nynev, they would have to make haste. He didn't know what would happen once they did reach Nynev—he hadn't left on the best terms. Would they blame him for the theft of the jewel?

BURIED

The first step after shifting was the hardest. The wield which had held the great sand dune in place over Nynev was gone, and so was the dune. Despite the subtlety of the wield, its absence had drastically changed the area surrounding Nynev. Most notably, Devlyn no longer felt safe—he felt exposed and in more danger than he had felt since freeing Krysenthiel of the Shroud.

The second step was almost as difficult. Where the great sand dune had risen like a dome over the hidden city, the canyons had been revealed and the surrounding sand now dipped into them. Red, orange, and yellow colorations streaked the stone as though done by a paint brush. Devlyn, Ellendren, and Viren went to the edge of the cliff. A river of sand buried the canyon's lowest level, swallowing most of the inhabitants and buildings.

Before he even had the chance to consider what had happened to the Dwonians here, he felt a spear prick his back. Viren's sword was already unsheathed and Falthion, still in his larger form, growled. Devlyn shook his head and asked, "What happened?" He had to hear it from someone who had been here, not from a Deurghol's deceptive tongue.

"Many hold you accountable for this tragedy. Some even say you came in the dead of night and stole the jewel yourself, the words from your own mouth," the sand warrior said. Devlyn thought he recognized her voice, but her urda made it impossible to determine for sure.

"Is that what you believe?" Devlyn asked.

"No. I saw Cairn fleeing the scene with twenty other deserters and a shadow elf."

"Did everyone manage to escape before the dune collapsed?" Devlyn asked.

"The sand would not kill the least of our numbers. We were born in the sand and we know how to survive it where many others would not." She lowered her spear. Devlyn had more questions but she interrupted his thoughts before he could speak. "Come, your presence is requested." She turned to leave, expecting them to follow.

Tapping his inner sense, Devlyn tried to get a better sense of the damage. Like the Dwonians who called Nynev their home, it seemed that the city was just as resilient. The sand would not be the end of Nynev. "Wait. Let me help in this small way."

Unsure of his intentions, the sand warrior turned cautiously about.

Devlyn knew he couldn't replicate the wield Ithendryl had created, nor did he think it was appropriate now. He didn't want to encourage Nynev to hide beneath the sand any longer than they already had. Their city was no longer lost to the outside world—the Erynien Empire had found them. There was no point in hiding again. That did not stop him from pressing into terys.

Something had to be done about the sand. Even as he tried to wield it, it slipped as though through his fingers. He'd imagined he could wield it similarly to water, stone, or air, a single wield and all the sand particles would follow the current of his wield. This was different though—much different. The sand acted independently, yet it was also tied together by an invisible force.

He focused on a small area of sand and wielded it up and out of the canyons, expending much more energy than he'd imagined was necessary. Realizing his intention, Ellendren joined him. The sand swooped up in a wave, mimicking an avian formation in the changing of seasons. Devlyn and Ellendren twirled their wields in the sky, admittedly being more showy than necessary before finding a safe place to deposit it outside the canyons. The sand wouldn't remain where they led it. Its nature was to dance on the wind and travel the desert currents.

"It appears I can't perform well-meaning gestures without you anymore, Elle." She smiled in return. She didn't have to say he was useless without her or entirely co-dependent on her, for he knew she also felt the same. Every day felt like a gift when they were together.

The awestruck sand warrior had watched the entire spectacle. "That would have taken us years. Even our wielders would not have managed what you just accomplished."

"We are not your enemies," Ellendren said, her tone convincing and empathetic.

"I am not the one you must convince. Come, they are waiting for you." The sand warrior led them to a stone outcropping.

Nynev might have been revealed to the elements once again, but that did not mean accessing the city would be any easier for an enemy. An invading army could hardly scale down a canyon face. They would be plucked off by arrows and fall to their doom. They would have to swarm Nynev if they sought to conquer it.

Still, Devlyn wondered how Cairn had gotten into the city in the first place. Had someone betrayed Dwonia and revealed its secrets or had he always known? Had the deserters passed down Nynev's secrets through the generations, hoping they might one day find the lost city again? The questions persisted until they reached the canyon floor. No longer dark and limited to filtered light, the sun had transformed the canyon and it gleamed burnt red in the sunlight.

Startled Dwonians trickled back into the city now that the sand was gone. Their whispers came easily to his ears. The hushed voices and rumors were as varied as the grains of sand that he and Ellendren had removed. Whether negative or positive, they were all tinted with a degree of skepticism. No one in Nynev trusted the elves, even if it had been one of their own, deserter or not, who had stolen the lucilliae and caused the sand dune to collapse.

Devlyn expected to find the chiefs waiting in the middle of the canyon again. Instead, the sand warrior took them to a building carved from the canyon face. They were near the center of the densest part of the city, and the upper levels looked like they might have been above where the sand had filled in. While the building had been pristinely carved from the rock, it had a cavernous quality on the inside. Whoever had built it must have thought an open portal was the only necessary entry, but it made the entry feel more like a cavern than a doorway.

Rectilinear reliefs, mimicking windows, adorned the only façade, but none of them punched through the rock. The interior of the building could be entirely unrelated to the exterior. The building might only span a single level or could be the full height of the canyon and reach the surface above. It could even delve into a mazelike structure deep below the canyon floor.

The sand warrior did not lead them to a stair, nor did they pass any as they stopped at the mouth of a hypostyle hall. Wide columns marched down in pairs to a grand portal, sealed at the far end. Simple carvings were etched into the pillars, seeming to tell a story. The sand warrior gestured at Devlyn and Ellendren to go on but stopped Viren and Falthion, now in his smaller form. "You cannot," she said.

"We'll be fine," Devlyn encouraged, receiving a grunt from Viren. He and Ellendren stepped into the hall. The columns felt as though they were beckoning him and Ellendren forward, but it also felt as though they could discourage someone from entering. Rocks and stone, even if carved, could not judge someone's worthiness. Still, that's precisely how he felt as he walked between the columns. The stone at Oma's cavern came to mind. Had that been the same? Oma said the stone never forgot. He considered testing that feeling now, and as he prepared to tap his inner sense, Ellendren stopped him.

"I would not," she warned, her voice echoing down the cavernous space. "Something about this place is weighing us—judging us. It's as though the stone here is still awake. I think I'm beginning to understand the Dwonians' relationship with Dwonia. Devlyn, what if Dwonia is…" A drumbeat cut her off, loud and resonating deep into their chests.

There was no telling where it came from. It sounded as though it had come from every direction, but also from within them. It thrummed again. Dust fell from the ceiling in reply.

A third beat sounded and the stone doors in the great portal slowly swung inward, heavy stone scraping against the stone floor. A fire in a simple stone basin was visible in the next chamber. The room must have been massive, for the fire revealed no more than a ring of flickering light around itself.

"Dwonia deems you worthy," came a voice.

"We are grateful," Ellendren said as they stepped into the ominous chamber together. "Dwonia isn't just the name of the land, is it?"

"Astute of you. We do not have the same relationship with our irythil as the elves do. Our history with Dwonia is old and our ancestors preserved it on the columns that you just walked through. In the days when Ramiel last walked free, our people suffered from his cruelty. Our cities and villages were burned and our people slaughtered. Dwonia heard our plight and witnessed our suffering. She took us past the gap which was later named after Dwota. Twelve tribes crossed the gap to the savannah. In our gratitude, we named our new land after her. She brought our first chiefs who had been born in Dwonia to this place—the place of her dwelling."

"That's why Nynev was not intended to be a residence. It's sacred," Ellendren said.

"Before Erynor drove a spear into us, forever dividing the tribes, Nynev was tended by our elders. Our chiefs made the pilgrimage here when they had need to consult the elders or come together in council. Nynev is also the place where new chiefs are recognized. And for that reason, there is no chief past the Gap. The deserters abandoned our way."

"What about Cairn? He came here, did he not?" Ellendren asked.

"He came but was not recognized. Dwonia did not find him worthy. He was not granted access to this hall. Enraged, he left with something else—that which we had denied you."

"Who are you?" Devlyn asked. He didn't recognize the speaker's voice and she was still cloaked in the shadows. The firelight did not reach her.

"Kodin, Chief of Tribe Fendur, was killed. The deserter would not challenge him—too cowardly to stand against him. Kodin did not survive standing against the shadow elf that came into Nynev. I am Chief Aesa of Fendur." Aesa stepped into the firelight. Her sharp cheekbones reminded Devlyn of the former chief. "Kodin was my brother."

Tura too stepped into the light. "A new age is upon us," she said. "For the first time since our beginning, a new tribe is recognized and embraced by Dwonia."

"Our three tribes will remain hidden no more," Genin said.

"What will you do now?" Ellendren asked.

"A shadow elf has not only defiled Nynev but has stolen one of our chiefs' souls. We cannot allow this crime to go unanswered. Tribes Fendur, Vadir, and Tura have called in our sand warriors. We march for the Gap and will rid Eklean of the deserters, starting with their pretender chief-king in Binton. Tye is in charge of organizing the runners to call back our sand warriors scattered across Dwonia. Erynor will not be pleased to be reminded why he first feared us all those years ago when he sought to weaken and divide us. We are joining your war. Dwonia will not be left behind as Eklean is reshaped."

"What of Nynev?" Ellendren asked.

"Erynor cares little for Nynev, even though he knows it's the dwelling of an irythil. Only the deserters desire to wrestle it from us and we intend to keep them preoccupied."

"And the lucilliae?" Devlyn asked.

"As I said, we were fools to keep it from you."

Devlyn paced the room he and Ellendren had been given in Nynev. Neither were sleepy, too focused on the impending march to Binton. They'd gone back and forth with options for hours.

"Come to bed, Devlyn. Your pacing is making me nervous." She patted the mattress.

"Are we sure we shouldn't bring this to the Guardian Senate or even to the aryls?" Devlyn asked as he sat next to her.

"And how long do you think that will delay us? Besides, the Senate hasn't been called into session yet. We still need to wait for all the dignitaries to arrive. No one from Qien, Ja'horan, or Charren has made it and neither have any merpeople."

"But what about the Eklean kingdoms? Thellion and Sorenthil will certainly want to be involved in deciding Mindale's fate."

"Myranda is busy reinforcing Gestoria's borders. Alex might be able to send help. I wish we had time to formally call a Senate session, but we simply don't know how long Erynor will let Cairn keep the lucilliae. We also don't know if they'll try to damage it or corrupt it somehow."

"Can Cairn do that?" Devlyn wrapped an arm around Ellendren as she nestled into him.

"I'd rather not find out." She rested her hand on his stomach; her fingers casually drew against his skin. "Perhaps we should go to the Ashton Wood first. Daphne and Henry are spearheading the resistance against Cairn.

"We'll also have to find out if Liam and the others have discovered anything. They've been in Mindale all this time."

Nynev was abuzz the following morning. The atmosphere had changed. The three chiefs must have spread their message and intent, for the Dwonians had a different attitude toward Devlyn, Ellendren, Viren, and Falthion. Their side-eyed glances and whispers had diminished, replaced largely by people smiling at them. Compared to Devlyn's first visit, the mood was entirely unrecognizable. Rather than setting themselves on an isolationist path, they all had a determination to set out from Nynev and confront those who had wronged them and had spat on their traditions.

Devlyn wondered how much the removal of the sand over the city had affected the Dwonians. The elders smiled as the sun reached the once buried city, and children ran around in the brightness. The canyon was a glow of burnt red, mixed with the determination of its people.

Tye came over to Devlyn, smiling. "Dwonia has accepted you, I hear," he said.

"Not enough to bring the seeds back."

"We'll have to leave it to the Sojourners to find the one. For all we know, it might very well be your sister and they're already persuading her to make the journey here."

"It's possible." Devlyn hadn't expected or wanted himself to be the one named in the Dwonian prophecy; he had enough prophecies revolving around him. "When will the sand warriors be ready to move against Cairn?"

"We'll be ready to march for the Gap in a week and if Cairn doesn't try to engage us there, we should reach Binton before the next moon."

"That quickly?"

"We are not knights with heavy arms or steeds to care for. Sand warriors are known for travelling light and quickly. Will we be fighting the deserters alone?"

"We hope Thellion will join this battle," Devlyn said. "The loss of Mindale would be a great defeat to Erynor. His retribution will be swift if we take it from his empire. We'll travel ahead to organize our allies. Will the sand warriors understand that we cannot march with you?"

"If they don't, they are more narrowminded than I thought." Tura stepped from behind Devlyn and Tye. "Our sand warriors might be strong and willing, but we are only three tribes. The deserters are a great many more. We need all the allies you can muster if we're to have a successful campaign in eradicating Cairn." Devlyn nodded, wondering what was keeping Ellendren. Quite unlike her, she was running late. As his mind drifted, he reached out to Liam, letting him know to meet them in the Ashton Wood.

Liam was quick to respond, excited to share some sort of news. Ellendren and Viren came out from one of the buildings. Her cheeks were flushed, and she seemed to be a mixture of tired and happy. He couldn't quite understand why she was so tired. They had slept fine the night before. "Are we ready?" Ellendren asked.

Tura went up to her, held her head and touched their foreheads together. Ellendren's eyes widened as she parted from Tura. Devlyn found the exchange odd but didn't comment on it. Whatever the shock was, it did not last, and curiously, her thoughts and emotions were still. Instead of explaining what was going on, she held her hands out for Devlyn, Viren, and Falthion. Together, they left Nynev.

CAUTIOUS JOY

A soft, cool breeze replaced the warm, arid air of Dwonia. Taking in his surroundings, Devlyn saw that he had shifted to the private gardens behind the Ashton manor house. His emotional connection to the Ashton estate had brought him here where dozens of settlings hurried about, elated at his and Ellendren's return. Oddly, they paid little mind to the men as they pressed against Ellendren, practically forcing a wedge between her and Devlyn.

"They're happy to see you," Viren said.

"I suppose so." Ellendren brushed their little bodies, careful not to disturb or damage the blooms on their heads. "We probably should have shifted to the entry though for a proper welcome, rather than showing up in the back gardens." Ellendren echoed Devlyn's thoughts.

"No matter, we'll make our arrival known." Viren and Falthion walked off before Devlyn could follow.

"That's odd. It's not like Viren to run off and leave us alone." Devlyn looked down the path Viren and Falthion had taken; none of the settlings had chased after him, too preoccupied with Ellendren.

"Not entirely." From behind him, she took his hand, drawing him back.

Devlyn was confused. Ellendren's thoughts and emotions were still closed off. Had something happened that Ellendren didn't want to share with him? "You would tell me if something was wrong, right?" He had never had a reason to doubt her, but he struggled to keep that doubt from his voice now. Something had changed. She had never guarded her thoughts from him before. "Elle?"

She smiled and as their eyes met, she released whatever barrier she'd deliberately placed between them. She didn't have to say anything, for Devlyn suddenly knew. The miracle of light and love and hope blossoming inside her stunned him speechless. A thousand questions flashed across his mind. But most notable was how?

"You know how *it's* possible," she teased, fluttering her eyelashes.

"I mean, I understand the *how*." He blushed at the number of times they'd explored the *how* and celebrated their love together. "But I thought you couldn't get pregnant yet."

"Would and could are quite different. We were ready and willing."

"Are we? We're at war; Erynor is on our doorstep and the Evil One might return any day."

"You've been more than willing," she teased again, softly this time. "Persistent is likely the better word." She laughed, making them both blush.

Viren returned with Daphne Ashton. "I trust you told him."

"You knew?" Devlyn rounded on Viren.

"I wanted to know if it was safe to shift," Ellendren answered.

"The settlings won't leave you be." Daphne offered a congratulatory embrace. "If you thought they were obnoxious before, carrying a child will be a whole other affair."

Devlyn held in a sigh. The onslaught of emotions was too much. One moment he was overjoyed and the next he couldn't breathe. It felt like a panic attack. He couldn't sort or deal with his emotions at present, so he pulled Ellendren into a deep hug and kissed her. "You're pregnant," he managed when their lips parted enough to speak. His smile was teary, the news still washing over him. "But the war...Erynor, the Evil One...how will we manage?" Before his ramblings could continue, a roar thundered somewhere in the near distance. Already on edge and feeling even more protective of Ellendren, he pressed into all the elemental erendinth and embraced the transcendental erendinth, forming a wield that would nullify any threat.

"Be calm," Ellendren cupped his face. "It's only Rusyl."

Devlyn reached out and a flood of relief washed over him that he hadn't unleashed his wield when he recognized Jaerol, Liam, and Rusyl.

A thump followed when Rusyl landed where Devlyn should have—in front of the manor.

"Should we see to our arrivals? They're not the only ones here, mind you," Daphne said. She took them inside, where she had been having tea with Queen Lara, Velaria, and Yelaris in her smaller form. Velaria's flowery leaves had grown since Devlyn had seen her and they shyly peeked past her sleeves.

Lara, Velaria, and Yelaris immediately knew that Ellendren was pregnant. They went over to her, hugging and congratulating her, sharing only a fraction of their joy with Devlyn. He was on the verge of asking what the Chair of Azurelle and the Queen of Evellion were doing in the Ashton Wood when Jaerol, Liam, and Rusyl joined them too. Rusyl had to hunch through the doorway, even in his smaller form.

Velaria took command of the situation the moment everyone settled and returned to their seats. "As eager as I am to learn about Aldinare, we must focus on Cairn and Mindale's future."

"What has happened in Mindale to attract Septyl's attention?" Ellendren asked.

"Our informants point to Erynor planning something consequential happening here. We haven't had any success tracking his forces' movements, but we fear he intends to launch an invasion on Krysenthiel from Mindale. Its borders are filled with more dangerous foes than Dwonian deserters." She looked to Jaerol, Liam, and Rusyl, somehow knowing that they had stayed in Mindale to monitor the area. "Did you learn anything?"

"Escaping Broid felt safer than prowling through Mindale," Jaerol said. "Erynor is definitely planning something. It appears the entire Dark Flight has assembled on the plains near Krysenthiel. And if dragons aren't enough, shadow elves have been feasting on the villages in the area; their sickening screeches can be heard throughout the night as they devour innocent people's souls. Liara and Prya are still tracking their movements."

"Are Deurghol involved?" Ellendren asked.

"I'm sure they are, but we didn't dare get near enough to find out," Liam said.

"Troubling," Velaria said. The look on her face indicated she was calculating how to deal with the Dark Flight and shadow elves so close to Krysenthiel.

"There's more." Devlyn paused as everyone turned to him. "Cairn has a lucilliae."

"How is that possible?" Velaria asked.

"It had been in Nynev and had facilitated concealing the city. I was angry at the Dwonian chiefs and elders for refusing to return it, and let slip the Evil One's name, revealing the city's location to those listening for it. A shadow elf killed the chief of Tribe Fendur and Cairn stole the lucilliae. With it gone, so too is the wield that hid Nynev under a massive sand dune."

"That is unfortunate," Velaria said.

"The Dwonians want revenge; they're sending a force past Dwota's Gap to confront Cairn for the murder of Chief Kodin," Devlyn said.

"Are both of the remaining tribes of Dwonia coming?" Velaria asked.

"There's three now." Devlyn explained how Tura started her own tribe to save Tye's life.

"Are we certain the Dwonians are in a position to fight?" Velaria asked.

"I believe so. They are determined," Ellendren reassured.

"If the lucilliae is in Binton, we'll have to set up a perimeter and ensure that neither Cairn nor the lucilliae escape the city," Velaria said.

"Henry already has Binton's western districts under siege. We've led the resistance ever since Lawrence was killed, not that anyone mourned his passing," Daphne said.

"Our military is mobilizing on our southern border. Alexander has agreed to support the Mindalean resistance and is sending more reinforcements as we speak," Lara said.

"Does he also support the Ashton's claim to the throne?" Velaria asked, shifting the conversation to another manner of plotting.

"*If* the throne comes to Henry and me, Alex has agreed to support us. But the nobles will fight for it. If it's not handled swiftly and delicately, Mindale could fall into a bloody civil war over the throne," Daphne said.

"And will Mindale join Thellion as Evellion has?" Velaria asked.

"I'll never understand your long desire to see Thellion restored, but yes, Henry and I did agree to become part of Thellion if Mindale's throne passes to us," Daphne said.

"Much will be decided on a strong Thellion," Velaria said, knowing more than she was willing to share.

"Is there any way Krysenthiel can support Mindale?" Ellendren asked.

"Septyl has met with the Guardian knights. Jeanne shares our fears, but the presence of shadow elves and the Dark Flight along Krysenthiel's borders greatly concerns her. The Guardian knights stand alert in Verenthyl should they be needed," Velaria said. "We don't have the luxury of a long, drawn-out siege. Cairn must be defeated swiftly."

"What about the Dark Flight? Surely they won't stand by while Binton is under siege," Ellendren said.

"They haven't drawn near any Mindalean city. They seem preoccupied with Krysenthiel's border—not that that's encouraging but it doesn't seem like the Dark Flight is interested in who rules a human city," Jaerol said.

"That doesn't bode well. If they're not here for Mindale's sake, then I shudder to think what they're plotting." Ellendren absently turned northeast, as though she looked directly at Arenthyl. "Perhaps the Guardian knights should remain in Krysenthiel?"

"I don't think there's a good answer. The cities are protected. Not even the Dark Flight can breech Krysenthien city wards. Still, we should relay what we know to Jeanne and get her opinion. Our combined forces might be strong enough in Binton without the Guardian knights."

Devlyn nodded. He didn't like this. The Dark Flight was planning something far too near Krysenthiel for his liking. If not for the lucilliae being in Cairn's possession, he would have shifted back to Arenthyl to prepare for an imminent invasion. Even without having any evidence of their intent, he wanted to plan a defense against the Dark Flight. But how were they supposed to defend against an entire dragon flight devoted to the Evil One's cursed tenebrys?

Worse, they had no idea what the Dark Flight was targeting. For all Devlyn knew, they could only be resting in Mindale before heading to their target. That could either be a Krysenthien city or any of the human cities opposed to the Erynien Empire. Those dragons could even be preparing to fly to Aldinare or the Eldin Wood for all he knew. At least the Dark Primus, Tolvenol, remained caged under a mountain in Qien.

They needed more information but had no means to gather it. Jaerol, Liam, and Rusyl had risked their lives investigating the Dark Flight's whereabouts, and Liara and Prya were still taking the risk.

"What's our next move?" Ellendren asked.

"We're of no use to the resistance here in the Ashton Wood. We should make haste to Henry's camp outside Binton." Daphne seemed eager to return to her husband.

"Agreed; the sooner this is resolved the better," Devlyn said, still torn between going to Binton or Arenthyl.

Little time was wasted in their preparations—Daphne had had everything organized. Devlyn had considered shifting directly to Binton, rather than accompany House Ashton's retinue, supplemented by

Queen Lara's knights. Binton was not far from the Ashton Wood, and even if they shifted there, they would not be able to start the attack until the Dwonians and Thellish forces arrived.

GATHERING STORM

The Ashtons' rebel camp was impressively large. While a great many noble houses were still aligned to the Erynien Empire, at least in name and in treaty, the Ashton banner did not stand alone against Binton. The Ashtons must have gathered support from the other Mindalean nobles after Cairn had stolen Lawrence's crown and taken one of the many princesses as his wife. The noble houses might have supported the Erynien Empire when their coffers were full due to that arrangement, but that had all changed when their new king had impressed a new tax on Mindale. Cairn cared little for what Mindaleans wanted, and even less so for their nobles.

Stretching his wings, Devlyn swooped above the camp, getting a last look at the horizon. The Dwonian sand warriors and Evellion's military were expected to arrive any day now, and Devlyn was doing everything he could to distract himself until they did. He had wondered aloud how difficult it would be to sneak into the city and castle to steal back the lucilliae. Ellendren and Viren both opposed that idea. The castle was bound to be packed full of deserters, loyal only to Cairn. Also, Devlyn had never been inside Binton's castle. It had been built during the height of Thellion, when the name Mindale was only recognized for the Plains of Mindale. Castles that old promised to be full of hidden passages and secrets known only to their inhabitants.

Cairn might not have been king long, but the Mindalean princess he'd wed would know those secrets. Whether or not she had shared them with Cairn was another matter. Based on what Jaerol and Liam had told him of the chief-king, the Mindalean princess was not his only wife. The fool was determined to bear children by multiple wives to enact a Dwonian prophecy, the same prophecy Tye had hoped named Devlyn as the one to return the seeds to Dwonia.

Devlyn wondered if Cairn's wives could be persuaded to betray their husband. Jaerol and Liam were under the impression that his Sorenth bride would bury a knife in Cairn's heart the first chance she had. Perhaps his Mindalean princess shared the same sentiment.

Taking a final look west, he caught the first signs of movement on the horizon. The Dwonians didn't have mounts; they relied on their swift legs to cross an unimaginably long distance on foot. Devlyn wondered who would be more eager to fight their way into Binton. The Mindaleans under the Ashton's banner might be done with living under the Erynien Empire's thumb but the Dwonians had suffered greatly from Cairn's treacherous thievery in the night. Ending Cairn's place in Mindale would further dispel Erynor's influence on Eklean.

Sparing a northward glance, he hoped to glimpse Evellion's banners. The northern horizon showed no movement, and he swept down toward the camp.

Devlyn was not the only one to have spotted the approaching sand warriors. The camp bustled with activity and two Mindalean knights, no longer loyal to their crown, escorted Devlyn to Lord Ashton's command tent, where, to Devlyn's surprise and delight, Alex waited. The Thellish king was speaking lightly with Henry and Daphne.

"Alex? When did you arrive? *How* did you arrive?" Devlyn broke into a smile.

"I was never far. Diana is furious with me for not returning with her to Elothkar after your coronation. She expects us to resolve this incident with Cairn as swiftly as possible and hopes for even quicker negotiations after." Alex waved a crumpled parchment and then gripped

Devlyn in a hug. "To no one's surprise, Velaria and the ei'ana have been occupied scheming Eklean's future."

"Scheming is a strong accusation, Your Majesty." Velaria swept into the command tent as though it was her own.

"I think I preferred it when you insisted on calling me Alexander," he scoffed, followed by a mischievous grin.

"And I believe you mean that." Velaria offered her own small smile.

"So Mindale is to become part of Thellion?" Devlyn asked.

"It appears so. I had an uncomfortable conversation with Myranda at your coronation—which was lovely—regarding Thellion's reach. And in no uncertain terms, she made it quite clear that Sorenthil would not have a suzerain," Alex said.

"A crown is not the only way to unite the human kingdoms in Eklean," Velaria offered.

"Then remind me why this one was thrust on my head," Alex said.

"Would you have preferred your uncle staying in power?" Velaria asked, receiving only a huff from Alex.

Wyn and Aren were hiding in a rocky crevice, at least, Wyn thought they were still in a crevice in the rocks. Everything about this place was dark. He could feel the Void pressing against him, wanting to change him. He wondered if Aren felt it too. It wasn't safe to speak, not yet. Wyn didn't even trust himself to share his thoughts with Aren or breathe too loudly. They had to stay hidden. He had no idea how they were supposed to do that when everything else in the Void was composed of tenebrys. The two of them must have stuck out like lit candles in a dark room.

Yloran's description of the Void had hardly prepared him for the first step. He had known his sight would be compromised, but he hadn't expected complete and total darkness. He waited for his eyesight to adjust, knowing it wouldn't. This place was nothing like night, even when the moon was new, and the clouds hid the stars. The Void was a different level of darkness, a place completely without light. It wasn't just without light; tenebrys clung to everything like oil.

Wyn had tried to wipe it off when he and Aren first crossed over. Even the cavern beneath Mount Cyngol had been diluted by tenebrys. Wyn wondered at what point they had left Teraeniel. He hadn't felt any transition between the volcano's roots to this place. There hadn't been any identifiable marker, but he knew without a doubt that he was in the Void now and that he breathed it in. Nothing like this could possibly exist in Teraeniel and Wyn made a quiet prayer to Anaweh that it never would.

While Yloran's words had done little to prepare him, she had helped him find his way here. More, she had shared where she believed Alethea would be held. By no accident, that place was the same place where her delight in her bodily senses was kept. Wyn was to retrieve it. He worried she had only directed him there for her own selfish reasons—Yloran Eth Gnashar was a Sha'ghol after all. She had made no allusions to following any moral code other than her own. And yet, Wyn trusted her and had set off on this foolish endeavor. What choice did he have?

He could already hear Alethea scolding him for coming here.

While he couldn't see the great and terrifying citadels of Tosk rising around him, he could sense them. He had to be careful with his thoughts and using Yloran's name. Jaris Iln Desaris was here. He was dead, but death mattered little for souls trapped in the Void.

"We can't stay here," Aren whispered.

He was right. Someone was bound to pass through the only known accessible route between the Void and Teraeniel. Holding his breath, he took another step into the Void. It was just as dark, but Wyn thought he could perceive variations in its density. They were slight, and the more he tried to focus his eyes, the less he recognized. He didn't trust the place enough to use his interior senses here. The Void might have already begun to influence him, but he would not grant it further access than necessary. He refused to let it touch or even graze his mind and heart.

"The fortress is this way." Aren had a better sense of their surroundings than Wyn did.

The more Wyn adjusted to his surroundings—if it could be called adjusting—as they walked through Tosk, the more he was able to discern the differences in the city. Nothing about the Void was physical or built—dorthl wasn't a physical substance here in the Void. Dorthl took on different traits depending on which realm it occupied. In Teraeniel, it mimicked an onyx stone and in Somnaeniel, pools of oil. But here in the Void, it felt like formless smoke.

How he and Aren had not simply fallen into nothingness was beyond him, but they were already in a realm of non-existence. The only thing that filled this Void was tenebrys and dorthl. Tenebrys wasn't a physical thing though. Ramiel had corrupted his power linked to umbrys with the Void. The shadow and darkness had formed into something new, something horrible, and it clung to Wyn and Aren's bodies. Wyn might have blocked off his interior senses, but he could already hear the Void whispering to him, trying to pour into him.

"Don't listen to the whispers," Aren said.

They pushed forward and Wyn saw where they were headed. A vortex of a fortress filled his vision. He hadn't yet sensed anything so dense in this cursed city. Even as his eyes focused, the dorthl fortress remained stable. Twisted spires clawed upward and every roof pitch looked as though it too was a lance. As they neared the fortress, Wyn saw that its gates were unattended. Guards mattered little in Ramiel's realm. All the souls here were empty husks. If their spirit still lived, it had dimmed to an indecipherable light, not even a flicker in this overwhelming darkness.

He had no idea whether they had passed any souls or walked through them. Did the souls here remember what life was? Had any of their memories survived the Void's onslaught on their minds and hearts, dousing their spirits' vitality?

Wyn couldn't help but wonder if that light could be reignited in the souls lost here. Would they ever find their way out of the Void and into Life again? The death that mortals feared so much was this place. Ramiel's deception about mortality had led anacordel to cling to the World-Below, and in so doing they had lost themselves here in the Void. They clung to their mortal lives, refusing to let go and believing Life ended with the deterioration of the body. The elves with Life Immortal had understood the cycle. That had all changed when the Cyndinari had succumbed to the deception in exchange for power.

Wyn knew he shouldn't be thinking of the lost souls, allowing them to distract him. He still wondered and worried about them though. He and Aren passed through the gates, his mind abuzz as they walked into a great hall. The ethereal architectural elements were somehow perceivable, even inside with nothing else for the tenebrys and dorthl forms to play against. Like the exterior, every element felt like a sharp and twisted weapon, making Wyn wonder if this castle was indeed meant to be a weapon of some sort. Did Ramiel intend to pierce the veil between the Void and Teraeniel? The more he observed, the more logical it seemed. This castle—Vasknir—had a purpose. Ramiel didn't need a castle in the Void. He had spent his entire imprisonment forging this castle into the perfect lance and Wyn was sure beyond a shadow of doubt that Ramiel intended to use it.

He shivered as the realization struck, and knew he had to tell someone. Vasknir didn't need to strike fear into the lost souls here. They were mindless and stripped of everything as they wandered directionless.

Do you intend to join them? A familiar voice quipped in his mind. *Don't reply. They'll know if you do. You should not have come here. I'm afraid it matters little now though.*

Wyn sucked in his breath at the message as he followed Aren deeper into the castle, sensing Alethea. She burned like a sun in this place of eternal emptiness and darkness. Her spirit had not faltered and her presence beamed forth like a beacon now that he was aware of her.

They hurried through the castle's halls and descended deeper into its hold. Wyn hadn't let himself believe that she was gone, that the

Void had snuffed her out as it had done with all the lost souls here. He couldn't even allow the possibility aloud. And as he and Aren pushed on, he saw Alethea and heaved in relief. She was alive. Her legs were crossed and she floated above the oily surface as though in a trance, surrounded by a globe of light. Tenebrys and dorthl pressed against her, but the Void's corruptive fingers could not pass through.

"Come into the Light, you fools." Nothing confined Alethea, no chains, shackles, or rope.

Puzzled, Wyn asked, "Why didn't you try to escape?"

"The way out is hidden from me. If I had attempted to find it, I would have become lost in the Void's endless stretch. There is no saying where I would have ended, but I do know that I would have never found my way back to Teraeniel. Even Lumaeniel would have been barred to me from here. So, I stayed where they brought me and have never withdrawn from the wield I formed in Teraeniel when they stole me away. I do not think I would be able to recreate it here, as none of the erendinth are in this place—only tenebrys."

"You've been wielding lumenys all this time?" Wyn asked in disbelief.

"Time—I cannot recognize it anymore. Do I dare ask how long I've been here?"

"Too long," Wyn said.

Alethea then noticed Aren. "You've been freed, I see."

"I was reminded of who I was—am."

"Devlyn has that effect on many." Alethea smiled. "It is good to see you whole again, my friend."

"You know each other?" Wyn asked.

"We were aryls at the same time," Aren said.

Alethea seemed thoughtful, but didn't share her inner musings before saying, "I trust you did not come here without knowing the way out."

"I will. We have to retrieve something first. Only then will the way be revealed to me," Wyn said.

Alethea brought her hand to Wyn's head, her fingers barely grazing his temple. He didn't fight the intrusion into his mind and memories. The familiar interaction with his mentor rekindled the relationship which had been absent for far too long. Wyn hadn't realized how much he had missed Alethea. He opened himself to her touch and she learned all that had transpired since she had been taken. Sorrow and guilt and blame rushed into his mind, followed by agony and dread. She didn't scold him for seeking out Yloran to rescue her.

"Very well, let's be off then. Stay in my light, it'll keep the Void from touching you, though I fear it has already done its worst."

FOREBODING

The Thellish army arrived the day after the Dwonians. Given the Dark Flight's disturbing presence near Mindale's border to Krysenthiel and their unsettling disinterest in Binton's growing siege, the Guardian knights stayed in Verenthyl. Letters were sent to the elven aryls, the dwarven schtams, and to every human sovereign, including those on other continents. A message was even sent to the Meridean Conclave; the merpeople could not avoid this war.

The Guardian Senate had sat idle long enough; for the sake of Teraeniel, the international body had to come together. No one was safe from Erynor's scheming. Devlyn and Ellendren had even reached out to the Ealyn of Tenethyl, imploring them to join the Guardian Senate, a move they had long declined when the Senate had last been in session. Their voice and wisdom would be invaluable in this conflict.

As Teraeniel held its breath, Devlyn and Ellendren were at a military camp outside Binton. While their mission was much larger than simply retrieving a jewel, Devlyn fretted over their choice to remain here. They should be in Arenthyl; he felt it in his bones. Ellendren agreed. A weight pressed down on them, warning them of the danger they were in. Despite that ominous feeling, they hadn't received any guidance from Auriel or Uriel. If something was brewing, the anadel were just as blind to it as they were. Even if they were in the wrong place, they couldn't simply abandon their allies here or the lucilliae in Binton.

Whether or not this battle was a mistake, it was too late to alter their course of action. The Dwonian sand warriors had formed attack lines on the southern stretch of the city walls, the Mindalean forces under House Ashton assaulted the western gate and the Thellish forces sieged the eastern gate. Their forces battered the gates and walls as arrows rained down on them.

While many of the Mindalean nobles had abandoned their city and new king, Binton's city guard had no option but to defend their city against their own people. Cairn and the deserters would have slaughtered the city guard's families if they abandoned their posts. The deserters had also supplemented the city guard to defend the walls and gates. Even if any of the city guard had a change of heart during the battle, they would have to deal with the deserters fighting at their side. There was no room for dissent. Any city guard who showed a shift in loyalty would be quickly pushed off the defensive walls to their death.

As the battle unfolded, Devlyn waited at the back of the lines with Alex. He could have easily wielded and destroyed the gates or even a portion of the defensive wall. It would not have been the first time he exploded one of Binton's gates. But Velaria had cautioned him against joining the battle too soon. His strength would be needed once they reached the castle. The Dark Flight might not care what happened to Binton, but Erynor surely would. He might not have sent a Deurghol to defend the city, but he had plenty of shadow elves to spare. He would not forfeit the city without a proper fight.

Horns sounded and bells rang, signaling the fall of one of the gates—the city was breached. It felt odd being on this side of a battle. Devlyn had always been inside the city walls, defending beleaguered allies from the Erynien Empire. Another flurry of horns echoed as another gate fell.

Something felt wrong about this. "Does this seem too easy to you?" Devlyn asked Alex.

"Perhaps the Mindaleans inside the city have turned on their occupiers. I doubt the deserters were ever trained to defend a city, only how to assault one," Alex replied.

"I suppose. Something doesn't feel right though." The wrongness pervaded his bones.

"It only seems easy because we're all the way back here and aren't the ones engaged in the actual fighting. I assure you it'll feel less easy once we join the battle ourselves," Alex said, just as a runner came up to them.

Devlyn expected confirmation of his suspicions about whatever that wrongness was. "The ei'ana are in position; they haven't detected any traces of tenebrys in the city." Ellendren was with Velaria, Lara, and Daphne. Other ei'ana were with them, having accompanied Lara from Everin and Velaria from Septyl. They were intent on protecting as many people as possible from whatever heinous wields might be launched at the attackers. But according to the runner, there hadn't been any.

"None? You're telling me there aren't any shadow elves fighting back in that city?" Devlyn frowned. His unease squirmed inside him; he feared a trap would spring as soon as their forces pressed into the city. Binton had thousands of citizens, regular people who had never wanted anything to do with the Erynien Empire. Whatever was about to happen, Devlyn refused to let them pay for their nobles' schemes and past and present kings' allegiance. He was done pretending that nothing was wrong. Erynor would never relinquish Binton without a fight. He tapped into his innermost depths and bonded with Aliel; the world bloomed in light.

"I thought the plan had us waiting until our forces breached the castle," Alex said.

Jaerol stepped forward. "You're not thinking of going alone, are you?" Rusyl let out a low growl, digging up the dirt with his claws. Jaerol pulled himself onto the blue dragon's back, extending his hand to Liam. They weren't giving Devlyn a chance to object.

Alex cursed under his breath. "Bring Dennion." The winged horse appeared a moment later, his feathered wings folded back. "I'm not answering to Viren for this." The Guardian knight had gone with Ellendren, having been assured Devlyn would be far away from a fight.

Devlyn irritably waited for Alex to get in the saddle before darting into the sky. Ellendren pressed into his mind, concerned. *What are you doing?*

Something is wrong. We don't have time to wait for this battle to play out, he sent back.

I sense it too.

I'm not going alone. Alex, Jaerol, Liam, and Rusyl are with me.

Ellendren sent an encouraging mental embrace. *Keep your mind and heart open to me.*

As though I could close myself off from you.

They flew toward the city. The wind past his ears buffered most of the sounds of the battle below as Thellish forces poured into the city. The noticeable absence of high-pitched screeching and laughter of shadow elves was less consoling than it should have been. They were never welcome company, but them not being here to defend Binton had Devlyn's mind burning.

What was Erynor planning? Where was he directing his efforts while this battle occupied Devlyn and Ellendren? Aside from Cairn and the deserters, the Erynien Empire's forces had been disturbingly quiet since the Luminari had reclaimed Arenthyl. Considering the constant assaults before the Shroud's destruction, their absence nagged, and he realized he should have been more concerned about their withdrawal earlier. They had not vanished to allow the Luminari elves to peacefully settle into their reclaimed cities. No, Erynor had other plans. But what? Devlyn was suddenly very grateful that they had not pulled any of the Guardian knights from their posts in Krysenthiel.

Not having to concern himself with launching an attack on the outer gate, he flew over the last defensive stone wall and landed in the castle bailey. Alex landed beside him and Rusyl thudded to the ground, swiping his tail at the deserters there and baring his teeth. Devlyn wielded aerys to deflect volley after volley of arrows, changing their course back toward the deserters.

A swarm of them filled the bailey and enclosed their small party in a tight ring. Jaerol and Liam were quick to press into the erendinth, giving the deserters little chance to change their tactics. Rusyl roared fiercely and fire flew out of his maw, barreling toward the castle gate. They might not have needed to go through the gate themselves, but reinforcements certainly would.

Pulling more of the erendinth from his verathn's strength, Devlyn wielded aerys and swiped an attacker sideways, knocking him and several other deserters off their feet and into a stone wall. Devlyn whipped the scepter back just in time to deflect a spear, the full strength of its owner pushing down behind it. From the corner of his eye, he saw Jaerol and Liam fighting close to each other. Their movements were like a dance as they wielded both sword and erendinth. They complemented each other as though they had practiced each step and strike together.

Just as Devlyn thought they were getting the upper hand in the bailey, more defenders swarmed out of the castle. None of them were shadow elves and Devlyn again fretted over Erynor's plans. Devlyn didn't have the time to be stalled here. This battle, and especially his and Ellendren's part in it, had to end. The need to return to Arenthyl consumed him.

Images from Rusyl flashed through Devlyn's mind, picking up on Devlyn's sense of urgency. Rusyl insisted Devlyn, Jaerol, and Liam push their way into the castle and find the lucilliae. Rusyl and Alex, who fought from Dennion's saddle, would occupy the deserters.

Devlyn didn't wait for Jaerol and Liam to sign whether they were ready or even agreed with Rusyl about leaving the dragon and Thellish king behind. They could take care of themselves, especially when there weren't any shadow elves or Deurghol or dark dragons present. Still, the Dwonian deserters were fierce warriors. Rusyl growled, impatient with

Devlyn's lingering.

Glancing at the castle windows, Devlyn grabbed Jaerol and Liam's hands and shifted with them to an upper level where the window was dark. He knew nothing of the castle's layout and wished he had at least seen a floor plan of it. For all he knew about the castle, he could have taken the three of them to the armory where more of Cairn's deserters waited.

That didn't seem likely though. This chamber had plush colorful carpet and thick window coverings blocking out the sun. The dimly lit room had a regal air.

"Now what?" Jaerol whispered then heaved, trying to catch his breath after the battle they had just left.

Devlyn looked around the room and saw a woman poke her head past a doorway to the adjacent chamber. She realized Devlyn had seen her and pulled back with a yelp. "Wait," Devlyn called, quickly crossing to her, hoping she wouldn't sound any alarm or call for the guards.

"Get away, beast!" Terror mixed with hatred spilled out in her expression as Devlyn drew near. The room's only exit seemed to be the covered window.

Remembering he was still connected to Aliel, he withdrew. He hoped a more normal appearance would be less frightening to her, who on closer examination, looked no older than himself. Aliel sang soothingly, trying to calm the richly dressed woman, but Devlyn's elven appearance was even more distressing to her.

"I said, leave me be, beast!"

"I'm not here to hurt you. We're here to oust Cairn and the deserters; I'm Ei'denai Devlyn Lorenthien, Exalted Aryl of Krysenthiel," he said, hoping his title would reassure her.

"I know who you are and you're not welcome here," she spat back.

Devlyn blinked in confusion. Why did this woman hate him? "I don't understand."

"Have you forgotten your last visit to our city? I haven't." She stared at him with cold, spiteful eyes. "From that very window, I saw the explosion you caused several years ago at the city gate." She pointed to the window on the far wall. "The whole castle shook from the blast. Do you have any idea how detrimental that was?"

"In what way?" Devlyn asked, trying to calm her. Despite his sense of urgency, he felt a need to gain this woman's trust and to prove he wasn't the monster she accused him of being.

"Trade came to a complete stop while the gate was repaired. To say nothing of your careless disregard for life. You are nothing but a monster, bent on destroying our home."

"We were blocked off by shadow elves; we had no choice," Devlyn explained, uncertain now why he was defending his actions.

"Shadow elves in Binton? Don't be absurd," she laughed.

"Are you not aware of Mindale's role in the Erynien Empire?" Jaerol asked.

"Of course, I'm aware," she said, insulted.

"Shadow elves answer only to Erynor." Jaerol's patience seemed as thin as Devlyn's. "Do you not realize what's happening across Eklean from your castle window?"

"I know more than you realize, elf. If the gate wasn't still under repair, Cairn and his deserters would have had more difficulty getting in to kill my father. His death is on your hands."

"Priscilla," another woman chided. "They're here to rid us of Cairn."

"And after that? Do they intend to wed us and use us as breeding stock too?" Priscilla stared daggers at Devlyn, Jaerol, and Liam.

"Um, no," Devlyn responded, somewhat abashed. "I'm married and just found out that my wife is pregnant, and Jaerol and Liam are…"

"Quite taken with each other," Jaerol said flatly.

"I see." Priscilla turned to the other woman whom Devlyn hadn't seen. "Do you know them, Amelie?"

"I met the Cyndinari once before." Amelie looked at Jaerol, surprised at seeing him again. "Cairn took that fire you caused as a direct message from his ancestors. He claimed it was providence that the old ways had ended, and he could be a chief-king. At least, that's the story he spun to the other chiefs and elders." Amelie clutched a dagger. "I told you that night it would be my dagger that would end him."

"Can you take us to him? We don't have any time to waste," Devlyn said. "He's stolen something; we can't leave without it."

"That orange jewel? He won't take it off. It's making him insane," Amelie said.

"Can the lucilliae have adverse effects on people?" Liam asked.

"Not that I'm aware of." Devlyn was concerned that the lucilliae might become corrupted under Cairn's influence. "Will you take us?" He pled urgently.

Amelie sheathed her dagger and pushed aside a velvet drapery on an otherwise bare wall. Devlyn had assumed it was only meant to soften the stone room or provide some added warmth. But behind opened a narrow archway. Amelie nodded and shared a look with Priscilla.

"We've barricaded the door. I should be safe in here. Are there any more elves who can appear in my chambers without using the door?"

"Only one," Devlyn said as he, Jaerol, and Liam followed Amelie into the secret passage.

Aliel gave off the only light as Amelie led them deeper into the castle. Pushing aside another tapestry, she went down a corridor, stopping before a heavy wooden door. "The throne room is on the other side. Cairn will not be alone," she whispered.

Devlyn nodded and stepped forward, only to be stopped by Amelie, barring the way. "Is something the matter?" he asked.

"I want to be the one to end him," she said, unflinching, gripping the dagger. "He took my life from me; I *will* return the favor."

"Fine." As Devlyn eased the door open, bellows came from a gaudily dressed man sitting on the throne. That had to be Cairn. A rich mantle of green velvet covered a more traditional Dwonian outfit, the rough leather trousers and open vest clashing with the robe. Worse was the pointy crown and a myriad of necklaces, bracelets, and rings. Cairn was weighed down with what looked like all the wealth of the kingdom he had stolen.

"Cowards! Erynor dares betray us after we gave him everything. We bled and died for his empire. Our ancestors abandoned Dwonia for him!" Cairn brandished a spear that seemed to suck in the light. Devlyn recognized it as a dorthl spear at once.

He froze at the door behind the throne. Had anyone noticed he had cracked it open? He could hear others in the throne room as they shifted under Cairn's berating. The chief-king was enraged about Erynor seeming to desert him, leaving him to defend Binton on his own. Devlyn again fretted over why, the sense of foreboding building.

"His Imperial Majesty has not forsaken you." Devlyn felt himself chill at the new voice. He had no idea who it belonged to, only that it was not the voice of a deserter. Jaerol also tensed. "His designs are larger than an insignificant human kingdom. The Master beckons him."

"So, he sends you here in his stead? To advise without supplying an army—without providing any shadow elves to fight back, not one, but three armies sieging *my* city! We have no defense against ei'ana without shadow elves!"

"You are a fool if you think I came here to advise *you*. These fractured kingdoms and their borders will mean nothing after today."

"Then why are you here?" Cairn said.

"I came to deliver a message." The stranger's voice hung in the air as he hissed.

"Go on then. What message does His Imperial Majesty deem me worthy of?" Cairn asked, spiteful.

"It is not for you, but for the boy-king who came to retrieve his bauble. A fitting distraction. The Master is pleased you at least managed that." Devlyn could feel the stranger's eyes despite not being able to see him. "I believe you've eavesdropped long enough, Ei'denai Devlyn

Lorenthien, Exalted Aryl of a soon-to-be darkened Krysenthiel, High King of a fractured and warring Eklean, and Prelate of an empty Senate. None of your titles will survive this day. A new era will reshape this realm."

WORDS OF SHADOW

For a split second, Devlyn considered running. He didn't know who this stranger was, only that he was dangerous, and a terrible power oozed off him like oil. A voice screamed in Devlyn's head to shift back to Arenthyl at once, but Cairn would undoubtedly escape with the lucilliae if he did. Mindale's future would remain ambiguous and whoever was speaking to him could decide he wasn't as willing to forfeit the human kingdom as Erynor was. The stranger could stay behind and wrench the crown from Cairn's head and place it on his own.

Containing his doubts and fears and mustering his confidence, he pushed the door fully open and stepped into the throne room. The lucilliae hanging from a chain around Cairn's neck caught Devlyn's attention first. The chief-king was by no means a weak man, but the lucilliae weighed him down, as though it too wanted to be rid of him.

The chill in Devlyn's bones permeated further when he saw the speaker who had first brought on that chill. "I did consider remaining here and striking north. So many rich and powerful kingdoms for the harvesting. Be at ease, I'm here only to deliver a message."

"Deliver Erynor's message and be gone so I can finally end that wretch." Amelie stepped forward, not realizing how dangerous this Cyndinari elf was.

"I do not speak for Erynor." The elf laughed. "The Master would like you. So much hatred in that heart of yours. You've bent your life on

revenge. Yes, he would like you. I do hope you don't try something foolish and get yourself killed. Not that that will matter after today."

Jaerol urged Amelie back into the hidden passageway. "Ah, and
Jaerol Solaris."

"Hello, Kynol," Jaerol answered, his voice remarkably steady. It
was all the more shocking because he spoke the name of one of the
Sha'ghol. Kynol Min Othstrin was known to be Ramiel's Mouthpiece
and rarely left the Sha'ghol's citadel on Cyndinare, drinking in the Void
that had consumed it. He held a position that brought him nearest to
the Evil One. Ramiel was said to whisper directly to Kynol. Yloran had
claimed the relationship had driven Kynol insane.

"You have upset Erynor more than the boy-king has. He knew the
woman concealed some sort of weapon, but he never imagined that she
hid Auriel in her fragile frame. An irythil hiding away in a mortal. Pitiful.
Is there anything more cowardly? The irythil of the Luminari hidden
away for all those centuries in the Lorenthien heirs. The elves of the rising sun heed a coward, powerless in the Master's shadow. You shall suffer
the same coward's fate, only there will be no hiding this time. None can
hide from the Master in his Void. This reforged war was the only thing
Erynor has done right. He's kept you all distracted, just as Cairn has
done. That which you've thought impossible will come to pass and there
will be only one Master—kings and gods will fall and tremble beneath
his gaze. And those who refuse will suffer an eternity."

"What has he done?" Devlyn asked, terrified. His suspicions about
the lack of shadow elves and Deurghol and dragons was proving well
founded.

"All will be revealed when the Light goes out and you forever wake
in Darkness." Kynol laughed as a cloud of tenebrys engulfed him.

A commotion sounded from somewhere in the castle. Clashing
swords and spears and shields rang through the halls beyond the throne
room, echoing with violent clarity. The battle had reached the castle.
Devlyn didn't have the chance to wonder which army had pushed

through the city when Cairn lunged at him, thrusting his spear forward.

"When the Light dies and twilight follows the sun's peak, this day will usher in a new dawn of eternal twilight." Kynol did not move to join the fight but allowed his tenebrys wield to swallow him. The warning hung in Devlyn's mind, distracting him from Cairn.

"You will not take my crown from me and the jewel is mine by right as chief-king," he growled, rolling his spear into another thrust. Jaerol and Liam fell into their synchronized stance, intent on keeping other deserters from helping Cairn as he challenged Devlyn. The fighting outside the throne room intensified and sounded as though it had reached its doors. How many deserters had taken up positions outside to prevent the invading army from pushing through?

Devlyn's verathn answered each of Cairn's attacks. It moved weightlessly through the air, its crystalline shaft singing as it whipped back and forth to fend off Cairn's dorthl spear. He had yet to bond with Aliel. Cairn might be a skilled warrior, but he was no shadow elf. Devlyn could have wielded ignys and set the chief-king ablaze, but he worried about the lucilliae. Whatever influence Cairn had had over it was enough to be of concern. What sort of heinous acts had he committed with it hanging about his neck? Devlyn prayed that the lucilliae wasn't susceptible to corruption.

Jaerol and Liam fought efficiently, the memory of their treatment at the hands of the warriors of Tribe Liath bringing their synchronized defense to the fore as they battled the warriors, wielding their swords and the erendinth in unison. They easily fought back the deserters, even as the throne room doors crashed open.

Devlyn couldn't see past the throngs though and couldn't tell who had just forced their way in. Aliel was quiet; a disturbed stillness permeated the phoenix. Kynol's warning was like a dagger in the phoenix's spirit. Then a sense of panicked urgency flooded from Aliel. Devlyn had to end this and quickly.

Reaching into the depths of his spirit, he bonded with Aliel and the room exploded in crisp golden light. The stormy sky had washed the throne room in a bleak grey, but now Devlyn saw the world as it was meant to be seen. He leapt into the air and hovered over the fighting below. "Surrender," he said. It felt like a whisper, but everyone stilled, his voice reaching into them all. Only one person did not stop, for the command to surrender had not been directed at her, and Amelie thrust her dagger deeply into Cairn's back.

Cairn fell to his knees and on the brink of death, saw something with his dying eyes. "We were wrong." His voice shook with remorse, but whatever he now saw went beyond regret; he was petrified as death clawed at him.

———————————

Wyn, Aren, and Alethea left the holding cell and went back up through the fortress. From inside Alethea's bubble of light, Wyn was able to see Vasknir differently. The fortress was still composed of dense dorthl and tenebrys, but he saw it as he would see a tenebrys wield in Teraeniel. The black forms were anything but static as they shifted and morphed. Just like the erendinth wove through Teraeniel, tenebrys was a force that wove through this realm.

More astounding to see from within the globe of lumenys, were the lost souls Wyn hadn't seen before. They didn't seem to notice or recognize the light, as though they were blind to it, and blind to those inside it. "We cannot help them," Alethea said, pressing forward, having seen where Yloran had instructed Wyn to retrieve her stolen treasure.

They reached the specified twisted tower where nine illumined prisms hovered over the dark floor, as it drank in the little light they gave off. Aside from Alethea's wield, they were the only other lights in the Void. Each prism belonged to a Sha'ghol, and none were the same. They weren't locked away and Wyn wasn't stopped as he reached out for Yloran's prism. Somehow, he knew it belonged to her, recognizing her essence.

"Predictable."

They spun around to find Jaris Iln Desaris hovering by the entry. Unlike the other souls, Jaris was not lost, but he was dead.

"So, you've come after all. Of course, Yloran would ask you to retrieve this for her. She never forgave me for losing it. She made her choice; we all did. Go on, take it. Retrieve what she sent you for in exchange for freeing your esteemed mentor." Jaris drew closer. "Hello, Alethea Lenwyn. You'll have to forgive me for not coming down to see you after pulling you in here. As I'm sure you're aware, you were not my intended target; it was the Lorenthien boy-king."

"Your absence was more than welcome, Jaris." Alethea spoke with a familiarity with the Sha'ghol that caught Wyn off guard. Of course, they would have known each other before the elves were forced to abandon their Skylands and the Sha'ghol's allegiance was revealed. They had once been the esteemed leaders of Cyndinare, emulating the aldarchs.

"Ah, and Aren as well. Our Master is not pleased with you. You will suffer for your choice."

"I am no stranger to pain and Ramiel was never my master," Aren said, longing for release.

Jaris sneered. "You know, I have half a mind to call out for the Deurghol or Erynel. I recall you and she were always so fond of each other. She is still bitter and rather furious with the Lorenthien aryl. She's enraged that they managed to dispel her Shroud. But it served our Master's purpose, even now that it is gone."

"How do you mean?" Alethea pressed.

"Do you honestly think our Master cared about blocking the Luminari from Krysenthiel? Truly, Erynel's idiot son is fortunate our Master hasn't ordered his Deurghol to dispose of him after all his blunders. If Erynor hadn't focused so much of his attention on being a god-like emperor during his last reign, our Master's vision would have come to fruition a millennium ago. We were so close—we had nearly carved through all the ice that froze the roots in place. Fortunately for Erynor, time means nothing to our Master, but his patience has grown thin."

"Verakryl," Alethea breathed, her face blanching.

"Even the wise Alethea Lenwyn has come to the conclusion too late." Jaris laughed and spun around them.

BURIED TWILIGHT

Skimp had never had a large presence; no minum did. His race barely stood above human hips. Dwarves weren't much taller but were three times as wide and ten times as loud. Everyone knew when a dwarf was in the same room, but no one seemed to notice Skimp any more. He'd never felt so invisible. Everyone pretended he wasn't there. They must not have any more use for his seguians. That was a relief. He was tired, but the extreme lethargy he had felt was now gone.

The Deurghol hadn't ordered him to open a seguian in quite some time. Skimp had hoped that he would have recovered better with the reprieve, but he hadn't—he didn't feel anything. He felt empty, as though he were wasting away. He didn't even have an appetite, nor could he remember when he last ate something.

Only the Deurghol gave Skimp any notice now. Neither the shadow elves nor legionnaires acknowledged his presence, not even scowling at him. The Deurghol didn't demand anything of Skimp, only glared at him when they were near each other. Had he upset the Deurghol in some way? Had the Deurghol commanded everyone in Lake Saeryndol's frozen tunnels to shun Skimp? To what purpose?

Skimp hadn't returned to the mass elven grave. While the sight had repulsed him, something else had kept him from going back. He felt a mental block that he didn't want to break through just yet. Something painful. Instead, Skimp swept through the icy tunnels like a specter. The

Erynien legion here had been digging continuously since they'd arrived. Whatever they were looking for, they only had so much time before the lake fully melted. Water already pooled in the tunnels and pits had to be dug to guide the water away from where the legion devoted their energy.

The excavation network largely remained the same, but the once-abandoned tunnels were significantly deepened. Many of the legionnaires complained about the productivity of the long-dead Luminari elves who had been enslaved here. They said they should have found what Erynor wanted during their time here. Skimp didn't think that was fair. Why would the Luminari elves from back then want to help the Erynien Empire?

Going further down a tunnel that had seen a lot of activity, Skimp followed the sounds of what seemed to be a celebration. Skimp had never seen the legionnaires celebrate before. They were a mean group of Cyndinari elves and Skimp had only ever seen them thrive on their cruelty.

He carefully navigated through the rough, jostling crowd. The cold light reflected off the ice, as it had throughout the excavation. But it changed the closer Skimp got to the end. The light didn't darken or lessen as it did in the other deep tunnels that reached the lakebed.

Whatever the Erynien legion was digging for, they must have found it. Curious, Skimp snuck past the many Cyndinari elves. The Deurghol was already present. He looked at Skimp—looked through Skimp—then said, "Inform the Emperor that we've found it."

"We won't need to. He'll receive the message faster than the minum was ever able to travel," said a deep voice, one of the Sha'ghol. Skimp didn't know who he liked less, the Sha'ghol or the Deurghol. The legionnaires backed away, forming a path between the Sha'ghol and the Deurghol. The Sha'ghol carried a sharpened stave that drank in the light, corrupting whatever it touched. Not even the legionnaires risked allowing the corrupted verathn, laced with dorthl, to touch them. Only death followed in its wake.

The Sha'ghol walked through the parted elves and toward the source of light that not even his stave could lessen. Skimp, trailing after him, saw the light's source. A massive crystalline root, frozen solid, snaked through the chipped away ice.

The light coming off the root thrummed, almost nervously. Skimp then realized what the root was and wailed, "No!"

"They cannot hear you." The Deurghol smirked as he looked at Skimp. "Not yet."

The Sha'ghol reached the frozen root, lifted his corrupted verathn, then stabbed down.

The world shattered.

A laugh peeled through the room. Was the Sha'ghol still here? Was he laughing at them while hidden in the darkness? A cry pierced Devlyn's soul. It did not come from Cairn. This wail was omnipresent—the cry of a god dying. It shrieked through every moment of existence and every heart felt its stabbing pain. There wasn't a chance to question it, for the world darkened and the ground shook. Even with Devlyn's illumined Phaedryn sight, everything went dark. Twilight descended on Teraeniel, just as Kynol had promised. Had the sun suddenly been blocked? Not like an eclipse, but worse. The light was simply gone, swallowed by the Darkness.

Cairn's body crumpled to the floor, but his spirit and soul remained; his specter knelt where his body had fallen. Devlyn could see the ghost, and Cairn's was not the only one. Wayward specters filled the throne room. All those who had died in the battle were still there, lingering, confused. They had not yet had the opportunity to pass to the World-Beyond. Their lives had ended so suddenly and violently while in their prime. They had not had the chance to make peace with their death, and so they remained, now visible to the living.

Devlyn came down, landing in front of Cairn's kneeling ghost.

The petrified expression remained. Whether Cairn could speak as a ghost or not was a mystery, but he was silent as Devlyn took the lucilliae from his corpse, Amelie's dagger protruding from his back.

––––––––––––––

Wyn turned to Alethea; he had never seen her so frightened before, not even when the Void had swallowed her. "What's happened?" he asked, feeling her terror.

"It is the dawn of eternal twilight and you are too late to stop it. The Tree is dead and the barrier between here and the other realms will be shattered. The Void will swallow all and you will never know the touch of Light again."

"Wyn, Yloran's prism, hurry," Alethea urged.

"You are too late," Jaris laughed again.

Even so, Wyn grabbed the prism and immediately knew how to escape, relieved she had not sent him to his doom.

"Trying to leave before the spectacle?" someone else said, accompanied by two others.

Wyn and Aren pressed closer to Alethea, who was struggling to maintain her wield of lumenys.

"We Deurghol required a shell to reach your realm. The shells Erynor sacrificed for our use, including his own son, were our gateways into your realm when they wrought the Shroud into existence. My shell was destroyed when that wretched woman and the concealed coward, Auriel, disposed of the elf. Like Ramiel, we could not pass the Tree. But now, we won't need a shell."

Wyn felt everything move as a powerful force swept through the fortress. If they were in a physical realm with anything but tenebrys and dorthl, a wind would have rushed against and past them. The still and quiet of the Void crashed against something foreign—something not of the Void. The castle did not break, but a great slicing sound sheared the air, followed by the sound of something shattering. A rush of explosions ensued; eruptions thundered as the Void tore into Teraeniel, no longer confined to a hidden-away pocket. The erendinth revolted at the immense influx of tenebrys.

"We Deurghol are free once more. The beasts of the Void are free, monsters which Teraeniel has not witnessed since the Elder Days, before we were locked away. Teraeniel will quake beneath their feet. All will bow to Ramiel," the Deurghol declared, the hiss of his voice turning into a scream as Vasknir's dorthl walls solidified in the physical realm. "Return to the people you *love*. Go to them and see if your precious *love* will save you. The Tree is dead!" the Deurghol shrieked in delight. "Anaweh cannot save you pitiful anacordel a second time. You will bow to your rightful god."

The ground trembled as they fled the tower and passed through the great hall with the empty throne. Something roared in the distance, the sound reaching deep into Wyn's bones. Vasknir had pierced a hole between the Void and Teraeniel and the monsters from the Elder Days were returning. As Wyn, Aren, and Alethea hurried out into the sulfuric air of the Shadow Mountains, on the slopes of Mount Cyngol, they realized that the fortress wasn't the only part of Tosk to have been wrenched from the Void and into Teraeniel. The whole city now clung to the volcano. Every structure was woven of dorthl, and now that they were in a physical realm, their smoky, ethereal forms had solidified into onyx lusterless stone.

Wyn shivered, seeing the sun's light doused; he reached out to Eolwn and Leithel. The griffins did not belong here, looking just as foreign in this city as Vasknir was in Eklean: even here in the Shadow Mountains it did not belong.

No ghosts or servants of Shadow tried to stop them as they mounted the griffins at the fortress' gate, Wyn on Eolwn and Aren behind Alethea on Leithel. The ground rumbled as more beasts clawed their way out of the Void—out of the volcano—and back to where they had first walked. Terrified, the griffins immediately took flight, carrying their riders away from Tosk and Vasknir.

Wyn glanced back over his shoulder; the dorthl fortress seemed a black void, making the Shadow Mountains appear almost vibrant in contrast. His heart sank as he realized what they were up against and if the Deurghol and Jaris had spoken true, with the Tree of Life dead, Anaweh would not be able to save them. And worse, if someone died, they would not pass over to Lumaeniel. Ramiel had sealed that path with the Void.

Ellendren rushed into the Mindalean throne room, escorted by Viren and Velaria. She didn't know which army had breached the castle, only that the battle had mattered little. The menacing laughter still hung in her ears just as the cry still pierced her heart. Everything had gone dark. She had only touched Verakryl once; the Tree of Life was a beacon of Anaweh's Light in Teraeniel. What she had not realized at the time was that the Tree of Life was Anaweh. And now, the Tree was dead.

As though Ramiel's release into Teraeniel was not harrowing enough, they were now without Anaweh. Ramiel had not only claimed Teraeniel with the Void, but he had killed Anaweh's presence in Teraeniel in the process. Ellendren's heart quickened. Did that also mean that Anaweh the Creating Light was dead in Lumaeniel? Had that realm of the Creating Light also darkened? Had Anaweh's Breath gone still in Somnaeniel?

Too many questions needing answers.

She pushed through the stunned men and women who had just been fighting and killing one another, thinking they were each other's enemies. She went to Devlyn, kneeling at what had to be the dead chief-king's body, kneeling in front of a ghost. The throne room was filled with specters. Sitting on the throne behind Cairn's ghost was the late King Lawrence Maroven's ghost. Ellendren wondered why he hadn't transitioned to the World-Beyond. Had he lingered because he had yet to find peace with his death, or had something else prevented him? Was he pre-vented from transitioning? Had the dead been blocked from travelling to Lumaeniel? She thought of her parents. How long had the way been blocked? Were they still lost in Teraeniel?

Too many questions.

"We have to go," she said, snapping Devlyn out of his trance. The lucilliae hung by a chain between his fingers.

He nodded. They were both still bonded with their phoenix, but neither saw the world as though it was lit by a thousand suns anymore. The Tree was dead and with it, the Light had gone.

HERE ENDS THE SIXTH PART OF

THE JEWEL OF LIFE:

MEMORIES OF TWILIGHT

LOOK FOR THE SEVENTH PART OF

THE JEWEL OF LIFE

APPENDIX A

GLOSSARY OF TERMS

ABBEY SCHOOL

The preferred system of education for children throughout Eklean. Those deemed capable are sent to higher studies, preferably at Gwilnor Academy.

AELISH

Native language of the elves. Largely forgotten, only used in academic circles.

AELITH

Group of Aldinari elves who have been corrupted by the Darkness on Aldinare and live in the cities.

AERETHYN

Orb holding the lived memories of Kien and Kiara.

AERODHAL

Royal Palace in Arenthyl. Residence of the Exalted Aryl of Krysenthiel.

AERYS

An elemental erendinth. The essence of air.

ALBIEN

One of the seven Schools of Septyl. Albiens focus on truth and care for many of Eklean's libraries. Motto: Truth is discoverable. Emblem: A naked male and female elf holding unraveled scrolls with an owl perched behind, cast in gold on a white field. The chair of Albien is known as the Seeker.

ALDARCH

Deific rulers of Aldinare who reigned from their sanctums.

ALDINARE

Western Skyland of the Aldinari, one of the four elven kindreds. Lost to the Darkness. Only a hundred Aldinari escaped the Skyland with their lives.

ALICORN

A legendary beast native to the Skyland of Aldinare. A winged unicorn.

ANADEL

Spiritual creatures that predate Teraeniel and Somnaeniel. Their native home is Lumaeniel. There are four known classifications of anadel: irythil, enthiel, lorendil, and naril.

Anacordel

Creatures of body, soul, and spirit.

Anaweh

The Creating Light.

Animys

A transcendental erendinth. The essence of spirit.

Aquaeys

An elemental erendinth. The essence of water.

Arantiulyn

One of the seven Schools of Septyl. Arantiulyns focus on strength and protection and oversee the Knights of Septyl. Motto: With fortitude, we will protect. Emblem: A naked male and female elf in a fighting stance with swords in hand with a lion prowling cast in gold on an orange field. The Chair of Arantiulyn is known as the General.

Arcane Gems

Sources of magic used by the Mages of the Kilnae Del.

Archsteward

Part of the Ei'ceuril hierarchy, they are elevated wise ones. Before kien wielders were restricted to the Temple of Ceur, archstewards lived in every major city of Eklean tending to those faithful to Anaweh, the Creating Light.

Arenthylean Bells

Twenty-four bells composed of four materials that ring every hour.

Aryl

The united head of an elven house composed of a king and queen or lord and lady.

Auburnis

One of the seven Schools of Septyl. Auburnises focus on inner peace. Motto: To love is our gift. Emblem: A naked male and female elf offering a garland with larks flying above, cast in gold on a brown field. The Chair of Auburnis is known as the Pilgrim.

Aurephaen

Feast day of the Luminari, commemorating Auriel and the dawning sun. Celebrated on the 15th of Aurenth, the spring equinox.

AZURELLE

One of the seven Schools of Septyl. Azurelles focus on the advancement and training of the erendinth. Motto: The zealous soul must be temperate. Emblem: A naked male and female elf wielding the powers with a dragon behind, cast in gold on a blue field. The Chair of Azurelle is known as the Blue Dragon.

BELIN'S WATCH

An Evellion city in the Vespien Mountains comprised of humans and dwarves. Named for Belin, the dwarf who sheltered Thellion refugees in their greatest hour of need.

BOREPHAEN

Feast day of the Eldinari, commemorating Boriel and the sleeping sun. Celebrated on the 15th of Borenth, the winter solstice.

BOWL OF THENIEL

Sea set apart by the merpeople as sacred. The place where Theniel brought the waters to Teraeniel.

CENTAUR

Anacordel dedicated to protecting the forests of Eklean, particularly the Illumined Wood. The upper body is like an elf's but broader and more rugged while the lower body looks much like a four-legged horse.

CEURENDOL

The Jewel of Life. Created by the Luminari by placing their life essence within seven jewels of incredible brilliance which allowed them to share their immortality with every race in 1.3a (7085.3E). Also known as the Light Diamond, the Lieben Stone, and the Heart of Hearts.

CEURENDOL WAR, THE

A cataclysmic war instigated by the Erynien Empire which began over a philosophical difference over the Jewel of Life and whether immortal life was proper for the 'lesser races.' The war divided Eklean in two factions, those faithful to the Luminari and those subjugated by the Erynien Empire. As the fate of the war grew clear, emissaries and merchants from other continents withdrew from Eklean, fearing the Erynien Empire. 322-500.3a (7407-7585.3E).

CEURENYL

City founded by the ei'ceuril. Home of the Temple of Ceur and Gwilnor Academy. The only city not to fall into Erynor's control when Krysenthiel was lost to the Shroud.

CEURTRIARCH

Leader of the ei'ceuril, known as High Archsteward and Arbiter of the Light.

CHANCELLOR

The head of Gwilnor Academy under the authority of and appointed by the Seven Chairs.

CHILDREN

When capitalized, refers to the proto-race.

CITADEL, THE

Seat of the Sha'ghol on Cyndinare.

COR'LERA

A small village in eastern Parendior and in disputed territory claimed by both Lucillia and Perrien. The vineyards of Cor'lera produce the coveted ice wine, the Cor'leran Blue.

CRIMSYN

One of the seven Schools of Septyl. Crimsyns focus on healing and run many hospitals and infirmaries throughout Eklean. Motto: Through healing, hope is given. Emblem: A naked male and female elf dancing with a dog, cast in gold on a red field. The chair of Crimsyn is known as the Physician.

CYNDINARE

Southern Skyland of the Cyndinari, one of the four elven kindreds. Lost to the Darkness.

CYNETHOL

Home of the Cyndinari, situated among the Kinzdol Islands.

DAERENETH

Continent south of Ogren and west of Ja'Horan. Tropical continent.

DAWN AGE

The time frame that the Qien Dynasty refers to following the period in their history where Tolvenol, the Dark Primus, ruled over the continent of Qien. The elves refer to this as the First Era.

DEURGHOL

The Cyndinari directly responsible for the Shroud. They are neither living nor dead. Also known as the Deathless.

DORTHL

Substance that manifests differently in the different realms, either as a solid, a liquid, or a gas. Nullifies the erendinth and boosts tenebrae.

Draelyn

A mixed race anacordel of dragon and elven origins.

Draelish

Native language of the draelyn.

Dragon

Legendary creatures bound to the erendinth.

Druids of Kweil Aitch, the

Secluded faction of humans who learned to walk Somaeniel, the World-in-Between early on.

Dwarf

Anacordel who sought the deep roots of the mountains.

Ealyn

Leaders of the draelyn of Tenethyl.

Ei'ana

An organized group of wielders. Since the Balance was lost during the Ceurendol War, there are only kiara wielders among the ei'ana. There has not been a kien wielder among the ei'ana for over a thousand years.

Ei'ana Counsels

A series of norms ei'ana are to follow in regards to wielding. The counsels prohibit men from becoming ei'ana due to their inability to wield safely after the Balance was lost. The counsels also require ei'ana to bring kien wielders to the Temple of Ceur for their own protection and the protection of their communities.

Ei'ceuril

A religious order, currently a majority of men, focused on serving Anaweh, the Creating Light. Because a kien wielder is not capable of wielding with control, every male ei'ceuril capable of wielding is confined to the Temple of Ceur.

Ei'denai

Elven lord serving as aryl with his spouse. Head of House.

Ei'ethil

Elven lord.

Ei'lythel

Elven lady.

EI'PHAENYL

Instructor of the Phaedryn on Phroenthyl.

EI'TEREL

Elven lady serving as aryl with her spouse. Head of House.

EKLEAN

Continent where the anacordel first stirred as Children.

ELDER DAYS

The Elder Days span from the beginning of creation until what the elves refer to as the First Era, following Ramiel being sealed away in the Void and the creation of the separate races.

ELDER ONES

Anacordel that evolved from the Children before the Great Blessing, at which time the different races were solidified.

ELDIN WOOD, THE

Home of the Eldinari.

ELDINARE

Northern Skyland of the Eldinari, one of the four elven kindreds. Lost to the Darkness. The Eldinari were the first to evacuate their Skyland for the lands below.

ELEMENTAL ERENDINTH, THE

Forces wielded to influence the elements. *See Erendinth.*

ELF

Anacordel who changed little when the different races were created. Because they wished to retain their original form, their immortality remained, and they were gifted the Skylands. There are four elven kindreds, the Luminari, Cyndinari, Aldinari, and Eldinari.

ELYA

Powerful wielders born of any race who learn to wield instinctively and are not limited to the restrictions common to normal kien and kiara wielders.

EMRADIEL

One of the seven Schools of Septyl. Emradiels focus on beauty and life. Motto: Only the prudent thrive. Emblem: A naked male and female elf gesturing with open palms toward the beauty around them with a stag behind, cast in gold on a green field. The chair of Emradiel is known as the Tender.

ENTHIEL

Anadel dedicated to one of the seven irythil. The enthiel are very involved with the anacordel. A single enthiel guides an entire people.

ERENDINTH, THE

The erendinth are the wielded powers believed to have created Teraeniel. Tradition says that there are seven powers, three transcendental: lumenys, animys, and umbrys; and four elemental: aquaeys, aerys, terys, and ignys. Much is forgotten or unknown about the full extent of the erendinth which are dependent on inner spiritual and emotional workings.

ERENDINTH GAMES, THE

A game of wielding created at Gwilnor Academy, involving the wielding of all seven erendinth.

FAUN

Short nocturnal anacordel with the hind legs of a goat from the navel down. Some fauns have horns.

FULP

Dwonian staple that is mashed into a starchy dish.

GIANT

Anacordel that were drawn to the frozen north. During the Great Blessing, their physical features became capable of withstanding the harsh tundra of Glacien.

GLACIEN

Northern frozen continent spanning the northern pole. Connects Eklean and Ogren.

GOBLIN

Anacordel native to the Kinzdol Islands. Known for their monetary shrewdness.

GOBLIN GUILD

Infamous bank and guild of Eklean. Regulates the majority of Eklean's currency. The Goblin Guild is based in the Kinzdol Islands with branches in every city and most villages.

GREAT BLESSING, THE

Event recorded in the Theseryn where Anaweh blessed the growing differences among the anacordel and solidified their choices by making each their own distinct race.

GRILAE

Red flowering fruit trees native to Cyndinare.

Guardian Knights

Order of knights once based in Krysenthiel that served and protected all the land from injustice. The Guardian Knights were largely composed of Luminari and were defeated during the Ceurendol War.

Guardian Senate, the

An international body, crossing countries and continents to ensure the wellbeing of Teraeniel. Disbanded toward the end of the Ceurendol War.

Gwilnor Academy

The foremost school dedicated to the education of wielders, located in Ceurenyl.

Holy Tomes

Volumes recorded by various ei'ceuril, some being prophets, and from which the ei'ceuril base their beliefs and practices.

Human

Anacordel that differ among themselves more than any other race. They traveled the furthest from the Valley of Saeryndol, migrating across the entirety of Teraeniel.

Ignys

An elemental erendinth. The essence of fire.

Ilithae

Silver leafed trees native to Aldinare. The only ilithae trees to survive the doom of Aldinare are found in the Wooded Hills of Thellion.

Illumined Wood, the

A vast forest with mysterious qualities and inhabitants.

Imperium

Selective school for Cyndinari youth. Its violent academic style educates the next generation of shadow elves.

Irythil

The seven anadel who, under Anaweh's guidance, introduced the erendinth, thereby creating Teraeniel.

Jadien

Island and city-state in the Erynien Bay.

Ja'horan

Continent south of Eklean. Inhabited largely by nomadic peoples.

JAHRO ISLANDS

Island chain in the Unarian Sea. Believed to be the home of pirates.

JIENZU

Heart, mind, and body practice of meditation, breathing, and body positions called forms, used by the draelyn and ancient elves to achieve balance. Largely forgotten.

JUDGES OF YANIL

An order that once ruled beside the Yanilean. The judges are now a secret organization that strives to uphold law and order with limited influence.

KEEPER

Head of the time wardens and possessor of the time key.

KIARA WIELDER

A female wielder. Kiara wielders learn to control the erendinth easily but require a kien wielder to reach their potential strength. Because the Balance was lost, kiara wielders are not able to reach their potential strength.

KIEN WIELDER

A male wielder. Kien wielders reach their potential strength easily but require a kiara wielder to learn control of the erendinth. Because the Balance was lost, kien wielders are not able to wield safely, and if any male begins to show an aptitude to wield, he is sent to the Temple of Ceur where wielding is impossible.

KILNAE DEL

Order of mages native to Charren, headquartered in the Charrenese capital, Karithel.

KINZDOL ISLANDS

An archipelago in southern Eklean, homeland to the goblins and Cyndinari.

KIRENAE

Gold flowering fruit trees native to Luminare.

KWEIL AITCH

Island east of the Illumined Wood. The place where the veil is thin between Teraeniel and Somnaeniel.

LAY VOTARY

A non-clerical class of ei'ceuril.

LETHIEN

A mixed race anacordel of elven and human origins. Largely extinguished by

Erynor during and after the Ceurendol War.

LORENDIL

Anadel that guard and protect individual anacordel. Some anacordel are known to communicate with their lorendil.

LUCILLIAN ALLIANCE, THE

An alliance of the Eklean kingdoms established to return peace and order to Eklean following Emperor Erynor's disappearance.

LUMAENIEL

The World-Beyond. Dwelling of Anaweh, the anadel, and those anacordel who have passed beyond.

LUMENYS

A transcendental erendinth. The essence of light.

LUMINARE

Eastern Skyland of the Luminari, one of the four elven kindreds. Lost to the Darkness. The Luminari evacuated their Skyland for the lands below where they established Krysenthiel.

MAR'ANATHYL

City on the Skyland of Luminare. Governed by the Lorenthien aryls.

MASTERS, THE (SEVEN MASTERS, THE)

Vigyl Vyoletryn, Cyrelle Azurelle, Lanielle Emradiel, Lyon Arantiulyn, Mainor Auburnis, Caelyn Crimsyn, and Saeyrn Albien are the founders of the Seven Schools of Septyl and Gwilnor Academy.

MERIDEAN CONCLAVE

Governing council of the merpeople.

MERIDEPHAEN

Feast day of the Cyndinari, commemorating Meridiel and the noon sun. Celebrated on the 15th of Meridenth, the summer solstice.

MERPEOPLE

Anacordel who longed for the depths of Teraeniel's oceans.

MIERVAE

Anacordel who longed to nurture Teraeniel's forests. Miervae are also referred to as Great Trees and begin their life as Settlings.

MINUM

The least of Eklean's anacordel. A short mixed race anacordel of goblin and human origins. Before the elves migrated to Eklean, they were enslaved, sold by goblins to humans.

Naril

Anadel reminiscent of the seven erendinth. There are seven types of narils and they are commonly known as nymphs.

Neridu

Group of Aldinari elves who have been corrupted by the Darkness on Aldinare and live in the wilderness.

Nymphs

See Naril.

Observant

Non-wielders who have dedicated themselves to one of the Seven Schools of Septyl.

Ogre

Brutish anacordel covering the vast majority of Ogren. Mixed race anacordel of giant and human origins.

Ogren

Continent east of Eklean and west of Qien. Mountainous land with a mixture of forests and deserts. Inhabited by giants, humans, and ogres.

Parenhal

Citadel of the Phaedryn in Arenthyl.

Phaedryn

Those bound with a phoenix.

Phroenthyl

Small Skyland that is home to the Gold Flight and base of learning for Phaedryn.

Purged Desert of Dwonia, The

A vast wasteland in western Eklean that was rumored to have at one point been fertile. Home of the Twelve Tribes of Dwonia.

Return

The final stage of formation of an ei'ceuril toward becoming a steward. Often occurring in the Illumined Wood.

Sanctum

Expansive complexes housing the aldarchs and their courts on Aldinare.

Sand Warrior

Dwonian guardian responsible for protecting Dwonia's tribes and lands.

Schtach

Language of the dwarves.

Schtam

(1) A dwarven people. (2) The dwellings of the dwarves.

Schtamite

The eight dwarven schtams.

Seguian

A portal created to traverse space and time. Traversing time is restricted and only the keeper can use the time key to traverse time.

Septyl

(1) The order of Ei'ana composing the Seven Schools of Septyl. (2) The city of the ei'ana in Krysenthiel and now lost in the Shroud.

Septyl Knights

Order of knights dedicated to Septyl. The knights receive their training at Gwilnor Academy and vow to serve one of the Seven Schools of Septyl.

Seraph

Six winged anadel in Lumaeniel.

Servants of Shadow

Secret organization carrying out the orders of shadow elves and, in some instances, the orders of the Deurghol.

Settling

Tree-like creatures that wander about in their youth until finding an appropriate place to settle their roots and grow into a Miervae, also known as a Great Tree. Settlings have unique vitality qualities.

Seven Chairs of Septyl, the

The leaders of the Ei'ana. Each of the Seven Schools elects its own Chair who leads his or her particular School and participates in the leadership of Septyl. Responsible for admitting student wielders into Gwilnor Academy and selecting a chancellor.

Seven Schools of Septyl, the

The order of Ei'ana, composed of Albien, Arantiulyn, Auburnis, Azurelle, Crimsyn, Emradiel, and Vyoletryn Schools.

SHADOW ELVES

Cyndinari who consume the spirit of others to prolong their own life.

SHA'GHOL

Past rulers of the Cyndinari. First to communicate with Ramiel after her was imprisoned and wield tenebrys.

SHIFTING

(1) The ability to teleport in Somnaeniel. (2) The Phaedryn ability to teleport physically in Teraeniel.

SHROUD, THE

A diseased-looking fog placed by the Cyndinari over the entirety of Krysenthiel. It severed the Luminari from the Jewel of Life, cutting them off from their life essence and making them mortal, as well as any others who had benefited from it. An unanticipated result was that the Cyndinari also lost their immortality with that placement of the Shroud over the Jewel of Life. The Shroud's mysterious origin is one reason no one has been able to remove it.

SKYLANDS, THE

Four island countries, Aldinare, Cyndinare, Eldinare, and Luminare, floating in the clouds thousands of feet above the ground. The dwelling places of the elves before they were forced to evacuate to the land below.

SOJOURNERS

The exiled of Dwonia who sought reentrance after forming an allegiance with the Erynien Empire.

SOMNAENIEL

The World-in-Between. A realm visited by dreamers. Gateway between Lumaeniel and Teraeniel.

SOPHILLIAE

Orbs that preserve knowledge.

SOPHILLIAN

Head Librarian of the Sophillium

SOPHILLIUM

The great library of Septyl that houses the sophilliae.

STAR WARDEN

An elven military unit, typically ensuring the protection of their lands.

Stellendae

Remarkably large trees native to Eldinare that now dominate the Eldin Wood and serve as dwelling places for the Eldinari elves.

Steward

A clerical class of ei'ceuril with the ability to wield.

Stewards of Shadow

Ei'ceuril stewards who forsook Anaweh to support Ramiel.

Temple of Ceur, the

Home to the ei'ceuril and pilgrimage site for the faithful. It is impossible to wield within the temple walls. All kien wielders are confined to the Temple of Ceur.

Temple Knights

Order of knights dedicated to protecting the Temple of Ceur and the city of Ceurenyl. Some of the temple knights are men who were brought to the temple when it was discovered that they could wield. These temple knights are prohibited from leaving the temple.

Tenebrae

An unrecognized School of Septyl intended to replace the other seven Schools. Its adherents focus on power and dominance. Motto: Might conquers. Emblem: A naked male and female elf standing triumphantly on seven broken emblems, cast in gold on a black field. The chair of Tenebrae is known as the Conqueror.

Tenebrys

A corrupted form of the erendinth, unrecognized by the Ei'ana of Septyl as one of the erendinth and absolutely forbidden to wield. The essence of Darkness.

Tenethyl

(1) Jeweled city of the draelyn hidden in the Illumined Wood. (2) City destroyed by Ramiel's forces before the Great Blessing.

Teraeniel

The World-Below. Composed of the continents Daereneth, Eklean, Glacien, Ja'Horan, Ogren, and Qien.

Terys

An elemental erendinth. The essence of stone.

Theseryn

Holy tome recording the creation of Teraeniel and the anacordel, written by the first Ceurtriarch of the Ei'ceuril. The Theseryn states that seven irythil, under Anaweh's guidance, introduced the erendinth thereby creating Teraeniel.

TIME KEY

An artifact created by the Luminari to restrict the ability to traverse space and time. It was entrusted to the minums, the least of Eklean's races.

TIME WARDENS

A select group of minums entrusted by the Luminari with the ability to create seguians, allowing them to travel to any place and any time.

TOSK

City in the Void.

TRANSCENDENTAL ERENDINTH, THE

Wielded forces to influence the ethereal realities of lumenys, animys, and umbrys. The ability to wield the transcendental erendinth is forgotten.

TREE SPIRITS

Narils who agreed to bond with the trees under Sariel's guidance.

UMBRYS

A transcendental erendinth. The essence of shadow.

URDA

Garment the Dwonians use to protect their heads from the sand, sun, and wind.

VAER

Fruit native to the Illumined Wood.

VALLEY OF SAERYNDOL

Birthplace of the Children, the first anacordel.

VERAKRYL

A crystalline tree within Mount Verinien which brought life to the world and is connected to Anaweh. Also known as the Tree of Life.

VERATHEL

Sprouts of Verakryl, the Tree of Life.

VERATHN

Weapons of power.

VESPEPHAEN

Feast day of the Aldinari, commemorating Vespiel and the setting sun. Celebrated on the 15th of Vespenth, the autumn equinox.

VOID, THE

A realm that existed before Teraeniel and Somnaeniel. Realm of Ramiel and the fallen anadel.

VYOLETRYN

One of the Seven Schools of Septyl. Vyoletryns focus on justice and diplomacy. Motto: With justice, peace. Emblem: A naked male and female elf holding a staff with an eagle soaring above, cast in gold on a violet field. The chair of Vyoletryn is known as the Watcher.

WIELDERS

Anacordel capable of wielding the erendinth.

WINGED HORSES OF THELLION

Ancestors of the grey coursers of Perrien.

WISE ONES

(1) Part of the Ei'ceuril hierarchy. There is no certainty how many are among the ei'ceuril. (2) Part of the Ei'ana hierarchy. There are seven wise ones for every School of Septyl.

YANILEAN, THE

The undisputed monarch of Yanil, always male. Used both as the monarch's title and as his name during his reign.

DAYS OF THE WEEK
(Based on the seven anadel involved in the creation of Teraeniel)
Gwynthaen–Thenaen–Uraen–Ramaen–Lerenaen–Saraen–Karaen

MONTHS/MOONS
(Based on the anadel attached to the elves)
Spring – Marenth, Aurenth, Delenth
Summer – Dynenth, Meridenth, Reventh
Autumn – Kyrenth, Vespenth, Orenth
Winter – Estlenth, Borenth, Lierenth

CURRENCY
Goblin Guild currency – 16 iron angots for a copper lewt. 9 copper lewts for a silver jent. 13 silver jents for a gold crown. 3 golden crowns for a lumol.
Luminari currency – 8 kenols for a narol. 4 narols for a lumol.

Appendix B

Dramatis Personae

Aaron Roendryn

Luminari. Ceurtriarch. Prince of Lucillia, brother of Ellendren. Ei'ceuril.

Abbie Wintyr

Human with emerald eyes. Student at Gwilnor Academy. Druid of Kweil Aitch.

Aen Finamarc

Lethien from Cor'lera, squire to Alex Vaerin.

Agnelle Phanstienne

Luminari. Ei'ana and Chair of Auburnis.

Aisa

Human from Dwonia. Member of Tribe Fendur. Sister to Chief Kodin.

Alesei

Queen of Tiel. Of the Royal House Ziera.

Alethea Lenwyn

Eldinari. Emradiel ei'ana and former Lenwyn aryl.

Alexander (Alex) Vaerin

Human from Perrien, whose family migrated to Cor'lera. King of Thellion. Betrothed to Diana Thellion.

Aliel

The first phoenix born since the fall of Krysenthiel, bonded Devlyn.

Alkesh

Human from Jadien. Prince of Jadien.

Amry Thellion

Former king of Evellion. Married to Queen Lara. *Deceased.*

Andrea Farneis

Human from Sudern. Septyl knight. Nephew to Duke Farneis. Known as Andrew.

Angennia (Ange) Soricci

Human from Yanil. Judge of Yanil.

Aorinol

Daer Senator.

ARBOL

A faun searching for settlings.

AREN LORENTHIEN

Luminari. Led a rescue party to Aldinare and did not return. Now a Dark Phaedryn in service to Erynor.

ARLYN

Ei'ceuril steward from Cor'lera. Devlyn's uncle on his mother's side.

BASTIEN

Human from Sorenthil. Temple knight.

BERNADETTE HAERT

Human from Briel. Princess of Briel. Sister of King Irvienne.

BERNARD

Human from Perrien. Ei'ceuril, librarian, and magister at the abbey school of Cor'lera.

BON LI

Prime Minister of the Qien Dynasty.

BYRON ROENDRYN

Luminari. Lord knight. Brother to Vernal.

CAIRN

Human. Chief of Tribe Laith. Son of Suin.

CATALINA TURLAN

Human from Yanil. Supreme Judge of Yanil.

CECILLE FARNEIS

Human from Sudern. Daughter to Duke Farneis.

CIAREN

Draelyn of the Gold House.

CLARA

Aldinari. Ei'ceuril, steward and abbess of the Monastery of the Poor Ladies in the Ashton Wood.

CLOVIS

Cyndinari. Attendant to Yloran. Known in Lankor as Bieto.

DANIELLE AERQUIN

Luminari of House Aerquin. Student wielder at Gwilnor Academy.

DAPHNE ASHTON

Human from Mindale. Lady of Ashton Wood. Emradiel ei'ana.

DAPHNEL

Human from Ceurenyl. Temple knight.

DEVLYN LORENTHIEN

Ward of Cor'lera's abbey school. Physical features indicate Lucillian ancestry.

DIANA THELLION

Princess of Evellion. Eldest daughter of Amry and Lara. Betrothed to Alexander Vaerin.

DOLAN LORENTHIEN

Father of Devlyn, Leilyn, and Liam. Husband of Evellyn. Son of Eldinari Leienya Lierafen and an unknown Cyndinari, although this is undisclosed. Raised in the human Telvin family of Cor'lera. *Deceased.*

DONOVAN ORITHIL

Human from Gestoria. Prince of Gestoria.

EAGAN WINTYR

Human. Druid of Kweil Aitch, and Abbie's brother.

EALYNDOL LORENTHIEN

Luminari. Former Ceurtriarch. *Deceased.*

ELAYNE THENREL

Luminari. Guardian knight.

ELIEL

One of the first Phoenix to cross into Teraeniel. Bonded with Kiara.

ELLENDREN ROENDRYN

Luminari. Princess of Lucillia. Student wielder at Gwilnor Academy.

ELYSE LORENTHIEN

Luminari elf. Phaedryn. Ei'phaenyl of the Phaedryn. Daughter of Kien and Kiara.

EMDIAN

Human from Sudern. Ei'ceuril steward.

ENRICO DESILLIO

Human from Yanil. Noble in the Yanilean's court.

ENTIEL TELVIN

Human from Perrien. Ei'ceuril, steward, and abbot of the abbey school of

Cor'lera. Devlyn's uncle on his father's side.

ERYNEL MERIDEN

Cyndinari. Former Sha'ghol and Erynor's mother. *Deceased.*

ERYNOR MERIDEN

Emperor of the Erynien Empire. Disappeared after Lucillia gave birth to the twins, Roendryn and Feolyn in 7857.3E. First Cyndinari born on Eklean.

ETIENNE JIETHEL

Human from Briel. Grand chamberlain to His Majesty, King Irvienne Haert of Briel.

ETRIEN FERNORIL

Aldinari elf.

EVELLYN LORENTHIEN

Luminari from Cor'lera. Mother of Leilyn and Devlyn. Widow of Dolan. Captive of Erynor.

FALTHION

Dragon of the White Flight.

FERINN

Merperson. Currently resides in Myrium. Consort and widower of the late Queen Karina Larviere.

FORVL VIII

Dwarf and patriarch of Oern Schtam. Son of Oma and Forvl VII.

FURYK

Dwarf of Undol Schtam. Son of Matriarch Muriel IV.

FYONA ORENDI

Luminari. Student wielder at Gwilnor Academy.

FYREH GLAEDA

Eldinari. Azurelle ei'ana and magister at Gwilnor. Twin brother to Myrah, husband to Suella, and father to many children.

GALITHINOL

Dragon of the Gold Flight. Father to Weilyn and grandfather to Thien, Vivien, and Theseryn.

GENEVIE DALIETH

Human from Briel. Brieli knight and lieutenant.

GENIN

Human from Dwonia. Chief of Tribe Vadir.

GORDON CARVIL

King of Torsil. Of the Royal House Carvil. Supporter of Erynor.

HANNAH TORIN

Human from Mindale. Azurelle ei'ana and chancellor of Gwilnor Academy.

HARNYL ROENDRYN

Luminari. Aryl of Lucillia. Married to Queen Vernal. Father of Aaron, Kaela, and Ellendren. *Deceased.*

HENRY ASHTON

Human from Mindale. Lord of Ashton Wood. Husband of Daphne.

IANTHOL

Cyndinari. Shadow elf. *Deceased.*

ILYNOR

Cyndinari. Shadow elf.

INDRYL

Luminari. Tenebrae ei'ana, once believed to be a Vyoletryn ei'ana.

IRVIENNE HAERT

Human from Briel. King of Briel.

IZARA

Ja'horan Druid Elder.

JAEROL SOLARIS

Cyndinari. Former Erynien emissary. Student wielder at Gwilnor Academy.

JAEK

Luminari. Lucillian sentry.

JARIS ILN DESARIS

Cyndinari. One of the Sha'ghol. *Deceased.*

JAX

Minum and time warden.

JEANNE DARKEL

Luminari. First of the Guardians.

JEHN

Luminari elf. Ei'ceuril. Secretary to the Ceurtriarch.

JENYD TARNETH

Daer of House Tarneth. Advisor to Senator Koth.

KAELA ROENDRYN

Luminari. Princess of Lucillia, sister to Ellendren and Aaron.

KAELIEN

Elder One. Queen of Tenethyl. Aunt to Gael. *Deceased.*

KAEYTH ILLIERO

Luminari. Ei'ceuril novice.

KARINA LARIVIERE

Former Queen of Sorenthil. Widow of the late King Dorian. Wife to Ferinn. Mother of Myranda. *Deceased.*

KARL OLNEY

Human from Perrien. Observant of Vyoletryn.

KEVN WEYVIEN

Luminari. Has studied to become either an ei'ceuril or an ei'ana.

KIARA

A mythical woman believed to be the first female wielder.

KIEN

A mythical man believed to be the first male wielder.

KODIN

Human from Dwonia. Chief of Tribe Fendur.

KYRENDAL LORENTHIEN

Luminari. First chancellor of Gwilnor Academy. Crafter of the verathn. Monk at the Monastery of Kyrendal. Son to Kien and Kiara.

LACUS

Human from Torsil. Ei'ceuril steward.

LARA THELLION

Queen of Evellion. Widow of the late King Amry. Azurelle ei'ana.

LAWRENCE MAROVEN

King of Mindale. Of the Royal House Maroven. Supporter of Erynor.

LEILYN LORENTHIEN

Sister of Devlyn, living in the Illumined Wood. Daughter of Evellyn and Dolan.

LENORA HANARYLD

Human from Ceurenyl. Ei'ana and Chair of Arantiulyn. *Deceased.*

LEX TELVIN

General from Perrien. Leader of the renegade Perrien Militia. Brother to Entiel, Vine, and Dolan, who was adopted. Uncle to Alex. *Deceased.*

LIAM LIERAFEN

Son of Dolan. Half-brother to Devlyn and Leilyn. Student wielder at Gwilnor Academy.

LIARA

Dragon of the Red Flight bonded to Prya.

LILLIANNA

Human from Mindale. Ei'ceuril and formerly an Emradiel ei'ana.

LORAL VICALEN.

Luminari. Attendant in the Narielle household. Father to Toryn.

LORETTA JAVIE

Human of Sorenthil. Ei'ana and Chair of Crimsyn.

LUCILLIA

The woman who gave birth to the twins, Roendryn and Feolyn.

LYREN FENTHYR

Luminari. Attendant, formerly in the Roendryn household before joining the Lorenthien household to attend Devlyn Lorenthien.

MALIND KOTH

Daer Senator of the Upper Tier.

MARA

Elder One that lived in Tenethyl.

MELANIE BIRKWELL

Human from Mindale. Ei'ana and Chair of Arantiulyn.

MILDRED THELLION

Human from Evellion. Duchess of Cyril and widow of Talyian, the late Duke.

MYRAH GLAEDA

Eldinari. Albien ei'ana and magister at Gwilnor Academy; twin sister to Fyreh.

MYRANDA LARIVIERE

Queen of Sorenthil. Student wielder at Gwilnor Academy.

MYRASHA

Dragon of the Purple Flight.

NADIA DESUANI

Luminari. Ei'ana and Chair of the Tenebrys School; former Arantiulyn ei'ana.

NAIEL

One of the first Phoenix to cross into Teraeniel. Bonded with Kien.

NAITHOS

Dragon of the Blue Flight.

NATALIE

Luminari living in Cor'lera.

ODUIN DUR SETHARA

Cyndinari. One of the Sha'ghol.

OLIVER PENAULT

Human from Perrien. Septyl knight of Vyoletryn.

OLIVIA

Cyndinari elf. Shadow elf and Jaerol's former classmate at the Imperium.

OMA

Dwarf of Oern Schtam. Stone seer.

ORANNA

Luminari. Azurelle ei'ana and former chancellor of Gwilnor Academy. *Deceased.*

ORENIEL

Centaur of the Illumined Wood.

PAOLO FARNEIS

Human from Sudern. Duke of Sudern.

PAUREL ROENDRYN

Luminari. Ei'ana and Chair of Azurelle.

PEVREL

Luminari elf. Attendant to Ellendren Lorenthien.

PHENDIEN SHENDIELLE

Eldinari. Ei'ana and Chair of Emradiel.

PRYA

Draelyn of the Red House. Bonded with Liara.

QIEN DI

Empress of the Qien Dynasty.

QIEN JI

Crowned Prince of Qien and Son of Empress Qien Di. Monk of Beishi Monastery.

QIEN KAI

Cousin of Empress Qien Di. Azurelle ei'ana and magister of politics at Gwilnor Academy.

RAELINTH

Cyndinari. Attendant to Yloran. Known in Lankor as Pico.

RALENIEL

Elder One that lived in Tenethyl. Married to Weilyn.

RAMIRA BIR GINTHOL

Human from Yanil. Supreme Judge of Yanil at the time of Nauto's Wrath.

RAZCUL MIETHEN

Cyndinari. Shadow elf disguised as an Eldinari assistant magister at Gwilnor. Known as Danyol.

REIA

Luminari. Arantiulyn ei'ana.

RENAUD LARIVIERE

Human from Sorenthil. Temple knight. Royal cousin to Queen Myranda Lariviere.

REZEKI

Human from Jadien. Son of Prince Alkesh.

RUSYL

Dragon of the Blue Flight.

SAECRIEN

One of the Children who watches over the Waters of Anaweh.

SAENDRE LIORITH

Luminari. Student wielder at Gwilnor Academy. Assistant magister to Kai.

SANJIN AL'SANHIR

Human from Charren. Crowned Prince of Charren of the Royal House Irithru.

SARA

Human from Briel. Auburnis ei'ana.

SELENYA WAEYN

Luminari. Ei'ana and Chair of Albien.

SKIMP

Minum and time warden.

STEPHEN

Human from Evellion. Temple knight.

SOPHIE

Luminari elf. Creator of the sophilliae and founder of the Sophillium.

SUIN

Former chief of Tribe Laith. Father of Cairn. *Deceased.*

TABITHA

Human from Sudern. Azurelle ei'ana.

TAEN TAERINIOR

Luminari. Ei'ceuril novice.

TARIEL

Phoenix bonded to Ellendren.

TERAN

Cyndinari. Uncle of Jaerol.

THAERWN

Aldinari elf.

THERRIL

Ei'ceuril magister of theoreticals at Gwilnor Academy.

THIEN

Draelyn of the Gold House. Married to Loren. Son to Weilyn and Raleniel. Grandson to Galithinol the Gold. *Deceased.*

TIERA WELDON

Luminari. Emradiel ei'ana.`

TINDOL

Human from Dwonia. Member of the Sojourners.

TODRICK CORVIN.

Human from Evellion. Duke of Overen.

TORYN VICALEN

Luminari. Lady of the Watch.

TRETHIEN NARIELLE

Luminari of House Narielle. Student knight at Gwilnor Academy.

TURA

Human from Dwonia. Member and elder of Tribe Fendur. Grandmother to Tye.

TYE

Human from Dwonia. Member of Tribe Fendur.

TYIEL

Phoenix bonded with Aren.

URSULA CORVIN

Human from Evellion. Duchess of Overen.

VELARIA TREYVEN

Cyndinari born in Lucillia. Ei'ana and Chair of Azurelle.

VERINIEN

One of the Children who never aged. Protector of the Tree of Life.

VERNAL ROENDRYN

Luminari. Aryl of Lucillia. Married to King Harnyl. Mother of Aaron, Kaela, and Ellendren. Direct descendant of Lucillia. *Deceased.*

VICTORIA ORITHIL

Human from Gestoria. Crowned Princess of Gestoria.

VINE VAERIN

Human from Perrien. Self-styled Queen Mother to the King of Thellion.

VIREN DEKENUREL

Luminari. Guardian knight.

VIVIEN

Draelyn and ealyn of the Gold House. Granddaughter of Galithinol the Gold, and daughter of Weilyn.

WALEISIUS

Merchant in Cor'lera, more commonly known as Walei.

WEILYN

Draelyn of the Gold House. Married to Raleniel. Son to Galithinol. *Deceased.*

WYN LIERAFEN

Eldinari. Grandson of Dalenya and Fendryl. Star Warden. Emradiel ei'ana.

XANTH

Cyndinari. Shadow elf.

YELARIS

Dragon of the Blue Flight. Bonded to Velaria.

YENIEL

Phoenix bound to Aren.

Yloran Eth Gnashar

Cyndinari. One of the Sha'ghol. Known in Lankor as Enna.

Ythinor the Black

Dragon of the Dark Flight. Bonded to his half-brother, Erynor.

Yvonne Kardol

Human from Yanil. Crimsyn ei'ana and Magister of the art of wielding at Gwilnor Academy.

Zara

Cyndinari elf. Former servant of the Erynien Court.

The Seven Irythil and their Associated Enthiel

Uriel – Lord of the Stars, whose name means Anaweh is my Light. Irythil who brought Anaweh's Light to Teraeniel.

> **Auriel** – The Dawn Star. Guardian of the elves of Luminare.

> **Meridiel** – The Noon Star. Guardian of the elves of Cyndinare.

> **Vespiel** – The Evening Star. Guardian of the elves of Aldinare.

> **Boriel** – The Night Star. Guardian of the elves of Eldinare.

Gwynthiel – Lady of the Lorendil, whose name means Strength of Anaweh. Irythil who brought Anaweh's spirit to Teraeniel.

Ramiel – Lord of Death, whose name means Arrogant toward Anaweh. Betrayed Anaweh and all creation. Irythil who brought shadow to Teraeniel.

Theniel – Lady of the Seas, whose name means Anaweh Heals. Irythil who brought water to Teraeniel.

> **Nauto** – Guardian of all humans living along the coasts.

> **Aquae** – Guardian of the merpeople.

Sariel – Lord of the Land, whose name means Command of Anaweh. Irythil who brought substance to Teraeniel.

> **Tera** – Patroness of harvest and nourishment. Often referred to as Mother Tera.

> **Mundi** – Guardian of the dwarves.

Lereniel – Lady of the Winds, whose name means Friend of Anaweh. Irythil who brought air to Teraeniel.

KARIEL – Lord of Peace, whose name means Who is Like Anaweh. Irythil who brought fire to Teraeniel.

SEVEN CHAIRS OF SEPTYL

CHAIR OF ALBIEN — Selenya Waeyn. Luminari. The White Owl.

CHAIR OF ARANTIULYN — Melanie Birkwell. Human from Mindale. The Orange Lion.

CHAIR OF AUBURNIS — Agnelle Phanstienne. Luminari. The Brown Lark.

CHAIR OF AZURELLE — Velaria Treyven. Cyndinari born in Lucillia. The Blue Dragon.

CHAIR OF CRIMSYN — Loretta Javie. Human from Sorenthil. The Red Dog.

CHAIR OF EMRADIEL — Phendien Shendielle. Eldinari. The Green Stag.

CHAIR OF VYOLETRYN — Paurel Roendryn. Luminari. The Purple Eagle.

HIGH LUMINARI HOUSES AND ARYLS

ARYL OF ARENTHYL AND EXALTED ARYL OF KRYSENTHIEL — House Lorenthien

ARYL OF LUCILLIA — Vernal (deceased) and Harnyl of House Roendryn

ARYL OF REINYL— Therrin and Zara of House Reyndien

ARYL OF OSTYL — Naesiv and Valerie of House Aerquin

ARYL OF WINSTSYL — Toral and Silvia of House Narielle

ARYL OF TENYL — Iridil and Enoria of House Taerinior

ARYL OF DELMIRA WOOD — Ciraenth and Aegian of House Ginielle

ARYL OF EANDYL — Enithil and Binoral of House Clarion

ARYL OF VERENTHYL — Kyiel and Fyona of House Lauriel

High Eldinari Houses and Aryls

Aryl of Lierthyl — Fendryl and Dalenya of House Lierafen

Aryl of Virathyl — Naerelle and Eohire of House Shendielle

Aryl of Drethyl — Vanoreh and Elialen of House Illia

Aryl of Ladrithyl — Indryn and Diera of House Allandis

Aldarchs of Aldinare

Gael of Quel'anir – The Reverend Mother, also known as the Nurturer. Her followers dedicate themselves to nature and caring for the ilithae trees, native to Aldinare.

Orien of Eln'dinai – The Just Father, also known as the Judge. His followers focus on upholding law in Aldinare.

Nialth of Dur'linos – The Philosopher, also known as the Learned One. Her followers dedicate their life to study.

Theseryn of Thas'thallas – The Faithful Servant. His followers devoted their lives to worshipping Anaweh, the Creating Light. Theseryn left his sanctum of Thas'thallas to establish the Ei'ceuril order and became the first Ceurtriarch.

Lerathel of Val'quin – The Artisan. Sister to Nialth. Her followers are practitioners of the arts and designed the great cities and sanctums of Aldinare.

Endruil of Kir'enon – The Shepherd. His followers are caretakers of the alicorns native to Aldinare.

Aeryth of Ai'lyr – The Rogue. Her followers prefer to hide in the shadows and wield the fabled Aldinari bows.

Irithel of Mel'inor – The Smith. His followers develop advanced weapons and tools, often forged from aldaryl.

Ealyn of Tenethyl

Vivien — Ealyn of the Gold House. Granddaughter of Galithinol of the Gold Flight.

Daela — Ealyn of the Amethyst House. Granddaughter of Myrasha of the Purple Flight.

Torik — Ealyn of the Onyx House. Grandson of Jiertha of the Grey Flight.

Mellory — Ealyn of the Ruby House. Granddaughter of Vulgath of the Red Flight.

Niron — Ealyn of the Sapphire House. Grandson of Naithos of the Blue Flight.

Allister — Ealyn of the Opal House. Grandson of Ithinol of the White Flight.

Helen — Ealyn of the Jade House. Granddaughter of Fenoral of the Green Flight.

Dragon Primus

Lyvenol — Primus of the Gold Flight. Warden of lumenys.

Eilynol — Primus of the Purple Flight. Warden of animys.

Orythnol — Primus of the Grey Flight. Warden of umbrys.

Aerinol — Primus of the White Flight. Warden of aerys.

Caephenol — Primus of the Blue Flight. Warden of aquaeys.

Thereinol — Primus of the Green Flight. Warden of terys.

Fyrinol — Primus of the Red Flight. Warden of ignys.

Tolvenol — Primus of the Dark Flight. Warden of tenebrys.

APPENDIX C

CIVILIZATIONS OF TERAENIEL

ALDINARE

Remnant of Aldinari rescued from the Skyland Aldinare by Aren and accompanying Phaedryn. They are considered part of Krysenthiel.

Race: Elf

House/Aryl: Avign, Eraen, Kenoril, Threilen

AUDUN

One of the eight schtams composing the Schtamite. Situated at the westernmost edge of the Laudien Mountains.

Head of State: Patriarch Dridn IV, son of Dridn III

Race: Dwarf

BRIEL

River valley kingdom situated between two rivers forming the River Reifen and the slopes of the Dead Wood.

Capital: Briel

Head of State: King Irvienne of the Royal House Haert

Motto: Seek the message

Sigil: Black raven on a yellow field

Race: Human

BRUNST

One of the eight schtams composing the Schtamite. Situated within the Vespien Mountains. Close friends with the Eldinari.

Head of State: Patriarch Thraen, son of Anuun

Race: Dwarf

CHARREN

A kingdom spanning across two continents, Ogren and Daereneth.

Capital: Karithel

Head of State: King Sanhir of the Royal House Irithru

Race: Human

DAER EMPIRE

Oldest continuous human empire in Teraeniel and advocate of slavery and colonialism. Situated on the continent of Daereneth.

Capital: Daer

Head of State: Body of the Daer Senate

Race: Human

DWONIA

Desert country once controlled by the Twelve Tribes of Dwonia. Only two tribes refused to ally with Erynor and remained in the desert.

Heads of State: Chief Kodin of Tribe Fendur and Chief Genin of Tribe Vadir

Capital: Nynev

Sigil: Red lion on a yellow field

Race: Human

ELDINARE

Eldinari society secreted away in the Eldin Wood.

Head of State: Aryl Fendryl and Dalenya of House Lierafen

Capital: Stellantis

Sigil: White tree on a green field

Race: Elf

ERYNIEN EMPIRE

Cyndinari empire founded by Erynor Meriden, its sole emperor. Responsible for the Ceurendol War and enslavement of the Luminari.

Capital: Broid

Head of State: Emperor Erynor Meriden

Sigil: Bronze sun on a red field

Race: Elf

EVELLION

The mountain kingdom where the Laudien and Vespien mountain ranges meet. Original inhabitants were the refugees of Thellion.

Capital: Everin

Head of State: King Amry and Queen Lara of the Royal House Thellion

Motto: The pure will soar

Sigil: White eagle on a blue field

Race: Human

FRIETON

The free city-state of Frieton. Given to the minums on their release from slavery.

Capital: Frieton

Head of State: The Keeper (identity unknown)

Race: Minum

GESTORIA

Fallen kingdom situated on the Plains of Orithil. Once great allies to Thellion and Krysenthiel. Obliterated during the Ceurendol War.

Capital: Quellion

Motto: Will triumphs pride

Sigil: White gold winged lion on a blue field

Race: Human

GLYOL

One of the eight schtams composing the Schtamite. Easternmost and only schtam in the Illumined Wood.

Head of State: Matriarch Vylma, daughter of Toreldn

Race: Dwarf

HAROL

One of the eight schtams composing the Schtamite. Situated in the Laudien Mountains.

Head of State: Matriarch Loewn, daughter of Brenola

Race: Dwarf

JA'HORAN, TRIBES OF

Nomadic civilization on the continent of Ja'horan.

Race: Human

JA'NALIHN

Short lived kingdom covering all of Ja'horan.

Race: Human

JOPHT

One of the eight schtams composing the Schtamite. Southernmost schtam in the Vespien Mountains and staunch defenders against the Shadow schtams from northern infiltration.

Head of State: Patriarch Oerth III, son of Oerth II

Race: Dwarf

KRYSENTHIEL

The kingdom of the Luminari. Currently lost within the Shroud. Translates to land of the golden flowers, named by a human trying to speak Aelish, the language of the elves, to describe the countryside.

Capital: Arenthyl

Head of State: Exalted Lorenthien Aryl

Sigil: Seven golden kryseniels blossoming from a larger central kryseniel on a white field.

Race: Elf

Lucillia

Kingdom of the Luminari after gaining their freedom from the Erynien Empire. Named after Lucillia, the woman who gave birth to the twins, Roendryn and Feolyn.

Capital: Lucillia

Head of State: Aryl Vernal and Harnyl of House Roendryn

Race: Elf

Mindale

A kingdom east of the southern Vespien Mountains.

Capital: Binton

Head of State: King Lawrence of the Royal House Maroven

Motto: Mind over body

Sigil: Brown ox on a green field

Race: Human

Nunstol

Shadow schtam that was cast off by the Schtamite for their actions in Mount Cyngol.

Head of State: Patriarch Uriden, son of Urodrn

Race: Dwarf

Oern

One of the eight schtams composing the Schtamite. Belin belonged to Oern schtam and sheltered Evellion and his people as they fled Elothkar.

Head of State: Patriarch Forvl VIII, son of Forvl VII

Race: Dwarf

Parendior

A hilly country north of the Laudien Mountains and west of the Illumined Wood. Most Parendians are farming folk, and when Perrien invaded, they had no means of defending their land.

Motto: Protect the harmony

Sigil: Purple doe on a beige field

Race: Human

PERRIEN

A kingdom north of the Laudien Mountains where the citizens overthrew their monarchy and replaced it with a council and doubled their territory by invading Parendior.

Capital: Gneal

Motto: Swift to action

Sigil: Grey rider and horse on a white field

Race: Human

QIEN EMPIRE, THE

Empire of the Hundred Kingdoms on the continent of Qien, west of Eklean.

Capital: Zhongshi

Auxiliary Capitals: Beishi, Dongshi, Nanshi, and Xishi

Head of State: Empress Qien Wei

Race: Human

SORENTHIL

A kingdom along the River Meyien.

Capital: Myrium

Head of State: Queen Karina of the Royal House Lariviere

Motto: Flow with the waters

Sigil: Blue dolphin on a light blue field

Race: Human

SUDERN

A city state on the Dagger's Point peninsula. After a bloody civil war with Josque, the inhabitants declared themselves independent.

Capital: Sudern

Motto: Hidden daggers

Sigil: Red ship and dagger on a white field

Race: Human

THELLION

The fallen Eklean kingdom covering all the lands east of the Vespien Mountains. Met its downfall through a civil war relating to succession.

Capital: Elothkar

Head of State: King Alexander of House Vaerin

Motto: Eternal wisdom

Sigil: Silver winged horse on a white field

TIEL

A southern kingdom bordering the Erynien Bay and the Unarian Sea.

Capital: Josque

Head of State: Queen Alesei of the Royal House Ziera

Motto: Eternal wisdom

Sigil: Orange serpent on a blue field

Race: Human

TORSIL

A weak kingdom with little influence on its neighbors.

Capital: Trest

Head of State: King Gordon of the Royal House Carvil

Motto: Stronger together

Sigil: Grey wolf on a red field

Race: Human

UNDOL

One of the eight schtams composing the Schtamite. Deeply religious and situated in the Laudien Mountains surrounding Lake Saeryndol. They have strong ties to the Luminari.

Head of State: Matriarch Miurel IV, daughter of Miurel III

Race: Dwarf

VORN

One of the eight schtams composing the Schtamite. Situated at the northernmost edge of the Vespien Mountains.

Head of State: Matriarch Tiltha, daughter of Tilma

Race: Dwarf

YANIL

Southern kingdom along the Erynien Bay. Yanil was once jointly ruled by the Yanilean and the Judges of Yanil.

Capital: Lankor

Head of State: The Yanilean

Motto: Deep as justice

Sigil: Black castle on a blue field

Race: Human

ZORIK

Shadow schtam that was cast off by the Schtamite for their actions in Mount

Cyngol.

Head of State: Matriarch Jiora, daughter of Jiorza

Race: Dwarf

About the Author

Ryan D Gebhart first started writing the Jewel of Life series in 2012 in Philadelphia, PA, shortly after concluding his undergraduate studies in philosophy. This unexpected passion evolved over the years and has remained a constant companion, developing into new LGBTQ+ Fantasy stories he's excited to publish. Ryan lives in Washington, DC with his husband and cat, where he also works at an architecture firm. Ryan D Gebhart is originally from Wilmington, DE.

Keep up with Ryan D Gebhart at www.RyanDGebhart.com

Milton Keynes UK
Ingram Content Group UK Ltd.
UKHW011136220424
441551UK00006B/607